Donna —
To my beautiful —
wonderful sister.
With
love,
Larry

Praise for Lincoln Raw

Other Fiction by DL Fowler

Lincoln's Diary—a novel of suspense

Sarah Sue Morgan's search for truth turns deadly when she learns that Abraham Lincoln's previously undiscovered private diary is missing from her mother's estate. Matters spiral out of control when she's accused of murdering a professor who spent his career trying to prove Lincoln planned his own assassination.

Ripples—a novel of suspense

(To be released - Spring 2015)

Amy's a prisoner. Jacob Chandler's been used to having things his way. When their lives collide in the rugged Sierra foothills people start dying.

About the Cover

The picture on the right is a copy of an ambrotype taken on May 7, 1858. Forty-nine-year-old Lincoln had just won the Duff Armstrong "Almanac" murder trial, and 22 year-old Abraham Byers stopped him in the street outside the courthouse. He and asked Lincoln to pose for a photograph. Lincoln protested that his rumpled white linen suit was not fit for a portrait, but the younger Abraham prevailed.

The cover is a reverse image of Byers' photograph, showing Lincoln's face as if viewing it in a mirror. The novel that follows is an attempt to interpret his life the way he likely perceived it.

Credit goes to Heather Steward Fowler for creating this cover, which with a single picture, captures the essence of **Lincoln Raw—a biographical novel**.

LINCOLN RAW

a biographical novel

DL FOWLER

Cover design by Heather Steward Fowler

For additional information visit http://dlfowler.com or scan
the QR code below:

Visit the author's blog http://dlfowler.wordpress.com or scan
the QR code below:

Library of Congress Control Number: 2013922631

ISBN 978-0-578-07768-0

Published in the United States by Harbor Hill Publishing

Dedication

Gertrude S. Baccus

(1908-2001)

My teacher, who inspired me, believed in me, and loved me, as she did for so many students over the years.

Author's Notes

The inspiration to write a novel based on Abraham Lincoln's life came in part from reading Jackie Hogan's *Lincoln, Inc.: Selling the Sixteenth President in Contemporary America.* As a sociologist, Hogan explores the ways we employ Lincoln today (as American culture has done since his death) in our political, ideological, personal, and national struggles; the ways we simultaneously deify and commercially exploit him; the ways he is packaged and sold in the marketplace of American ideas. In *Lincoln, Inc.* we see our proclivity for projecting onto Lincoln the way we see ourselves, who we think we are, and who we wish we could be.

Lincoln Raw is a biographical novel in which I attempt to look at life through Lincoln's eyes as he was coming of age. I focus on his humanity by dramatizing his responses to the world as he likely saw it, filtered through his sensitivities, emotions, and values. As we look at the events of his life—beginning with childhood—and keep our focus on how he responded to various forms of disorder, injustice, and abuse, we can better understand the passions that drove many of his policies and decisions as president.

I build Lincoln's story around events that have been described by those who were close to him. When confronted with different versions of emotionally charged events, I do not discount those incidents, but synthesize the accounts to produce scenes which seem consistent with his development at the time they occurred. I am indebted to the biographical works of Michael Burlingame and Joshua Shenk, among others, for their insights into Lincoln's personality and the events that shaped his character.

Every character in the novel—except one—is a real person with whom Lincoln interacted in some way. In each case, they are presented in a manner consistent with the way in which they were regarded by Lincoln. For example, throughout his life Lincoln demonstrated an attitude toward his father that suggested the elder Lincoln was abusive and unfair. The son's assessment may not have been accurate, but it was the perception that he lived by. Lincoln also probably saw his marriage as being less blissful than might have been the case. As with all of us, perception is reality. We respond emotionally to our perceptions, and those responses contribute to the development of our character.

Writing about Lincoln is tricky, in part because today's author must reconcile three distinct periods of Lincoln scholarship that take different slants on who he was and what he believed.

During the first period (the demi-God era, including biographies written from the time of his death until the early 20th century), Lincoln's wife, Mary Todd, and son, Robert, wielded a great deal of influence (some say censorship) over what biographers should say in molding his legacy. The image Mary championed seems to have differed from how she treated him while he was alive. Robert, who was often embarrassed by his father's backwardness (his unkempt appearance, frontier style of language, and lack of formal education), likely wanted to recreate his father in the image of the man he wanted to remember. After his father's death, Robert committed his mother to an insane asylum for a brief time and destroyed many of her private papers and letters. Biographers of this period were also sensitive to the nation's need for a narrative that would facilitate healing after the assassination and Civil War.

The result of these influences was a tendency to discredit perspectives that were not in sync with the needs of the era. Casualties of such biases included two people who knew Lincoln intimately: Billy Herndon, his law partner, and Hill Lamon, his friend and bodyguard. It was Herndon who first exposed the Ann Rutledge story based on extensive interviews with members of her family and people who lived in the small village of New Salem. Objections to the Ann Rutledge stories by Mary Todd and Robert contributed greatly to the efforts by biographers to discredit Herndon.

Ironically, in the current era of Lincoln studies, that discrediting has been discredited, and today's leading

Lincoln scholars such as Michael Burlingame and Joshua Shenk suggest that sufficient evidence exists to support the hypothesis that a close bond between Lincoln and Rutledge existed. They also argue that proving whether the relationship rose to the level of an engagement is trivial compared to understanding the role her premature death, combined with the deaths of his sister and mother, played on Lincoln's psychology.

The second era of Lincoln (the Romantic period) was dominated by efforts to convert the demi-god into a folk hero. Carl Sandburg made an indelible contribution to Lincoln's legacy by spotlighting his meager beginning (though he soft-pedaled it to a degree) and his meteoric rise to power.

The third era, beginning about the middle twentieth century, has focused on Lincoln's psychology and asks the question, what made this man?

Lincoln Raw draws mostly from the current era of scholarship and tries to show Lincoln's personality development by looking at events through his eyes. By most accounts he was emotionally sensitive, introspective, and melancholy. In his time, those characteristics often attracted awe, admiration, and respect. During Lincoln's time, melancholy people were considered to possess special insights and consequently, were regarded as exceptional, rather than deficient.

Lincoln's misunderstood, almost conflicting, views on slavery and abolition are part of what attracted me to his story. In his speeches over decades in public life, he was equally critical of radicals at both ends of the spectrum. Despite his professed life-long hatred for slavery, Lincoln discouraged abolitionist policies. Instead, he repeatedly declared slavery should be allowed to die a slow death and drew a hard line against allowing "the extension of a bad thing [slavery]." To him, slavery was wrong, specifically because of its unfairness—*It is wrong for a man to eat bread from the sweat of another man's brow.* Nonetheless, he held that it was protected by the Constitution where it was in place when the country was formed.

The same level of conflict that appears in his politics also shows up in his religious views, which when explored honestly and wholly, should give all of us pause when we claim that God is on our side. Lincoln declared more than once that he was not Christian (most prominently in a conversation with Newt Bateman which is captured in the latter third of this book), but he articulated and lived the teachings of Christ more fully than most people who claimed to be faithful in his day.

Much of the dialogue in these pages is drawn from original sources, including letters, speeches, journals, and notes from interviews with Lincoln's contemporaries. Some original material, particularly italicized excerpts from speeches and writings, has been edited for clarity.

Like most of us, Lincoln employed a variety of voices. For instance, his oratorical voice, which matured over the years, was distinct from his conversational voice, just as his storyteller voice differed from his letter writing voice. He sounded different when engaged in formal conversations than in casual banter with an intimate. In *Lincoln Raw*, his narrator voice falls somewhere between his storyteller voice (especially in the use of present tense) and the style he might have employed when writing a letter. In each case, given how much language has changed over the past two centuries, I have found it helpful to adapt Lincoln's voice so it is more attuned to modern readers. Even so, I tried to maintain as much as practical the colloquialisms and language style that were true to Lincoln's times and usage. I was particularly surprised to learn that the expression "what's up?" was in common usage in mid-nineteenth century America.

If reading *Lincoln Raw* prompts you to investigate his life in more depth, you'll find an abundance of scholarly material in the sources I have listed at the end of the book under "Additional Reading."

I hope you enjoy reading *Lincoln Raw—a biographical novel* and I look forward to your comments.

DL Fowler
March 25, 2014

Lincoln Raw

a biographical novel

That which does not kill us makes us stronger.

Friedrich Nietzsche

Chapter One

The Executive Mansion, Washington City - April 14, 1865

People gossip about my face. Some say I'm steeped in gloom over little Willy's death. Others insist this great conflict weighs on me like an oxen yoke. According to my copper-headed Kentucky playmate, Austin Gollaher, I was melancholy even as a baby.

In my youth, neighbors called me lazy. Cousin Dennis Hanks pronounced me a dullard. Today, some contend my countenance betrays uncommon wisdom, while others argue I'm simple and indolent, a gorilla posing as a man. A man's shadow merely betrays his presence. To know him, we must probe the stripes from which he bleeds.

Still in my faded dressing gown and broken down slippers, I look out my office window upon the city. Traces of last night's pyrotechnics hang in the air, and yesterday's mantle of gray has yielded to splashes of red, white, and blue. Flags and buntings announce the Rebel Army's surrender while reflections from the morning sun dance on the Potomac like scattered jewels.

The river's stench must have stopped General Lee's men from crossing over when they had the chance, warning them of an invisible plague lurking in its waters. Seeds of disease are deposited in the Potomac by rivulets of human waste and refuse that flow along our streets and into its currents. Even this great mansion is no safe harbor from the pestilence. Our little Willy was taken by an epidemic of fever, and Mother is almost insane from grief.

I covet the luxury of mourning in the same fashion she does. Willy is not the only son I've lost since assuming this Office, and with every soldier's death, a piece of me dies also. The blood of those who've perished in this great conflict could fill the little Knob Creek near my boyhood home, and their families' tears would flood the fields around it.

I give a letter to my secretary, George Nicolay. Hardly more than a boy, he's entirely trustworthy, and nothing escapes his keen eyes. On our walks through the city, he can spot mal-intended ruffians from blocks away, though if we were set upon, reckon I'd be the one protecting his bony frame.

The letter is a reply to General James Van Alen who complains I exposed myself carelessly while visiting Richmond this week. Nicolay thinks it best to assure him appropriate precautions will be taken in the future. My friend Ward Hill Lamon, Marshall of Washington City, a massive man equal to me in height but much greater in girth, reminds me daily of those who want me dead. Hill claims there are more than eighty plots against my life. There are times he could have added me to that list. Nonetheless, were it not for my decision to dispatch him to Richmond on Wednesday, he'd be haranguing me over Mrs. Lincoln's plans to attend theatre this evening.

A recent dream buoys me; its details are etched in my memory, carved there by repetition. Invariably, it foreshadows momentous events. The morning would be made even brighter if it heralds the much anticipated news from General Sherman that the remaining rebel units under General Johnston have capitulated.

In my vision, I float at a rapid pace across a dark expanse of water to an unknown destination. But this time, unlike the previous occurrences, Austin Gollaher appears and calls me back to a memorable Sunday morning of our boyhood.

• • •

In 1816—my seventh year as I am told—we live on a tiny farm near the Gollaher family in Hodgenville, Kentucky. Once a wilderness, now this patch of earth is regarded as a peaceful valley. Surrounded by spiraling hills and deep gorges, our place lies along a branch of the Rolling Fork known as Knob Creek. Father tells us stories of the times before the Indians were vanquished from these parts—a time when they tormented people as far east as Virginia. He witnessed their inhumanity when he was a child.

When not tending the farm, Father works at the distillery down where the creek and Rolling Fork join together. That is, unless he's hunting, or out in the woods brooding, or dreaming up schemes to make a better life.

Last year's winter lingers as the next one begins. The few sprouts that emerged from our late-May planting succumbed to aberrant snows and frosts in June. We replanted, only to suffer more crop-killing frosts through late July and August. A half-inch layer of ice stayed on the ground through most of September, but has finally melted during a brief interlude of moderate October weather. The resulting runoff swells our little branch to its brim.

As the morning sun breaks over the horizon, a biting wind whistles through our cabin, confirming that the year-long winter has merely taken a respite and lurks nearby, ready to resume its assault. I roll out of my cornhusk bed to find Mother fixing breakfast. She's a rugged woman, but today she's decked out in her best Sunday dress. Her coarse black hair cascades onto her shoulders. It's the dress that snugs around her waist, rather than draping loosely from her bony shoulders to her narrow hips. She wears it when she hauls us down to the holy-roller camp meetings to hear preachers who've come through these parts; she can whoop it up with the best of them. It's also what she wears when Father is away and she sets about on affairs of her own.

I exchange glances with my sister Sally. Her eyes are deep-set and grey like my own. In spite of her being two years older, she looks up at me, and me down at her. She's stout like Father, but that's the only way they're alike.

We don't ask what sort of business Mother is up to, but at breakfast, she tells us Mrs. Gollaher will be calling today.

I cock my head. "And Austin, too?"

"Yezzun. The two of y'all 'll have the whole day to play. Father done gone off scoutin' for land 'cross the 'hio River."

"How long he be gone?"

"He be back when he be back, as always," she answers.

Folks often talk of Providence smiling on them. When that happens, their insides must get warm the same as mine do when Mother tells me Father is away.

After breakfast, I take a perch on our split-rail fence and wait for Austin. He's three years older than me, but not taller. We'd rather be dead than apart, even though we don't always see eye to eye on things.

Once, while we're playing at his cabin he says, "You loose a coon or fox from your father's traps again, I'm tellin'."

I say back, "We've no right takin' more 'n we need. It's mean to harm animals for no reason."

We argue until Mrs. Gollaher takes his side and scolds me. It doesn't matter what they think. Right is right.

A week later, Father hauls me along to check his traps. He gets a coon in the first one, and about a dozen yards away a fox struggles to get free from a snare. Father yells, "Ha!" and crows about his trappin' skills. Then he loads his flintlock and aims at the coon's head.

My shoulders grow taut.

The rifle's report sends a sharp pain ricocheting through my throat and head.

I choke back tears as Father walks over to the next trap and bends down to inspect the fox. He crouches like a thieving pirate digging through his plunder, shakes his head, and sends me to the next trap thirty yards away. The trap sits at the end of a game trail, which winds through a thicket and comes out near the creek. In it he has caught another fine fox.

I'm standing there telling myself it's wrong to kill two handsome foxes on the same day when another report from Father's rifle sends tremors down my spine. Tears seep down into my throat. After a moment, I straddle the wooden cage and bend over to open it. At first, the critter hunches down, recoiling toward the rear of the trap. I slap the back of the cage with my hand a few times to coax it, and finally it springs out and races into the brush. I'm still astride the cage, smiling, when Father walks up and cuffs me on the side of the head.

"You stupid boy," he mutters. Then he grabs my ear in his meaty hand and drags me home where he whips me. On hearing the whaps of the switch raising welts on my back, Mother races outside and grabs Father's hand.

She snarls, "This time ya done gone too far."

Father flings his switch down next to my bare feet and glowers at her. After a long silence, he storms away, muttering. *He ain't none of mine.*

"Where ya goin'?" Mother shouts after him.

"Huntin'," he shouts back.

His words ring in my ears. "He ain't none of mine."

What I'm always eager to hear Father grumble is, "Git jeself down to Hodgen's Mill with a sack of corn. Yer ma says we're gittin' low on meal." The Miller Hodgen, a large man whose nickname is Mr. John, grinds our corn by hand. He lives with his plump mother Missus Sarah in a spacious home built of stone and evenly sawn boards.

Missus Sarah's first question whenever I arrive is, "Hungry, Abraham?" And without waiting for my answer, she serves up a fancy plate loaded with sweet cakes. While I'm devouring her pastries, she sits next to me at the finely carved table. Smiling, she opens *Robinson Crusoe* and reads aloud. At the end of each page, she coaxes me to sound out the words and prompts me to take a stab at reading a line on my own.

"When you speak, dear boy," she tells me, "do so properly like Mr. Crusoe in the book. Well-spoken men go far in this world."

Though we read for over an hour, it seems like only a few minutes have passed when Mr. John comes in from the mill, carrying my sack of meal. That's Missus Sarah's clue to put aside her book to set the table for supper. I'm always invited to join them.

Sometimes, they let me stay with them for days, sleeping in a bedroom all to myself on a real bed. Mr. John often says they wish Mother and Father would give me to them for good. But when the homesickness sets in, they always send me off well fed and smiling.

Once, Austin and I are down at the mill together when Ol' Zack Evans, a swarthy, near-skeleton of a man, rides up on his blind rickety nag. When the beleaguered animal balks at the platform, Mr. Evans kicks her hard in the sides. The burly miller jumps down from the platform, seeming to shake the earth, and pulls Mr. Evans off his mount, pinning him to a post.

Mr. John's nostrils flare. "If ever you kick a horse again, I'll give you a thrashing you'll never forget."

Mr. Evans stares at the ground.

I pull back my shoulders, straightening from my slouched posture, and say, "Mr. Evans, the other day your boy tears off a bird's head and throws it at my feet. At first, he laughs, and Austin, here, warns him he'll get a good whuppin' if he doesn't say he's sorry. Your boy just shakes his head and says, 'Abraham don't never fight no one.' I ball up my hands into fists, clench my jaw, and stare hard at him 'til he buries his face in his hands and cries. Then he confesses he behaved shamefully. Now, your boy oughten not do such as that, and neither should you kick any more horses."

Several days later while returning from the mill alone, a brown-and-white dog is lying on the trail at the base of a precipice. Its shallow breathing is the only sign it's alive. I kneel beside it, set down my bag of cornmeal, and stare up to the top of the bluff. It's a long drop. The little fellow whimpers as I pet him, and his right foreleg shakes. His eyes look like he's been crying. No way he can walk far. It's a good thing he's not too heavy to carry.

After a while, though, my arm tires, so I drop the sack of cornmeal under a shade tree and lay my dog on the ground. A few yards away, there's a small spring where I fill my cap with cool water. Honey, that's my new pet's name, laps up badly needed refreshment while I fashion a crude splint for the injured leg, winding straps of soft bark from some nearby pawpaw bushes around a couple of saplings I've cut down to size. Mr. John made one just like it once. My doctoring is good enough for Honey to hobble behind me the rest of the way home.

I'm within hailing distance of the cabin when I stop and tie Honey to a tree using the leather tie on my sack of meal. Since Father won't be at all happy about my new pet, Mother must approve before he sees him.

In near darkness, I steal up to the cabin and peer through the window. Father is asleep by the fireplace, so it's not hard to slip in and whisper to Mother, "Down by the big sycamore, I've tied up a dog. His leg's broke. Please, let me keep him in our empty pig pen. Father says we ain't gonna have no more hogs for a while, and it's got a roof to keep the rain out."

Mother smiles and asks where the dog came from.

I explain how I found him and beg, "Father won't like my dog; he'll see its broken leg and complain he's useless, but you and Sally will love him. Please, tell Father not to shoot him or give him away."

She rubs my coarse, black hair. People say we favor each other in looks and in temperament. Nothing of that sort is ever said about Father and me.

She says, "Seems ya loves the poor critter. I'll make sure your pa doesn't do it no harm."

Mother and I collect Honey from his hiding place and make him a home in the old pig pen. True to her promise, Mother convinces Father to let me keep him. But just the same, he's mean to my dog and always calls him ugly.

Every time Father looks askance at Honey, it makes me cringe. I'll never forget the darkness in his eyes when he discovered the first pet I brought home.

Back during the springtime of my sixth year, a litter of new born pigs catches my fancy over at the Hodgen's farm. I take them up and hold them one by one, stroking their cute little snouts. The smallest one nuzzles up against my chest and makes little loving squeaks. He so captivate me that Mr. John cannot get me to put him away. Finally, he says, "Abraham, you can have it if you can get it home."

My heart almost bursts. "Ya made this the best day of my life."

Mr. John chuckles. "What you gonna name him?"

"Let's see ... why ... how about, Friday after Mr. Crusoe's man in the storybook?"

"Well, take good care of Friday," he replies.

I gather up the hem of my tow-linen shirt forming a make-shift sack and carry him home cradled against my bosom. To make a bed for him, I line a hollow log with corn stalks, shucks, and leaves.

The poor piglet squeals all night, bringing grunts and muttering from Father who tosses about in his bed. In the morning, the first thing he says is, "That pig's gotta go." I hope he's just hungry and rush outside with corn meal, bread, and milk, but Friday doesn't touch any of it. He just continues his relentless squealing.

At last Mother says to me, "Ya best take that pig back to its mama; it'll die if ya keep it here."

It breaks my heart, but what Mother says is always the truth and the law to me. With my head bowed, I take Friday back to the Hodgens.

When the little fellow goes in the pen with his mother, she snorts with delight. He scurries to her teats, making joyous little squeaks. After she suckles him for a while, he looks happy and becomes so playful. I beg Mr. John to let me take him back. He nods, and I gather up Friday in my shirt and carry him home again.

On my return Mother plants her hands on her hips and glares at me. "How would ya feel if'n somebody took you away to a strange place and ya never saw yer ma or sister ever again?"

My heart pinches and my throat turns raw. Tears roll down my cheeks.

Mother rubs my head. "Now, if ya really loves that pig, you'd want him to be at home so he could be happy."

I continue blubbering, begging her to let me try him one more day. "When he sees how much I loves him, he'll change his mind." But the next day he still won't eat, and Mother convinces me to take him back once more. This time, however, she agrees to let me carry him back and forth. That way, we can play together by day, and he can suckle on his mother and sleep with her at night.

After two weeks, he finally learns to eat on his own,

and Mother lets me bring him home for good. I play with him and teach him tricks. We even play hide-and-go-seek. He always peeps around the corner of the cabin to see if I'm coming after him.

Father comes beside me one morning during Friday's feeding time and pours out a pail of corn. He says nothing, but licks his lips as he watches the pig devour its breakfast. Each morning thereafter he joins me in the feeding ritual, increasing his offering as the little fellow grows. Eventually, Friday gets too heavy for me to carry around and starts following me everywhere—to the barn, the plowed fields, even the forest.

We spend most days in the woods where I teach him how to brush leaves aside to find acorns and nuts. Sometimes he takes a lazy spell, rubs against my legs and stops in front of me to lie down. I can decipher his language when he says to me, "Why don't you carry me like you used to do?" When he grows a little larger, the table turns and he carries me. He does so as happily as I ever gave the same service to him.

One night Father stares darkly at his plate of venison stew and says, "That hog's fat enough for slaughterin'. Think we'll do the business tomorrow."

My breath hangs in my throat.

Mother asks, "Abraham, is somethin' the matter?"

I leap off my stool and run to bed without finishing my meal. I lie awake weeping, plotting to rise early and steal poor Friday away to safety. If Father thwarts me … there must be some way to punish him for his cruelty.

Come morning, despite being famished, I pass up breakfast and hurry outside to check on Friday. The sight of Father filling a barrel with water, and the smoldering fire nearby for heating stones to make it scalding hot, takes my breath away.

My heart races as I slip past Father and coax Friday to follow me to the forest. When Father discovers us missing he hollers, "You, Abraham, fetch back that hog! You Abraham, you Abraham, fetch back that hog!" The louder he calls, the farther and faster Friday and I run until we're out of hearing range. We stay in the woods waiting for nightfall. On our return, Father scolds me and switches me with a stick until my back oozes. He ties my pet to a tree stump and threatens to whip me twice as hard if I interfere again.

After another restless night, I rise early and sneak outside, planning once more to take Friday to hide in the woods. My heart sinks. Father is up before me again, his eyes narrow and dark as he prepares my pet for slaughter. Without breakfast once again, I start for the woods—this time alone.

Not long afterwards, Friday's squeals stab at my heart. I take off running, gasping for breath through mucous and tears, as if it's my life Father wants to take. A half mile away, at the creek, the sound of flowing water covers distant noises, and I race along its bank, finally in control of myself, breathing in unison with the current's rhythm. Calm settles over me when I stop to rest and distract myself by floating twigs downstream. Now and then, my serenity is disturbed by thoughts of how to mete out the punishment Father deserves. My mind often ponders what kind of world lies beyond our little Knob Creek farm. Maybe I'll run away.

By noon, my stomach growls, and I start for home. From the edge of the clearing by our cabin, Friday comes into clear view; he's split open, gutted, and hanging from a pole. Mist covers my eyes, blurring Friday's image. My stomach wrenches into knots, and my heart is heavy. I turn and race back into the woods and keep running along the creek side, determined to put as much distance as possible between me and Father's treachery.

A mile deep into the woods my legs grow weary, and hunger pangs prick my stomach. I stop and forage for acorns to stay my appetite. Once my hunger is abated, a tall hickory tree offers shelter from the glaring sun. My eyes sting from the saltiness of my tears. I rub them and blink, then rub them some more and blink again. The stinging subsides, and I gaze up at the overhanging branches, studying the leaves' shapes and following patterns in the rippled bark of the limbs. In time, sleep overtakes me. When my eyes open, dusk is settling over the forest. I get up and wander home, resigned to accept whatever punishment Father has in store for me.

A couple of months later, we're all settled in for supper when Mother sets cured ham on the table. The sight of it makes me gag. Forgetting any thoughts of hunger, I make a beeline for bed and burrow under a layer of animal skins to block out everything around me.

The next morning I glare at the spot where Father had slashed Friday's throat. Tears trickle down my cheeks. With a chip of bark, I scrape into a pile every grain of soil that had taken in Friday's blood and heap twigs and hot coals over the little mound. Pain gnaws at every bone in my body as the fire burns down to a bed of fine white ashes. I gather up the hem of my tow-linen shirt, forming a make-shift sack, and collect some soft dirt from the edge of the clearing to spread over the ashes, covering the earth's memory of my pet's murder.

So when Father looks askance at my new dog, something pinches at my heart.

One time, on our way to Hodgen's mill, Honey sets off after a coon. In no time, he gets himself stuck in a hollow log, and it takes me considerable effort to extract him. On arriving at the mill, Mr. John says we're last in line and the wait is long. Instead of going in with Missus Sarah to read, I pass the time exploring a nearby cave.

A few yards inside, I find myself wedged between two large rocks. Faint glimmers of daylight cast shadows off the jagged walls around me. For some time, I struggle to get loose, exhaling the last wisps of breath still in my lungs, contorting and angling myself every which way, trying to pry the boulders apart with my hands, but they don't budge. No effort is successful. I cannot gain my freedom.

All the time I'm wrestling with those rocks, Honey is whining and darting between my confinement and the mouth of the cave. But once darkness engulfs us, he races off, barking. When he doesn't return after several minutes, thoughts of dying in the pitch of night, or being eaten by a bear, weigh on me. On considering the first prospect, my body quakes, on the latter, my eyes shut and my throat seizes up.

About the time I've given up hope of being found, Honey's barking is back, and shimmers of light reflect off the cavern walls. Next, come echoes of Mr. John's anxious voice calling my name. I let out a holler. Before long, my dog and my friend are standing in front of me. Being big and strong, Mr. John makes quick work of pulling me out. At one point, however, I'm resigned that my salvation will come at the price of leaving a patch of my hide on the coarse surface of the rocks.

Outside the cave we're greeted by a large search party, including Father. The good miller glares at Father and speaks sharply. "Now, Tom, Abraham here is my prisoner. You must promise not to whip him or even scold him. The trouble he's been through is lesson enough. I doubt he'll be going into that cave again."

Father tightens his hands into fists and says, "I'll raise my boy how I sees fit."

Mr. John puffs out his large chest. "I've told you before, me and my Ma would be grateful for you and the missus to give us young Abraham. We love him like a son and would take right good care of him. Now what I'm tellin' you is, if ever you raise a hand to him about this matter, I'll come and fetch him away and never give him back."

Father knows Mother would never forgive him if the Hodgens take me in for good. On top of that, he'd have no one to slough off chores on. Once home, he heeds Mr. John's warning, but his meanness comes out in other ways. He works me long hours each day at tilling the fields and whips me if I work too slowly. He says to me, "That nosy miller cain't blame me fer beatin' the laziness outta ya. It's fer yer own good."

In early autumn of that same year, an itinerant preacher, the Rev. Mr. Gentry, visits our settlement. His face glows to match the shine of his bald head as he inspects the outdoor church we've built under the shade of a large maple. "It's perfect for camp meeting," he says. "God led you to build the church in this spot for the special purpose of winning souls." Its pulpit is carved out of a stump, and the benches are whipsawed from felled trees.

Under the sway of Rev. Gentry's fire and brimstone sermons, Father makes another trip to the mourner's bench, repenting of his sinful ways. Afterwards, he gets called upon to pray aloud before the entire congregation. Our neighbors whisper among themselves they hope it sticks this time. He proves their sentiments are anchored in fact when one night, after making a public prayer, he comes home and kicks Honey's bad leg.

The next morning I confess to Austin, "Don't know 'bout Father's religion."

"What makes you say that?" he asks.

I tell him about Father kicking my dog and say, "All Honey did was lay his nose on Father's knee, tryin' to be friendly. Can't believe anybody with even a little religion would kick a dog, 'specially kick its bad leg that's all twisted from a fall."

"Maybe your father thinks it's no harm to kick a dog. Could be he s'poses God don't care much for dogs."

I wrinkle my nose. "Why, he'd be a mighty funny God if he doesn't like a good dog."

If Father's behavior isn't enough to shake my faith in his religion, Rev. Gentry makes me doubly wary. Later that same morning, the parson knocks on our door and asks to borrow a hat to cover his head. He says his blew off in a stiff gust, landed in the creek, and got carried away. Mother offers him my coonskin hat which he promises to return.

In the afternoon when we gather as usual for the sermon, Rev. Gentry doesn't show.

Folks speculate he got a calling out of the blue to carry the gospel to a more needy flock.

I turn to Austin and say in a low voice, "Seems to me it's called stealing a perfectly good cap. No God who allows dogs to be kicked or a boy's hat to be stolen is of much use."

Austin whispers, "Those words would kill yer ma."

"She shan't hear them," I vow.

Chapter Two

Austin hollers as soon as he rounds the bend in the trail. His mother waves as he takes off, sprinting up the hill to our cabin.

"Haloo, Austin," I call out, leaping off my perch atop the split rail fence and race down to meet him.

Within minutes our mothers are giving us their usual cautions before we take off into the woods.

Austin leads.

Every day should be like this.

Down near the creek branch, I recall spotting some partridges the previous day. Hunting doesn't appeal to me much, but Austin fancies it a lot.

I point to the knoll across the branch. "That's where the birds were yesterday."

He pulls out his sling shot then studies the current. "Crick's too wide to cross here."

He's right. Even though my legs are longer than his, it's still too far to leap across.

I spot a foot log upstream and sprint to it. "Let's try this."

"No, Abe. Log's too small."

I glare at him. "Don't call me that. Call me Abraham just like my grandpa. He was a hero in the Revolution."

"Don't see what's wrong with Abe."

"Abe sounds dumb."

"Everyone calls you Abe."

"Sally doesn't. Father and Mother don't."

He shrugs. "You can't make everyone stop calling you that."

My shoulders sag. "S'pose you're right."

He saunters up to the log, scratching the back of his neck. "Nah. Won't do."

I puff out my chest. "It'll do just fine. Come on. Don't be a chicken."

He squints. "The bark's slippery."

I nudge it with my bare foot. "It ain't slippery."

He checks the fast flowing stream again and shakes his head. "Ah ... dunno."

"Dare you."

He jerks around and glares at me, then plants one foot on the log, testing it. After a moment, he spreads both arms like wings and eases across, bending his knees a bit and keeping his body centered over the log.

Now it's my turn. The water's seven, maybe eight, feet deep. The current's so fast it'll suck me under and drag me away.

Austin laughs. "Coon it."

No way I'm going to take the coward's way— straddling the log and scooting across it on my tail.

My first step is just like Austin's, half squatting, except I teeter. After getting my balance, I slide one foot forward then drag the other right up behind it, repeating the same until I'm about halfway out.

Austin laughs. "Come on slow-poke."

I glare at him and swing my back foot around to plant it in front of my forward foot. My front knee wobbles, and back foot shoots out one way while the rest of me tilts the other.

Austin hollers, "Don't look down. Look at me."

I glance down. During dry-spells a person can jump across in most places. But when the weather turns stormy, the creek tests its banks, and the water rushes downstream like a gale pounding us from the east. The tallest, strongest men can't stand against it. My arms flail in the air, but there's nothing to grasp onto.

"Coon it," Austin shouts again.

But before I can blink, I'm in the creek, limbs

thrashing. I call out to Austin. Water pours into my mouth. The current coils around me and drags me into its cavernous throat. A chill penetrates me, drawing every muscle taut as its icy sting riddles my bones. I kick and stretch my arms upward, grasping for the surface. My breath rushes out of me, bubbles erupting from my nostrils and swirling past my ears, sounding like the devil's laughter. I want to scream, but my lungs are empty, burning. My heart aches as if struggling against a vise.

An eternity later, a bough slaps the water in front of me. My senses fade away. No sight, nor sound, nor touch, nor taste, nor smell, only the sensation of floating in darkness, as if in a deep sleep.

Next, Austin is yelling, "Abe, Abe, stay with me." He's yanking on my arms and shaking me.

I jerk about, gasping and coughing up water.

He laughs. "Lord, thought you was dead."

"Me too," I rasp, shivering. A host of prickly hairs sprout all over me.

"Better let our things dry. Our mothers gonna switch us if they find out you fell in that crick."

"Spank me she will, but she's never laid a switch to me." I undress and hang my clothes on a bush.

Naked, I tiptoe to a sunny patch of ground and sit, drawing my knees up to my chest. The sun filters through the October chill, warming my bare skin, yet my mood remains shrouded. My mind wanders to my infant brother Tommy who died a few years back. Will this raging creek sweep him out of his grave and swallow him up? Folks around here tell of corpses being washed up out of the ground and floating off during storms. Even without melting ice or snow, and without a drop of rain here in the lowlands, the runoff from storms in the hills can fill our streams and swamp our fields. It's like the great flood that Mother's *Bible* speaks of; a flood that once destroyed all mankind, except for a chosen few.

I look over at Austin, wanting him to rescue me from my melancholy.

He meets my gaze and says, "Remember that game of hide 'n seek? When you hid up in the big sycamore tree."

We laugh together.

My dark mood has lightened. "Remember that prank I tried to pull on you?"

His eyes get big. "Sure do. I wander up the tree and sit down right under ya, pretending you've stumped me. I say out loud, 'Think this is a good spot to rest 'til ol' Abe shows his face.'"

"I barely keep myself from splitting a gut and falling off that limb."

He bounces to his knees. "You don't see your hat's tucked in the waist of my britches. You'd dropped it on the trail."

I shake my head. "When you start to nod off, I undo my pants and aim right fer yer head. But jest as my load drops, ya prop my hat upside down and catch the whole stinkin' mess."

Austin slaps his knee and lets out a whoop. "You was so surprised ya almost fell down outta that tree. That look on yer face when I jumps up and hollers, 'It's not every day someone gets the best of you, Abraham Linkhorn.'"

I laugh, forgetting I'm naked as a jaybird. Austin is rolling on the ground, jerking about like he's been touched by the Holy Ghost—except he's not convulsing from Satan's legions fleeing the name of Jesus. No hollering, spitting, kerchief-waving itinerant preacher has brought him to this state. He's contorted from giggling.

By the time I'm dressed and we return to the cabin, the memories of the dark hollow of death that nearly consumed me down at the creek are gone. Instead, I'm relieved at finding our mothers so deep in conversation that we slip past them unnoticed. This time, we escape our just punishment.

Early the next day, Mother again dons her Sunday best. When she calls for Sally and me, my melancholy spell has returned. Again, visions of Knob Creek's chilly throat close in on me, and storm clouds darken the sky over our little valley.

Mother looks at Sally. "You keeps an eye on Abraham whilst I be gone a bit."

Sally gives me an evil eye. Then she glares at Mother who shushes her. Mother may not look it, but she's as rough-and-tumble as most men in these parts. People laugh about her mixing it up with men.

Each of us nods.

As Mother disappears beyond the trees, I take off.

Sally calls after me. "Abraham Linkhorn, where do you s'pose you're goin'?"

I stop and look down, poking at the muddy ground with my bare foot. "Nowhere particular."

She shakes her head and groans.

I turn and start for the woods.

She hollers at me, "Stay away from that crick."

Hackles go up on the back of my neck. I spin around. "I'm seven. Nearly a man. Stop babyin' me."

"You're far from a man, Abraham, and you should know to mind your elders."

"Jest 'cause you're nine, that don't make you my elder. Elders are smarter, not jest older."

"If that's so, why do ya mind Pa?" She grins.

I look off into the trees. "'Cause he's bigger and stronger, for now."

She turns and marches into the cabin.

"Know-it-all," I mumble.

Even when Sally gets uppity with me, I love her. She used to carry me through mud and rain to the one-room log school—half the size of our little cabin, but with the same dirt floor. I only came up to her shoulders, then, and she kept watch over me so the bigger boys wouldn't bully me.

On our first day at the Riney school, Mother made me wear a sunbonnet and tow-linen shirt that hung below my knees. As usual I wore no pants. When we stepped through the rough hewn doorway, a curly-haired girl blabbed, "Don't he look jist like one of 'em darkies out on the big road?" One of the older boys blurted, "Yeah, some ol' mammie gittin' herded off to her new massa down Cumberland way mus've left him behind." Other children joined their teasing.

A girl with blonde hair sneered at me. "Lookie how dark his face and legs are," she said. "He mus' be a little Negro boy."

Sally made them stop, and when we returned home,

she convinced Mother to braid me a manly new hat out of straw. Mother said not much can be done about my slave-boy, tow-linen shirt, due to our poverty.

Until yesterday, the roiling water of Knob Creek never sparked fear in me, but these woods always make me shiver. I keep watch as I creep along. My heart beats faster, haunted by visions of Indians stalking me, lurking behind every tree. They'd be ghosts of the ones who slaughtered Grandpa Abraham and would've killed Father, as well. He was just a tyke at the time.

That Indian, his tomahawk poised, hovering over Father—just a boy—is more than a dream to me. Grandpa dying at his side. Uncle Mordecai firing the flintlock, cutting the savage down before he can wreak more terror. Folks say the Indians are long gone from these parts, but thinking about them chills me.

The big sycamore tree Austin and I laughed about just yesterday makes me laugh again. The knots in my back begin to unravel. This old tree chases away the pall that hangs over me—its branches reaching down like the arms of a gentle father.

Weeks later, Father returns from his excursion across the Ohio River and says we have to leave our home. My playtimes with Austin end, and my boyhood dies.

I catch a whiff of the approaching winter storm. Darkness settles over the woods even though it is barely noon. Knob Creek thrashes against its banks, already filled with icy runoff from the deluge that blankets the nearby hills. I envy the freedom with which these waters flow, even though their abandon makes me fret, not only over Tommy. A few days ago Mrs. Gollaher and Austin carried Mother and me in their wagon to Tommy's grave where we bid him our final goodbyes. Mother wants to be laid next to him when she dies, but her wishing is in vain now that Father says we must remove to Indian Anner. That's what I called it before Missus Sarah corrected me.

Father's voice breaks through the roar of rushing water. "Abraham, git yeself up here. There's work to be done if we're gonna make Indiana 'fore winter."

He's wrong. Our cow is already haltered, and all that's left is packing the horses that'll carry our sparse provisions over a hundred miles to our new home. Father will return in the spring for our pigs; in the meantime, Mr. Gollaher will keep an eye on them.

On the other side of the Ohio, the bulk of our personal belongings wait for us, as do the barrels of whiskey Father will use to pay for a new farm. He must've bought the whiskey from Mr. Boone at the distillery down where Knob Creek spills into the Rolling Fork. "Uncle Boonie" treats us well. Likely, he sold Father the whiskey at a favorable price, or gave it to him for missed wages he never got paid for making barrels.

When it's time to leave, Austin and his family come to say farewell. As we clutch each other, my tears dampen Austin's shirt, and his soak mine. I promise to remember him every day for the remainder of my life.

Father, Mother, Sally, and I say nothing to one another until the Ohio River comes into view. While storm clouds cast their shadows on the river's cold gray waters, Father tells us the Linkhorn name will stay behind in Knob Creek. We will call ourselves Lincoln in our new home. One more part of my childhood is wrenched away.

Chapter Three

As the year-long winter resumes its assault, we arrive at our new homestead near Little Pigeon Creek in the Indiana wilderness. Without unloading our belongings, Father races against an impending storm to make a scant shelter, tucked up against a thicket of bare-limbed trees. It's called a half-faced camp—fourteen foot sides, framed with stout poles, and covered on three sides with smaller poles and brush. At the open end, we build a fire for cooking. The embers provide warmth, and the fire's glow keeps hungry animals at bay.

A lull in the storm gives Father time to hunt, but fierce winds and snow trap us in our shabby lean-to before he can cure enough game to last until spring. A few days later, our fire dies out from want of kindling, and we hang animal skins across the open face—our only defense against the elements.

Sally and I huddle under animal pelts on a mattress of dried leaves and twigs piled at the foot of our parents' crude bed. Our teeth clatter, and our tears are dried up from a bone-aching cold that has sucked moisture out of everything. A hungry panther's scream keeps us awake late into the night. If it doesn't get us first, we're sure to become supper for a bear or pack of ravenous wolves.

Sally drapes her arm over me and whispers, "Snug up closer. We'll be warmer."

I burrow against her. "Should've drowned in that stupid crick. Would've been over an' done with."

"Shh ...." Her voice is nearly lost in the howling storm. "Try dreamin' 'bout Kentucky."

"If we see morning, Father will insist God's Mercy has saved us from our own foolishness."

Sally giggles. "Mother will argue we're in the hands of Providence."

Near my eighth birthday in early February, tiny patches of bare ground checker the snow in front of the half-faced camp. I peer between the animal pelts hanging over our entry and spot a small flock of turkeys mingling among the trees, scratching about for acorns or frozen bugs. Father is out setting traps. He left his muzzleloader behind, propped just inside the opening. He's been teaching me to shoot and keeps hounding me about becoming a man. Tells me it's time to put aside childish ways, just as Mother's *Bible* says.

A voice inside my head telling me it's wrong to kill. "Mother, would Father be angry if I shot a turkey?"

She nods and says in a low voice, "He'd be proud."

My hands tremble as I fumble with the ramrod, trying to pack powder, waddling, and shot down the gun's barrel. I draw a deep breath and raise the stock to my shoulder, taking aim. Tiny beads of sweat line my brow, and the muzzleloader weighs heavy in my clammy hands. My conscience twinges again, but I quell it once more and whisper, "... put aside childish ways."

The charge explodes, pummeling my ears, and my eyes slam shut. When I open them, the turkey is flailing and making an ungodly noise. "I've murdered it," I whimper.

I collapse to my knees, sobbing.

Mother tries to console me.

Tears roll down my cheeks. "Father can be proud of me if he wants, but I hate myself for what I've done. Never again will I pull a trigger on anything as large as a turkey."

Spring's arrival finds Father building a permanent shelter from logs he harvests out of the dense forest. He says it's going to be at least two times bigger than the half-faced camp. I do my best to help, but never enough to please him. He no longer teaches me to shoot, instead he puts an axe in my hands and gives me long hours of practice felling trees. To help Mother and Sally, I keep the fire going and trek a mile each way down to the creek whenever the water pails are empty.

If Father's in a good mood, or if he's out tromping through the woods, Mother recites stories to Sally and me from the *Bible* and *Aesop's Fables*, books we spirited away from Kentucky without Father's knowledge. The passages are ones that were read to her as a child, which she committed to memory. As Mother recites, Sally and I follow along in the books. In this way we build on the meager skills we gained at the ABC schools back home. Mother encourages me to practice writing as well.

Warmer temperatures allow us to plant corn and vegetables among the tree stumps left from cutting timber for logs. By late summer the new cabin is up, and our first crop is ready for harvest. I begin regular trips on horseback to the grist mill a couple miles away. Often, waiting for my turn to grind our corn into flour takes hours. My idle time is filled reading books I've borrowed from neighbors.

One afternoon, I return from the mill to find Father back home from gathering the pigs we'd left behind at the Gollahers' in Kentucky. That was one of Father's few sound choices. The unruly animals would have slowed us down, preventing our arrival in time to build even the sparsest winter shelter. Survival would have been impossible. Of course, if storms had set upon us along the way, we all might have died before reaching our destination, anyway.

I grin broadly and bring the old mare to a halt. The Sparrows, relatives of ours who lived near Knob Creek, are unpacking their belongings and moving into the half-faced camp we've recently abandoned.

Dennis Hanks, a cousin, is ten years my elder, lean, and only a scant taller. He calls out, "Haloo, Abraham."

"Cousin Dennis," I holler back as I jump down and dash toward him, forgetting the sacks of flour draped over the horse's neck.

Father scowls. "Mind yer manners, boy. Give due respect to yer elders, first." He points to Aunt Betsey and Uncle Thomas. They raised Mother from the time she was a girl, and now watch over Dennis because his mother died, and he's a Hanks bastard.

I straighten. "Good day, Uncle Thomas, Aunt Betsey. Have you quit Kentucky, also?"

"Good day, Abraham," says Aunt Betsey who bears a resemblance to Mother. She smiles at Father. "Your Nancy's workin' to make a fine gentleman outta this one."

"Time'd be better spent makin' him useful, rather than wastin' it on readin'," Father grumbles. "Gittin' too smart for his britches. Always got his nose stuck in some book. Startin' to soun' like one too."

Dennis breaks in. "Abraham, help me unload."

As we rush off, Dennis mutters in my ear, "Yer ol' man's still mean as a polecat."

"No difference 'tween him and those slave traders back in Kentucky, except I don't reckon they yoke or beat their own sons."

That evening at supper when Mother sets a kettle on the table, I examine the sparse offering of potatoes, and scowl. A quick glance toward the fireplace dashes my hopes that another pot of vittles is simmering away. That would be quite a trick, since we just have the one pot that's already on the table. The only other thing coming from that hearth tonight is a touch of warmth. Of course, any heat from the fire makes a quick escape through the doorway that's still in want of a door.

Father calls for us to bow our heads and offers a blessing for the food.

"These is mighty scant blessings," I mutter.

Father glares at me and pounds his fist on the table.

Mother shouts, "Thomas!"

He looks at her, and she stares him down.

We eat the potatoes and go to bed without a word spoken among us.

Next morning, I ask Mother where Father is off to.

"Huntin' with Dennis," she replies, adding she can't understand why he always waits for our stomachs to ache with hunger before he hunts.

I mumble low enough she can't hear, "Maybe now he has a son who'll make him proud."

After a couple days, Father and Dennis lumber home carrying a single, scrawny deer.

Chapter Four

U nlike the half-faced camp, our cabin's fireplace is protected from direct assault by winter's frigid storms, but its walls are still a sparse defense against icy gusts. Instead of slicing through loosely stacked poles, the wind whistles between logs which are not yet chinked with mud and grass. Snow drifts that pile up inside our open doorway eventually melt, making a mud hole of our dirt floor.

Mother's nagging about these deficiencies has no effect on Father. He and Dennis spend the bulk of their time wandering the woods for game. Father gets something now and then, Dennis hardly ever. When not hunting, they swap stories in front of the fire, Dennis being more of a chatterbox than a storyteller. I devote the long winter nights to reading long passages from the *Bible* or *Aesop's Fables* which come easier to me now, and in my head I act out portions that catch my fancy.

When the weather warms, Father finds new excuses to neglect our cabin's needs. Extending the fence takes precedence over making a door or chinking our walls. I'm still not much good with the finer points of wielding an axe, so Father has me drag rails from the pile to the fence and lift them into place.

One sweltering afternoon near Independence Day of my ninth year, a party of strangers driving a large wagon comes by as I'm helping Father split fence rails.

I climb onto the fence and hail them. "How long you been on the trail?"

"Weeks," one of them says.

"Where do you hail from?"

He grins. "Maine. North-most part of the country."

"What's it—"

Father cuffs me on the side of my head, knocking me to the ground.

I turn away to hide a solitary tear trickling down my face as Dennis crawls between the fence rails and helps me to my feet.

By the time I'm standing, Father has apologized to the strangers for my insolence.

I run to the cabin to check on Mother, who's sick once again. Except for my feeble attentions, I'm certain she'd be ignored completely. Father is always preoccupied, and Sally is overwhelmed carrying Mother's burden as well as her own.

Mother is in bed, her eyes closed. Frontier life has drained her. Father should have never made us leave our Knob Creek farm.

Her forehead, clammy to the touch, means the fever has subsided; her face is ashen. "How are you?"

She looks up at me and rasps, "Better, son."

Her hand is cold, bony. My voice cracks. "I worry."

"Ya shouldn'. I'll be up an' 'bout soon."

"I know." Something tells me it's not true, though.

"Abraham," she murmurs, "fetch me some water?"

"Yes, Mother."

After returning with a cup of water, I sit on the edge of the bed and watch her sip, her lips trembling. Mine quiver as well.

Mother whispers, "Abraham, I won' always be here for ya ... to teach ya right 'n wrong. Promise you'll be good. 'Specially, obey Father and be kind to Sally. Learn from books, even if it makes Father angry. Grow to be a fine man, a preacher or teacher, someone special."

My throat grows raw. "But you're not going to leave us any time soon."

"We never knows the Good Lord's intentions," she tells me. "Jest do as I says."

"Yes, Mother." I lay my head on her frail chest and weep.

Father calls me from outside. I wipe my tears and kiss Mother's forehead. He calls again, impatiently.

"Coming, Father."

When I stand at the doorway, he stares at me. "Fetch some corn from the storage 'n get down to the mill. Sally tells me the flour is runnin' low."

"Yes, Sir."

I fill up two sacks with corn from the storage bin and tie each of them to opposite ends of a leather strap. After draping the strap over our old mare's withers, I climb on board and goad her into a trot. When Father can no longer see us, I rein her in and recite *Bible* verses the rest of the way to Noah Gordon's Mill.

Upon arriving at the mill, Miller Gordon—he's a shadow of Mr. John from Knob Creek—he tells me the wait is long. A book I've smuggled in one of the sacks of corn fills my idle time until my turn comes near sundown. I hitch the old mare to the wheel arm of the grinding stone and sit atop a rail, coaxing her around the circle.

After a few turns, the old nag becomes sluggish and stubborn. Each time she passes my perch, she gets a smack on her rump and a goading, "Git up, you old hussy." A couple of turns later, I swat her again, and as I'm saying "Git up—" she bucks and plants her unshod hoof into my forehead. Folks say I was unconscious through the night and presumed killed. Family and neighbors gathered in our little cabin to keep vigil, poor Mother not only sick with fever but stricken by grief.

Upon waking late the next morning, I jerk upright and blurt out the rest of my refrain "—you old hussy."

The resulting deformity of my skull leaves my left eye unfocused and drifting upward—a constant reminder of my near death. My quickening from that premature mortality also endows me with an abundance of mental energies. Lengthy passages from Mother's *Bible* come to me with greater ease, and the entirety of *Aesop's Fables* rolls off my tongue without a single line misspoken. I remember almost everything without effort.

Weeks later, Father catches me reading in the middle

of chores, my axe propped against a tree. He complains I'm lazy as a possum and whips me with a strap until my back is raw. A few days later he rips up one of my poems and grinds it in the dirt with his heel. In spite of being threatened with more lashes, reading books and writing verse are irresistible temptations. The more I read, the more Father's ignorance embarrasses me. When I correct him on even a small error, he gives me the back of his hand, or sometimes his fist. Mother is too weary to protest.

As the chill of autumn blows through the prairie, milk sickness descends on us, taking our neighbor, Mrs. Brooner, as its first fatality. Uncle Thomas and Aunt Betsey are afflicted soon after.

About noon one day, Mother returns to our cabin—not much more than a skeleton now—exhausted from tending the sick. She nods at Father, and for once he seems to know her thoughts. He takes down a whipsaw from the wall and turns to me. "Come along, Abraham." I follow him to the log pile and watch as he examines several specimens. He selects one and motions for me to help. We lift it off the stack and set it on the ground. Next, he picks up the saw and tells me to grab one end. First, I rub my clammy hands on my pants.

As we begin cutting the log into boards, I ask if we need Cousin Dennis' help.

Father says to let him be.

My throat tightens. "Are Uncle Thomas and Aunt Betsey getting better?"

Father yanks on his end of the saw.

I barely hang on to mine. I don't repeat my question, not wanting to hear him confirm what I dread to know—they're already dead and Mother's time is coming soon.

When we're done sawing the first log, he chooses another that we cut into more boards. We repeat the process again until Father decides we've made enough, and he shows me how to bore holes in the planks. As I proceed, he whittles pegs from scraps he digs out of the trim pile.

Once finished, we assemble the boards into two long, narrow boxes. Tears trickle down my cheeks. The boxes remind me of the one little Tommy was put in to be buried.

I return to the cabin and sit on the bed beside

Mother, taking her hands in mine. They're cool. Her forehead is chilled, more so than the time weeks ago.

"Fetch me a pail." She winces and clutches her stomach.

When I return with the pail, she begins retching.

Soon, Sally joins me at Mother's bedside, and we help her sit up. My sister cups Mother's chin and tilts her head back. Her tongue is white, as if it's coated with milk. Sally shakes her head. Mother grimaces as we lay her back.

Over the ensuing days Mother's condition worsens. Her tongue is now dark, nearly black. She has no control of her arms or legs. Her head wobbles when we help her sit. It's been seven days since she left her bed. Cramping and dry heaving come regularly. Her bowels are empty.

Late that afternoon, she whispers for Sally and me to draw close. "Love each other and God," she says. After a deep breath she adds, "Be good to Father."

Sally and I cry.

Mother reaches for my hand, but her arm falls limp at her side. Her mouth quivers.

I move closer and turn my ear toward her lips.

She rasps, "Be ... special ...."

I recall the promise she asked of me weeks ago.

Father comes into the cabin and stands at Mother's bedside. None of us speaks for the longest while.

Mother strains to prop herself up on her elbows. Failing, she falls back on the bed, mumbling. Sally and I lean forward wanting to understand her words, but it's useless. Her breathing becomes shallow, sporadic. After several minutes, she gasps one last time, then breathes no more.

Sally closes Mother's eyes.

I lay my head on her hollow chest, choking back tears, begging her not to leave us.

Sally strokes my hair and whispers, "Shh ...."

Father hangs his head and shuffles toward the doorway. At the threshold, he stops and speaks my name without turning. He waits for me to follow him to the woodpile. As we saw boards for her coffin, I bite my lip, fighting back tears, but a trickle escapes, tracing the edge of my nose until it finds the corner of my mouth. My tongue tastes its saltiness. When Father thinks we've cut enough boards, I bore holes into them, and he whittles pegs. My head throbs as we cobble together the long, narrow box for Mother's burial.

At Father's instruction, I pick up one end of her coffin, and together we carry it into the cabin. My eyes are swollen and raw. I stumble, unable to see my way. At Mother's bedside, I wipe away tears and focus on her ashen face. No longer is it contorted by disease. Her lips are cool to the touch of my trembling fingers.

As we lift her body, wrapped in a threadbare dress she wore most every day, she almost floats into the coffin— light, like the skeleton of a tiny sparrow that's fallen from its nest and died. What reason is there to live on? If the milk-sick disease should claim me soon, it would be a welcome escape.

That evening we bury Mother alongside Aunt Betsey and Uncle Thomas in a dale not far from the cabin. Once the last shovel of dirt is thrown onto her grave, I kneel and erupt into convulsive sobbing.

Father mutters, "Come along. There's work to be done."

Sally follows him, stopping for a moment to kiss the top of my head.

Weeks pass without Father speaking a word about Mother's death. He spends much of his time in the woods, often alone but sometimes with Dennis. Regardless, there's little meat on our table. Preparations for the winter are also ignored; our cabin still lacks a door, and the gaps between logs remain unchinked.

Sally rises each day before dawn and works long into the night, cooking, cleaning, and mending. She says little, except making an occasional complaint that she can't manage the household alone. I keep the fire fueled for her, and fell trees or split logs to bury my grief.

When the skies darken, turning daytime into a near-night, torrents of rain beat on Mother's unmarked grave, threatening to wash her body up from the ground. On those occasions, I sit on the sod above her, railing against Heaven, praying to whatever God there is to keep her safe from flooding. In the evenings, under the dim light of the fire, I painstakingly etch out a letter to Rev. Elkin, a preacher Mother knew back in Kentucky, and implore him to attend to her proper burial as soon as he can brave the wilderness and come to us. Her body could be swept away by flooding before her soul is delivered safely into the Almighty's hands.

The misery of another winter taunts us like a panther toying with its prey, and we still have no answer from Rev. Elkin. I take up an ax and devote the short hours of daylight to felling more trees and splitting firewood. Father is more distant and brooding than ever.

We are often hungry, except for Sally, who no longer has any appetite, and we're always cold. At night, Father and Dennis sit at the table bantering about matters of little consequence while I lie by the fireplace reading Mother's *Bible*. Sally huddles in the corner under layers of animal skins, her sobs mingling with the moans of icy winds blowing through our cabin.

By spring, our strength is nearly dissipated, and our spirits are crumbling. Then one sunny afternoon, Rev. Elkin arrives to preach a sermon at Mother's grave. Some twenty neighbors join in prayers for our family and for Mother's soul, but the warmth of the moment is soon gone.

During the planting season, I lack the energy or the will to challenge Father, so I put aside my reading and writing, and tend to chores. He fills my idle time with trying to teach me his trade of carpentry. He says it's a son's calling to follow his father's footsteps. My heart's not in it. Father grows frustrated and invests no further effort in my apprenticeship. He leaves undone the cabin door we were making, and I become little more to him than a set of arms for wielding an axe.

Soon after the corn sprouts, Father slaughters our meager herd of pigs—a bear has already feasted on our cow. After he cures the meat, he sets out down the Ohio on a rented flatboat, intending to sell the pork. Since pork fetches a better price than wild game, he leaves none of the pork for Sally and me to eat. Besides, he tells us, he won't be gone long, and our supply of corn meal and cured game should be sufficient during his absence.

If need be, he says Cousin Dennis can hunt, notwithstanding his lack of skill and the continued scarcity of game. Much of the wildlife perished in the unending winter that lingered over the world for an entire year before we left Knob Creek. Back then we didn't know why summer never came, but now folks say it was due to the mountains that exploded half a world away—somewhere called the Dutch East Indies.

Once Father is gone, my days are filled with wandering the woods, writing poetry, and reading. When Sally asks, I grind corn by hand into flour and keep the fire going. Sometimes the embers die out, and I make more smoke than fire getting it restarted. Sally cooks as best she can and cleans. Dennis makes himself scarce, scouring the woods for game to little avail. When not hunting, he often boards with one of our neighbors, leaving Sally and me unattended.

As weeks stretch into months, Sally demands more help from Dennis and me. Dennis scowls and reminds us, "Men hunt. Women and children keep the house and tend the crops." He turns and struts away.

She calls after him, "The least you can do is make us a door for the cabin."

He shouts over his shoulder, "It cain wait 'til your pa gets home."

Sally stomps into the cabin, muttering about its naked doorway.

I lumber down to a stand of cornstalks, peel back a few husks, and find the kernels withered and pale. Just the same, I snap off the ears and hold them in my shirt. The harvest goes quickly as planting was sparse.

I carry the crop up to the cabin where Sally is sitting at the table, trembling and crying, her face buried in her hands. I drop the corn on the table in front of her and lay my hand on her shoulder. "What's the matter?"

She looks up at me. "Father's not coming back. I'm convinced of it."

"He wouldn't abandon us,"

"No, but something might have happened. This is wild country."

I search her face for any hint she can be consoled.

She drops her head. "He could have been killed by Indians. Or eaten by a bear or wolves."

I stroke her hair. "He can take care of himself."

She pounds the table and screams, "Abraham, he's never been gone this long before. What are we going to do for food if he doesn't come back?"

"He'll come back, and if we run out of food before he does, Dennis can hunt."

Sally laughs, her voice strained by bitterness. "Dennis is useless," she says. "Just like Father, he'll wait 'til our stomachs are knotted with pain before he picks up a gun to hunt. And when he does, he'll come back empty-handed as always."

My heart sinks. I am ten years old. Dennis Hanks, ten years my elder, is more of a child than me. If the survival of this household is on my shoulders, we're doomed. I walk to the uncovered doorway and stare at the horizon. I can't even make a door.

In due time, Father returns, but he doesn't stay long. Having sold all our pork, he's off to Kentucky to find a new wife. Now it's November, and the weather is turning foul. If winter's fury holds off for a week, it'll give him time to make it to Kentucky and its comforts.

Sally and I are not so fortunate. Our food stocks are low, and if we were fortunate to have a gun, I'm unskilled at hunting. I'm more useless at setting traps. One day as I'm making my usual trek to the creek to draw water, the skies unload a torrent of rain and sleet. In my haste to escape the storm, one of my boots gets lost in thick mud. The sole of the other is already worn through.

On seeing me stumble into the cabin, Dennis teases me. "Got yer head in them clouds again, Abraham? If ya come down here with the rest of us, ya might notice ya got one boot missin'."

My feet sting from the cold. "Not funny."

Dennis stands, shaking his head. "Off to the Turnhams to see if theys got spare vittles. When I git back I'll give ya a hand makin' some mocksakins."

Shivers run through me. "How long will you be?"

"Be goin' huntin', too." His eyes widen. "Plan to git a big deer, so likely be gone a while."

Sally glares at him. "Well, be quick about it. Pickins getting mighty slim."

He grins. "A week, maybe."

Days later Dennis still hasn't returned, and Sally and I wake to a smattering of snowflakes flying about in an icy wind. Hoping to beat the storm, I rush out in bare feet to gather kindling. By the time I return to the cabin, the snow is up to my ankles, and my toes are nearly frostbitten.

A few nights later, during another fierce storm, Sally sets two half-full cups of gruel on the table. "This is the end of our corn meal," she says, wiping a tear from her cheek. She drops onto her stool and bites her lip.

"Dennis is bound to scare up something soon."

"He's as lazy as Father." She laughs and points to the neglected doorway. She and I already tried hanging animal skins to keep out the storms, but the pelts were no match for winter's merciless assault.

I gaze about the cabin. Our woodpile is exhausted, and a mound of gray ashes in the fireplace is all that remains of the once glowing embers. Snow blows through our uncovered doorway, and a bitter wind howls through the still unchinked walls, sounding like a horde of ghosts.

After licking the final scraps of gruel from our bowls, Sally and I huddle in bed, covering ourselves with animal skins, both of us quivering from the cold. Her body quakes from crying, as well. I nuzzle closer to her and whisper, "Shh...."

She turns over and faces me, wiping away tears. "You know it's all Father's fault—even Mother's dying." She mutters, "If he hadn't brought us here, chasing after such foolish dreams ... we were happy in Kentucky."

"I know."

She buries her face in my chest and continues weeping. I wrap my arms around her and rehearse in my mind the scolding I'll give Father when he returns. In time her quaking ceases, and her whimpering gives way to quiet, rhythmic breathing. My heart aches for her. She's my only remaining love.

Sleep is the only relief we have from the pain in our stomachs and the fear in our hearts. At dawn, our aching returns, but neither of us has energy enough to rise. In time our bodies become weary and surrender to numbness. Instead of leaving our bed to tend to the necessities of toilet, we lie in our own piss. For the ensuing days, the only blessing we can count is that our need to relieve ourselves is lessened by the emptiness of our bladders and bowels.

When Father finally arrives with his new wife and her brood in tow, she gathers Sally and me to her side and smoothes our lice-ridden hair. She's smaller than Mother had been before her sickness, but she's sturdy as an oak. I gaze at her face, sweet and calm as an angel, her eyes warm and blue like the summer sky. Her gentle hand makes me forget my aching stomach. Winter's chill evaporates from my half-naked body.

Many times since Father left us to court the widow Johnston in Elizabethtown, I've wondered if a stepmother would make life less miserable, or more so. I've thought of Heaven with its golden streets and mansions, and wondered whether it would be better to die. Our new mother directs Father to gather wood for the fire, and she attends to bathing Sally and me. She dresses me in her eldest son's clothing, and Sally dons one of our new mother's own dresses. Once we're refreshed and spanking clean, she prepares a feast from provisions brought from Kentucky and food Father gathers from our neighbors at her insistence.

Chapter Five

I n the spring after I turn eleven, Mama, as we call her, sees to it that the cabin door is hung, wooden floors are laid, and a window is cut in the wall and covered with shutters. Our cabin is filled with furniture she brought from Kentucky, which Father would sell if he had the chance.

She tells him, "There's no excuse for a man's family to want for the basics of life, even on the frontier." She also makes fine new clothes for me and Sally, but her greatest gift is that I'm allowed to read and write without interference. All of us attend school when there's a teacher, and no longer borrow books in secret.

Father has taken a shining to Mama's eldest, John, who is two years my junior and something of a dullard. He's short and stocky, a likeness of my father that I am not. He might make me jealous, except that when John and I make mischief together, we get away with a great deal more than I would alone.

One evening, John talks me into sneaking out with him and some other boys on a midnight coon hunt. They need one more for a proper contingent, but I won't have to do any killing. They'll let me just tag along. Our attempt falls short, however, when Father's useless house-dog, Yellow Joe, sounds his alarm. We just get a mild scolding, since John confesses the excursion was his idea. He winks at me when Father looks away.

Several nights later, John's ready for another try at hunting coon and gets the idea of taking Yellow Joe with us. Come time to make our move, Yellow Joe follows us willingly, tail a-wagging. We meet up with the other boys and quickly snag our quarry. When they're done skinning the furry critter, someone suggests we sew the hide onto Yellow Joe as a joke. That's exactly what they start doing. I turn my eyes away to avoid seeing the needle going into the poor dog's hide. Even so, its whimpers pinch at my heart, though the discomfort doesn't prompt me to intervene. Instead, I allow their evil deed—tit for tat, torture Father's favorite dog to pay for my pig's death.

When they let go of the desecrated mutt, he scampers off, whimpering. The boys all howl with laughter as we follow. There's no catching Yellow Joe, though, and we figure he'll find his way home in time.

Come morning, Father's hollering wakes us. John and I climb down from the loft and stand shivering in the doorway. Outside, Father is on his knees surveying Yellow Joe's mauled carcass. Portions of the coon's hide are still attached.

John whispers to me, "A pack of large dogs must've mistook him for a coon."

I bite my lip, and my shoulders droop, weighed down by guilt. Of course, watching Father mourn isn't what grieves me. My grief is over my complicity in a cruel act. I've shown myself no better than ol' Zack Evans who abused his blind, decrepit horse that day at Mr. John's mill back in Kentucky. I'm also no better than Father who kicked my dog Honey on his twisted leg the evening before Rev. Gentry went off with my hat.

Father experiences another renewal of his zeal for religion, but I'm not as impressed as Mama. In spite of my skepticism, I tag along as we begin attending services with regularity. Even though the preacher makes no sense, I recall his words precisely. Sometimes, I mount a stump and gather the other children around, distracting them from their chores, to deliver a parody of the sermon. My step-sister Matilda, who's angelic like her mother, leads everyone in singing and I offer a prayer for the Lord to provide the chickens with stockings come winter.

On one such occasion, I recite a particularly ridiculous Sunday sermon.

> *Brethern and sistern. I rise to norate ontoe you on the subject of the baptismal. Yes, the baptismal! Ahem. There was Noah, he had three sons, ahem, namely, Shadadavack, Meshisick, and Bellteezer! They all went intoe Dannels den, and likewise with them was a lion! Ahem.*

At that point, I mimic the wild-eyed parson as he surveys his inattentive congregation. When the children begin to giggle, I continue.

> *Dear perishing friends, ef you will not hear ontoe me on this great subject, I will only say this, that Squire Nobbs has recently lost a little bay mare with a flaxy mane and tail, Amen!*

Father runs up and chases the children back to their chores. As for me, he dishes out a double portion of work. In no way does this change my ways. Mama will come to my rescue if he punishes me too harshly, and she'll remind him, "The boy needs to be about his readin' and cipherin'."

In my twelfth year, Father conscripts me to help construct the new church building. I show myself no more talented at carpentry than the summer after Mother died. When he grumbles, Mama turns a deaf ear and demands we continue. She's delighted to be gaining favor with the elders, so I fumble my way through until the job is done.

My passion for reading the *Bible* wanes as other volumes, which are easier to comprehend, capture my imagination. *Pilgrim's Progress* belongs to Josiah Crawford—we call him Old Bluenose on account of the purple veins in his large nose.

He's also a surly old miser. When the copy of Weems' *Life of Washington* that he lends me becomes damaged in a urain storm, he makes me pay with three days labor at twenty-five cents per day. In the end he lets me keep it, as he prefers to by an unblemished one for himself. On hearing the Ramsey biography of Washington is better than Weems', I borrow a copy of it from another neighbor.

Around my fourteenth year, I pose a question for Cousin Dennis while we're taking a break from felling trees "Why do folks call you *another* Hanks bastard?"

Dennis plops down on a log and laughs. "'Cause no one knows who my pappy is."

I sit down next to him. "You don't have a father?"

"We all got pappies," he says. "Jest some of us don't know who they is."

"Wish I had a different one."

He shakes his head. "Watch what ya wishes fer. Us bastards always get the crumbs."

I pick at a loose patch of bark. "At least you get to keep the wages you earn. No father is waiting for you at the end of the day to snatch them out of your hands."

"I'd trade my wages for a real pa any day."

A mosquito lights on my neck; I slap at it. "Just the same, it's a sin to eat bread from the sweat of another man's brow, that's what the *Bible* says."

"Yeah, but when ya gits out into that big world ya keep dreamin' of, where ya gits to hold onto yer own wages, ya don't want people knowin' yas a bastard. They'll treat ya like them lepers in the *Bible*. No bastard's gonna get a good wife or be let to make a good life."

A bank of thick black clouds fills the sky, closing in on us. "How do you know if you're a bastard?"

"Well, from some of the stories folks tell ...."

I stare at him blankly.

Dennis goes on. "Rumor has it yer pa was nowhere around when you was born'd. Folks say ya was named after a young neighbor named Abraham Enlow."

I jump to my feet. "I'm named after my grandpa, Abraham. He was a hero in the Revolution."

He shakes his head. "Sure, that's what yer pappy tells folks, but others say different."

I pound my forehead with the heel of my hand. "But a bastard can never be someone special."

"Ah, ya jest thinks yer better 'n the rest o' us. Truth is yer nuttin more'n a Hanks bastard yerself."

I start pacing. "But I promised my angel Mother when she died ... and the Weems book says 'every youth may become a Washington.'"

Dennis laughs. "Ha—maybe yer pa is right 'bout one thing. Ya reads too much."

I stop pacing and study his expression. "So, you mean when Father calls you *another* Hanks bastard, I'm the other one."

"Heavens boy, 'eres not jest two o' us. My mammy has six by herself. Bastards run in the Hanks' blood."

I run into the woods, tears streaming down my cheeks. When my legs give out, I sit under a tree and write a verse to salve the gashes Dennis' words left in my heart.

He speaks the cruelest words yet said
As storm clouds gather o'er my head.
No more dreams of Washington,
Naked I stand in bastardom.

At supper that night, a storm is raging, and I hardly touch my soup.

Mama says, "Ya won't be able to hear ya' self read later over the growling in yer stomach."

I stare at Father and ask, "What do you mean when you call Dennis *another* Hanks bastard?"

"Eat yer soup," he says.

Dennis chimes in. "'Cause ere's so many of us Hanks bastards."

"Shut up," Father says.

I stand and glare at Father. "Why do you call Dennis *another* Hanks bastard?"

Father points to my now cold soup. "Sit. Eat."

My lips tremble as I bolt for the door.

"Abraham," Mama calls.

Her voice stops me. I turn and glare at Father. "Is that why you hate me? Am I a bastard, too?"

He looks at me coldly.

His expression is all that's needed. I break for the door and rush outside, slogging through the driving rain.

Mama calls after me. At the edge of the woods, near the stump where I often mimic the itinerant preachers, I collapse, weeping and shivering. Before long, Mama is kneeling next to me wiping the rain from my face.

My words are almost incomprehensible through my blubbering. "I can't keep my promise."

"I know ya misses yer ma. She was an angel."

"I do miss her. I love you, too. Sally and I wouldn't be alive if you hadn't come to save us."

Mama clasps my face in her hands and tells me, "I loves ya, too. Jest wants ya to know it's okay fer ya to loves her and me both."

Her face is barely visible to me, my eyes blurred by tears. "Mother's dying isn't why I can't be someone special."

She takes my hands in hers. "But ya is special."

I pull away from her and hang my head. "No, Mama, bastards ain't special. They're not even fit for pig slop."

She brushes my wet hair from my eyes. "There, there," she whispers. "Ya ain't slop ... and, yer no bastard."

"You're just sayin' that."

"No, the gossip ya pro'lly hear Dennis Hanks spoutin' about ol' Enlow bein' yer pa is rubbish."

I shake my head. "Father wasn't with Mother when I was born."

Lightning streaks through the sky followed by a clap of thunder.

Mama takes my hands again, kissing them. "A couple days before ya was born, yer pa went to Elizabethtown, where I hail from, on important business. Before he could head home, the great blizzard of that year comes along, and he's stuck there for several more days. By the time ya come poppin' outta yer ma's womb, the fire is dead and there's no food in the house. Yer ma is so weak and yer sister so little that all of yas almos' perish."

She wipes the rain and tears from my face. I look up, gazing into her eyes.

She goes on. "Fortunate for everyone, the neighbor, Isom Enlow, stumbles upon the cabin where he finds ya all huddled in bed freezin' to death. Yer ma begs him to save her baby which he thinks is yer sister ... but when he pulls back the covers, he finds yer grey shriveled little body and can't tell if ya got any breath. Fer sure though, he's got to git ya warmed up in case yas still alive, and he rubs yer tiny body til ya begin a faint whimper."

I bite my lip.

"After that, he goes out and collects wood to start a fire, then he scrounges around the cabin for food. Finding none anywhere, he reaches in his pocket and pulls out a jar of turkey fat he carries for cleanin' his gun. He dips a string in it and holds it as ya suckles on it."

Salty tears drain into my throat.

"Yer ma is so grateful for Mr. Enlow saving her baby she agrees to name him Abraham after his son. 'Course yer pa claims he only allows it on account of it's yer grand pappy's name, too. You cain't say he don't love ya. The worst ya kin say is he sometimes is lax in caring fer the ones he loves ... but I'm fixin' that."

I jerk away. "No, he hates me."

Mama puts her hand to her mouth. "Ah, he don't hate ya, Abraham. He's angry at the whole wide world. Seems he's always drawin' the short stick in life. It's just some people's fate. I knowed yer pa before you was born. He's a good man. Why, when he came courtin' me, he paid off all my debts so we could marry. Most men wudda turned their backs on me and gone off lookin' for another wife."

I roll back on my heels. "That was money he got from selling the last of our food. He left me and Sally with nothing. We could have died while he was courting you."

Mama buries her face in her hands.

I stand. "Well, I can't love a man I don't respect. A man who can't read or write, or who kicks a dog. I don't want any part of someone who always leaves his family wanting and drags them to a God-forsaken wilderness where their mother shrivels and dies."

Mama reaches up and takes my hand. "I's so sorry, son. He's a good man."

I squeeze her hand. "Then let him show me."

She gazes toward our cabin.

After a long silence we release hands. "Who are the other Hanks bastards?"

She wipes the rain from her brow and takes a deep breath. "I lernt about yer ma and the Sparrows when yer pa started courtin' her. Ya see we all lived in Elizabethtown back in those days. Yer pa proposed to me afore he went after yer ma and I worried I broke his heart. So I kep' askin' folks how he was farin'."

Lightning pierces the night sky again. I let the thunder finish before asking, "What do the Sparrows have to do with anything?"

"Jest like they did for yer cousin Dennis, yer Aunt Betsey and Uncle Thomas took in your ma when she was a little girl. A lot of folks called her Nancy Sparrow."

"What happened to her ma and pa?"

"Her ma was all alone; father refused to say the baby was his. She couldn't manage raisin' a child by herself, so the Sparrows took yer ma in and raised her."

I drop my head and begin crying again, my tears mixing with the rain streaming down my face. "Then I'm the son of a bastard. What's the difference?"

"Shh ..." she whispers. "Nobody knows her pappy's name. Folks say he's rich. A planter down Virginia way. Well-bred and intelligent."

My throat is raw.

"Abraham Lincoln, ya come from the finest stock, and cain't no one take that away from ya."

"How can I become someone special when I don't even know who I am—who I belong to?"

"Oh Son, don' say sech things."

When I help her to her feet she wraps her arms around my waist.

I clutch her tight and say, "I promised Mother I'll become someone special—and I'm going to keep that promise if it kills me ... but as soon as I'm a man, I'll put as much distance as I can between me and Mr. Tom Lincoln."

Chapter Six

Gloom settles over me as the summer of my fifteenth year edges toward autumn. Sally, whom I've always turned to for comfort in my melancholy, spends much of her time at the Grigsby's working as household help. She also has designs on their eldest son Aaron, who's conceited, six years older than her, and, according to his family, too good for her. My head aches anytime I see them together, which happens whenever I'm visiting Nathaniel, Aaron's younger brother. Nathaniel inherited what little goodness there is in the Grigsby name.

In the midst of my anxiety, Father is steeped in debt again, and I'm the solution to his predicament.

Mama pulls off her apron and throws it on the table. She glares at Father. "You promised he could keep up his schoolin'."

Father glares back at her. "The boy's near sixteen. He's done learnt more 'n he needs."

"That boy's gonna be somebody, if we let him."

"Time that he stepped up to bein' a man, putting in a full day doin' a man's work, every day of the week—payin' his own way."

She plants her hands on her hips. "Ya mean payin' off yer debts?"

His nostrils flare. "Ain't payin' fer no more schoolin'. Thomas Carter's expectin' him straight away. Needs a boy to cut corn."

I start to object, but he raises his fist.

"Yer pay is ten cents a day. Bring home every penny of it. In the meantime, I'll be lookin' for better wages. A boy yer size is worth more than ten cents."

He turns and walks to the door. I follow.

A week later, Father sends me off to work for Old Bluenose Crawford, who pays twenty-five cents a day for clearing land, splitting rails, building fences, and helping around his farm. My chest tightens at the sight of his miserly face. When he shorts my pay, he complains I love money more than working. For several days afterward, images of the Savior driving money-changers from the Temple invade my mind, and each swing of my axe dissolves my anger a bit more than the last.

In the spring, James Taylor employs me at the rate of twenty cents a day to run a ferry up and down Anderson Creek, more for chores around the farm. On top of that, he feeds me and gives me a bunk. He lives some twenty miles away. After supper each night, I take a candle to the loft and read until midnight. In the morning before everyone else rises, I build a fire for Mrs. Taylor and put on a pot of water.

One sweltering summer day Mr. Taylor puts me on the hog slaughtering crew, and I retch at the sight of blood spurting from the slit they make in a poor sow's throat. My convulsing increases as the ground turns deep purple—the same color that stained the earth where Father murdered my pet pig years ago.

The others keep working while Mr. Taylor takes me aside. "What's wrong?" he asks.

Tears trickle down my face. "I can't bear it."

"Can't bear what? The blood?"

I shake my head. "The cruelty."

"Look at me," he says.

My eyes meet his.

"Get used to it. It's part of life. I'm payin' you thirty-one cents a day to work on this crew. Your pa says you need the money."

I stare off, not fixing my gaze on anything.

Mr. Taylor's shouts, "You don't want the money?"

I snap my head around to look at him.

"Well, do you want to be paid?"

"It's not my money to keep. Father takes every cent of it."

He shakes his head. "That's between the two of you. My question is, do you want to keep working for me or not?"

If I refuse to help slaughter hogs, he'll sack me on the spot, and if I return home jobless and empty-handed I'll get lashes from Father's leather strap. My shoulders droop. "I'll do it."

He hands me a club and points to a pen full of hogs. "Then get to work."

I trudge over to the pen and stand outside the fence, staring at the poor animals.

Mr. Taylor shouts at me. "No dawdling."

I climb into the pen and eye a surly old sow.

He calls over to me again, "And when you're done, you'll be hanging 'em, bleeding 'em out, scalding 'em, and pulling out the bristles. Pay attention and learn."

That night at supper Mr. Taylor says, "I'll only use you for slaughtering when there's no other choice."

"What about Father?" I ask.

"I'll tell him you're too good a ferryman to waste on farming." He winks.

Several weeks later while I'm docking a small boat I cobbled together for Mr. Taylor, two fancy dressed men rush up. One is short and thick, the other lanky. "Say there, lad," the stout one hollers. "We require passage out to a steamer. You and your boat for hire?"

I examine the two trunks they plop in front of me, then survey all fifteen feet of my little boat. "I'm at your service."

"Fine," he says, dabbing his brow with a lace kerchief.

I whisk up each trunk in turn and stow them before helping the men aboard. After shoving off, my arms yield long, steady strokes as we make good time down Anderson Creek and into the big water of the Ohio.

"There she is, dead ahead," the tall man shouts, pointing to the anchored steamboat.

I gaze over my shoulder, taking a bead on her.

The current pulls hard on us, drawing my boat downstream. My oars bite hard into the water, as I angle in the direction of the steamer. When we're finally tied up to the larger vessel and my passengers unload, each of the men tosses a half dollar coin to me. Although the whole dollar goes to Father, my chest swells knowing someday those wages can be mine.

Not long afterwards, I'm sued by Mr. John D. Hill, a ferryman from the Kentucky side of the Ohio River for operating a ferry without a license. When I stand before Justice of the Peace Samuel Pate in the parlor of his home, my mouth is as dry as the windblown prairie. Perspiration glues my shirt to my back.

I tell Judge Pate, "Sir, I'm ignorant of any requirement for a license to ferry passengers from the creek bank out to a steamer anchored in the middle of the river."

The sour taste of the word "ignorant" lingers on my tongue.

Stern faced, Judge Pate stares at me. "Young man," he says, "you cannot be ignorant of a law that does not exist. The requirement for a license to ferry pertains to transporting passengers from one shore of the river to the other. Since your ferry service terminated in the middle of the river no such license is required." Rapping his gavel on the desk, he says, "I find in favor of the defendant here, young Mr. Lincoln."

I sigh, relieved, but the bitter taste of ignorance continues to haunt me.

Shortly after my trial, Mr. Turnham, the local constable, hires me as a laborer. In addition to my wages, he lends me his volumes of *The Statutes of Indiana*, of which I become an ardent student, determined never again to be ignorant in matters of the law.

Father snarls whenever I mention the law within his earshot. Even so, he brings me a paper one day, asking me to read it over before he makes his mark. Our neighbor, Thomas Carter, has drawn up the document to settle a dispute between our families. He is the same neighbor to whom Father hired me out for a paltry ten cents per day. Upon reading the paper, I see it requires Father to convey the deed to our farm to Mr. Carter. When Father hears we'll be thrown out of our home and off our land if he signs the paper, he rips up the document and tosses Carter out of our house.

My chest swells as Father boasts to his friends that I saved our family's farm, and the law brings me an understanding of the world that nothing else provides.

However, Father's appreciation for my reading skill is short lived. One evening, when work thins out and wages are sparse, he decries my "excess of eddication" and collects all the books he can lay his hands on. As he snatches up the Weems volume he wags it in my face. "And this," he says, glaring at me. "Ya cain't be nuttin' like General Washington. You was put here to farm like me and my pa before me, and his pa before him. God decided these things 'fore he made the world, and there's no changin' his mind. It's a sin even to think 'bout doin' anything else." Then he takes the whole stack of books and throws them out into a raging storm.

I clamber outside with Father's words trailing after me. "Leave those books be!"

Nearly blind from rain, I mutter to myself, "If only one can be saved, let it be Weems." Passing up the other books, I scramble until the prized volume is in my hands. My crying turns to laughter, and I tuck it into my pants, shielding it from any more damage.

Father's continued shouting becomes a faint din as I pluck up book after book, blinking away the raindrops. Once I've recovered the remaining volumes, they're stashed in the hollow of an old tree. As for Weems', I shove it up under my shirt and cradle it in my arms on my way into the cabin. I brush past Father and go straight to bed, holding *The Life of Washington* close to my chest.

Even if Father doesn't value my reading, neighbors beg me to read aloud the letters or papers they receive. When they marvel at my skill, I try to maintain a humble countenance, just as Washington would have done. Some folks also dictate correspondence to me, which gives me practice in organizing their thoughts for clarity. In so doing I learn to harness the power of well-chosen words and logically arranged ideas.

Early one morning while Father is away, I climb atop our old mare and venture to Boonville. It's the seat of Warwick County where court sessions are held twice each year. According to rumors, a skilled attorney named Brackenridge is arguing a murder case.

In the early afternoon, Mr. Brackenridge finally rises to his feet and begins addressing the court. Never have I imagined anyone so skilled with words, so possessed of logic or so eloquent in delivery. For more than an hour, every word and gesture of the tall, fancily dressed lawyer holds my rapt attention. My pulse matches the cadence of his rich, baritone voice.

When the court session ends, I jump to my feet and press forward to shake Mr. Brackenridge's hand, wanting to congratulate him for his speech.

He surveys me and sneers. "What is this?" he asks an aide who carries his papers.

His attendant shrugs.

Mr. Brackenridge raises his chin and struts off with a crowd following him. I stand alone, considering my gangly, rough appearance. Presumably, men of his station can catch the scent of a bastard or bastard's son even at a great distance. I hang my head and shuffle out of the courthouse. On my ride home, everything is as colorless as my gray eyes.

The next morning throughout my daily chores, my shoulders sag, and my gait is lumbering. The younger children are playing, and step-brother John is chopping wood. My step-sister Matilda comes along side me and offers a word of encouragement. My chest tightens as I pick at loose threads on the sleeve of my tow-linen shirt.

In the afternoon when Sally comes out of the cabin after helping Mama with housework, Aaron Grigsby makes an appearance. I don't want my sister to become like the other Hanks women, wooed by wealth only to be discarded as trash.

What value can rich families place on their hired help beyond profiting from their labor? None of the Grigsby women will ever accept Sally as anything more than their seamstress. Much worse they won't tolerate a bastard's blood in their family line.

I hop onto a nearby stump and yell for everyone to gather around. It's a good time to start practicing to become as fine a speaker as Mr. Brackenridge.

"Ladies and Gentlemen, cruelty to animals is wrong, and there can be no right in it. An ant's life is as precious to it as ours is to us." My step-brother John meets my stare. "Those who toss and smash terrapins against trees," I peek at Aaron Grigsby out of the corner of my eye, "or who terrorize cats and maim dogs, should refrain or be held accountable." Some of the younger ones' faces hint their hearts may be aligning with mine, but Sally blushes as she steals glances at Grigsby.

Heat rises from under my collar as I step off the stump and saunter up to Sally before she nuzzles up to Aaron. "Sister, let's talk a minute."

"What about?" she asks, peeking past me at Grigsby.

I nudge her. "It's something private."

Aaron taps my shoulder, and I turn my head, scowling.

Sally pouts and looks again at her beau. "Sorry, Aaron. We'll just be a minute. I promise."

I guide her away so we can't be heard. "Is it true you plan to marry him?"

Sally looks down, fidgeting. "He hasn't asked Father … yet."

"I've warned you before, these Grigsbys are bad news. They use people and throw them away when they're done."

"You seem to get along with his brother Natty."

"That's different. Natty wouldn't hurt a fly, but this one—he's even meaner than his old man."

Sally shakes her head. "You're just jealous."

"That's not true. You mean the whole world to me, and I don't want to see you hurt. To the Grigsbys you're just hired help, and don't think he's going to treat you any different once he's bedded you."

"Abraham Lincoln, you're the one who's evil."

"I'm sorry, Sally." I grab her hand.

She yanks away.

"Look, you deserve to be treated like a queen, not a chamber maid. Over at the Grigsbys one day, I overheard his aunts talking about the two of you. One of them said, 'Can you imagine the scandal, a Grigsby marrying the hired help? Shameful.' That's exactly what the old biddy said."

Sally glares at me.

"I don't want you to turn out like Mother. Remember how Father wore her down to the nubbins?"

Sally rushes past me to Aaron. I watch over my shoulder as she wraps her arms around his waist. A lump rises in my throat.

Not many months later, Sally and Aaron Grigsby are married. At the wedding, the Grigsby family is cool toward her at best, and we Lincolns are relegated to the rear benches to witness our finest led to slaughter.

In spite of my dislike for Sally's new husband, I seize the chance when she invites me to board with them in their new cabin. Aaron has no choice but to treat her with respect when I'm around. The other benefit of boarding with them is I'm out from under Father's roof, though I still turn over my earnings to him at the end of each week.

Chapter Seven

In the spring of my eighteenth year, my step-brother John Johnston presses me to join him in going down to work on the Louisville-Portland Canal. A two-mile long channel is being dug so large boats can bypass the falls on the Ohio River. It's one of President Adams' internal improvement projects which Father rails against, but he doesn't mind me bringing home a good wage to pay off some of his debts. He says under the law I have no choice but to work wherever he sends me.

Not long after we settle into the laborers' colony, I say to John, "By the time we get back home, Sally will be skin and bones with her pregnant belly drawn so taut it could split with a feather's touch."

John shakes his head. "You sound like an old gossip. Girls are meant for marrying and bearing children. Your broad-beamed Sally can handle her duty just fine. She's stout and hard-working like a wife ought to be. When my sister gets hitched to your cousin Dennis you won't find me sniveling about it. It can't happen soon enough."

Months later when early winter storms impede our work, John and I pack up and go home—him to Father's cabin filled to the gills with Mama's brood, me back to Sally and Aaron's place. To my distress, Sally is pregnant and haggard. I threaten to thrash Grigsby over her mistreatment, but she insists I calm down. She says, "He'll be on his best behavior with you around."

A few nights later, I come in from splitting wood at Father's and find Sally and Grigsby arguing. I lay into him with a verbal lashing, but she comes to his defense. She insists she'll be all right and begs me to do nothing more to rile her husband. She's too weak to bear the weight of any more discord. Nonetheless, I continue to give him a piece of my mind, and he kicks me out of their home.

It's been the better part of a year since I've slept under Father's roof for two consecutive nights, and Mama lights up at seeing me walk through the door with my sparse belongings slung over my shoulder. Father, on the other hand, pretends to ignore me. This night is no different from many others I've spent in the cramped cabin, reading by the fireplace under the glare of disapproval.

I rise early the next morning and set out on foot for the day-long trek to Mr. Taylor's place on Anderson Creek. I break out in a broad grin when he says he needs a ferryman. The river life has gotten in my blood. There's even time for reading during waits between passengers.

In early January of the next year, during a weather-created lull in ferry traffic, I'm up at Father's, and Mama conscripts me to cure some freshly butchered pork. Father's off hunting or whatever he does when he's in one of his melancholy moods. Hunched over, draping strips of meat over rows of pegs, I push down memories of my pet pig's slaughter years ago.

When I'm summoned out of the hut, the frigid ground is still spotted with remnants of last week's snow. The brittle grasses crunch underfoot. Smoke itches my eyes and hangs in my throat. Redmond, the youngest of the Grigsby boys, has been sent to deliver the news. A knot forms in my chest as the gravity etched on his face sinks in—his mouth drawn and chin quivering. He speaks haltingly. Sally and her infant son died in childbirth.

I collapse onto a nearby log and bury my face in my hands, sobbing. As tears roll down my cheeks, a wave of heat flushes through my body. I jump off the log and race two miles to the Grigsby family's home where Sally has been staying in recent weeks. Redmond barely keeps up with me. I crash through the door and charge at Aaron, not even glancing at Sally's lifeless corpse. I grab him by the shoulders and shake him. He pulls back. My hands reach for his neck.

"What did you do to her?" The pitch in my voice climbs with each word.

Natty—the only good Grigsby—and his father lunge at me, wrapping their arms around my waist and chest. I throw them off.

Aaron stumbles backwards stabbing the air with his finger as he points at me. "Are you mad?"

The veins in my neck pulse. "Did you even send for the doctor?"

Natty answers for him. "We sent for the doctor, but he was drunk, passed out, useless."

Old Man Grigsby chimes in. "We did everything we could. We did our best to save them."

I turn to him, "You never wanted her or her child to be a part of your family. You're just as happy to see them dead and your boy, here, marrying someone else you think is more fit."

The room is hushed except for the buzzing of the Grigsby women huddled in a corner. My shoulders slump and my head droops as I walk slowly to Sally's body. Tears trail down my cheeks as I gaze on her pale, angelic face. Gone with the color from her cheeks are the last remnants of my faith and hope. Providence is against me. Of course, Fate was not the sole author of her demise. There is plenty blame to go around—the Grigsby clan for their negligence, Father for dragging us into this God-forsaken wilderness, and me—for bringing a wretched curse onto the precious angels I love.

The Grigsbys see to Sally's prompt burial, assuring God's Grace—if there is such a thing—will do its duty. Nonetheless, I lie awake on many stormy, windswept nights cringing at the thought of snow falling on her grave, hoping she rests deep enough and on high enough ground to keep her secure from flooding.

Months after Sally's death, a local merchant, James Gentry, offers me eight dollars a month to accompany his son Allen, a long, lean fellow like myself, on a twelve hundred mile float trip down the Mississippi. We're to carry cured pork and other merchandise from Gentry's store to markets in New Orleans. I accept his offer and busy myself helping Allen build a forty-foot flatboat for our trip. The work keeps my mind off of Sally.

In mid-April we launch our rustic vessel into the unruly Ohio River at Gentry's landing, waving good-bye to Allen's sweet wife, Anna.

Only a few nights previous, Allen, Anna, and I had been sitting on the deck of the nearly finished flatboat, reminiscing about my dear Sally. After a time, I grew sullen and fell silent. Several moments passed without anyone speaking before Anna pointed to the moon and said, "Look, the moon is going down."

"That's not so," I replied. "It doesn't really go down— it just seems to. You see, the Earth turns from west to east, and the revolution takes us under, preventing us from seeing the moon. We do the sinking. The moon's sinking is only an appearance."

She laughed and called me "odd."

I stood and told her she's "silly," then left her and Allen sitting on the boat.

Two hours into our voyage, Allen and I confront the first evidence of the river's guile; along the flooded shoreline another flatboat has gotten caught up among some partially submerged stumps in slack water. We throw them a rope as we pass, taking care not to get too close lest we meet the same calamity. Allen scurries to secure one end of the line to our gunwales as the men on the other boat do the same on their end. I plant my feet flat on the deck and put every sinew of my back into the ten-foot rudder pole in order to keep us in the current.

As we pull the stranded boaters free, Allen quizzes them about their experience on the river. They've made three previous trips from Louisville down to New Orleans and warn us of dangers ahead. Allen studies their boat as it catches the river's current and reminds me he has as much experience as the fools we just rescued.

I stare at their cargo, half a dozen Negroes shackled together with chains. "Those poor fellows could drown if they fall into this river, weighted down by those irons."

Allen shrugs. "Not our problem."

"Aren't their lives as precious to them as ours are to us?"

"No sense borrowing someone else's trouble."

I continue gazing at the slave trader's boat and wonder whether President Adams, the abolitionist, can realize his vision for our country.

On our journey down the Ohio—before reaching the great waters of the Mississippi—we tie up to shore each afternoon as the sun drops behind the trees. If we wait until dark to make land, we could miss spotting shoals and other obstacles. At dusk, good landings are hard to pick out along these wild, unsettled shorelines. It's even harder with the river swollen beyond its banks. Experienced flatboat-men we've encountered tell us flooding is as bad as anyone can remember. They warn that whirlpools and eddies close to shore are uncommonly hazardous.

Four days out, we approach the Ohio's confluence with the Mississippi. Our course widens, nearly doubling in volume and increasing in speed and turbulence. Allen warns me of the behemoth we are about to encounter and how it will test my strength, which he claims is unmatched by any man he's ever met.

I mutter, "There are greater things than strong backs."

Our hull creaks and groans as we bob up and down over swells and dips. One plunge jolts us so hard I nearly lose my footing. I grip the rudder-oar tighter and wedge my boots into the gaps between deck planks.

Soon a vast sea opens before us without a hint of shore in the distance, and a thunderous roar pummels my ears. The chop of the Ohio launches us headlong into the churning, swirling Mississippi. A whirlpool half the size of our boat gapes, intent on sucking us into its throat. The rudder thrashes in my hands as if possessed by demons, yanking my arms almost out of their sockets. Throwing my whole body into the pole, I remember the ravenous bowels of Knob Creek that nearly swallowed me up as a boy. It would have been the end of me if it wasn't for good ol' Austin Gollaher. I tell myself, "This one's not going to get the better of me."

Allen clutches the corner post of the shelter at our stern. In an instant, the giant swirl whips us around and shoots us almost halfway across the Mississippi. As we float sideways, Allen sets the oars, and I feather the rudder. Once he's got them set, I grab one oar in my left hand while managing the rudder with my right, and he mans the other oar. We row feverishly toward the current.

By the time the Mississippi takes us into its bosom and sweeps us along its course, my back is wracked with spasms, and I'm gasping for breath. I kneel and watch the river carry us along. To our left, the clear waters of the Ohio are shackled to the stronger, murky current. In less than two miles the Ohio's whole identity is lost, consumed by the great, wide, muddy waters of its master.

Soon the Mississippi calms and flattens. Its meandering course creates the perception that the sun is shifting positions in the sky, peering at us first from one direction, then another, and again another. The shorelines are mostly wilderness until we reach the fledgling town of Vicksburg on our left—a handful of newly raised brick homes and a church perched atop a cliff. According to Allen, "Under the Hill" is what they call the area along the bank below the bluff. It's normally teeming with commotion—commerce, slave trafficking, and debauchery. Today, Under the Hill is partly submerged in flood waters, so human activity is sparse.

Near nightfall, we put in at a place known as Rodney, also called "Petit Gulf," where the waterfront contains one surprise after another. Even the visiting boatmen have donned colorful costumes in reds, yellows, greens, and blues to match the riverfront inhabitants. Allen tells me these alien appearing folks are Cajuns—a half-breed mix of French Acadians and local Indians.

I talk Allen into standing guard over our cargo while I explore the carnival of activity. I'm drawn to a large flatboat docked nearby which does double-duty as a theatre. A family named Chapman performs plays onboard each evening. When I hear they'll be doing Shakespeare's *King Lear* at nightfall, I rush back to our boat for a bushel of corn to trade for admission. Allen needles me about wasting valuable cargo on idiotic entertainment. There's only wonderment and no foolishness that night as the actors perform their solemn scenes on the torch-lit floating stage.

From Rodney we slow our pace and keep a keen eye out for opportunities to sell our wares or trade for anything we think will command a better price in New Orleans. We stop at any landing that isn't inundated by flood waters. My heart is pinched at the sight of slaves being led in chains through the waterfront marketplaces or laboring in the fields. They remind me that Father owns the wages for my toil on this great river.

Three weeks into our journey we anchor along the Sugar Coast about sixty miles above New Orleans. We linger in the area for the next several days, selling stock and bartering with the local plantations for sugar. The last evening before continuing on to New Orleans, we tie up along the shore at Madame Busham's Plantation, six miles below Baton Rouge.

During the night, Allen and I awaken to a ruckus on deck. In the moonlight, we see seven burly men with glistening black skin rummaging through our cargo.

Allen jumps out of our shelter to challenge them. I'm right on his heels.

Allen shouts, "Get off our boat."

They drop our goods and turn to face us.

Again, Allen orders them off the boat.

They charge us.

I lunge at the largest one, locking my arms around his massive chest and lifting him off his feet.

He bangs his forehead into mine, drawing blood from just above my eye.

I hurl the big Negro onto two of his cohorts.

As the bunch tumbles to the deck Allen yells, "Abe, get the guns."

Even though we have no weapons, I charge back into the shelter, doing my best to sell Allen's ruse.

With no further ado, the seven jump off our boat and scramble through the water to shore.

We collapse to our knees, breathless. Allen wheezes, "Thought we were as good as dead."

I nod. "Wonder where they came from."

Allen rubs the back of his neck. "Runaways."

"What do you think they were up to?"

Allen grunts. "Killing us. Stealing food and weapons, if we had any. Taking anything they'd need to outrun their masters."

"Running to where?"

Allen stands up. "North. Canada. Freedom. 'Course most likely, a patrol will catch 'em and drag 'em back for a good whipping."

I get up and gaze at the plantation. Beyond the fields of cane and rows of shanties, the mansion is lit up like a priceless jewel. "Think they'll be back?"

"Not a chance," he says. "They're running as fast and as far away as they can."

I shake my head and wipe the blood from my brow. "Just the same, I'll feel safer dodging snags on the river at night than tied up here."

Allen agrees, and we weigh anchor with due haste, finding the heart of the current before either of us can blink. Even as we keep a keen eye out for obstacles in the water, our thoughts remain pinned to images of those Negroes and their intent to murder us.

New Orleans is a full eight to ten hours away—a good half of that time we're casting about blind. Two hours down river I chuckle and turn to Allen. "Counting the day I was born, that's the fifth time I've almost died, and there were three other times I wished I had."

On approaching the Port of New Orleans late in the afternoon, Allen points to the grand homes perched on the high ground to our left. A bit later, we come to the beginning of the flatboat-stores docked end-to-end along the wood-planked wharf. They line the river's course as it sweeps east then bends north. Allen tells me to keep out in the current while he scans the shore for a vacant slot. We've plenty of time, he says. Most of the activity is about a mile downstream.

As we float past the array of docked boats, the waterfront gets more crowded and we inhale increasingly foul odors. Allen explains that most flatboat merchants live on their vessels and dump their spoiled cargo and human refuse directly into the river. As the river turns and the current flows northward, their garbage lingers in slack water and rots. Allen says the city tries to hold down the dumpage by imposing a five dollar per day fine on flatboats that stay past eight days after docking.

A half mile later he warns me we better find a spot soon. The Frenchmen who rule the city have their homes downriver from Notre Dame Street. If we put in past there, we'll be fined twenty dollars. On top of keeping us away from their upper-class district, another purpose of the steep fine is to prevent itinerant vendors like us from encroaching on the shopping districts that lie beyond Notre Dame. The local merchants fear that our lower prices will lure customers away.

Allen points to a boat pulling away from the dock, and I angle toward the newly vacated spot, fighting the current as it tries to drag us downriver. Allen helps me pull, and with a mighty effort we maintain our course. However, we're not the only ones intent on mooring there. Another flatboat closer to shore is challenging us, though it's farther upstream. When we reach shallow enough water, Allen does the oaring singlehandedly while I grab a pole and push us along in earnest. It's a close call, but we win the race, cutting off the other boat by a hair. At that point, I bring the bow around so we're aligned with the wharf. After checking to make certain there's ample clearance to avoid collisions with the boats forward and aft, I pole sideways to the dock.

Allen jumps ashore to tie us down while I stow my pole and begin looking around at our neighbors. On the forward boat, two uniformed men are rummaging through crates and barrels.

I nod toward the officials and ask Allen, "What's up?"

"Inspectors," he whispers.

I glance aft at our other neighbor's deck. No officials onboard. One of the crew is dangling ears of corn from strings tied to a pole. "Haloo there," I call out.

The man waves.

"Where from?" I ask.

"Kaintuck'" he says, unsmiling.

Cursing erupts from the forward boat. I turn. A burly, redheaded crewman is restraining a companion who's shouting and waving his hands in the air. The inspectors are off-loading the boat's cargo.

Allen steps back aboard our boat. "If they find damaged or spoiled goods, they confiscate them and auction them off. Proceeds go to the Port." He bends down and unties a barrel of pork we'd secured for our journey downriver.

"Any other rules?"

"Can't smoke meat on board."

The unsmiling crewman to our aft calls over to us. "Been hearin' stories 'bout some fellow burnt up his boat last month. Cookin' on board. Cudda set the whole wharf and half the city ablaze." He turns away, shaking his head.

A ruckus grabs my attention from several boats away. A sow and her piglets are being offloaded from a flatboat. After watching the buyer herd the critters up over the levee, my gaze wanders. Docked upriver, is the pilot we pulled out of slack water up on the Ohio. He's leading the Negro slaves he's brought down from Kentucky off his boat—all shackled to one long chain.

I turn to Allen who's wrestling with another barrel of pork. "What do you reckon that fellow is doing with those Negroes?"

He follows my hand.

"Looks like he's headed towards Hewlett's Exchange."

My jaw tightens.

A large Negro woman's voice rises above all the other noises as she trundles down the levy toward the dock. Her billowing dress, imprinted with purple, red and, green flowers, grabs my attention as does the strange babble spilling from her lips. She's followed by an equally dark-skinned man wearing a loosely fitted black suit, white shirt, and a tie.

"Hey you," she calls out, or at least that's what it sounds like she says.

I turn to Allen. He whispers, "Colored Creole. Accent is French."

I look back at her. Her companion is standing to one side behind her, his head lowered.

She laughs. "Yes, Ugly. I'm talking to you."

I glare at her.

"Where you boys from?"

Allen stands up straight. "Indiana."

"You got any bacon? Pork? I'll give three dollars a barrel for pork."

The unsmiling crewman in the next boat shakes his head.

"Make it five. Need the extra to buy a mask to cover this 'ugly' face."

She snorts a laugh. "I'll do four, not a cent more."

I glance again at our neighbor and get a nod.

I look at Allen who taps his nose with his finger.

"Sold," I say.

Allen adds, "Let's see your money before your man touches that barrel."

The Creole woman stuffs her hand into her ample bosom, digging for money.

I look at Allen, "Is that Negro with her a slave?"

He nods. "They're Colored Creoles, not from Africa, different from other Negroes. Some own slaves. Down here, they're mostly treated like white folks."

An angular little man in a gray, tailored suit is carrying a chicken by its feet, its wings flapping. He darts aboard and makes a beeline for a barrel of corn. Allen collars him while I take the woman's payment.

"Sorry, Ma'am," I say. "This won't do."

"What's wrong?" she demands.

I wave the bills at her. "There's only three here."

"Can't none of you backwoods boys count?"

"My ciphering isn't the problem."

A scruffy urchin boy races onto the boat and scrambles for an open barrel of sugar.

I lunge and snatch him by the collar.

The Creole woman orders her man to collect the barrel of pork.

I block him, still holding the boy.

The man stops in his tracks.

I glare at the woman. "One more dollar."

She scowls as she pays, and I let her man pass.

As for the boy, I take an ear of corn from one of the barrels, give it to him, and send him on his way.

The next morning, Allen and I agree to take turns manning our floating store. He does the first shift and shoos me off to explore the city. I head in the direction the slave trader took his Negroes the evening before, and soon stumble onto a coffle of slaves being led away to market. I follow behind them.

The slaves are herded through a door into a two story, red-brick building near the intersection of St. Louis and Charles Streets. Around the corner at the front entrance to the building, a man stands on a platform under a banner that says *Auction.* His slick black hair is combed straight back, and he's wearing a freshly pressed tan suit. A bright red kerchief hangs out of his breast pocket.

He points with a riding crop at a girl standing next to him. She's wearing a light blue satin dress and white gloves coming up to her elbows. A silk shawl covers her shoulders, and her straight brown hair is coiled on top of her dainty head. She appears no older than my step-sister Mattie. Her angelic face turns ashen when she's directed to drop the shawl. Her lightly-tanned skin is as fair as many folks in the crowd.

The tan-suited man gives each of her breasts a squeeze and announces with a lecherous grin, "Ample, yet firm. This quadroon is quite the fancy girl."

I turn to a young man next to me who's sporting a brocaded vest, under a black waistcoat with tails. "What's a quadroon?"

He studies me, first my hands then my hair. With a sneer he says, "A slave who could almost pass for white. Except, the skin's a little off, and the hair's a bit coarse— like yours."

I clench my teeth.

The man on the platform asks, "Shall we start the bidding at five-hundred dollars?"

The brocade-vested man shouts, "One thousand." The pitch of his voice betrays his excitement.

My stomach turns.

An older man a few yards away calls out, "One thousand-two hundred."

A portly fellow with rosy cheeks and reddish tufts of

hair ringing his bald crown blurts, "Can I inspect the merchandise close up before bidding?"

The man on the platform shakes his head. "Sorry. Inspections were all done inside beforehand. Should've been here earlier."

"Fit for breeding?" the fat man asks.

The auctioneer grins. "Very."

"One thousand-seven-hundred." The brocade-vested man's voice, louder and more pitched than before, sends chills down my spine.

A collective gasp rises from the crowd.

"Sold," the auctioneer announces.

The winning bidder turns to me and whispers, "I have a fantasy or two to indulge with that one."

My stomach knots as he goes forward to collect his property. I turn to another man nearby and ask, "How can a woman so fair be a slave?"

"S'pose she was born a slave," he says.

"But why wouldn't she be set free? She'd make someone a fine wife."

The man wrinkles his nose and squints at me. "Where you from?"

"Indiana."

He snorts. "Figured as much."

I look back toward the platform.

The balding, portly fellow leans in and says, "She's worth a small fortune as a breeder, to say nothing of the pleasure she'll bring him." He leans close to me and whispers. "Fancy this. Any dalliance he conjures up can come true with just the snap of his fingers." He backs away and strokes his chin as he gawks at the girl. "Imagine how fine her offspring will be with that planter's white blood mixed in. She'll earn back his investment a dozen times."

My jaw drops. "He'd sell his own children?"

He laughs. "He wouldn't make them his heirs, not that fellow. I mean, if a man plants a sugar cane field with his own hands, wouldn't the crop be his to sell the same as if his slaves planted it?"

I glare at him.

He tips his hat and presses toward the platform. "I'll be bidding on this next lot."

As the quadroon girl disappears with her new owner, she's replaced by a family. The man is tall, shirtless, with skin as dark as I've ever seen, his massive chest and arms glistening. The woman wears a loose-fitting dress; her hair is bound up in a scarf. Two children, a boy and a girl, cling to her waist.

The auctioneer motions for the man to step to center-stage. "We'll start with him."

The woman wails, "Please, please. We's fambly. My Mistress promise a'fore she die, you take us all together. I's would be the best slave ever. Obeyin' everthing— the chilluns too. Work day 'n night. Please."

The auctioneer unhooks a long whip from his belt. "Shut up or I'll take you inside and give you the whip."

The woman hunches over and keeps wailing.

The auctioneer motions to the man. "Turn around." The son still clinging to his mother, stretches one arm out to his father.

As the large Negro stands with his bare back to us, the auctioneer points at him. "See, no marks. This one's never been flogged, though his woman is gonna be if she don't shut up."

When the slave turns around to face us again the woman's moaning gets louder.

The auctioneer continues. "This boy does what he's told. Not going to find a better worker for your sugar cane fields."

I turn and head toward the wharf. I've not taken more than a dozen steps when someone from the crowd calls out, "One-hundred."

"We've got us some mighty serious bidders today," the auctioneer chortles.

The woman's moans echo in my ears on my way toward our boat. My own dull skin causes me to wonder if any Negro blood runs through my veins. I glance at others around me, taking note of their complexion. If I ever get the chance, I'll hit this injustice squarely in the head just as that old mare did to me years ago. I'll just do the job more thoroughly than she did.

After the last of our cargo is gone, Allen and I dismantle our flatboat and sell our wood to the Port. They'll use the lumber for repairing and extending the docks. Who knows, someday I may return and walk on those deck planks again. Allen insists on staying a few days to explore the city. I indulge him, though I'd rather book passage on the first steamboat up river to home. For me, anything we see here will be tainted by visions of that slave market.

Chapter Eight

Work is scarce when I return from New Orleans, so Father insists I stay at the farm and help tend the fields unless I'm out looking for paying work. When I do find a job, he continues his practice of taking my wages at the end of the day.

My step-sisters still live with Father and Mama, joined now by their new husbands, adding two more bodies. Elizabeth is married to Cousin Dennis Hanks. Mattie has wedded Dennis' half-brother, Squire Hall.

These days, the tiny smoking hut for curing meat would feel less confining than the cabin. What's more, I've gone from sleeping on a bed too short for my body to curling up under animal skins on the floor. When everyone's up and about, there's no straight path from one end of the cabin to the other.

Except for me, everybody belongs to someone else.

To avoid chores I trek into Gentryville, a couple miles away, to search for any work that pays a few cents an hour. Any job that will take me out from under Father's roof is preferable. Crewing on a steamboat would be ideal, but my age is against me. Operators don't want anyone who's younger than twenty-one.

Often on my way to town, a little ditty comes to mind that reflects Father's political views, which are shared by many of our neighbors. I'm not sure, though, that I agree with the sentiments any longer.

Let auld acquaintance be forgot
And never brought to mind.
May Jackson be our president
And Adams left behind.

Most days there's no paid work to be had, so I linger at Jones' General Store and peruse the only newspaper to be had for several miles. When customers are scarce, the proprietor—a pudgy, blue-eyed bookworm named William Jones—engages me in conversation about Shakespeare, great books, politics and events reported in the news. After a few weeks Jones hires me to clerk in his store on the rare occasion when business is brisk.

I begin staying late after the store closes, jawing with Jones and other young men about the week's news. Stories about President Adams, The Abolitionist, grab my fancy. I become firmer in my belief that it's Jackson who ought to be left behind. Four more years of Adams could bring an end to slavery, and every man would be paid for his labors. Schools would be built so children everywhere can learn to read, write, and cipher. We'd have new canals, bridges, and roads to speed commerce across our growing nation.

One autumn evening I yield to Mama's plea to make it home for supper. During our meal Father looks up from his plate and rails against President Adams. "The ol' crook is fixin' to tax us poor folks and sell off public lands to pay for another of his pipe dreams."

"What's wrong with more canals and roads?" I say. "Seems sensible to me."

"Rumor is ya been readin' trash newspapers over at Gentryville. Wastin' time and fillin' yer head with dung."

I roll my eyes. "Maybe you should learn to read. Broaden your horizons."

"Too much nonsense rollin' around in yer head jest makes ya stupider and—and lazy. What this country needs is a man like Jackson. Git rid of the bank. Let us ordinary folk live our lives. Stay outta our hair."

I lean back on my stool. "He'll keep slavery spreading, costing ordinary folks like us the chance to work for fair wages."

"I'm agin' slaves like any other good Primitive Baptist. Ain't votin' fer no head-in-the-clouds Whig. Give me a common sense Jackson man any day."

"But Adams is against slavery, and Jackson's a slaver. It's men like Jackson who keep slavery going and hold back families like ours so we can't get ahead."

Father pounds his fist on the table. "I'm a Jackson man. No different from our neighbors. No different from my upbringin'. If'n ya had any respect fer yer upbringin', ya'd be a Jackson man, too."

"Next year there'll be an election. Reckon we'll find out then how the folks feel about progress."

He glares at me. "Just so Adams don't cheat Jackson outta it like he did last time."

I get up from the table and start for the door, remembering a verse from the *Proverbs* in Mother's *Bible*.

Answer not a fool according to his own folly, lest thou also be like unto him.

"Where ya goin'?" he grumbles.

"Out."

The air is nippy as I study the western horizon on my two mile trek into Gentryville. Even without company, a thousand-plus mile flatboat trip down the Mississippi couldn't be any lonelier than this place.

Jones' store is sitting alone on the wood plank porch of his store when I arrive.

I point to the empty crates. "Where are the rest?"

He chuckles. "They only come to hear you spin yarns and tell jokes."

I take the crate next to him and have a seat. "Doesn't matter. All they want is entertainment."

"Thought you like putting on a show."

"Naw, storytelling just makes my isolation tolerable. It distracts me from the emptiness in here." I lay my hand on my chest. "You're my only true friend, the only one I find pleasure in talking with."

We sit in silence for a long while—me staring into the horizon, him reading.

After a while I look at him. "What're you reading?"

He closes the cover, using a finger to mark his place, and shows me the title.

"Ah ... *Hamlet*."

He peers over his spectacles. "Reminds me of you."

How weary, stale, flat, and unprofitable seem to me all the uses of this world!

I shake my head.

He stands and starts inside the store. "Do you need anything?"

"Whiskey."

"Thought you didn't drink."

I stand up, too. "Maybe it's time I started."

After we spend several hours drinking and talking *Hamlet*, I stumble home.

A few weeks later, everyone in the community—except the Lincolns—is invited to an infare celebrating the double wedding of two of the Grigsby's sons, Reuben, Jr. and Charles. To feed my lingering resentment, I recruit one of the guests to help me pull off a prank.

During the wedding feast my co-conspirator sneaks upstairs and exchanges the beds which have been deliberately prepared for the two couples by the elder Mrs. Grigsby. When the celebrations are finished, and the bulk of the guests have drifted back to their homes, attendants escort the brides to their respective beds, which they at once identify by their familiar furnishings. Upon hearing the attendants' word that the girls are ready to receive their husbands, Mrs. Grigsby directs her sons upstairs according to her earlier arrangement, one to the bed on the right and the other to the left.

As the family lounges downstairs, their ears peeled for the sounds of marital consummation, they're accosted by a frantic commotion. Racing upstairs, they find the two boys in a pile on the floor as their brides sit wailing in their beds, covers drawn up to their chins. When the confusion is unraveled and the crying abates, the family stands ashamed over the egregious error.

Not content for the scandal to remain a secret among the Grigsbys, I write a satirical account of the matter in biblical style. My piece finds broad circulation in the community. The townspeople come to call my composition *The Chronicles of Reuben*. Some claim it is more widely read and memorized than the *Bible*.

Encouraged by folks' reactions to my publication of the *Chronicles*, I heap injury upon insult with the following rhyme directed at another of the Grigsby boys, William, ridiculing his ineptitude in relations with the fairer sex.

> *I will tell you a joke about Joule and Mary*
> *Tho' it's neither a joke nor a story.*
> *For Reuben and Charles has married two girls*
> *But Billy has married a boy.*
> *The girls he had tried on every side*
> *But none could he get to agree.*
> *All was in vain, he went home again*
> *And since that he is married to Natty.*

William's humiliation is so complete he insists we settle the score with our fists. When I point out the unfairness of such a contest and the unlikelihood of him prevailing against someone of my size and strength, he agrees to fight my step-brother John in my place.

Nearly all the young folks from Little Pigeon Creek show up at the designated site over in Warrick County. It's outside our local constable's jurisdiction and beyond the reach of any grand jury. Several boys hold me back from the fracas, but as John is getting himself thrashed, I break free and charge Grigsby. After throwing him off, I proclaim myself "the big buck at the lick," only to draw the whole crowd into a general melee.

Chapter Nine

The advent of my twenty-first year finds me slump-shouldered as I tread through Little Pigeon Creek. My long-awaited emancipation has been delayed. Mama begs me to accompany her and Father, who has decided to remove some two hundred miles west to Illinois. This announcement comes in spite of our having recently started building a new cabin on the Indiana homestead.

I search Mama's face and join in her distress. Father is too old to take on the journey and carve out a new home in the Illinois wilderness unassisted. His various infirmities of age will not allow it. I agree to go. Besides, there's little promise for me here in Little Pigeon Creek.

Dennis Hanks and his wife, Mama's daughter Elizabeth, have already moved their young family west to join up with another of Mother's cousins, John Hanks. After the milk-sick disease struck our community for a second time, Dennis set his mind on leaving. He endured enough misery when an earlier epidemic claimed his surrogate parents and my angel mother. John Hanks claims there are abundant opportunities out west, and Father's scheme to settle there suits Mama, who yearns to reunite with her daughter and grandchildren.

As soon as winter starts to thaw, Father sells off his livestock, except for a team of oxen, and uses the entire proceeds to pay off his debts. Penniless, he trades the farm for a horse. For our conveyance we use a crude, hand-built wagon with wheels made of three-foot wide, solid oak rounds, somewhat uneven in size. It'll carry the three of us, my dog, and a few possessions.

Along our journey we encounter ice-laden rivers swelling over their banks. I often jump down from the wagon and drive the oxen by foot, stumbling in knee-deep mud, or I put my shoulder to a wheel and help them along. When the road turns and runs along the Kaskaskia River, I lead the oxen through long stretches that are submerged by flood waters. As the current churns past, I ponder our best course.

Between the thundering stream and my deep concentration, the argument between Mama and Father escapes my attention. At least it eludes me until Father yells, "We ain't turnin' back."

I slog back to the wagon and find Mama crying. "What's goin' on?"

Father mumbles. "She wants to turn back."

Her face is pallid; her eyes beg me for assurance.

"Mama, everything will be fine."

She nods as she wipes away tears.

I walk forward and lead the oxen ahead. Within a few hundred yards, a portion of the road has been completely cut away, and rapids are raging over our intended path. My fingers ache as I grip on the oxen's lead and forge into the rising current with its icy spray soaking my shirt and face. The water quickly deepens, reaching the animals' chests. The wagon starts to drift.

One of the oxen stumbles, and I yank on the lead, drawing it toward the near bank in hopes of guiding it to more secure footing. The other ox falters, as well. I grab onto the yoke and pull with all my might. Once the wagon's back on solid ground, I drop to my knees and pant from exhaustion. Mud and sweat drip from my forehead, and my shirt clings to my aching shoulders and back. I catch my breath and stumble back to the water's edge to splash myself with clean, chilly water.

A few miles later we come to a less treacherous spot where the road crosses the river. After making it to the other side without incident, my dog starts yelping from the opposite bank. He must have jumped out when we stopped to survey the best route for our crossing. As I turn back and wade into the frigid water, Father berates me. I pay him no mind and trudge across the current to retrieve the poor mutt. As I carry him to the wagon, my wayward pet licks my face.

Two weeks after our departure, our trek ends near Decatur, Illinois at the homestead of Mother's cousin John Hanks, a round-faced affable fellow, seven years my senior. He preceded Dennis in moving here from Indiana about four years ago, convinced that opportunities are greater here than in Indiana. After a hearty meal and good night's rest, John guides us to the homestead he's staked out for Father. In the ensuing months, he also helps us raise a cabin. As I'm now expert with an axe and have a keen eye, I'm the one notching up the ends of the logs and making sure the corners fit snugly.

We finish the cabin and clear the fields in time for a late spring planting, but the crop will be sparse and Father isn't well. I look for paying work to support him and Mama and turn over my wages even though it is no longer a burden of the law. It's a gamble I take, hoping Father will finally make a go of it once the coming winter has passed and he has a good harvest next autumn.

Although jobs are not plentiful, I earn enough to keep us from starving by hiring onto crews for splitting rails, clearing land, and building cabins for other new settlers. Most of the work is several miles away, adding to my already long work days. On occasion, an employer provides meals and lodging on top of a meager wage. One kind woman sews me a new set of clothes on noticing my only pair of pants is worn through in both knees, and my one shirt is torn and threadbare.

When I board away from home I'm not weighed down by Father's oppression, which I should have thrown off by now. I'm also cheered whenever there's an audience to hear my jokes and stories. I've become proficient at telling them—like one Uncle Mordecai taught me. He was the one who saved Father's life when the Indians scalped Grandfather Abraham.

A country meeting-house, that was used once a month, was quite a distance from any other house.

The preacher, an old-line Baptist, was dressed in coarse linen pantaloons and a shirt of the same material. The pants were the old fashion type with baggy legs and a flap in the front. They were held to his slight frame without the aid of suspenders.

A single button at the collar kept the shirt from falling off his narrow shoulders. On one particular occasion, he rose up in the pulpit and with a loud squeaky voice announced his text thus: "I am the Christ whom I shall represent today."

About this time a little blue lizard ran up his roomy pantaloons. The old preacher, not wishing to interrupt the steady flow of his sermon, slapped away on his leg, expecting to arrest the intruder. Unfortunately, his efforts were unavailing, and the little fellow kept ascending higher and higher.

Continuing the sermon, the preacher loosened the central button on the waistband of his pantaloons, and with a kick, off came the easy-fitting garment.

Meanwhile, Mr. Lizard had passed the equatorial line of the waistband, moving northward, and was calmly exploring the part of the preacher's anatomy that was covered by the back of his shirt.

Things were now growing interesting, though the sermon was merely grinding on. The preacher's next move was to undo the collar button, and with one sweep of his arm, off came the tow linen shirt.

The congregation sat for an instant as if dazed; all the while the preacher kept sermonizing. At length, one old lady in the back of the room rose up, and, staring at the excited preacher, shouted: "If you represent Christ, then I'm done with the Bible."

During the summer election canvass, a few political candidates make the rounds of the newly plowed prairie farms. Among them is a Methodist circuit preacher by the name of Cartwright who aims at becoming a state legislator. When he stops at the farm where I'm working, his voice booms out a speech that's too dogmatic for my liking. I look him over; he's a square-jawed, weather-faced man dressed in the finery of a bishop. He surveys me, as well, thinking I'm an ignorant farmer with whom he can have some fun. When he engages me in debate, I best him on every point of argument. After we finish, he asks how I've come to be so articulate and well informed.

Days later, another candidate named Posey draws a crowd near John Hanks' place where I'm helping split firewood. Hanks and I drop our axes and wander over to see what the man has to say. Posey's speech is poorly given and shallow in content. John turns over a crate and says to me, "You can do better than him."

I scratch my head. "If folks promise not to laugh."

Urged on by several bystanders, I step up on the crate and make a strong case for navigational improvements on the Sangamon River. Their applause is so raucous I fear for Mr. Posey's embarrassment. He's not the least bit chagrined, however, and encourages me to persevere in my studies and to practice my oratory. He says I could make a bright future for myself and anyone who cast his lot with me.

On my hike back to Father's that evening, I consider Mr. Posey's assessment. How different his vision is from my reality—an impoverished young man encumbered by the obligation to care for aging parents. The day of my emancipation cannot come soon enough.

As summer progresses, my dream becomes even more distant. An attack of malaria spoils Father's effort to open up more land for farming, and his hunting suffers as well. Every time he seems to recover, he falls back into fever, chills, and melancholy. Mama is afflicted as well, but her condition is not as grave as Mother's was when she died of the milk-sick. Just the same, I'm gripped by fear over the prospect of losing another angel I love so dearly. My burden is lightened by Mama's daughter Elizabeth, who has a brood of her own. Although she suffers from fever, too, she attends to our parents until I'm home from a full day's work to nurse them through the night.

By November, their misery is so complete that Father vows to "git outta thar" as soon as both are well. His plans are ruined, however, as early winter storms set in before their health returns. While unexpected snows drive out the disease-ridden mosquitoes, our food stores are fast depleted. A sparse harvest and my meager wages have not been sufficient for us to store enough food to make it through until spring.

My chest tightens as I join Mama's son, John, to hunt for game. My boyhood vow to never again shoot anything as large as a turkey must be broken. Father's flintlock resists me like an anchor when I pick it up and rest it on my shoulder. My stomach knots up like it did the day Mr. Taylor put me to work slaughtering hogs.

After a bit, John and I split up so we can cover more ground. Not much later, I come across a deer at the edge of a small brook, trapped in thin ice. On seeing me, the critter thrashes all the harder, hastening to extricate itself. Its struggle is to no avail. At last, it drops its head and pants from exhaustion.

I tell myself, "These animals aren't faring any better than the rest of us."

Tears cloud my vision as the rifle stock comes to rest in the fold of my shoulder. I nearly choke on the lump in my throat and then hold my breath for what seems like an eternity.

The gun's report rattles my jaw. My eyes slam shut, and my head throbs as if I were the one shot. I have no memory of squeezing the trigger, but when my eyes open, my treachery is evident. The deer lies still in the water, the current lapping at the ridge of its back. Blood-stained shards of ice float downstream.

From behind me, twigs snap under John's weight as he makes his way down to the creek. He pauses at the bank and surveys our prey. Still looking down on the critter he says, "Was worried the spring thaw would get here before you mustered the nerve to shoot."

After hauling the deer home and dressing it, I beg at a neighbor's for grain. Running low himself, he points me to the bins where he keeps his store of corn. With my near-frozen hands, I sweep up loose kernels at the base of the tubs and scoop out no more than what we need to survive a few more days. My head hung low, I brace against howling wind and hike for miles toward the nearest mill, pushing through biting cold and deep snow. After passing a farmer who's for digging in snow drifts, scavenging for frozen ears of corn, I reflect on his advantage over me. At least he has his own corn and not scraps gleaned from a neighbor's harvest.

As the snows begin to melt in the early part of 1831, Father and Mama start back to Indiana, abandoning the farm to creditors. Dennis and his brood, along with my step-brother, John Johnston, remain in Decatur. Mama wraps all my earthly belongings in a blanket, ties the ends together to make a bundle, and runs a long stick through the knot. With the sum total of my wealth slung over my shoulder, I kiss her goodbye and leave my Father's house for the last time.

John Hanks takes me in, and we cast our lot together cutting and selling cords of wood as well as splitting rails for fences. When we collect our pay, I tuck mine in my shirt and grin from ear to ear. For the first time my wages are truly my own.

Several days later, Hanks tells me about a man named Denton Offut who does business up and down the Sangamon River. Mr. Offut has asked him to run a flatboat loaded with merchandise down to New Orleans. Hanks tells me he's been pondering the idea and intends to give an answer straight away. The only hitch is he'll agree to take the job only if I join him. I push aside memories of New Orleans slave markets and contemplate the adventure to be had floating down the Mississippi.

I consider Hanks' invitation for a couple of days before accepting it, and on condition that we recruit my step-brother, John, to accompany us. Hanks agrees and says Mr. Offut intends on having his boat ready in early March. We'll each be paid fifty cents per day plus sixty dollars.

Hanks and I continue hiring out our arms and axes until one morning he says, "Time to go and see if the boat's ready." We say good-bye to his family and head over to the Sangamon where we procure a canoe and paddle downriver to a landing five miles from Springfield. It doesn't take long to find a buyer to take the canoe off our hands before we walk the remaining distance into town to meet up with John.

Mr. Offut is not easy to find, but we eventually locate him entertaining associates at the Buckhorn Inn. In stature and frame, he reminds me of Father, but unlike Father, he gives the initial impression he'll do whatever work it takes to achieve his dreams. On closer inspection, however, his glazed eyes and rosy cheeks suggest he's a drunken likeness of Father. His condition brings to mind the humiliation I suffered in Little Pigeon Creek over drinking too much apple-jack. I fell face down in a creek and would have drowned if I'd not been discovered by pretty Lizzy Tuley. I fancied her at the time, but her father wouldn't allow her to see me anymore. I pled for forgiveness, pointing out it was my only moral lapse, but Mr. Tuley was resolute, and Lizzy obediently ended our friendship. The thought haunts me still—if I'd been one of the handsome boys in town, her father might have overlooked my transgression.

Offut's words are all a slur as he makes excuses for failing to have our boat ready over by where Spring Creek joins the Sangamon. Hanks, who's an experienced riverman, turns to me and says, "Lincoln, here, once helped build a flatboat out by Pigeon Creek. Took it all the way down to New Orleans. Ain't that so, Abe."

"After a fashion."

He looks at Offut. "It'll cost ya for our labor, but we can build ya a boat."

Offut belches, wobbles, and says, "How does twelve dollars a month suit you fellows?"

Hanks extends his hand. "We'll build your boat."

Offut grabs Hanks' hand and jerks it up and down. "You've got a deal."

I rub the back of my neck, "Any place near the river to cut timber?"

"Sure," Offut says, pulling back his shoulders. "There's some federal land northwest of here, by Sangamo Town. Kirkpatrick's mill is close by. When it's finished, you can float it down the Sangamon to the Illinois."

Down at the so-called Congress land, we slap together a shanty to sleep in and begin cutting timbers. I'm elected camp cook. Before I was big enough to swing an axe, I used to sit in our cabin and watch Mother make soups, bread, and other vittles, but I scarcely remember how she went about it. Hopefully, my cooking doesn't kill the lot of us. I reckon they could also die from my smutty stories and jokes, but they seem to like them. One of their favorites is another one I learned from Uncle Mordecai:

There's Busey. He pretends to be a great heart smasher. Claims he does wonderful things with the girls. I'll venture he's never entered into anyone's flesh but once, and that's when he fell down and stuck his finger into his own.

The boat is bigger than the one Allen Gentry and I cobbled together three years ago. For this one, we cut down two of the tallest trees in the area and mill them into beams for the eighty foot gunwales. We use the trim pieces plus other milled lumber for floorboards, sideboards, decking, and roof planks.

Smaller trees measuring about eighteen feet are used for girders that run across between the gunwales. Once the girders are attached, we fasten the floorboards then haul the boat down to the river and turn it over. Next, we lay the deck planks and add studs to the ends of the girders to create the framing for our sidewalls. Longer studs are attached at the ends of the girders at the vessel's midsection so we can add a roof. The area under the roof is partitioned to separate the sleeping quarters from the section where we keep livestock and perishable cargo.

After four weeks, the boat is ready for launch. Offut is nearly delirious when he brings a supply of libations from the Buckhorn Inn to help us celebrate upstairs in the home of one of his friends. The evening's entertainment is provided by a traveling juggler who is also a magician. To his chagrin, however, we get distracted by political banter. Our spirits are so high we find Jackson men and Whigs agreeing on a few things, a feat of magic in itself. Any other time or place, each side would swear the other does the devil's bidding.

To commandeer our attention, the juggler asks for a hat in which he says he'll cook some eggs. John offers mine—a humble, low-crowned, broad-brimmed affair—which I hesitate to hand over. The others complain loudly that I'm being haughty.

I hold the hat close to my chest. "I'm not protecting my hat; it's out of deference to the eggs that I object."

After much cajoling, I give up the hat, and sure enough, out of it he pulls two cooked eggs. His trick yields plenty of laughter.

As the evening continues, I take a seat in the back of the room, drawing my knees up to my chest in as compact a form as I can manage, and watch the revelry.

The following day we load the boat with hogs, corn, bacon, and barrels of cured pork, as well as other merchandise. Then we use one of our two twenty-foot poles to push off from shore. The poles can be converted to oars by pegging flat boards onto the ends. Forked branches anchored on either side of the roof serve as oarlocks. Another longer pole set up in a similar way serves as a rudder for steering from the roof. It's Hanks' idea to build sails out of leftover lumber and some cloth. His sails don't provide much propulsion, but do give spectators a source of amusement.

Offut is on board with us, since he intends to conduct business at towns along the Sangamon. His first stop is the fledgling village of New Salem about ten miles downriver from our launch site. As we approach shore at the small bluff-top settlement, a submerged wooden mill dam catches us hard. We all tumble to the deck.

I turn and look aft. My breath catches as water covers our stern. All the cargo has shifted back and pushed the rear of the boat down, leaving our bow pointing skyward. The boat begins to rock as we teeter on the dam.

Offut and Hanks begin arguing over who's at fault. "Stop," I shout. With everyone staring at me I begin giving orders. "Unload everything that's weighing down the stern."

Hanks stuffs his hands in his pockets and asks, "How do you propose we do that?"

I point to a boat tied up on shore. "Find the owner. See if we can borrow it to hold some of the cargo. I'll go ashore and ask whether anyone has an auger to lend."

I look up at the crowd gathering near the mill on the bluff above and say to Hanks, "Reckon we're today's amusement."

He shrugs.

As the gallery of spectators grows, a slender girl, with golden hair framing her comely face, makes her way to the front. An aura about her captivates me from the start. When she looks at me, I glance away.

Offut takes hold of my arm and guides me over to a small boat that someone has rowed up alongside us. He tells me to go up into the town and ask for a local cooper named Onstot; he'll be happy to lend us an auger. He says to simply tell him I've been dispatched on an errand by Mr. Denton Offut.

After being rowed to shore, I climb the trail to the bluff-top, recalling how some neighbors would shake their heads when they learned Father had sent me to work on their farms. Mr. Onstot—who resembles the barrels in his shop—dispels my apprehension when he lauds my employer's head for business.

Back at the boat I use the auger to bore holes in the forward floorboards. Once the cargo is removed from the stern, the bow tilts down over the dam, and water swamps forward, draining out through the holes. Several townspeople help us coax the boat off the dam and tow it to shore where I plug the drain holes using pitch and wooden pegs, also provided by Onstot.

Offut boasts of my ingenuity to all of New Salem's assembled residents. He expresses his delight with our recovery from near disaster by announcing his plans to build a steamboat to run on the Sangamon, declaring I will be its pilot. Everyone cheers, including the golden haired girl in whose direction I continue to steal glances. It would be best if she did not take notice of me, however, given my gawky frame, untamed hair, pantaloons some four inches short of my ankles, and shirttail barely tucked into my waistband.

I lean over to Offut. "Who is she?"

As if there is only one girl in the crowd who could evoke such an inquiry, he whispers, "Her name is Ann. Daughter of John Rutledge, one of the town's founders. He owns the mill here. It's his dam you freed us from."

"Ann is a good name.".

"You kind of fancy her?"

"Naw. I'm sure she's got a beau. Anyway, she wouldn't look twice at a homely fellow like me."

Not long after leaving New Salem we moor at Blue Banks to load some pigs Offut has bought from a man named Squire Godbey. His swine are the most uncooperative sort. Every time we round them up they turn and run back past us. After several tries, I say to Offut, "Once they tire out we should cover their eyes. Maybe it'll be easier to herd them aboard."

He looks at me with a grin. "You give me an idea. Round them up one by one." Tapping my shoulder he says, "Lincoln, take their heads. Johnston and Hanks, you two hold their legs while I sew the eyelids shut."

My jaw drops as Offut reaches into his bag and pulls out a sewing kit.

"Go. Do it," Offut says, waving his hand in the air.

If Father barked such an order, I'd balk, digging in my heels, but I give Offut the benefit of the doubt and do as he says. Once we have collected the poor creatures, we try our best to still their squirming bodies as "Doctor" Offut performs his crude—if not cruel—surgery. I turn my head and keep my eyes shut. The earsplitting shrieks remind me of the abuse Father's poor dog, Yellow Joe, suffered during that coon hunt John led.

After he sews the first pig's eyes, I carry it, squealing, aboard our boat. I wince and snip the twine then remove it from the critter's wounds, restoring its sight. When I turn it loose it behaves as if its trauma never happened, though my eyelids remain tortured by the pain it endured. As Offut finishes sewing each pig, I repeat my part of the ritual. On finishing the last one, I take a deep breath.

The Sangamon River snakes through the wilderness between our launch site and the Illinois River as if it's aiming for no particular destination, nor constrained by anyone's timetable. What is thirty miles as the crow flies, winds around to become more than sixty. That doesn't count the constant maneuvering to avoid sandbars, snags, and submerged logs that hide in the shallow waters.

We're fortunate to have company for this portion of the journey. Another boat owned by a man named Clark floats alongside us until we get to Beardstown just after we start down the Illinois. We camp together at night on the Sangamon, since it's too dangerous to navigate after dusk. One evening I remark to Clark's son Phillip that Beardstown would make a fine place to settle someday. Of course, New Salem might have its advantages, as well.

Three days into our journey we join the broad, stable current of the Illinois, and eight miles later we float past the young city of Beardstown, named after its founder, Thomas Beard. It's built right on the water's edge, a tidy geometrical form, seven even blocks long and three deep. On one end of town, a column of white steam rises out of a sawmill's chimney. Not far from the mill, a steam powered paddlewheel boat is nestled up on the sandy riverbank.

I study the town's layout as it fades into the distance, eyeing the uniformity of its blocks. "Reckon you have to be someone special to have a town named after you. Maybe someday I'll build a town, just like Mr. Beard or Mr. Rutledge."

A hundred-twenty miles south at St. Louis, we dock and part company with Hanks, who books passage on a steamboat for home. The month we spent building this boat consumed most of the time he planned to be away from his farm and family. Continuing on to New Orleans with us would double the length of his absence.

Downriver, Offut, John, and I make better time than expected. The government has removed most of the logjams and snags that once slow navigation. They've also cut away the overhanging tree canopies that blocked late afternoon and early morning sunlight and shortened travel days. We make landings in Memphis, Vicksburg, and Natchez. All three of these bluff cities look down on Under the Hill districts where flatboatmen tie up to trade their wares. Steamboats unload passengers and collect new ones. Vicksburg appears much different from my first voyage when the waterfront was under flood waters.

After our business at these ports is finished, we float along the Sugar Coast without mooring, not even for the night. I gaze at the miles of sugar plantations as we pass by, my jaw tightening over the injustice they represent. My shoulders knot as we drift past Madame Busham's Plantation. My brush with death at the hands of runaway slaves on the previous voyage is an event I'd like to forget, but the scar above my eye reminds me whenever the memory starts to fade.

When we arrive in New Orleans, Denton Offut's experience and acquaintances are indispensable. We're sold out in less than a week and he's so pleased that he hires me on to clerk at the store he plans to open in New Salem. Though I'm eager to head home, passage on a northbound steamboat takes several days to arrange. While the others indulge in the city's saloons, gambling tables, and sideshows, I find other diversions. I seek out bookstores and become fascinated with a shop that displays surveying equipment, similar to what General Washington used in his youth.

John pressures me into accompanying him on one of his excursions. We have great fun until we come across a slave auction. My thoughts travel to the pretty quadroon girl who gained her seller seventeen-hundred dollars from the brocade-vested planter. I turn away and call over my shoulder to John, "I'm getting out of here."

He hurries after me—his short legs making it hard for him to make up ground. When he catches up, he bobs along next to me, telling in hushed tones of a Creole witch who tortures her slaves, mutilating their bodies, even drinking their blood. My back twitches and my stomach turns. John says he's picked up stories about the witch from patrons in the city's saloons. I wonder what's become of the quadroon girl.

Welts pinch at my flanks—memories buried beneath my skin—as I tell him about my previous visit here. I repeat my earlier oath, "If I ever get the chance, I'll hit this injustice hard."

"How do you plan to do that?"

"Don't know, but I promised Mother when she was about to die that I would become someone special. Once that path is clear to me, I'll put everything into stopping men from stealing the wages of another man's toil."

On my way back to the boarding house, I encounter more slave sales. Everywhere, auctioneers prod men, women, and children, goading them to prance around a stage to demonstrate their agility and obedience. Fancily dressed men bid for the right to profit from others' bondage. For the remainder of my time in New Orleans I linger at our boarding house, telling stories, reading, and recalling Weems' admonition in his *The Life of Washington*.

> *... every youth can become a Washington ... in piety and patriotism ... in industry and honor ...*

Even sequestered, there's no escaping the city's darkness. At the hotel, while I'm seated in the parlor reading from Shakespeare's *Merchant of Venice*, another boarder bursts into the lobby with gruesome news. A teenaged slave was just hanged for murdering his master, and another boy—the poor slave's friend—died of convulsions, mourning at the foot of the gallows. My body tightens, and my stomach wrenches into knots.

I bolt from the chair and run to my room. As the door shuts behind me, my back twitches again, recalling the sting of Father's strap. I press my back against the door, hoping to stop his assault, and out of nowhere I'm overwhelmed by a dark shroud. When my senses return I'm crumbled on the floor, my skin itching as if laced with scars, having no memory of the past hour.

For the rest of my time in New Orleans, I venture out only to attend an exposition of a revolutionary locomotive steam carriage. According to the newspaper, the demonstration dispels all doubts that such a conveyance can be propelled by steam. Its promoters say their steam locomotive is designed along the lines of one in England which recently dragged a string of loaded carriages over a distance of twenty-five miles in only two hours. Compelled to examine this new wonder, I walk briskly toward the wharf, keeping my eyes fixed ahead, looking neither left nor right, lest I again become a witness to human cruelty.

Chapter Ten

T he prairie sun beats on the back of my neck as I lumber through dusty New Salem in late July on my return from New Orleans. At each open doorway I take off my sweat-soiled, broad-brimmed hat and inquire about Mr. Offut. No one has seen him since our flatboat got caught up on the mill dam on our way down to New Orleans. I ask to be pointed in the direction of his store.

They reply, "What store?"

I scratch my head. He should have made better time than me, him traveling all the way from New Orleans to Beardstown by steamboat, and me off-boarding in Memphis, then hiking nearly four hundred miles through wilderness to Father's new home in Coles County. Not only did my detour cost time, but I gave Father my wages to help alleviate his financial distress. He'd run out of money before making it to Indiana, so he and Mama settled in Coles County where some of her family lives.

Mr. Onstot, the cooper, remembers me and recommends I inquire about lodging at the Rutledge Tavern across the way. A corpulent, pink-skinned customer, who's inspecting some of Onstot's new casks, overhears our conversation and introduces himself as Judge Bowling Green, Justice of the Peace. He asks how long I'll be staying in the village, and I tell him about Offut's store.

He shakes his head.

Onstot reminds Judge Green of the incident with our flatboat and the mill dam. "This is the young chap who took control of that calamity and got the thing unstuck."

The judge studies me, sober-eyed. "You don't say .... Then I suppose you're quite a bright enough lad. Come on up to my place for supper this evening and we'll get better acquainted. Unfortunately, we're stuffed to the rafters with children and don't have a spare bed. Though if you'd like, we can make a spot for you on the floor by the fireplace, at least for one night."

I pull back my shoulders and smile. "Sir, I'm grateful for your hospitality. And if it helps, I enjoy playing with children."

Judge Green turns to the cooper. "A well-spoken young man at that. He might do a fine job of arguing cases in my court someday."

Later during supper, I say, "The only time I've been this close to a Justice of the Peace was when I got sued."

Mr. Green's large belly shakes when he laughs. "A lad like you got sued? Over what?"

I tell him about ferrying two passengers to a steamboat out on the Ohio and say, "I never again want to be ignorant of the law, or anything else, for that matter."

He points to several thick books stacked on the mantle. "My library is yours for the borrowing, anytime you like." He goes on, telling me he uses the public room at the Rutledge Tavern when he hears cases. His Justice of the Peace duties only require his attention part of the time; otherwise he's busy tending his farm.

I thank him, and our conversation turns to Offut's plans for his store. The Judge says others have preceded Offut in setting up businesses in the village. Besides the grist mill, cooper shop, and tavern which provides lodging but doesn't sell liquor, there's already a grocery, three general stores, a wool-carding mill, and two doctors' offices. The town also has a blacksmith, shoemaker, carpenter, hat maker, and tanner. Some twenty families live here, sharing common pastures and kitchen gardens. Among the hodgepodge of wood-framed buildings and log cabins is a log schoolhouse, which is also used on Sundays as a church.

The next day I make the acquaintance of John Cameron, a square-jawed preacher with an aristocratic nose. He's Mr. Rutledge's partner in the tavern. While he's unwilling to give me a room in the establishment without payment, he offers me lodging in his home until my affairs with Offut are settled. In the meantime, I continue to take my meals with Judge Green and his family, giving me the opportunity to learn more about how to pursue studying the law.

I leave Mr. Cameron and stop in at the grocery and dry goods store, reputedly the best stocked mercantile around. A slender young fellow seated on the wood-plank porch in a chair made out of branches, greets me with a hardy "Haloo."

I lean against a sturdy timber supporting the overhang roof. "How do?"

He stands and offers a handshake. "Sam Hill, one of the proprietors."

I shake his hand. "I'm Lincoln."

He looks up at me through his spectacles. "Well Lincoln, what can I do for you?"

"I've just landed in town and decided to get acquainted with folks."

"Well, welcome to New Salem," he says, smiling. "We're the biggest merchants around. Carry both groceries and dry goods. Got a root cellar around on the side. The other places only handle your basic supplies and staples. Some sell whiskey, too." He directs me inside.

I gaze around at the packed shelves and the rows of barrels lining the walls, jammed tight against each other. "With all this stuff, it's good your place is so big."

He points to the ceiling. "We live upstairs. Me and my partner, John McNeil."

"Look forward to meeting him."

He shakes his head. "Don't be too sure."

"Why's that?"

"Just my opinion. He's good enough at business, but we haven't gotten along since he swept the prettiest gal in New Salem off her feet. Thought for sure she'd be mine."

I shake my head. "Bad luck."

He frowns. "Usually don't lose with the ladies."

I laugh. "Wouldn't know what that's like. Not accustomed to winning."

A few days later, Offut shows up and tells me he's waiting for delivery of goods for his store and won't require my services until the inventory is on hand. On the bright side, though, he lets me sleep in the empty store if I wish to do so. He'll even procure a cot for me.

Offut's earlier introduction of me to the townspeople—that being on the occasion of our flatboat getting stuck on the mill dam—pales in comparison to his present accolades as he saunters around town making his plans known to everyone. He boasts that I am the strongest and smartest young man ever to cross his path. The latter compliment helps me gain an appointment as the assistant elections clerk.

Election Day arrives in early August, and all the able bodied men from miles around forgo a day's work to come to the village and cast their ballots. As they mill about, I engage them in conversation, hoping to make new friends. When several are gathered together, I entertain them with stories such as the one about the blue lizard that accosted the old preacher.

Mentor Graham, the town's spritely school teacher, offers to help with any studies I might care to do. After the teacher, Colonel James Rutledge introduces himself as co-founder of the village, as well as proprietor of the grist mill, the tavern, and one of the general stores. He's tall, a serious man, gentle in manner, and able to put strangers at ease with his warm gaze. His daughter is the golden-haired beauty who watched us free our flatboat. I gladly accept his invitation to attend meetings of the debating society he presides over, but I become anxious when he tells me his daughter is one of the town's most skilled debaters. My mind will likely turn to gruel in her presence.

As the day approaches for the debate society meeting, my idleness is joined by melancholy. If I could somehow hasten the arrival of goods for Mr. Offut's store, or if I could find some other work to occupy my hands, my gloom could be tamed.

One afternoon, while sitting in the doorway of the empty store, I distract myself by reading from a volume of

Robert Burns' poetry. It's a copy I borrowed from my newly acquired friend, a free-spirit named Jack Kelso.

> *I've notic'd, on our laird's courtday,*
> *An' mony a time my heart's been wae,*
> *Poor tenant bodies, scant o' cash,*
> *How they maun thole a factor's snash;*
> *He'll stamp an' threaten, curse an' swear*
> *He'll apprehend them, poind their gear;*
> *While they maun stan', wi' aspect humble,*
> *An' hear it a', an' fear an' tremble!*

On turning the page I look up and see several young men approaching me. Their swaggers suggest they're an exception to the good-heartedness and hospitality of the general population. In the midst of them is an ox of a man, his dark eyes trained on me and his mouth drawn in a frown.

As they proceed in my direction, leaving a trail of dust in their wake, a crowd led by Offut gathers behind them. When all arrive at the store they hover like an impending storm. I'm told there's always trouble when Jack Armstrong and the Clary's Grove Boys appear.

I look down at the page of poetry, pretending to be indifferent to their presence.

One of them shouts at me, his words slurred by too much whiskey. "So yer the one they says can lick the meanest bull in the field?"

I stand and study the whole lot of them, holding my place in the Burns book with a finger.

One of the ruffians offers Jack a jug, but he pushes it away.

"What?" the boy with the jug says. "Got nothing to say fer yerself?"

Offut jumps in front of me and faces the crowd. "Jack Armstrong, here, has challenged young Lincoln to a fight. Says there's no one who can beat the toughest of the Clary's Grove Boys."

The crowd begins to buzz. I fix my eyes on the ox.

Offut announces, "Ten dollars says my friend Lincoln, here, will take down Jack."

"Who holds the purse?" someone calls out.

"That'll be me," Offut says, waving his hand.

Pandemonium breaks out as people place bets. Some wager money, others drinks, and at least one puts up his prize knife. I pull Offut aside. "I don't fight for sport."

"Hold on, son," he says. "These Clary's Grove Boys are hell-raisers. They need to be set straight or they'll just keep terrorizing good people. Don't think of it as sport. It's ... well, it's ... law and order."

I gaze over the crowd. They've suddenly become quiet.

The words form slowly in my mouth. "I accept."

They roar their approval.

As I step down from the doorway, Armstrong strides toward me, and the onlookers draw away to give us space. Standing six-feet-four-inches, I tower over my adversary. He glares up at me, the veins in his thick neck pulsing. His frame is so compact and his mass is so solid that getting a firm hold on him won't be easy.

The spectators shout their impatience as we size up one another.

He digs in his feet, and a grunt rises from his throat. I stand my ground as he charges, absorbing the impact of his lunge with only the slightest movement. Neither does he so much as flinch from the impact. We struggle to gain purchase on one another, all the while twisting and turning to avoid the other's grip. Armstrong kicks at my ankles in an effort to take my legs out from under me and drop me to the ground.

To counter, I grab for his waistband and strain to lift him off his feet. We wrestle to get the better of each other until his breathing becomes labored. I take a deep breath, grit my teeth, and set my jaw. Recalling Offut's words, "law and order," I muster the strength to raise him off the ground. With his legs kicking and arms flailing, I draw in another breath and lift him over my head. Again "law and order" echoes in my head and I throw him into his gang of thugs. They all tumble to the ground in a heap.

The crowd turns silent as Armstrong's men exchange bewildered glances.

Spectators begin chanting, "Abe! Abe!"

I grin at the sea of admirers, willing to forgive them for using the nickname I hate; however, the Clary's Grove Boys are determined not to be denied their victory. They pick themselves up off the ground and rush at me all at once, growling like a pack of wolves. I back up against the side of the store and shout, "I'll take you on—one-by-one."

They stop in their tracks and look at each other as if silently plotting their attack.

I hold the stare of the one closest to me and say, "Let's keep the fight fair."

Still on his knees, Jack Armstrong shouts, "Stop!"

His boys turn and watch him, waiting for his word.

Armstrong stands and walks toward me with his hand extended. He says in a loud voice, "Abe Lincoln is the best fellow that's ever set foot in New Salem. He's one of us, now."

With a handshake we become friends, and I'm welcomed like a kinsman by all the townspeople. One of the first to step up to greet me is a stocky, well-dressed fellow named McNeil. On his arm is the sandy-haired beauty, Miss Ann Rutledge.

I look down into her sky-blue eyes, and she beams up at me, forming her full lips into a bright smile. My composure goes into full retreat, but once McNeil introduces her as his fiancé, my anxiety evaporates, and my shyness dissolves. Having lost Mother and Sally, I fear I'll jinx anyone whom I love. As for Miss Ann, that burden of worry is now lifted. She belongs to another; she's safe from my curse.

At the debate society meeting that evening, I rise to speak and greet the members with a timid smile. They gaze at me with anticipation etched on their faces, no doubt expecting to be entertained with some humorous story. Among them is Miss Ann, sitting a bit forward between two boys on the bench right in front of me.

Instead of amusing them with wit, I advocate in earnest for internal improvements such as roads, canals, and navigable waterways. Everyone applauds, and Mr. Rutledge commends my argument as pithy and well reasoned. Miss Ann's eyes gleam as she turns to congratulate me before stepping forward to take her turn.

From the very first word, her melodic voice captivates me. When she takes her seat at the end of her speech I commend her, even though I can't recall anything she said. Her beauty distracted me.

Mr. Rutledge approaches Miss Ann and me after the meeting and suggests that she and I, his two prize students, practice our oratory together. She looks down as she waits for my reply.

I fidget with my shirt cuff. "With Mr. McNeil's approval, of course."

She twists a lock of her hair in her fingers. "I'm sure he won't mind. He's quite secure in his position."

Mr. Rutledge grins and adds, "As a man of his accomplishments and charm should be."

"Yes," I say, "a merchant and landowner. Any girl would be lucky to marry such a man."

Miss Ann blushes. I relax, assured that our time together won't be strained by the awkwardness of romance.

"By the way," she says. "Friends call me Annie."

A few days after the debate society meeting, a prominent doctor employs me to run a flatboat down to the confluence of the Illinois and Sangamon Rivers, carrying him and his family. They are removing to Texas and have contracted with another pilot to take them the remainder of the way from Beardstown. Our trip proceeds without incident, and once I'm paid for my services, I walk thirty miles back to New Salem.

On my return, Offut is giddy as he greets me. His goods have arrived and he is open for business. Next to him stands a baby-faced, sandy-haired lad named Billy Greene, no relation to Judge Green. Offut has hired him to assist me in the store.

Offut says, "Billy, here, can sleep in the store. His father has a farm a couple of miles out of town, but the old man's illiterate and drinks too much. One of you can bunk on the counter, unless you want to share the cot."

I throw a bear hug on Offut and pick him up off his feet.

"Save your strength," he says. "There's whiskey barrels that need lifting."

As the weeks pass, business at the store is never

brisk. I often sit in the doorway reading, only taking my eyes off the page to get a glimpse of Annie Rutledge when she passes by on her way to and from her father's grist mill. Saturdays are busier than usual. That's when farmers and their farm hands come to town to do some trading and raise Cain. We close our doors around three o'clock on those days, since by then, everyone's consumed by a variety of drunken amusements which last until they can't stand up any longer.

On weekdays, we lock up at seven o'clock, and Billy and I hike to Judge Green's home for supper. Mrs. Green is a renowned cook in these parts, so the table is always crowded with visitors. During one meal I'm seated next to the school teacher, Mentor Graham, to whom I say, "I've been thinking about studying English grammar."

"If you expect to go before the public in any capacity," Graham says, "it's the best thing you can do."

"Well, if I had a grammar I would commence studying right now."

"I don't have a grammar myself," he says, "but I know John Vance has one."

With that, I excuse myself from the Green's table and hike several miles to Vance's farm. Mr. Vance gives me a copy of Samuel Kirkham's *English Grammar in Familiar Lectures*. He says it's the best available anywhere. When I get back to the store, Billy Greene is already asleep on the cot in the backroom. I stoke the fire and stretch out on the floor and begin studying.

It's a real puzzler. Four, five, and six headed rules, about as complicated to me as the *Longer Catechism* and the *Thirty-nine Articles* are to young ministers. It consumes me day and night—while clerking, or when I lie under a tree on the hillside overlooking our village. Evenings, I study stretched out by the stove at the store.

One Saturday, while tending store, I've no time to study, and after work, I find the athletic games too tempting to pass up. My long legs give me an advantage in jumping contests, and my arms, like a pair of low-hanging pendulums, serve me in weight throwing. Out of respect for me, the Clary's Grove Boys pass on wrestling matches, giving me easy victories over all comers.

I'm more than happy to stay out of the cock-fighting as a fair trade for their courtesy, but owing to my reputation for fairness, Jack Armstrong insists I referee when his gang's birds are in play. In honor of our mutual friendship, I agree. After hunting game for survival when Father was ill, and having passed through a hot summer day of slaughtering hogs while under his bondage, I suffer less pain than I once did when animals are abused. Still, a twinge of it still inflicts me.

Tonight's contest is between roosters owned by Tom Watkins and Babb McNabb. Poised inside a ring formed by spectators, I steel myself against the protests of my conscience while the boys agitate their birds into a frenzy. When McNabb's bird surprises everyone by shrinking from the fight, my chest swells and I cannot contain my smile.

McNabb, red with embarrassment, jumps into the ring, retrieves his entry and throws the bird back over his shoulder onto a woodpile. On landing, the rooster puffs out its chest and begins to crow. McNabb throws up his hands and hollers, "Yes, you little cuss, you're great on dress parade, but you ain't worth a damn in a fight."

For all the activity Saturdays bring to town, sales at the store are barely adequate to pay salaries to Billy and me, let alone pay the mortgage on the store. Anxious over his financial situation, Offut expands his enterprise by renting the grist and saw mills from Mr. Rutledge, adding additional responsibilities for Billy and me to share. Even though the added chores interrupt my reading, work at the mills keeps me busy—wrestling logs onto the saw carriage, trimming boards, and grinding kernels of grain into flour.

I'm especially delighted when Annie stops by and asks me to accompany her to the grist mill to grind up corn for her father's tavern. Our friendship blossoms and I become her confidant in matters she's too nervous to share with McNeil. In return, she tries to pair me with some of the single girls in town. I admire her persistence in such a hopeless endeavor.

Chapter Eleven

Offut's expanded business endeavors keep me busier than ever, but I still find idle time to jaw with the likes of Jack Kelso. In addition to our mutual liking for poetry, we share a dislike for menial labor, though he is able to survive without having to work for wages. When business is slack, Jack and I talk about fishing, read Burns, and plumb the depths of Shakespeare's verse. The Bard's plays intrigue me and inspire me to commit long passages of *Hamlet* to memory.

As January of the new year draws to a close, our monotony is broken by news that Captain Vincent Bogue of Springfield has plans to run a steamboat called *Talisman* up the Sangamon, turning Springfield into a port city. His letter of January 26 as published in *The Sangamo Journal*, claims,

> *I intend to ascend the Sangamon River immediately on the breaking up of the ice. I should be met at the mouth of the river by ten or twelve men, equipped with long-handled axes and under the direction of some experienced axeman. I shall deliver freight from St. Louis to the new port at Springfield for thirty-seven and a half cents per hundred pounds.*

I'm not alone in following reports of Captain Bogue's progress. The whole town is abuzz, and there is much talk about New Salem becoming a boom-town on account of his venture. Some folks insist a canal is needed to bypass much of the Sangamon's snake-like course coming out of Beardstown. Others fear the cost of such a project would be exorbitant and urge dredging the bottom and clearing away overhanging trees and logjams. My experience, having taken three flatboats down the river, fuels my passion for making the Sangamon's waters safer and faster for transporting goods.

By February, a gloom settles over me. My friends' wives claim it's due to my increased idleness. Offut's store is floundering, there's little call for lumber to be cut, and the grist mill warehouses an over-supply of meal and flour. Our wages have been suspended on account of Offut's foolish speculation in corn and cottonseed he imported from Tennessee.

One morning near month's end one of Offut's creditors confronts me on my arrival at the store. "Is Offut around?" he asks.

"Reckon he's at his cabin."

The man scowls. "I've been there. He's not. Neighbors haven't seen him since yesterday afternoon."

I run my fingers through my hair. "He didn't stop in last night to check the receipts, so the last time I saw him was the night before."

His eyes narrow. "Did he say where he was going?"

I shake my head. "Didn't say he was going anywhere."

He hands me some papers.

"What's this?"

"A judgment," he says. "It lets me take anything I need to satisfy the debt."

"Afraid you'll have to wait for Mr. Offut."

The man hangs around for several days. Offut doesn't show. I stay away from the store out of shame over my employer's abrupt departure.

Lying in bed one night, I recall once overcharging a customer. After locking up the store, I walked three miles to return the six-and-a-half cents she was owed. She told me to keep it as a reward for my honesty. I refused. All the way back I held my chin high, delighting in the reputation

I'd earned for Mr. Offut's enterprise. Now I weigh the damage he leaves in the wake of his cowardly escape.

My spirits are buoyed by Bowling Green, James Rutledge, and schoolmaster Graham who all laud my efforts at self-improvement. They praise the efficient manner in which I managed Offut's enterprises and are quick to absolve me of any blame for his business failures.

Judge Green keeps me busy serving as a juror and drawing up deeds or other papers for townspeople who need the aid of a lawyer. I refuse compensation, allowing that I'm not licensed to practice law, but I'm encouraged by their appreciation. Still, their gratitude does nothing to lift me out of my poverty.

One afternoon while I'm studying some law books at the Judge's home, he sits with me and insists on discussing what he calls a matter of great import. He takes the book from my hands and snaps it shut.

"Lincoln," he says. "I've been talking with some stalwarts around town, particularly Rutledge, Mentor Graham, and Dr. Allen. We are all of one mind."

I look down at the floor. "Yes, Sir."

"The business we all would like to see you pursue...." He clears his throat. "We think you would make an excellent candidate for the state legislature."

I look up at him and swallow hard. "I don't understand. There have to be many ...."

"There are always others, but the point is, you're every bit as good, if not better."

My face grows warm. "I'm honored."

He stands. "Then it's settled?"

I cock my head. "Can I think about it?"

"Don't take too long," he says. "The *Sangamo Journal* will be publishing the candidates' platforms in next week's edition. If you want to finish among the top four names on Election Day in August, you best have something ready for them to print."

Mother's words, "become someone special," echo in my mind as I contemplate Judge Green's proposition. After a couple sleepless nights, I conclude that serving in the legislature can be the way to leave the world a little better for having lived in it.

On March 9, I announce to the people of Sangamon County my intentions to be a candidate for the state legislature. My platform appears in the *Sangamo Journal* alongside those of a dozen other candidates.

The next day, I'm picking up some wages by filling in as clerk at Sam Hill's dry goods store when Charles Maltby, who used to help out at Offut's store, stops by. He urges me to make up a speech.

"What shall I say?"

"Why not say what you put in the newspaper about your plans?"

"No. That's too long."

Maltby pats me on the shoulder. "Then use only the first part."

I scratch my head and pick up a copy of the paper. After pondering it for a spell, I take up the quill and ink I always carry with me to write letters and legal papers for neighbors. I cross out the lines that don't seem to make good speech material.

"How's this?"

He reads it aloud.

Fellow Citizens, in accordance with an established custom and the principles of true republicanism, it becomes my duty to make known to you my sentiments with regard to local affairs.

No person will deny that the poorest and most thinly populated countries would be greatly benefitted by the opening of good roads, and in the clearing of navigable streams within their limits.

"Very direct," he says. "Direct and to the point."

I cock my head. "Then, should I expect you to vote for me?"

Maltby strokes his chin. "If you make it to the legislature and get a bill passed to improve navigation on the Sangamon, New Salem would make a fine shipping point. It would be perfect for servicing Captain Bogue's steamboat business. What do you say we rent a log building to run a storage and forwarding enterprise?"

I immediately agree, and in a matter of days we acquire the necessary accommodations.

Not many days later, word arrives that the 150-ton, 136-foot long, double-decked *Talisman* has left Saint Louis and is steaming up the Illinois River. Storekeeper Rowan Herndon, a hardy fellow two years older than me, takes the lead, and a dozen of us follow him to the rendezvous point at the mouth of the Sangamon just north of Beardstown. Once there, we make quick work of breaking up the ice with our axes.

On the vessel's arrival, Bogue introduces his pilot, Captain Pollock, decked out in a colorful uniform, and surveys the group of us. Seeing that we're a fit crew, he hires us to clear the channel for the *Talisman* through the Sangamon's gauntlet of twists, turns, and hazards. As the gathering disperses, I approach Bogue about the storage and forwarding venture Maltby and I have organized. He gives me a firm handshake to seal his intent to avail himself of our services.

The steamer's progress upstream is slow, as logjams must be cleared and overhanging limbs need to be cut away due to the ship's height. As we approach the mill dam at New Salem I keep a keen eye on the water line along the banks, worried the massive vessel might get hung up. The river's level, swollen earlier by the spring runoff, has already dropped several inches in just a few days. When the boat makes it to the dam, my anxiety lingers on account of the rate at which the Sangamon continues to drop. We still have to sail back over the dam on the return trip to Beardstown.

When we arrive in Springfield about ten miles upstream, a marching band with shining brass instruments and drums, all decked out in vibrant colors, joins a large crowd heralding the *Talisman*'s maiden journey. But during the evening's celebration, Bogue becomes incensed with his pilot's intoxication and scandalous behavior. Pollock's guests, two bawdily dressed, painted women, are an embarrassment. Bogue sacks the old seadog on the spot, leaving the boat without a seasoned skipper to see her back to Beardstown. Faced with the Sangamon's rapidly falling water levels, Bogue acts swiftly, employing Rowan Herndon as his new pilot. Rowan, who previously ran a ferry on the Ohio River, takes me on as his assistant.

As we leave the port at Springfield, the water is already so shallow we have to back the boat downstream to find a spot wide enough to turn around. Once underway, we make only two or three miles per day over the short distance to New Salem. We must disengage the ship's paddles through the shallower depths, leaving us to drift along at the current's languid pace. As we float over the shallows, I scurry up and down the deck on whichever side is closest to shore, manning a long pole to push us back if we get close to the bank. At this point, the touted steamboat is no more than a monstrous, unwieldy flatboat.

On our approach to New Salem, I lean over the forward corner of the deck railing to see if the water is getting murky from silt deposits collecting behind the dam. When the water is too cloudy to see more than a few inches below the surface, I signal to Rowan that we're almost there. He blows the whistle and engages the boat's wheel in reverse. Seconds later, the *Talisman* strikes the mill dam and I'm thrown to the deck. The grinding of the hull against the submerged obstacle makes such a groan that everyone in town rushes to the bluff to gawk at our catastrophe.

In his agitation, Bogue demands we remove a portion of the dam. Mr. Rutledge, the mill owner, refuses permission. Bogue asserts that the Federal Constitution prohibits the damming or obstruction of any navigable stream. I stand back and listen to each side, hoping to chime in with a voice of reason, but I'm in a bind. Rutledge is my friend and Annie's father, and Bogue is my employer. Anything I say is likely to backfire. In the end, Bogue prevails, and with the help of several men from town, we remove a section of the dam. Rutledge assures me he doesn't hold me responsible for any part of the affair. Once we pass through the dam, we continue to Beardstown without further incident.

After Rowan and I each collect forty dollars for our services, Bogue laments that conditions on the Sangamon are not conducive to steamboat navigation. He no longer plans to continue his venture, which means the storage and forwarding business Maltby and I had high hopes for is dead before it starts.

As Rowan and I trudge through the woods back to New Salem, I make mental notes of a possible canal route. When I'm certain of a course which could be dug to improve a section of the river's navigation, I sight in on a landmark. Rowan doesn't speak to me for the entire thirty miles; he only shakes his head now and then.

On April 19, only days after our return, word comes that Governor Reynolds is calling up a militia to deal with a band of Redskins crossing the Mississippi into Illinois. We all fear Chief Black Hawk has set out to reclaim land ceded under a previous treaty. Every able-bodied man volunteers for service, though some must stay behind to defend our settlement, which is particularly vulnerable as it lies near the westernmost edge of the frontier. The men drill in formation, some toting brooms in place of muskets, others brandishing hoes or other farming implements. Women huddle together comforting each other, and children cling to their mothers' frocks.

I join the volunteers, knowing that means suspending my campaign for the legislature. The $6.66 per month stipend for militia service is a badly needed source of income now that Offut's store has winked out. We all head to Beardstown where our company joins the brigade led by General Samuel Whiteside, commander of the Illinois militia.

The General is a seasoned soldier, having fought in Tecumseh's War, as well as the 1812 war against the British invasion. His recruits, on the other hand, are neither experienced nor disciplined. Many of us don't even possess our own weapons; we have to requisition thirty muskets from the Federal army to fully arm our company. Once we are mustered in, the rifles are provided to us as well as meager rations, and the task of establishing order begins.

Each company of the brigade is directed to elect its own captain. William Kirkpatrick, a local sawmill owner, offers to lead the Sangamon County volunteers, and the glint in his eye broadcasts how badly he wants the honor.

Not long after I arrived in New Salem, Kirkpatrick hired me to move some logs with a cant hook which he was about to purchase for two dollars. I offered to handle them with a simple spike hook if he paid me the two dollars on top of my wages. After I moved the logs he refused to pay.

I see an opportunity for revenge and huddle with the Clary's Grove Boys to explain my complaint against Kirkpatrick. They tell me they're not about to take orders from anyone, but they would relish putting Kirkpatrick in his place. The Boys see to it that three-fourths of the men come over to my side and elect me captain. As they line up behind me, and I read the dejection on Kirkpatrick's face, I puff out my chest and grin broadly.

We train for a week before setting out to engage the enemy, and the Clary's Grove Boys try to set themselves up at the top of our company's pecking order. They begin with a threat that anyone ruffling their feathers ought to be careful about taking a battle position forward of their muskets—the offending parties might fare better rushing head-long into a volley of enemy fire. At least if they died charging the enemy, their corpses wouldn't give the appearance of having been shot in the back while deserting the battlefield.

A couple of days into our training, the gang chooses to put my leadership to the test. We're under orders from the brigade commander to take a ten mile march out from camp carrying heavy packs, and to return by dusk. The Clary's Grove Boys begin grousing after only a couple hours. Before noon, they drop their packs and announce that after resting, they're heading back to Beardstown to find some whores. When I order them to fall into formation and resume the march, they all laugh.

I remind them they'll be arrested if they don't return with their unit, and besides, I say, "You have wives back home who won't like hearing about you cavorting with prostitutes."

Armstrong reminds me they're his boys, and anyone who gives them up to their wives will regret it.

I take off my hat and scratch my head. "If you catch the syphilis, no one will need to tell. You'll go insane and maybe even die. Can't hide that evidence."

"We ain't had none in weeks," he says. "And anyway, we'll be careful. Pay enough for high quality merchandise."

His buddies chortle.

I glance at the rest of the company. Their eyes are fixed on me.

"Armstrong," I say. "You and your boys leave me with little choice. Reckon I'll have to let you go. But first, give your rifles and rations to the rest of the men. They belong to the government."

Armstrong grins. "That just makes our load lighter." The Boys nod their heads.

"Fine," I say, and direct the others to collect the Boys' gear.

After relieving the Clary's Grove Boys of their burdens, I order the balance of the company into formation, walk over to the gang, and lower my voice so as not to be overheard. "Boys, you'd best keep a watch out for Indians after we split up. The General worried that some of the men might desert if they knew our true mission, so he ordered all the company captains to keep it secret. You see, scouts have reported Indians out this way, and we're on this march to sniff them out. Kill any we see if they should engage us."

The Boys' eyes widen as they exchange glances.

I continue. "Now if you get in a tight spot, you should see to it that one of you escapes to come back to camp. With his help we can chase the savages down and get revenge."

I walk away.

Armstrong calls after me. "Lincoln."

I stop, but don't turn back.

"Lincoln," he repeats, "let's talk this over a bit."

I turn and take a couple steps toward the gang.

Armstrong scratches his head. "Look, we don't like folks ordering us around."

I turn my palms up. "What do you want me to do?"

"We'll come along, but we don't want you to make us look bad."

The others nod.

"Fine," I say and turn to the company telling them, "The Clary's Grove Boys talked among themselves and decided the rest of us would need their help if we're attacked. All of us would probably get scalped if they weren't along to protect us."

Armstrong plants his hands on his hips. "That's right. We got to thinking how selfish it would be to abandon you out here in the woods with Indians and whatnot running loose."

I turn back to the Boys, holding back a smile. "We're most grateful for your thoughtfulness. Now if you're sufficiently rested, can we resume?"

"Reckon," says Armstrong.

I turn again to the rest and say, "Good. Out of gratitude for their sacrifice, we ought to carry the Clary's Grove Boys' packs and guns for them. Just be ready to hand them back if we get ambushed."

We encounter no Indians along our march.

On the last day of April, our brigade begins marching out of Beardstown. We cross the Illinois River and head toward Rushville, about ten miles north, where we make camp for the night. The following morning, we break camp and continue north, headed for the mouth of the Rock River. We reach the river several days later, having seen no signs of Indians along the way. The rations, including whiskey, that we'd been promised aren't waiting for us when we arrive. Bored and disillusioned, my men become unruly.

I can hardly blame them for lacking confidence in me. Some think my bargaining with the Clary's Grove Boys showed weakness. On top of that I'm totally unfamiliar with military maneuvering, and twice I've been disciplined by my superiors for breaking rules. Both times, I discharged my musket in camp, which they claimed was negligence.

One day we're marching across an open field toward a fence. We're in a front, twenty men abreast. I want the company to pass through a gate in the middle of the fence, but I realize I don't recall the proper order for getting them into single file. In desperation, I call the men to a halt and dismiss them with an order to reassemble on the other side of the fence in two minutes. All but the dullest of the men laugh at me when I call them back into formation.

In time, General Whiteside orders us on a two-day march northeast to an Indian outpost called Prophet's Village with instructions to burn it down. It is reputed to be a haven where Black Hawk's band enjoys protection from a Redskin spiritualist who is aligned with the British. Rumors abound that the British will aid Black Hawk in his assaults against our towns and families. I remember Father's stories about the Indian raid in which his pa died.

We find Prophet's Village abandoned, empty of inhabitants and their belongings. We follow through with our orders and set fire to every structure so the place can no longer serve as a threat. I am relieved we avoid a bloody confrontation, and suspect others feel the same.

Next, we head for Dixon's Ferry, another day's trek northeastward, following the southern bank of the Rock River. The ferry house is a large log structure on the opposite shore. There we learn that a company under the command of Major Stillman has just left Dixon to engage the Black Hawk band at Old Man's Creek, a long day's march north.

Rather than following Stillman, we're told to wait at Dixon's Ferry for the balance of General Whiteside's brigade to join us. Two days later, as Whiteside's units arrive, more than two hundred men from Stillman's company come scurrying back to Dixon's Ferry with horrific stories of an assault on their encampment.

Whiteside orders our entire brigade to reinforce Stillman at Old Man's Creek. When we arrive, the field is littered with fallen militiamen, scalped and mangled. I stand, mouth agape, and gaze at the carnage—flies swarming around a dozen disemboweled, beheaded bodies. My legs quiver. Unsure where to begin, I stoop to pick up a detached head, its cloudy eyes still open and its mouth formed as if in mid-scream. My head wobbles and I sway from side to side. Unable to keep my footing, I fall to my knees and bury my head between my legs.

Throughout the day, as we go about the task of burying the dead, men stab at the earth with their shovels, as if the ground were their enemy. When they speak to one another, their words cut like sabers, and their tones deepen. Each time I lay one of the brutalized victims into his grave, I grind my teeth and imagine punishing the savage that killed him. In the evening, as we sit around our fires, numb from fatigue and mourning, a patrol of scouts reports that Black Hawk's band has moved north. Little is said among us except for occasional angry outbursts and open derision against those in command.

Near dusk on the second day of our encampment, a grey-haired, leathery Indian wanders into camp seeking refuge. He carries a letter vouching for his trustworthiness, written some months ago by President Jackson's Secretary of War. Several of the fellows grab their muskets and aim at him. I step between the visitor and my men, staring them down. "We're instructed to give him refuge and safe passage."

Someone yells, "We've been sent to kill Indians,"

"Not this one."

"You're a coward, Lincoln," another calls out.

"Afraid to kill, are ya?" someone yells.

I straighten and rise up to my full height. "Anyone who thinks I'm a coward can fight me right here."

Some murmur. Others snicker.

One of them says, "No fight would be fair. You're bigger than the rest of us."

I hold out my hands. "Then pick any weapon that suits you."

They look at each other for a moment and shrug in near unison. One by one they walk away and restack their muskets. I escort the old Indian to General Whiteside's tent and show his aide the Secretary's letter.

Ten days later our company is disbanded, and we are mustered out of service. Most of the boys return home, but I reenlist, needing the money and thinking there's little danger of seeing any fighting.

This time I stay a private, and as expected, the next thirty days pass without our unit engaging in combat. After thirty days, we're discharged from duty.

On my third enlistment I borrow a horse and join an independent spy company under the command of the boisterous Captain Jacob Early. We're assigned to scout and spy on the enemy, but have little success.

One morning up in the Michigan territory, we come

on a place called Kellogg Grove where we're to join a small company of spies camping there. As we come out of the woods, a broad valley opens before us, and the morning light paints the entire scene with a crimson cast. The soldiers' bodies lie in a row on the ground in front of us, each of them with a round red spot on top of his head about as big as a dollar. A wave of nausea washes over me. One of the dead boys is wearing buckskin breeches like mine. I rein in my horse, wondering if this sight is akin to the one Father witnessed in his boyhood when savage Indian raiders scalped Grandpa Abraham.

On July 10, my military career comes to an end as Captain Early's company is disbanded, and we are discharged from service. None of the blood I've seen has been mine, except that which flowed from battles with mosquitoes or an occasional self-inflicted wound—a result of shaving or being careless with my knife. Furthermore, my experience has produced neither great honor nor profit. I rise on our last day of service to discover my horse has been stolen. George Harrison, a friend from around New Salem, has suffered the same fate. The value of mine is almost equal to my three months' stipend. That money goes to the friend who loaned me the horse.

Horseless, Harrison and I trudge through the wilderness from our encampment in the Michigan Territory to Peoria in Illinois—some one hundred and fifty miles. There we purchase a canoe and paddle down the Illinois River to the little town of Havana. After selling the canoe, we hike the final twenty-three miles to New Salem. My arduous journey home dims the images of carnage stamped on my memory and dissipates the fog of war.

Arriving in New Salem, I'm welcomed as a hero. Having gone to war and returned is enough to inspire some folks, but I remain restless, not having yet satisfied my yearning to become someone special.

A lump rises in my throat when Annie tells me McNeil confessed in my absence that he settled here under a false identity. He claims to have taken the name McNeil to avoid being dogged by his father's financial distress. His true name is McNamar. Now having secured his fortune in New Salem, he has gone back east and promised to bring his parents and younger siblings out west to join him. Annie sympathizes with him and is confident his promise to marry her stands, though their wedding must be delayed until his return.

I wrestle over telling her that I have known of McNamar's true identity almost since my arrival in New Salem. He put his real name on the deed I witnessed when he purchased John Cameron's half interest in the Cameron-Rutledge farm located a few miles from the village at Sand Ridge. I keep silent and encourage her to hope for his soon return.

With only two weeks left before voting, I resume my campaign for election to the state legislature. Among the other candidates is John Stuart. Nearly as tall as me, he's an articulate lawyer from Springfield with an aristocratic bearing. He's also an incumbent state legislator and former comrade-in-arms during my enlistment under Captain Early. Stuart wins election while I fall short. My defeat comes in spite of garnering three-quarters of the votes from the men in New Salem. I fare poorly among voters in the outlying regions where my name is not known.

I journey to Springfield to ask Stuart his opinion on whether I should continue to pursue politics. He encourages me to do so and tells me to prepare by devoting myself to reading the law. He offers to lend me some of his books and points me to a set of volumes titled *Blackstone's Commentaries on the Laws of England.*

Even though I master the first forty pages in a single afternoon, I'm full of gloom. The obstacles before me in the study of law are insurmountable. Mr. Blackstone insists a lawyer should be a man of breeding, who subdues the rules of grammar and becomes schooled in the great literary works of the English language.

On my return to New Salem, my misery is compounded by Annie's despondency over McNamar's failure to write to her. She wraps her arms around my waist and presses her face into my breastbone, sobbing. Her weeping pinches my heart.

As I cradle her head against my chest, the twinge in my heart grows into an aching. I lift my head and stare into the vast blue sky, beckoning memories of my dear

Sally. I search for some image to reassure me our embrace is the kind shared by siblings—not lovers.

Days later, McNamar's first letter finally arrives from Ohio, confirming not only his safety, but also his enduring love for Annie. He says his previous failure to write was due to a protracted illness from which he is at last recovered. Another letter comes a few weeks later, reporting his arrival in New York City and bringing news of his father's death.

Annie's eyes grow misty as she reads his letter.

Careful not to tread on her devotion to another, I offer her my kerchief to daub her tears.

Chapter Twelve

Annie asks, "Did you know that McNamar sold his interest in the dry goods store to Sam Hill before going East?"

On this question I can answer honestly. "No."

She stares up at me. "Why would he do such a thing if he planned to come back?"

Sweat collects across my brow. "He and Sam were not getting along. Maybe they decided to part ways."

"Certainly, he would have said something to me. He says he plans to make me his wife."

I take her hands. "Annie, I'm sure he had good reasons. He's a man of industry and good business sense. When he gets back, he'll have great plans for your future together."

Tears stream down her cheeks. "How can I be sure? He used a false name. He doesn't write. He sells his business. What else is there I don't know?"

I draw her close and wrap my arms around her. "He's a good man. He'd have to be a fool not to come back for you, and we know he's no fool."

She shakes her head. "I feel so alone."

I pull back and look down into her eyes. "Why don't I take a room at the tavern? That way I'll be nearby when you get blue, and you can cry on my shoulder as much as you want."

She laughs. "Abraham, you're a gem."

I scurry to find any kind of work that's available to pay for my lodging. When idle, my favorite remedy for my gloom is observing trials in Judge Green's court. We have no resident lawyers in New Salem, so unless an attorney from Springfield happens to be in town, parties in most lawsuits appear without representation. I'm often asked to assist one side or the other.

During one session, a visiting lawyer asks me to vouch for the veracity of a witness whom I know to be of questionable reliability. Judge Green's bench creaks under his weight as he leans forward and nods at me to respond.

"He's known as 'lying Peter Lukins.'"

The lawyer shakes his head. "How do you come by such knowledge?"

I point to the judge. "Ask Esquire Green. He's taken Pete's testimony under oath many times."

Green pipes up, "Never believe anything the man says unless someone else swears to it as well."

When Judge Green and I begin laughing, the lawyer knows his case is lost.

In late autumn, James Herndon sells his share of the store he runs with his brother Rowan to Willie Berry—a shrewd lad, two years my junior. Willie and I served together in the Black Hawk War. His principal fault is that he's overly fond of whiskey.

For Rowan the transaction wears like a burr under his saddle. In a short time, his differences with Berry become so severe he offers to sell out his share to me. I have no money, so Rowan adds up his inventory and takes my promissory note in exchange. Among the store's advantages is its location. During slack times, I can linger in the doorway and watch Annie as she tends the garden outside her father's tavern.

Shortly after the New Year, my friend Billy Greene buys Reuben Radford's grocery. Billy gives Radford his notes for four hundred dollars in payment for the inventory and store building. Billy's venture is not long lived. He makes the mistake of thinking himself too big a man to have to tread carefully around the Clary's Grove Boys. When he crosses them, they ransack his store, emptying casks of whiskey, slicing bags of flour, smashing jars, and overturning the counter. I try to console him, but he's undone. He jumps from his stool and cries out, "I can't do this. You and Berry can have this place."

I palm the back of my neck. "How would we pay you?"

He grabs a tuft of his hair with each of his trembling hands. "Just take over my notes."

"Let me give you something to cover the damages."

He laughs. "You don't need to do that."

"Look, Berry and I will promise to pay your notes to Radford and give you our own chit for two hundred in addition."

Billy's eyes widen. "That's more than fair."

Once word gets out that Berry and I have consolidated two of the four general stores in New Salem, Mr. Rutledge offers to sell us his on credit. We're giddy. Almost overnight we hold a near monopoly. We bring all the stock together into a two-story frame building with two rooms and rough-hewn boards for siding.

Our business requires me to make several purchasing trips to Springfield, which give me opportunities to call on John Stuart. He encourages me to persevere in my law studies, piling books in front of me to consume. One day on my wanderings through the city I stumble across an auction of a deceased lawyer's estate. My pulse quickens as I read the title embossed across the tattered leather bindings—*Blackstone's Commentaries on the Laws of England*.

I dig in my pockets, scrambling for enough money to bid. Fortunately, I turn out to be the only bidder for the *Blackstone* volumes and wind up with enough money left over to purchase a tattered copy of Euclid's *Elements*, a treatise containing a system of rigorous mathematical proofs, which are universally recognized as the basis for logical thought.

When winter sets in, a lull in business gives me plenty of time for reading the law and other studies. I also find time to indulge in Burns and Shakespeare with Jack Kelso. Of course, meager sales mean outside work is essential, though it isn't plentiful. When odd jobs like chopping wood or rescuing livestock from snow drifts come along, I leave the store for Berry to handle alone.

As spring approaches, Berry lays out a scheme he thinks will save us from financial disaster. He proposes we get a license to sell liquor by the dram—without a license we can only sell it by the cask or by the quart. A dram at a time will bring us larger profits. Before I consent to the plan, I talk with Annie. Her father is a firm temperance man, neither imbibing nor selling, although that doesn't dissuade his Presbyterian minister nephew John Cameron from keeping a barrel of whiskey around the house. Selling by the dram would make us something akin to a saloon, and I want to make sure there will be no hard feelings with the Rutledges if we make that leap.

Annie's counsel is to go directly to her father. After a lengthy conversation with him, he assures me he'll not hold the matter against me; however, he warns he'll never abide Annie keeping company with any drunkards. I assure him no whiskey will ever touch my lips. In fact, the Clary's Grove Boys often tease me for not having touched the stuff since coming to live in New Salem—an accusation which is largely true.

By March, we have our license and business starts to pick up, but not enough to carry us without my continuing to look for extra work—plowing during the planting season, felling trees and splitting rails when new settlers move in, or whatever other odd jobs there are between those. All the time, I hope our prospects will improve when men's thirsts go into full heat, come summer. With little free time, I pursue my studies by forgoing sleep or while tending store. Sometimes I become so engrossed in reading that patrons express their impatience by taking their business elsewhere. Those are the times I wish Berry were more dependable.

We hire a clerk who demonstrates we're better off when Berry is out of the store. My partner's laziness is eclipsed only by his drunkenness; he not only offends customers, he also squanders our inventory of whiskey. While Mr. Rutledge's speeches on abstinence have not yet swayed me, Berry's excesses have driven me to the brink of becoming a full-blown temperance man myself.

Not only is my patience at its limits, I'm worn to the bone. My friends point to my sallow complexion and sunken, bloodshot eyes. They complain that my countenance gives them cause to worry that I'm at the end of my rope. Nonetheless, my work and studies continue at a feverish pace.

In May, I receive an appointment as postmaster for New Salem. Every other week a courier delivers mail to the store. When the Sangamon floods and the courier is unable to cross, I go to the Post Office in Athens, ten miles away to collect our delivery. I usually take the mail to people's homes, though some collect theirs at the store. Folks often ask me to read their letters aloud, a habit which keeps me abreast of events in their lives. I also read newspapers delivered by mail—another benefit of being the town's postmaster.

The pay is low, so I continue taking additional work that's available. Of course, all my wages go to paying our clerk's wages and keeping the store running. In that way, it's like working for Father.

One day during summer while I'm splitting rails in the woods, Pollard Simmons, a local farmer, finds me and tells me that Sangamon County Surveyor John Calhoun wants to appoint me deputy surveyor. It is a good opportunity, paying three dollars per day—more than half the Governor's salary.

I shake my head.

"What's the matter?" Pollard asks.

"Why would an avid Jackson man such as Mr. Calhoun want to give a Whig such as myself a prized appointment?"

"Suppose party loyalty is a big enough matter for an up-and-comer like yourself, but Mr. Calhoun probably thinks it's a small thing."

I bury my axe blade in a log. "Well then, reckon I should go ask him."

Pollard snickers.

The twenty-mile walk to the County Surveyor's Office in Springfield gives me plenty of time to think. On my arrival, I stand in front of his desk, hat in hand and ask, "Sir, you should know that I'm a staunch Clay man and am unclear about why President Jackson would allow you to give me an appointment."

Calhoun leans back in his chair, his pursed lips curl upward, and his angular features soften. "I assure you that your politics won't matter to President Jackson."

"Then why would you want me to have this appointment?"

"My dear fellow, your part of the county is expanding rapidly, and I'm in desperate need of a deputy surveyor. Folks out there tell me you're the brightest, most honest and dependable young man to be had. I don't give a hang about your politics."

My fingers trace the rim of my hat. "You won't press me to change my views or shrink from speaking forthrightly?"

He leans forward. "My only concern is having accurate, honest surveys made with all dispatch. As long as that's done, you're free to engage in whatever political matters you see fit."

Satisfied with Calhoun's sincerity, I thank him and take my leave.

Shortly after my return home, Annie appears in the doorway of the store, holding a letter to post, her eyes darting between the stack of mail and my face. "Hello, Abraham. Is there anything for me?"

I sort through the mail, already knowing the answer to her question. As soon as the courier delivered the small batch of letters, I checked, as usual, to see if McNamar had written.

I shake my head. "Sorry, Annie. There's nothing here. Maybe next time."

She wrings her hands. "Something unthinkable has happened to him."

"Don't worry." I recall the assurances my sister Sally and I used to whisper to each other in Father's absence. "He's fine. Delivery from back east takes time."

She sniffles. "You're such a sweet fellow, Abraham Lincoln."

I fumble for my kerchief and give it to her. "It's just a matter of time before you hear from him."

"I hope so," she says, wiping away tears.

A lump forms in my throat. "I know so. He loves you greatly."

Her lips draw into a tight smile as she turns toward the door.

I call after her, "They made me Deputy Surveyor for the county."

She turns back, her eyes moist. "That's wonderful. You'll be working for Mr. Calhoun?"

"Reckon he doesn't mind hiring a Clay man."

"Will you still take care of the mail?"

I smile. "Oh yes, I'll still be Postmaster."

"Very well." She tucks the letter intended for McNamar into her apron pocket. "See you at debate society tonight?"

"Wouldn't miss it."

As Annie leaves, Betsy Abell—a short, stout woman—squeezes through the doorway past her. The toddler on her hip begins to wail. Betsy's father is a wealthy planter in Green County, Kentucky who gave her the best education his money could buy. He thinks she married beneath her station. This frontier prairie life is the kind of thing he hoped she wouldn't fall into.

"Abe, mind looking after little Mary for a bit?" she asks, lifting the baby up to me.

"Ah ... no. Not at all." I brush the little one's hair off her face.

"Suppose I owe you some sewing for all the times you've watched my babies."

"If money wasn't so scarce, I'd do it just for the pleasure."

"You should get yourself married up so you can have a family of your own. You'd make a fine papa."

I cock my head. "I'm doing the world a favor by not procreating another face like this one."

She laughs. "Want to come up for supper tonight? You can bring the young one back then."

I make a face at little Mary. "Sure."

As Betsy starts for the door, I dart from around the counter and follow after her. "Say, do you and the husband have room to take on an occasional boarder? With my appointment as Deputy Surveyor, I'll start spending a great deal of time up near Petersburg. I'm sure there will be nights I'll need a place to stay rather than hiking all the way back into town."

"You're welcome anytime, Abe. You know that."

"Thank you, I'm most grateful to you and Mr. Abell."

After supper that evening with the Abells in Petersburg, I return to our store in the village and stretch out by the stove with Flint's *System of Geometry and Trigonometry with a Treatise on Surveying.* My head aches over the mathematics and geometry problems I must master. I close it and pick up Gibson's *Theory and Practice of Surveying.* Mr. Calhoun directed me to study these texts to prepare for the examination that's required before I start work as his deputy. I break a sweat, pacing the tavern floor while tangling my mind in formulas, calculations of angles, and wondering why there are so many names for four-sided shapes. In my confusion, I snap up the books and make tracks for Mentor Graham's cabin.

Mr. Graham invites me in, despite the late hour, and offers me a seat by the fire. I'm nearly in tears. He pours me some tea, and I take tentative sips as he assures me the task is not insurmountable.

"You can certainly learn all that's required to be a surveyor," he says, "just as Washington did in his youth."

"But Washington enjoyed the encouragement of a gentle, loving father, and I have had no such privilege."

"Ah, my young friend," he says, "therein lies your advantage over the great general. You are equal to him in intelligence, but in desire you are clearly his superior. He prevailed because he could not do otherwise, whereas you shall succeed because you must."

For the next six weeks I devote every evening to studying with the school teacher, sometimes not stopping for sleep. Even while walking about town my nose is buried in either *Flint* or *Gibson.* Once, five-year-old Oliver Armstrong enjoys a ride tucked under my arm while I'm studying a book that's in my other hand. It's anyone's guess where or when I scooped up the little fellow.

Only one brief distraction interrupts my focus. Miss Mary Owens, who pays a visit to her sister, Betsy Abell, is the most intelligent and cultured gal I've ever met. While

Mary's charm has me wanting more of her attention, her sister's persistent maneuvering to see a relationship blossom between us annoys me. Even so, after Miss Mary returns home, I tease Betsy. "Your sister should have stayed around and married me."

With a gleam in her eyes Betsy says, "We'll see to it that she does so on her next visit."

I laugh. "Reckon we'll have to do that. Of course, I'm not sure I'd marry a woman who's fool enough to have me."

At the store, our liquor sales are brisk, but our profits haven't improved markedly, and Berry is unable to keep up even when he's sober. We hire a second clerk, Isaac Burner's son Daniel. I reciprocate by giving Isaac a hand at his still house up at the head of a nearby hollow. Ours isn't the only business suffering. Rumors are that Mr. Rutledge's tavern is not doing well, and he might have to sell out.

I wish Annie could have more of my attention, but we see each other less and less. My nights are consumed with studying, and she no longer comes by the store. McNamar hasn't written in some time, and she's stopped posting letters to him as well.

As winter deepens, neighbors call attention to my weathered skin, turned sallow, and my gray eyes, sunken deeper and lined with red. They beg me to rest; however, I keep pressing myself and pass Mr. Calhoun's examination when the time comes.

My surveying duties begin in January of 1834, and since most of the work takes me miles out of town, I buy a horse on credit. The Abells' home, near Petersburg, becomes my home several nights each week, though I keep my bed in town at the Rutledge Tavern in hopes of seeing Annie now and then. Her mood is often blue, and the sight of her in such despondency brings me no end of worry.

The surveying work takes me throughout the county, allowing me to make many new friends beyond the boundaries of New Salem. As my reputation for fairness and honesty spreads, I make another run for the state legislature. The salary for a legislator is $150 for the two month legislative session, and most of all, it may be the best opportunity for doing something noteworthy.

Voting is scheduled for early August, but before the canvass for votes begins, our business winks out. Unable to pay our bills, Berry and I exchange bitter words. We have no choice but to sell our inventory to two brothers, Alexander and William Trent. Since they have no cash, they promise to pay our debts in full as consideration for the purchase. Sam Hill, who owns the grocery and dry goods store, gives me space to receive and hand out the mail. He also hires me to clerk on occasions when he gets busy.

Within a month of selling our inventory to the Trents, they skip town without ever paying a dime to our creditors. Berry and I are left owing more than one thousand dollars on the notes we gave to purchase the Greene and Rutledge stores. We have no means of repaying them. I call our burden "the national debt." The sum is equal to almost half the Governor's annual salary—and far more than my earnings from surveying, which so far are a fraction of what I'd hoped they'd be.

Berry, who's also lodging at the Rutledge Tavern, is nearly incoherent from constant drinking. One day after coming in from the field, I barge in on him and say, "Get a hold of yourself. You need to clean up and get some work so you can help pay our debts."

He stumbles around, mumbling nonsense and rummaging through his belongings as if searching for something he's lost.

I throw up my hands. "What are you looking for?"

"None of your business," he slurs.

I grab him by the collar. "What are you going to do to help out?"

He turns and glares at me. "I'll ask my father for some money."

"He says you have to get sober before he gives you another dime."

His nostrils flare. "He helps everyone else."

"He's a preacher. A temperance man ... and you're ... you're a drunk."

His knees wobble. He leans against the wall, nodding, as if he'll fall asleep standing up.

I shake my head and leave.

When I ask Judge Green for advice on our situation, he clears his throat, sending ripples through all three layers of his chin. Peering over his spectacles he says, "Let this be a lesson. The frontier is full of men who have more ambition than sense ... or honor."

"Reckon I should have learned that from my father's debacles."

"Well, let's hope this setback doesn't sting too badly. Maybe the men who hold your notes will be patient."

"What do you suggest?"

"For now, tighten your belt and do what you can to make them happy."

In this calamity there's both good and bad. The good is that there's no longer a reason to labor over the choice between apprenticing some trade such as blacksmithing or studying the law. I must do the latter to earn enough money to repay my obligations. The bad is that lodging at the Rutledge Tavern when I'm in town is no longer affordable.

Jack and Hannah Armstrong give me lodging and board at their place when I'm not out surveying. "Aunt" Hannah—as I call her even though she's my age—is kind enough to mend my clothes while I study the law and rock little Duff, their newest offspring.

Jack treats me more rudely. He says he can't understand why I prefer the attention of married women over that of the young, single gals. He teases, "Suppose, that way you're saved the embarrassment of being thrown over in favor of one of the more handsome young bucks."

I tell him my romantic interests are none of his business.

He chortles. "You must satisfy your carnal needs by cavorting with the married or nearly married ones. Hell, for all I know you could be little Duff's pappy."

His broad-beamed, illiterate wife isn't at all attractive to me. But to preserve our friendship, I say, "Ain't a woman alive who'd want to bear a child after my likeness. As a matter of fact, I was once accosted by a man waving his pistol in my face. He said he promised to shoot anyone who was uglier than he. I said to the fellow, 'Then hurry up and shoot me. If I'm uglier than you, I don't want to live another second.'" Of course, the story isn't true, but I never let Jack know.

Nothing—even work—interferes with my reading. I always have a book in hand, usually one I've borrowed from John Stuart over in Springfield. One time, I'm picking up some extra wages cutting wood for Squire Godbey—the fellow who sold the pigs whose eyes Offut sewed shut. Godbey finds me perched atop a pile of logs and asks what I'm doing. I glance up from my book, scratch my head, and say, "It appears I'm reading." He shrugs and says, "Well, you are certainly the oddest fellow I've ever had for a farmhand."

During late spring and summer, the candidates for the legislature begin riding up and down the county canvassing for votes. We make speeches wherever folks gather—in a grove of shade trees, at a market or fair, at a schoolhouse, in a church or in a home, whether modest or lavish.

Sometimes I try to stand out by showing my physical strength by lifting a barrel of whiskey over my head or by burying an axe in a log deeper than anyone has ever done. When we stop at the edge of a harvest field to solicit support from laboring farmers, I grab a scythe from one of them and cut a swath so wide and long that their mouths are agape.

Folks think of me as a Whig candidate in what is mostly a handshaking campaign. Although measures aren't as important as how well a man is liked, my positions are popular. I favor construction of a canal between Beardstown and New Salem and dividing Sangamon County into two. The later measure would bring self-governance to fledgling towns like New Salem. My support for universal suffrage, by no means excluding women, is largely ignored.

One matter of great concern to many residents is personal. Isaac Snodgrass, whose name fits his stern face and sour disposition, leads a campaign to defeat me, alleging I'm a religious skeptic.

On hearing Snodgrass' charges, Annie asks me if I'm Christian. I'd like to pacify her parents, whose views on temperance have persuaded me to shun alcohol, but I can't deceive a friend. I tell her, "Much of what's in Scripture is not reasonable. I don't deny the Almighty, but merely wonder how much of what is said about Him is true."

Her eyes narrow, causing my heart to skip. "Abraham Lincoln, sometimes you're too honest for your own good. Try not to be so direct when expressing your views on the matter, especially if you're out canvassing for votes. And for Heaven sakes! Don't mention the writings of men such as Paine or Volney or Voltaire. They scare most common folks."

My chest tightens. "Do you think less of me for my views?"

She wrinkles her nose. "Of course not. Candor is a great thing between friends. I respect you for it."

I scratch the back of my neck. "It would be dishonest of me to hide the truth if someone asks."

"Do you discuss all your feelings when you canvass?"

"No."

"Do your feelings on religion make any difference on matters like internal improvements and breaking away to form our own county?"

"No."

She looks away. "Then say nothing more about religion."

"Snodgrass and his crowd will make a devil out of me if my views are not made clear."

She snickers. "He'll make a devil of you, nonetheless. You won't have to worry, though. Mentor Graham will take him to task on that—even if the straight-laced schoolmaster has to exaggerate your awe for the Almighty."

"It wouldn't do for him to lie for me."

She laughs. "He wouldn't be lying. He'd just be embellishing—like he always does when his passions overtake his reason. Anyway, people will listen to him before they pay any mind to what that old persimmon Snodgrass has to say. They love you."

I take her hand. "McNamar is a lucky man. I can only hope to be so fortunate someday."

There's a gleam in her eye. "To the contrary, Mr. Lincoln. It is the gal who will be privileged to have you."

My pulse races.

Of more than a dozen candidates on the ballot, the top four of us will go to the legislature. The Jackson men think they can win three, but not all four places, and they don't want the fourth seat to go to my friend John Stuart, an incumbent. They approach me with a strategy that will allow them to concentrate their energies on beating Stuart. They propose withdrawing two of their candidates and throwing their support behind me.

Unwilling to betray a friend, I go to Stuart and lay out their offer. He is strong in his conviction that he will win a spot in spite of their maneuvering, so he tells me to accept their proposal. He says, "That way we'll have two anti-Jackson men from Sangamon."

I follow his advice and place second. Stuart places fourth, and the Jackson men win only two seats.

After wrapping up the campaign, I call on Annie. Her mood is gloomier than ever, presumably on account of her father's business failures and the family's removal to Sand Ridge near Petersburg, several miles out of town.

We sit under a large live oak. "Annie, it burdens me to see you so."

She begins to cry.

I pat her hand. "Your father has weathered setbacks like this before."

She turns away and folds her arms across her chest. Shaking her head, she murmurs a few unintelligible words then draws a deep breath. In a measured tone she says, "McNamar has abandoned me."

I lay my hand on her shoulder. "That's nonsense. No sane man would turn away a girl as lovely as you."

"He's been away for nearly three years, and he hasn't written me in months." She lets out a hollow laugh as she wipes her tears. "All the women folk are right. I should have seen it. He's a fraud. He so much as told me so before he left, and I wouldn't hear of it. I'm such a fool."

She trembles as she continues sobbing.

I put my arm around her and whisper, "Shh, all will be well. Your man will come back to you soon."

"No," she says. "I'm done with him."

After a time, her crying ceases, her body is limp from exhaustion, and she looks at me. I help her up and take her hand in mine as we walk her to her house. At her doorstep, we say good-bye, and I promise to return every day until the legislative session starts in Vandalia. I almost never break that pledge, and she forgives me when I do.

Chapter Thirteen

On an uncommonly balmy afternoon in late November, I peer out the window of the Springfield-Vandalia stagecoach. Whereas I should be full of excitement over attending my first session as a legislator, my embarrassment a few days ago in Judge Green's makeshift courtroom haunts me.

When Berry and I gave Billy Greene our note for the purchase of his store, he assigned our debt to Reuben Radford from whom he had previously bought the business. Radford then endorsed our note—without our knowledge—as collateral for a loan made to him by Peter Van Bergen, a keen-eyed businessman. When Radford failed to pay his obligation, Van Bergen brought suit against Berry and me.

As Judge Green looked at me from his bench, he lamented that he had no option but to award the tight-fisted Van Bergen a judgment against my horse and surveying tools. I'd have to come up with cash to pay him—nearly four-hundred dollars—or everything I owned would be sold at auction. Only my books escaped lien because Green ascribed no value to them; he winked at me as he rapped his gavel. I slumped and walked away. What good are books when my future is to be wrenched away?

John Stuart, my mentor and a fellow anti-Jackson legislator, is seated across from me in the coach. His unperturbed countenance speaks of his familiarity with the proceedings soon to begin. I, on the other hand, expose my inexperience with a line of perspiration collecting along my newly starched collar. At the urging of several New Salem friends, Coleman Smoot advanced me two hundred dollars so I could buy a new jeans suit and accoutrements. The townsfolk didn't want to give Vandalia's citizens the impression that a bumpkin clad in worn buckskin was the best Sangamon County had to offer.

Since leaving New Salem, I've squirmed about in my seat, and not only on account of my scratchy new clothes. Before I left home, friends—Dr. John Allen in particular—admonished me to temper my oratory on slavery questions. "You might as well be heading off to the capital of South Carolina," he told me. In fact, folks in the bottom half of the state are so southern, and they have dominated state politics to such an extent, that we have laws for the inspection of hemp and tobacco crops, even though neither is raised within our borders.

Judge Green warned I can forget re-election if I vote for any measure that imposes taxes; although I can't fathom how we'd meet the public cry for internal improvements without a means of paying for them. He also discouraged me from supporting laws that benefit Negroes—"folks want to keep them in their place." Much of what I've read in our Illinois Constitution and statutes makes it clear that this is probably the most pro-slavery free-state in the Union.

"Black Laws" were entered onto the books immediately after our Constitution was adopted. One of these laws prohibits slavery while allowing indentured servitude. Another requires that a slave found ten miles from home be arrested and punished by thirty-five stripes. Our first legislature passed a law that fines a person twenty dollars for permitting slaves or servants to assemble for dancing or reveling, whether at night or during the day. All sheriffs, judges, coroners, and justices of the peace are required, on viewing such an assemblage, to commit the slaves to jail and to order each of them to be whipped on the bare back, not exceeding thirty-nine stripes. The thought of these injustices raises welts on my back.

After jostling about in the stagecoach for nearly thirty hours, we are now approaching Vandalia's post office in the heart of the capital. The smattering of log cabins that peek through dust clouds rising out of the town's dirt streets are interspersed with occasional brick and clapboard houses.

Minutes later, the coachman lets out a blast on his horn as he pulls his team to an abrupt stop at the edge of a public square. It's the first evidence I've seen that we're in a place better suited to be the seat of government than New Salem. A good number of Vandalia's eight hundred residents spill out onto the dusty street from the nearby buildings and swarm around us as if summoned to greet royalty.

Stuart smirks and says, "They aren't here to gawk at us. They're scrambling to be first in line for mail delivery."

I shake my head. "Reminds me of when the mail arrives in New Salem."

Stuart steps out of the coach as soon as the footstool is in place. His trunk is the first one passed down from atop the coach. The crowd begins to buzz as folks take notice of his greater than average height and handsome appearance. When I unfold myself from the cramped compartment and crawl out of the carriage, they fall silent. People stare as I tower over Stuart. They must think of me as some sort of freak. I turn away from them and wait for my bag—one of the last pieces to be unloaded.

"Follow me," Stuart says, his bishop's nose leading as he starts full stride toward a large frame house marked with a sign declaring *Vandalia Inn.* I take a few quick steps to catch up and match his stride.

He glances at me. "We're sharing a room."

The next morning on my way into the eleven year old capitol, melancholy drips from my pores the way bricks fall from the building's two-story façade. The sagging corridors smell of mildew, waterlogged plaster, and rotting timbers. Inside the House Chamber, chunks of plaster have fallen wantonly from the ceilings and walls, littering the floors. As I snug my shawl around my neck to ward off a dank morning chill, someone says that by afternoon it'll be as stifling as a smokehouse.

My shoulders droop more than usual as I shuffle toward my desk, past the pail of drinking water with tin cups we share that dangle from its rim. Arrayed around the room are buckets of sand we use for blotting ink, though the tobacco chewers also use them for spittoons.

John Stuart walks over and stands next to me as I take my seat. "Lincoln," he says, "Hope you don't expect your dour countenance to put you in any better favor with these Jackson men than it does with the young women of New Salem."

I look up at him. "Berry is dead."

He furrows his brow. "Who's Berry?"

I drop my head and mumble, "My old partner from the general store."

Stuart shrugs. "Isn't he the one who caused you more grief than good?"

"Yes. Just received news this morning."

"Why the gloom? What's it to you that he's dead?"

I knead my brow with the heels of my hands. "With him dead, the entire burden of paying off our indebtedness falls on me. As if that weren't enough, while we were traveling here by stagecoach, my horse and surveying tools were being sold at auction by the Sheriff." I shake my head. "How can I earn a living? I'll never afford the education to become a lawyer."

"Listen to me, Lincoln. No defeat is ever as final as it seems." He clutches my shoulder. "That's a lesson you need to learn fast if you're going to make a name for yourself around here. Leaders don't bask in the glory of their victories; they squeeze every lesson they can from their defeats. Folks back home care more about a man's character than they do about the measures he stands for. Persistence is the thing. The battles you win or lose don't count as much as being known for fighting and never giving up."

The Speaker raps his gavel.

I raise my head.

Stuart leans close to me and whispers, "We'll talk at supper. That gavel means we have business to attend to."

At supper, Stuart says that much of the legislature's business isn't conducted while we're in session. After legislators and hangers-on conclude their various evening entertainments of drinking, singing, parties, and theatricals, private bargaining over small measures takes place at bars and around tavern tables. Larger bills like the Illinois-and-Michigan Canal and the State Bank are threshed out by candlelight in the lobby of the House Chamber. During these informal sessions, senators and representatives aren't shackled by official rules. As the anti-Jackson floor leader, Stuart usually attends these lobby sessions along with state officials, speculators, and small-fry politicians looking to curry favors.

After a few days of mundane business, a report on internal improvements lifts the melancholy that weighs me down. My first bill as a legislator, one authorizing Samuel Musick to build a toll bridge across the Sangamon River near the new settlement of Petersburg, has been passed by the Senate after having cleared the House of Representatives.

Shortly afterwards, a moment of levity is created when we learn that our earlier appointment of Samuel McHatton as surveyor of Schuyler County was made when no vacancy existed. One of the members responds by offering a motion to "vacate" the nomination. I rise to make my first speech before the body.

> *As I understand the opinions of legal gentlemen, there appears to be no danger of the new surveyor ousting the old one as long as the current office-holder persists in not dying. May I therefore suggest we let matters remain as they are? In that way, if the old surveyor hereafter concludes to die, there will be a new one ready-made to take office without troubling the legislature.*

My motion is greeted with robust laughter, even though it is quickly voted down. Next, debate ensues on a resolution to rescind Mr. McHatton's appointment. When that resolution is laid on the table indefinitely, the result is the same as would have resulted from my motion.

The Speaker seems to have appreciated my humor. Previously, I had been largely ignored, but now I'm appointed to serve on special committees and am frequently recognized to make important motions. Consequently, in late January near the end of the legislative session, the Jackson men try to take me down a notch. After I give notice of my intention to introduce *An Act Relative to a State Road*, John Dawson, an arrogant Sangamon Democrat who chairs the Internal Improvements Committee, takes credit for the bill, introducing it under his own name. As a result, the bill's passage does me little good in gaining favor with the voters back home.

Stuart lays out a plan for me to garner recognition by staking out a claim on one of Dawson's bills, *An Act to Improve the Navigation of the Sangamon River*. After the House passes Dawson's navigation bill, I make a motion to change its title to *An Act to Authorize a Special Election in Sangamon County*. My maneuver succeeds, and his bill becomes law under my title.

In late February, the legislative session ends with the State Treasurer reporting our nearly insolvent state holds a meager $296.66 in its accounts.

On my return to New Salem, I learn I'm in better financial condition than the State of Illinois. My friend "Uncle Jimmy" Short —whose stature matches his name and who's hardly older than me—tells me he bought my horse and surveying tools at the Sheriff's auction. When he delivers the news he asks, "Do you give me your word you'll reimburse me when you're able?"

Tears well in my eyes; my lips quiver. I nod.

Uncle Jimmy pats me on the arm. "Abe Lincoln, you're the most honest man I've ever met."

The only words that spill out of my mouth are, "Thank you."

He points to my horse with saddle bags draped over its withers. "She's all yours."

After thanking him again, I gallop off to meet with each of my creditors as Stuart suggested. All of them agree to accept satisfaction in modest installments.

Later in the day, I ride out to Uncle Jimmy's near

Petersburg and find Annie has taken on work as his housekeeper. She had stayed down the village to manage the tavern after her father sold it, but now she lives at the family's farm, about half a mile east of Uncle Jimmy's place.

"How do?" Uncle Jimmy says when he sees me in the doorway. "Will you be staying the night?"

"Yes. I've some surveying up here in the morning. In fact, I'll be staying for a few days if that's all right."

He nods.

I turn to Annie and ask if we can talk in private. Uncle Jimmy's place is large by New Salem standards, and she leads me to a quiet corner. In hushed tones, I tell her about my financial distress and my plans to study the law in earnest to earn a good enough living to pay back my debts and make someone a fine husband.

She reaches up to place her hands on my shoulders. I stoop to meet her touch. Gazing up at me, she says, "Abraham, any young woman would be more than lucky to have you ... and as far as your obligations are concerned, if ever there was a man who could be trusted to keep his word, it is you. You're certain to make good on your studies and become a fine lawyer. Maybe even a judge, someday."

Her pink cheeks brighten and her soft lips curl into a smile. "Why, people even talk about you becoming governor."

I look away and fumble with my hat. "Well, if people hear you saying such nice things about me, they might question your good sense, if not your sanity."

She smacks me on the arm. "You stop that kind of talk, Mr. Lincoln."

I gaze overhead at the long tie-beam spanning the length of the roof. "Have I ever told you that you're ... quite an ... an intellectual woman?"

She laughs. "No, can't say you have. No one has ever said anything so nice to me before."

"Annie, I'm not much to look at ..." a lump rises in my throat "... especially compared to McNamar ...."

She reaches up and puts a finger to my lips. "Shh ... Mr. McNamar has passed up his chances with me."

My stomach tightens. I rake my fingers through my matt of hair and stare again at the rafters. "I've had a thing on my mind since leaving for the legislature ...."

"Well, if you intend to ask about courting me, don't expect me to wait as long for you to get to it as I waited on another gentleman to keep his promise."

I wring my hands. "Well ...."

"What I mean to say is I'll do the asking, if that's what it takes."

We laugh together. "No," I stammer. "Uh, yes, that's what I intend to ask, but I'll do it. You shouldn't have to."

"Fine, then. My answer is yes, but there are some conditions."

"I'm all ears."

She reaches up to pinch them. "That you are."

I press her hand against my cheek.

She looks up. "Now first, you should finish your law studies, right?"

I nod.

"And I plan to enroll in the Female Academy in Jacksonville."

"When?"

"In the coming fall. My brother David is a student at Illinois College—the schools are practically next to each other. He says I can board with him."

My eyes widen. "I can matriculate at Illinois College. We'd both be in Jacksonville."

"What about the legislature?"

"I'll take classes when the legislature's not in session. Berry attended there, and Billy Greene's been studying there, as well."

She squeezes my hand.

I squeeze hers. "Are you ready for the entrance exams?"

"Not yet," she says, "but Mentor Graham has a friend in Athens. His name is Colonel Rogers. He led an infantry unit in the War of 1812. Mentor says the Colonel's daughter can tutor me."

"I'll escort you to Athens. Colonel Rogers' inn is the pick-up point for the mail when the Sangamon is flooded and the courier can't make it to New Salem."

She lets go of my hand. Her smile dissolves. "There's one other thing."

My heart skips. "Yes?"

"Before we broadcast our courtship, Mr. McNamar must release me from our engagement. It's official, and that means ...."

"I know. It's a contract. Under the law he must release you from it. It's only right ... but what ... what if you never hear from him?"

"I'll write to him straight away to ask for his release. That's sure to get his attention."

"Annie, dear." My heart thumps in my chest. "I shall never be unhappy again. With you at my side, I can make a great mark on the world."

She wraps her arms around my waist. "Mr. Lincoln, I love you earnestly."

"I love you and always shall."

Uncle Jimmy calls out from across the room, "Ain't it getting to be about time for supper?"

"Yes, Mr. Short," Annie says.

Uncle Jimmy bellows, "Abe ... you ain't exactly company, you know. You best set about giving the girl a hand."

"Yes, Sir."

Her smile returns, and her eyes twinkle.

A week later, we dismount on arriving in Athens for Annie's first tutoring session with Arminda Rogers. I take Annie's hand, lead her over to my horse, and reach into my saddlebag to draw out my copy of Kirkham's *English Grammar* in which I have inscribed—*Ann M. Rutledge is now learning grammar.* When I present it to her, she beams. I lean down, and she kisses my cheek.

The warmth of her kiss stays with me throughout the day and into the evening, even after we return to Sand Ridge. When *Blackstone* makes no sense to me, I turn to the *Statutes of Indiana* and later sift through Flint and Gibson's treatises on surveying. It all becomes scrambled in my brain. I consider venturing over to the Rutledge place to borrow the *English Grammar* I've given Annie, but the sight of her would make a further rat's nest of my thoughts. I cram my head with more mathematics of surveying, and my weary imagination rebels. An all too familiar refrain—*those whom I love are cursed*—echoes through my head. Part of me argues I cannot live without her while the rest protests that Providence will steal her away at some unexpected hour. Long after midnight I'm exhausted and drift off to sleep.

Frigid winter days yield to torrents of rain in March and April. While stormy days bring more gloom than bright ones, long hours of work and study keep me from spiraling into melancholy as we wait for McNamar's reply. Regardless of the weather, my day almost always begins and ends in solitude. I rise early each morning with a fresh determination to rein in my thoughts and prove I'm their master. Before Annie arrives to do her chores, I'm off pounding stakes, measuring, and dragging my surveyor's chain through the woods and tall prairie grasses. Early evenings are given to studying with Annie at her father's farm, careful to avoid appearances that would compromise her reputation. I return to Uncle Jimmy's and study late into the night.

One day each week I lay aside my surveying tools and ride to Athens with Annie for tutoring, taking supper those evenings at the Rutledges. After eating, we study grammar and ciphering. Even those days end with my solitary studies of law and surveying.

Continued downpours through May and June make a soggy mess of everything. Dragging my surveying chain through the muck wears me down, and constant blinking to clear my vision sets my temples to throbbing. Uncle Jimmy and the Rutledges, especially Annie, worry that I'm overtaxing myself. They point to dark circles under my sunken eyes and call my complexion jaundiced.

When blistering heat greets us on Independence Day, Annie convinces me to take a break from my labors and join her at a quilting bee. While sitting beside her, the only man among a gaggle of women, I slide my hand under the quilting frame and onto her knee.

She kicks my leg. When I frown, she cranes her neck and whispers in my ear, "Do not make a display."

I turn to the fair-skinned Fanny Bailes, still a teenager, giggling on the other side of me and tease her.

She looks away and sets about sewing in earnest, so much so that she lodges the needle in her finger. I lean toward her, take her hand in mine and withdraw the needle.

Annie continues diligently with her sewing, avoiding my gaze.

I return my attention to Fanny and dab a bead of blood from her finger with my kerchief. "Is it better?"

After hesitating, Fanny bats her eyes. "Thank you, Abe. You have the gift of healing."

I look across the quilting frame at Mrs. Herndon who's staring at me. "I'm in a quandary and hope you can lend some advice. Which of these two girls should I marry?"

Annie glares up at me and proceeds to stitch with frenzy, staring straight ahead, not bothering to look down at her work. Her long, irregular stitches are a funny sight, and I point at them. "Why Annie, your needle has gone off on its own."

She jumps from her seat and throws her needle onto the quilt.

I reach for her hand, but she jerks it away.

My cheeks burn. "I was only teasing."

Without acknowledging my awkward apology, she runs off crying and disappears around the corner.

My heart fills with shame.

Chapter Fourteen

W e swelter under oppressive heat and lingering humidity as the rains cease in mid-July of 1835. Disease-ridden mosquitoes swarm at us from every mud hole, their bites raising welts wherever they find bare flesh. Many folks are stricken with typhus.

Each evening, after a day of dragging my surveyor chain through woods and fields, I rush back to Uncle Jimmy's hoping to catch Annie before she finishes her housekeeping chores. His answer is always the same. "She left earlier."

My refrain is, "Where?"

"I'm not her father or husband. As long as she does her work, I'm happy."

I sulk off to bed.

He calls after me. "She put up supper for ya."

I mumble. "Not hungry."

Rather than reading the law or studying the surveying volumes, my night is spent scribbling out a pamphlet that lays out my personal gospel.

I have no faith in things that cannot be demonstrated before my eyes. I am so constituted, my mind so inclined toward organization, that I can believe nothing that neither my senses nor logic can reach.

All things, both matter and mind, are governed by universal, absolute and eternal laws. I believe in universal inspiration and miracles only as evolutions under those laws. Law is everything. Mystical interferences are merely shams and delusions.

I claim not to have controlled events, but confess plainly that events have controlled me. Law fates all things and forgives nothing. Forgiveness is an absurdity.

When the first morning light draws a faint line across the eastern horizon, I take up my saddle bags and venture down to the Rutledge's well to wait under a large tree at the edge of the clearing. My eyes are as heavy as my heart. I've barely slept since my great Independence Day blunder.

Twigs snap under Annie's feet, alerting me before she comes into view. When she appears, my breath catches in my throat. The shimmer of sunlight arcing over the horizon behind her casts an aura over her sandy hair, a halo. Shame taunts me for having behaved so stupidly toward her.

On seeing me, she stops and draws back a step.

I'm quick to my feet. "Please."

Her tone is icy. "What do you want?"

"I was a fool. Don't know what came over me."

She walks briskly, angling toward the well. "You certainly are a fool."

"Everyone knows I'm clumsy around the girls."

She rests her bucket on the rim of the well.

"Can you forgive me? You have the right to shun me, but please, I can't bear knowing you shall forever—."

"After you embarrassed me at the quilting bee, I told Arminda to have her father hold my mail in Athens. I pick it up on my lesson days."

I hang my head.

"When I was there two days ago, she handed me a letter from McNamar. He will be returning in just a few weeks."

I look up. "What are you going to do?"

"Haven't decided. It seems I'm stuck now with the choice between *two* fools."

"Annie, I'm sorry."

"Do you know what this means? What if he still loves me and finds that I have not been faithful? That I threw his love away on a man who was merely trifling with me."

"Annie, if there is anything I can do to redeem myself, please tell me what it is."

She strains at lifting the overfilled bucket; water sloshes out onto her shoes. I rush over to lend a hand, but she backs away, spilling even more.

She sneers. "When I figure it out, I'll let you know."

"May I call on you?"

As she begins walking toward her father's house she glances back over her shoulder and says, "Considering how consumed you are with work and studies, I doubt you'll find the time."

"I'll make the time."

She pauses at the edge of the clearing and turns to face me, wearing a frown. "I'm afraid I'm terribly busy with all the sickness going around."

"I'll help."

"Help or hover?" she asks.

"Help."

"Do you realize there are only twelve doctors to care for hundreds of sick people? And folks are dying. There'll be over a thousand ailing if the fever keeps spreading."

"I ...."

"I suggest you call on Dr. Allen. He probably can use your help."

She turns and walks away.

After watching her disappear through the trees, I race back to Uncle Jimmy's, throw my saddle bags over my horse, and gallop to town. Dr. Allen is just climbing into his buggy as I ride up.

"Dr. Allen, Annie tells me you might need a hand tending to all the sick."

He lifts his hat to scratch his head. "See my nurse inside. We've set up an infirmary in there. We're doing one over at the tavern, as well."

"I'll do anything you need."

"Thank you." He straightens his hat. "Need to be on my way."

I see only shadows as I walk through the door into Dr. Allen's cabin. The windows are draped with blankets; only a few shards of sunlight trace the edges of the shades. When my eyes adjust to the darkness, I recoil at seeing sick neighbors lying on cots—a few are delirious with fever, muttering nonsense as they pick at imaginary insects crawling over their bedclothes. At my feet lies a gaunt little girl, blood leaking from her nose, her face so drawn and hollow its unrecognizable. A nurse rushes past me with a chamber pot.

A man lies listless a few feet away, his mouth hanging open, perspiration covering his brow. He stares blankly at the rafters. His frame and stature remind me of Father. I can't make out who he is.

A shriek resounds from across the room. A woman is being attended to by a nurse. The poor soul's face is drawn in agony. She's squatting over a chamber pot clutching her stomach—either her abdomen is terribly distended or she's pregnant. After a loud groan, she drops her head and begins to pant. Mother's image looms in my mind.

A baby whimpers in another corner of the room, reminding me of my little brother Tommy's plaintive cries during the few days he visited this earth.

The nurse pulls the chamber pot from under the woman and carries it toward me. When she stops and thrusts it into my hands, it's filled with a pea-green stew of waste. I gag from the stench as it combines with the odor of human sweat and the bitter tang of urine.

"Empty it," she says. "There's an open pit around back."

I hold my breath and rush outside, careful not to slosh any of the contents on my hands.

The sickness doesn't relent during all of July and continues to lay siege on New Salem in the early days of August. On my return to Uncle Jimmy's one evening after surveying a plat near Petersburg, his usual cheerful countenance is grim. I presume he's frustrated over the clutter building up around him. Annie hasn't been available for housekeeping for a couple of weeks. Caring for our sick neighbors has become a full-time affair.

I set my saddle bags on a chair and take a deep breath.

"Abe," Uncle Jimmy says, "One of the Rutledge boys stopped by a bit ago. Seems that Annie is down with the fever."

The distress on his face sends a sharp pain through my chest. "She's going to come through it, isn't she?"

He avoids my eyes. "I'm sure she'll be fine in no time."

"I should go see her."

"Her brother David says it's best if we stay away right now."

"But I must."

"She needs her rest. That's the best help we can be."

I hang my head, holding back tears. "My curse."

As the days crawl by, every task is drudgery. I sight in on a stake and moments later forget where it is. Measurements have to be done and redone as my memory constantly fails me. I end my work early and hurry back to Uncle Jimmy's, hoping for word of Annie's recovery, but fearing I'll hear the worst. It's always the same; he knows nothing new about her condition.

Often, I retire without eating, burying myself in books—geometry, Euclid's *Elements*, treatises on the law, Volney, Voltaire, Paine, Shakespeare, Burns, anything. Nothing dulls the pain of impending tragedy. I even resort to prayer, even though it's absurd to believe praying will do any good. If God truly exists, His purposes were set when time began, fixed in universal law, and prayer will not change His mind.

On a sweltering afternoon late in August, David Rutledge appears at Uncle Jimmy's door, holding his hat at his waist. I follow Uncle Jimmy toward the door, but hold back after only a few steps. After they whisper to each other for a moment, David looks past Uncle Jimmy at me. "Abe," he says, "you best get over there. She's asking for you."

Nausea washes over me, leaving me lightheaded.

"Abe," David repeats.

I look past him, through the doorway, transfixed on the path to the Rutledge farm. Nausea surrenders to panic. I bolt for the door, nearly bowling over both of them as I explode out of the house. Minutes later on arriving at the Rutledges' porch, I stop and press my forehead against the doorpost, catching my breath. My sides ache.

David walks up behind me and drapes his arm over my shoulders. "Let's go in," he says, opening the door with his free hand and nudging me ahead.

I choke back tears.

He leads me to Annie's room where we find her sleeping as she has for the better part of the past few weeks since taking ill. Her face is pale. Her breath is shallow and slow. I tiptoe up next to her bedside and take her hand. Her eyes flutter.

"It's Abraham," I say softly.

Her eyes open wider, the blue now milky, almost gray. "Abraham," she whispers.

I lean down, choking back tears. "My dear Annie."

"I ...." Her lips quiver.

I caress her face. "Don't say anything. Just rest."

She pants. "I've missed you ... love you."

My words hang up in my throat, trapped there with my breath. "I love you, too, and always have."

I sit with Annie for nearly an hour. Talking is difficult for both of us. Her voice is little more than a whisper. Mine is strained from salty tears draining into my throat, rendering it raw. What little we say in words is overshadowed by the volumes we fill tenderly gazing into each other's eyes.

She squeezes my hand. Her eyes flitter and close. I continue to sit and watch as she sleeps, her chest rising and falling with shallow breaths as her mouth forms a faint, blissful smile.

During the next week as Annie languishes, Betsy Abell takes me in hoping she can restore my appetite. Everything about Betsy—her stout frame, kind eyes, dark, curly hair, soft voice—remind me of my sister Sally, but nothing consoles me. My desire for food is as sparse as foliage in the dead of winter. I have not slept more than a few nods in days.

On the twenty-fifth day of August, Annie's brother David finds me hunched in front of the Abell's fireplace, wrapped in quilts as if it's a cold December night. His words overwhelm me with the kind of chill that only accompanies our winters of deepest snows. His voice is shaky and pitched. "She's gone, Abe."

I nod, signaling that I've heard his bitter news. He comes next to me and lays his hand on my shoulder. I bring my hand up to rest on his. Our tears flow and our bodies quiver with grief. After a long time, David pats my shoulder then turns away and treads to the door. His short, measured steps are barely audible.

After a few moments, I rise and lay the quilts aside.

"Can I get you something?" Betsy asks.

I wave her off and trudge outside.

"Abe," she calls after me.

"I'll be fine. Don't worry. Just need to walk."

Indeed I walk. How far or where, I can't recall.

The next day after we bury Annie, my eyelids are too heavy to prop open. For the first time in days, the idea of sleep comes to mind, and now it comes with an irresistible force. My hope is, that once slumber overtakes me, Providence will never allow me to be stirred awake again.

The next morning my eyes open. I close them again and draw the quilt up around me, my shoulders curled toward my chest as if it were possible to somehow disappear into myself.

Hours later, acknowledging the truth that, for now, sleep will have nothing more to do with me, I dress and set out for the woods, aware only of my grief. Color does not exist for me, nor taste, nor smell—nothing. As the trail bends toward the Rutledge farm, I fall to my knees, whimpering, "No ... don't ...." I stare, unseeing, into blackness. My body trembles. Pulse throbs. A sound like the wind rushes through my ears. My eyes shut. Silence.

I snap my head around, no idea how long I've been kneeling alone in the woods. My heart races. Rain cascades onto my shoulders, spilling from the brim of my hat. Must get to Annie's grave.

I leap to my feet and run. The driving rain stings my eyes, and seeps through my teeth. My lungs burn. Finally at the cemetery, I throw myself like a blanket onto the fresh sod where she's buried and lie face down in the mud, sobbing, until the torrent ends.

After returning to the Abell's place, Betsy draws a hot bath and takes my shirt and trousers out to the trough to wash them. When I'm done bathing she gives me a quilt to cover myself while my clothes dry by the fire and hands me a sweet cake and cup of hot tea. She strokes my hair. "You miss her terribly."

I stare into my tea. "Annie would have been the woman my angel mother never had the chance to become. When Mother died I was nine and thought my life was over, but I survived. Even cheated death on my own account on a few occasions. Then Sally died, and I was overcome by bitterness and resolved to make them both proud. Now, having lost all three women whom I've loved with all my heart, life has no purpose."

Betsy cradles my head against her chest. "You're hurting right now, but life will go on and it will be glorious."

"My heart is buried with that dear girl, and I can't bear the thought of rain falling on her grave."

In the ensuing days, my despondency increases. Judge Green takes me under his care, and I'm not allowed to wander off alone. My knife is taken away, out of fear I'll do myself harm. My idleness gives me time to refine the personal gospel I began before Annie's death.

The muggy days of August soon give way to crisp September mornings, which are supplanted by October's chilly nights. Sam Hill, who's equal in size to about half of me, takes his turn as my guardian, and I tag along when he heads down to his store to tally up the day's sales. Our breath hangs in a mist in front of our faces, a reminder that winter is close at hand.

After checking the storage bins in the back room, I toss Sam a small log to stoke the fire. Flames lick the freshly split wood as I repeat for Sam what I'd already told Betsy. "I can't stand the thought of rain or snow beating down on Annie's grave."

"Thought you were finally coming out of your melancholy," he says. "You're not backsliding, are you?"

"As long as I'm busy, I can keep my spirits up. Reckon I'll be fine."

Sam rubs the back of his neck. "Does McNamar know about you and Annie?"

"We haven't talked since he got back. Annie told him in a letter she wanted to be released from their engagement."

He pokes at the fire. "It must have been hard on him. He brought his mother and sister and their furniture all the way out here from New York. Just like he promised her."

I sit on the floor. "It would have hurt him more if Annie had lived to tell him we were to become engaged."

"Suppose you're right." Sam sits next to me. "You know there's been no love lost between me and McNamar since Ann chose him over me back before you came to town."

Neither of us speaks for a minute or two.

Sam breaks the silence. "Got any plans for the legislative session coming up? You know, folks didn't send you down there just to sit on your hands and watch."

"Was just getting my bearings last winter. Learned a lot with Stuart's help. Have some big bills planned for this session, though. They're a bit radical, but might get them passed just the same. About time I did something folks will remember me by."

"Don't go too far out on a limb. People don't need big ideas. You're big enough as it is. Billy Greene tells me the college boys down in Jacksonville still talk about the first time they ever saw you."

I take off my hat and pull out the paper on religion I've been carrying around.

"What's this?" he asks as he unfolds it.

"It might give those boys down at the college in Jacksonville some fodder for a lively confab." I watch his face. At first his eyes are bright and eager. As he reads further his lips pucker. "What is this?" he demands.

I puff out my chest. "A pamphlet explaining my ideas on religion. I'm going to publish it."

"You've run off track." He waves the pages in my face. "No special creation ... the Bible is not God's revelation ... miracles are just evolutions under natural laws ... prayers have no effect ... Jesus is not Christ ... not the Son of God! If folks see this, insanity is what you'll be remembered for."

"It's the truth."

"It may be the truth, but it'll get you tarred and feathered and probably ridden out of town on one of your own fence rails. Hell, it may even get you shot." He springs to his feet and opens the stove.

"What are you doing?"

He turns to me waving the pages. "Burning the damn thing. What do you think I'm doing?"

I lunge at him, landing on my knees, and reach for the paper. "No! Don't...."

With a sweep of his arm, Sam tosses the pages into the fire.

I crawl toward the stove, pushing him aside with one arm and reaching toward the flames with the other.

He bounds up off the floor and climbs on to my back, wrapping his bony arms around my neck and yanking me backward.

I buck him off, like an unbroken mule throwing a first-time rider.

Struggling to his feet, he grabs hold of my suspenders and pulls with all his might. Unable to deter me, he succeeds in slowing me down. Before I can reach into the fire and retrieve the papers, a bright orange flame laps up the last of my pen strokes. My body goes limp and I prostrate myself on the wood plank floor.

Sam crawls next to me and pats my shoulder. "Abe Lincoln," he says, "you need to get laid. It'll do you a world of good."

I turn over, propping myself on my elbows, and squint. "Just because I'm an infidel doesn't mean I have no morals."

He laughs. "Just trying to cheer you up."

I force a smile.

"That's better," he says grinning.

In the ensuing days my caretakers are pacified by

my feigned contentedness. When pretend smiles fail me, I recite an old joke or tell one of the stories that always help brighten my gloom. Shortly before I head to Vandalia for the legislative session which commences in early December, my friends are satisfied with my mental state and allow me to wander about. I take advantage of my new freedom and trek into Beardstown where rumors are that men can purchase services of women who are skilled at soothing their troubled spirits.

On my previous visits to Beardstown, I've not spent much time exploring its amenities. Twice I spent a night at the public house called the City Hotel, located at the corner of Main and State Streets, a short block from the riverfront. It's the most prominent structure travelers see when steamboats nestle up onto the sandy river bank, and it's operated by the town's founder, Thomas Beard. He's six feet tall with a straight, muscular build and says I'm one of the few fellows he has to look up to.

Tonight, as I stand in front of him at the lobby desk with my rain drenched hat in hand, my shoulders soaked and hunched, he must regard me as a pitiful sight. "Can you spare a room for a weary traveler?"

"That'll be fifteen cents," he says.

"Is that the sharing rate, or ...?"

"Twenty-five if you're looking for some privacy," he says, assessing me with his calculating blue eyes.

"I'll take the twenty-five." My resources are all but depleted, not having worked for several weeks. The balance of my three dollars will go to buying a night's worth of companionship.

I lay my coins on the desk, and Beard hands me the room key. "Anything else?" he asks.

I look down. On my previous stops at his establishment, I've heard it whispered that Beard is not sufficiently prudent in the matters of husbanding to keep a wife. The women I've seen wandering in and out of this place are proof enough of his weakness toward temptations of the flesh.

"I was hoping ...."

His smile broadens into a grin. "Hoping to get a little?"

I glance away then back at him, and try to read his face. "How much? Just have a little more than two dollars."

His tone is less friendly. "That's not going to buy my finer merchandise."

"I'm not particular."

He brushes his hand through his hair. "Might be able to find something for two-fifty. A couple of new girls just landed in town a few days ago. Come up from St. Louis."

"That'll do."

"I'll send one up."

"Thanks."

Once upstairs, I shed my waterlogged coat and yank a woolen blanket off the bed to wrap myself. I sit on the bed, shivering, and wait.

An hour later, there's a knock. I get up, gather the blanket up to my chin and open the door a crack. A thin, almost emaciated girl, about my same age, stares up at me. Dark circles ring her eyes. "You're expecting me?"

As she wedges past me, I peek down the hall to be sure no one is watching. After shutting the door, I latch it and turn to face her. She holds out her hand and says, "Two-fifty." Her coat is already off and a dainty cotton shift hangs loosely on her pale shoulders.

I pull out two one dollar coins from my purse, hand them to her, and continue digging for the fifty cents. She unfastens a single button just above her breasts; her garment reminds me of the tow-boy shirts I wore as a lad. Her flimsy shift floats to the floor, exposing her wispy frame.

"Don't have all night," she scolds. "Not for two-fifty. You'd best get yourself undressed."

I unwrap the blanket from around my shoulders and spread it over the bed, then fumble with the buttons on my shirt.

She shakes her head. "Your first time?"

My throat tightens. "All my women friends are married or spoken for. This face must scare away the rest."

She laughs and points to my crotch. "Pretty faces don't matter as much as what's down there."

I unbutton my pants, and they drop to my ankles.

She steps toward me, twisting her long brown hair into a cord, which she drapes over one shoulder so it cascades over her breast. "It'll do," she coos.

"What's your name?"

"Look, yer buying my time, not me."

I lie on the bed, on top of the blanket, motionless, staring at the ceiling.

She joins me on the bed. "Well?"

I swallow hard. "I reckon you'll have to take the lead."

Chapter Fifteen

On a snow-covered December morning, about two weeks after arriving in Vandalia for the special legislative session, I notice a blemish on my genitals. I shudder. Syphilis? I've heard folks talk about it. Rashes. Hideous deformities. Eventually, insanity.

Back in Little Pigeon Creek where Mother died, a young man named Matthew Gentry lost his mind. One of my playmates said it was the syphilis meting out God's judgment for his iniquity. Gossip was he maimed himself, fought with his father, even tried to kill his mother. Then one day, he began howling and flailing his arms as he ran through the village—his eyes aflame. All the women and children ran for safety while the men folk, en masse, wrestled him to the ground and bound up his limbs. Once subdued, he sang a mournful dirge all through the night. Poor Matthew, once a bright boy, a favored child, became a haggard madman, locked in a mental night. Was his insanity caused by a moment of devilish passion—a moral lapse such as my own?

I'm in a sweat even without pacing the room. It's a good thing John Stuart's out and not here to see me in such a state. John Stuart, my roommate—that's it. He would know. He always has an answer when I'm in a tight spot … but I can't go to him about this. Nor can I let Dr. Allen back in New Salem know about it. What if I die? I've achieved no measure of greatness with my life.

I pick up a book of jokes, hoping it will distract me, and slump down in a wooden chair in the corner. After reading a few entries, I pull down my hat to cover my eyes. Darkness sweeps over me like storm clouds blackening the sky before unleashing their wrath. After a great rushing sound, everything is silent.

Perhaps hours later, my eyes fly open. I rare back in the chair, swing one foot over onto the opposite knee, and roar with laughter.

A voice from across the room penetrates my hilarity. "Lincoln!"

I turn and stare at Stuart, sitting on the bed, watching me. It's as if he appeared from nowhere. "A great story, huh?"

"Lincoln," he says as he gets up and walks over to me, "do you do this often?"

"What?"

"It's the second time I've found you like this. All drawn up in your chair, completely still for hours."

"I was just sitting here reading."

"No, you weren't. You always read aloud—even when you're reading the law—and not a sound was coming out of your mouth."

"Maybe I read silently when no one's around."

He laughs. "Lincoln, I tried to stir you an hour ago, and you gave no response. I peeked under your hat. Your eyes were open and transfixed, as if gazing on eternity or reflecting some deep agony."

I shrug.

He shakes his head. "In any case, now that you're back among the living, let's write out a couple of bills for you to introduce. We'll start with a resolution to relocate part of the state road between William Crow's place up in Morgan County and Musick's Bridge in Sangamon."

"Good. Something to keep my mind occupied." I dig into my saddle bags looking for a pen. "Oh, and can we amend the *Act for the Relief of Insolvent Debtors*. I've been over it, and it brings too much misery to hardworking common folks."

He also helps me draft bills for building roads, dividing Schuyler County, and incorporating the

Sangamon Fire Insurance Company. Once the bills are in the hopper, I watch Stuart bargain for votes. Some of his deals make my skin crawl. He tells me it's the only way things get done. I bite my tongue. If I aimed at being no better than my teachers, I'd still be splitting rails on Father's farm. Stuart's methods have some merit, though. His bargaining wins me an appointment as chairman of a special committee to look into digging a canal along the Sangamon River valley.

Stuart's tactics also help when a boy-faced, twenty-two year old bantam rooster, named Stephen Douglas, swoops into Vandalia with the aim of whipping the Jackson men, who now call themselves Democrats, into a unified voting bloc. He's not even an elected representative, but they obey him like bondsmen. I tell Stuart, "His plot ought not to be tolerated in a republican government."

Other Whigs complain that his methods are a great danger to the liberties of the people.

Douglas' success is remarkable, since he's the least man I have ever met. In some ways, he reminds me of Father—both ask others to do their heavy lifting, and neither expends even a small amount of energy on plumbing the depths of logical thought. They differ in the respect that Father is indolent while Douglas is ambitious, but arrogant.

A bill to change the method of appointing the State's Attorneys is Douglas' pet. He prefers they be selected by the Democrat controlled legislature instead of the long standing procedure of being appointed by the Governor. I'm certain his complaint against our tradition is that the current Governor is a Whig.

When Democrats introduce a bill to carry out Douglas' wishes, Stuart rises to protest. He derides them for yielding to the whims of a smooth talking supplicant who is likely too young to vote for any of them. Stuart's objection falls on deaf ears, and the bill passes with all the Democrats voting for it. Douglas then executes the second part of his scheme. He slithers through the halls angling for an appointment as state's attorney for the First Judicial Circuit. With little effort he succeeds in supplanting a well qualified incumbent.

I make a motion to build another bridge on the Sangamon River, but it fails. Another measure of mine passes—a bill to incorporate the Beardstown and Sangamon Canal Company. Douglas refrains from opposing the incorporation bill, and the rest of the Democrats stand down as well. I turn to Stuart who's seated next to me and whisper, "Why do these Jackson men allow a mere boy to lead them around by the nose?"

He shrugs. "Don't look a gift-horse in the mouth. Maybe he's playing for votes in Sangamon County. Who knows what future ambitions he has? Anyway, you've just fulfilled a promise you made in your first campaign for the legislature. Be thankful."

When the session ends in late January, I return to New Salem to begin surveying a new plat out at Petersburg, not far from Annie's grave. Each morning I visit her and leave a winter nosegay or bouquet of early spring flowers at her headstone. Some days I kneel on the ground next to her and shed tears, sifting through bittersweet memories. On other days, I report to her on the mundane events of life.

My pilgrimages continue during March when I lay out the new town of Huron on the left bank of the Sangamon, twelve miles north of New Salem. Speculators from Springfield are keen on the prospects for a settlement there as it sits at the eastern terminus of the proposed Beardstown and Sangamon canal. The rapid growth of Petersburg and Huron comes with a cost, however. Not only is New Salem withering away—many of my friends have started resettling in the new communities to the north—my post office is to be closed, as well. My notice of closure, posted in the *Sangamo Journal*, lists the names of sixty-four people who must pick up their uncollected mail.

In payment for my Huron surveying services, I receive title to several lots in the plat. Hoping to make a windfall to pay off debts, I use my $162 stipend from the legislative session to purchase an additional forty-seven acre tract only a mile from the proposed canal. I purchase the lots from the government at the minimum price of $1.25 an acre—$58.75 for the forty-seven acres. I also buy stock in the Beardstown and Sangamon Canal Company.

On March 19, a day after I post an advertisement in the *Sangamo Journal* regarding my horse that has been lost or stolen again, a letter announcing my candidacy for a second term in the legislature is published. It's shorter than my declaration two years ago.

> *I go for admitting to the right of suffrage all whites who pay taxes or bear arms (by no means excluding females).*

> *If elected I shall consider the whole people of Sangamon my constituents, those who oppose as those who support me. Whether elected or not, I go for distributing the proceeds of sales of public lands to the several states to enable our state, in common with the others, to dig canals and construct railroads without borrowing money and paying interest on it.*

Still unable to afford buying a horse, once summer comes I often walk more than five miles between events in blistering heat to canvass for votes. Including the trek to and from, a single campaign event could consume most of a day.

While giving a speech one muggy July day at a rally in the Springfield courthouse, Mr. George Forquer is seated in the front row. He recently bolted from the Whig Party to take an appointment from President Jackson to run the local Land Register Office. With his appointment comes a three-thousand dollars per year salary and a fine house, complete with a lightning rod—a new fangled accoutrement the likes of which no one in these parts has ever before seen.

Though Mr. Forquer is not a candidate, he rises at the conclusion of my speech and points at me. "This young man must be taken down, and I'm afraid the task devolves upon me." Reckon I should be content that he does not consider any of the Democrats' candidates worthy of standing for themselves.

His speech is laced with condescension and sarcasm. Heat rises under my collar. At his conclusion, I stand and rebut.

*The gentleman has seen fit to allude to my being a
young man; but he forgets that I am older in years
than I am in the tricks and trades of politicians. I
desire to live long and earn a place of distinction;
but I would rather die now than, like the gentleman,
live to see the day that I would change my politics
for an office worth three thousand dollars a year,
and then feel compelled to erect a lightning rod to
protect a guilty conscience from an offended God.*

On the eve of the August election, a dense crowd
once again jams the oven-hot corridors of Springfield's
courthouse for a final round of speech-making by the
candidates. One of our Whigs, Ninian Edwards—a young
fellow of my age who walks about the corridors as if he's
royalty—is the son of a former governor. As opposed to
myself however, he is handsome, vain, short-fused and
hates democracy as much as Satan is said to abhor holy
water.

During his address, Edwards is interrupted several
times by the hot-tempered Democrat Dr. Jacob Early,
under whom I served in the Black Hawk War. After having
his fill of Early's rudeness, Edwards jumps off the platform
and engages the Democrat in a nose-to-nose argument.
When they almost come to blows, I force my way between
them and demand they address their differences in a civil
manner. They glare at each other, neither seeming to want
to have the next word. I take up the subject myself and
give it a fair treatment.

The next night after election results are announced, I
copy down the tally on a scrap of paper and carry it with
me to Annie's graveside. It's hard to believe it's been almost
a year since her death. When I give her the news of my re-
election, her voice echoes in the gentle breeze telling me
she's proud. I promise to protect her from rain and snow.
"Don't neglect your studies," she whispers.

A month later, on the day I'm awarded my license to
practice law, I return to her graveside and tell her, "Now I
can begin repaying my debts." A crack of thunder fills the
blackened skies. I take off my coat and spread it over her

grave, then flee to a nearby tree for shelter until the storm passes. If only my grief could be so brief.

When Betsy Abell returns from a trip to Kentucky, accompanied by her sister, Mary Owens, Betsy beams. "Here she is. I've done my part, now you must do yours."

I stand, my jaw unhinged. What happened to the comely girl with dark hair and large blue eyes who visited her three years ago? The woman before me now is corpulent with lines creasing her face.

"Well, Abe," Betsy says.

I remove my hat and say, "How do, Miss Owens?"

She returns my greeting.

I continue to stare.

Betsy takes me by the arm, "You'll excuse us for a moment, dear Sister, won't you?"

Mary nods, and Betsy ushers me out of earshot.

In hushed tones she says, "Abe Lincoln, what's the matter with you?"

"Sorry, Betsy."

"Well, three years ago when she went back home, I told you I'd bring her back some day if you would marry her."

"I ... but ...."

She peers up at me. "You agreed didn't you?"

My pulse quickens. "Yes, but I never expected ...."

"You are a man of honor?"

"Yes, by all means ... a man of honor."

Beads of sweat line my lips.

"She is quite in earnest about this, you know."

I glance at Mary. "Yes, reckon so ... coming all this way."

"Fine," Betsy says. "Let's begin this thing."

She tells me she's planned an outing for Mary and me to get better acquainted. We are to join friends for horseback riding in the country.

The next afternoon on our excursion, we come to a creek with a rather difficult crossing. The others in our party go first, each fellow taking care to assure his partner gets over safely. I, on the other hand, guide my horse straight into the water and never look back at Mary, who's following.

Once we are on the opposite bank, she rides up beside me and says, "I suppose you didn't care in the least whether I fell off and broke my neck."

I laugh. "Figured you were plenty smart enough to get over on your own."

She rides ahead to join the others. Though she engages the others in gay conversation, she doesn't speak to me for the remainder of the ride.

Over the next several days, I visit Annie's grave and commiserate with her over the pickle I'm in. As one would expect, she keeps silent on the matter.

Mired in guilt over my behavior, I call on Miss Mary again. When she refuses to receive me, I ride into town and wander the streets with my shoulders slumped and head hanging. Nancy Green, Judge Green's spritely aged mother, stops me as I'm leaving Sam Hill's store and says, "You seem a little blue."

"Reckon I am a bit ashamed of myself."

She throws back her head. "It wouldn't have to do with Betsy's sister, Miss Owens by any chance?"

"Why do you ask that?"

"It's just that I've been hearing gossip."

"Such as ...."

"Such as, Miss Mary's miffed because you've been paying more attention to Annie—who's been in the grave for more than a year—than you've shown her. I'd say that's a pretty poor attempt at courtship."

I scratch my head. "I've been a bit of a heel."

"Seems so."

"What should I do?"

She shakes her head. "Well, if you're ever going to snag a wife, you'll have to figure that one out on your own."

I want a wife, but Mary Owens is not the gal. Nonetheless, a promise is a promise.

Chapter Sixteen

In December 1836, John Stuart and I step out of the coach in Vandalia and gaze at the new capitol building caged in scaffolding. John says to me, "They're going through a lot of trouble to erect something that'll be abandoned in a couple of years."

As we walk toward the hotel, I point to the laborers hurrying to finish construction before the legislature convenes. "They best keep that scaffolding up in case the place collapses."

He laughs. "What do you mean? The last one stood for a good twelve years."

I snicker. "Every year it sagged a little more. By the time we left here last summer, the west wall was sunken four inches, and the north wall bulged out almost a foot."

He shakes his head. "Yeah, and the floor in the Senate chamber was nine inches down at the center. Imagine how rickety this new one must be. They've slapped it together in less than three months."

"I once built a good, sturdy flatboat in less than thirty days."

When we stop at the hotel door, Stuart turns to me and says, "If they're trying to convince us to keep the capitol in Vandalia, that building won't help their cause. Can you believe the legislature didn't even get a chance to approve the expenditures? That will cost them votes when the relocation bill comes up."

I put my hand on his shoulder. "Not sure I like the rule that makes good men like you quit the legislature to seek federal offices. It hurts all the more that you didn't win the seat in Congress."

"Well," he says, "I'm not abandoning you entirely. I'll just have to watch things from the gallery. Besides, you're going to like our new member, Dan Stone. You two have a lot in common."

I shake my head. "Won't be the same, you in the gallery and Douglas on the floor. Last session it was the other way around. Now that he's an elected legislator, he can keep a tighter rein on his troops."

"I'll keep myself busy enough in the lobby, bargaining." He winks.

I follow him into the hotel. "You know how I feel about trading votes for favors."

"Relax," he says. "The internal improvements bill is going to pass with or without us. Our chances for lining up votes to move the capital to Springfield will come in committee where we can bargain over the specific ventures that go into the bill. People all over the state are clamoring for bridges, canals, roads, and especially railroads."

"Those projects should stand on their own merit."

He nods. "Exactly. We'll hand out some favors to men who have good projects, but little support. At a minimum we'll be able to get their help on procedural votes to keep the capital relocation bill moving forward."

When we stop to pick up our room keys, I say, "Okay, I'll keep my eyes and ears open, but I won't betray my conscience."

"That's all I ask. And by the way, Stone will represent Sangamon on the Internal Improvements Committee. We need you to focus on making Springfield our next capital. It needs to be closer to the center of the state, especially now that the population is spreading northward."

My desire to see the capital moved to Springfield is partly personal. Stuart has offered me a partnership in his law office there once the legislative session ends. There is little left for me in New Salem. Not only is Annie gone, but her father died of a broken heart months after her death.

Most everyone else has moved on to Petersburg or beyond. Even Annie's mother sold the rest of the Rutledge-Cameron Farm to McNamar and removed to Iowa with her unmarried children.

On the morning the session is to begin, we're told the hall is unsafe. Workmen are still slathering the ceiling with plaster, and the stoves for heating are not yet installed. With nothing better to do, I write a letter to Miss Mary that sounds as dry and gloomy as my spirit. She likely won't be any more sympathetic to my professed shame for sending it than she'll be with my complaining about the legislature's idleness. I tell her of my dread over spending ten more weeks here. Any place would be better.

When the session finally begins, we mire ourselves in trivial matters. In the lobby during a morning recess, I tell Stuart, "I shall never gain any greater distinction than my father did."

"Stop moping," he says. "Have a little patience."

Our first completed business is repealing the "little bull" bill, which should never have passed during the last session. I was opposed to its nonsense, and sixty-six members who voted for it lost their seats in last fall's election. Under the "little bull" bill, owners of bulls over one year old that ran at large out of enclosure were fined— the fines falling mostly on poor farmers. The fine money was paid to owners of the three best bulls, three best cows, and three best heifers in each county—often the wealthy.

At supper Stuart assigns me to manage the petitions for and against carving Sangamon County in two. When I complain that hardly anyone will notice my efforts on such a small matter, he tells me that's good news—at least I won't be squandering any political capital in the process. Then he tells me I've been chosen to give a speech on the Democrats' bill to investigate the State Bank. It'll be my first big speech in the legislature.

Stuart says, "Usher Linder is introducing the bill."

I swallow hard as he hands me a copy of the bill. "He's no small game."

He nods. "The resolution is ninety-nine written lines. The first thirty-three lines relate to the distribution of the Bank's stock."

I look up from reading the bill. "What business is it of the people's? If a man thinks he's entitled to stock which he was denied, let him take the matter to court."

Stuart leans forward. "They're trying to lay a case that the Bank was unconstitutional in its formation."

I shake my head. "This investigation will cost some ten-thousand or more dollars."

After reading a bit I say, "It seems like these capitalists are always cooperating to fleece the people in one way or another. Here they want taxpayers to pay money for settling a quarrel in which the people have no interest. As folks say, he who dances should always pay the fiddler. If any man thinks his money is such a burden that he chooses to lead off this dance, I am opposed to using public funds to pay the fiddler."

Stuart chuckles. "I like that. Use it." He tells me the bill lays out several insinuations that the Bank's actions inflict great injury on the people at large.

I look up. "How is it that the people should be writhing under such oppression, but not one of them has raised a complaint?"

He nods. "This is exclusively the work of politicians."

"Politicians as a lot are one long step removed from being honest men."

Stuart glances over his shoulder. "I'm not sure you should insult the other members."

I straighten up. "Don't see how anyone can take it personal without imagining that I'm condemning myself."

He shakes his head. "Suppose you're right."

"It says here the Bank's commissioners are guilty of corruption."

Stuart glances at the page and shakes his head. "That's their justification for setting up a committee of legislators to investigate the bank. Of course, Linder will be chairing the committee."

I grin. "I've some choice words for them on that."

Stuart nods. "That's why we want you to give the speech. You're quite good at making your opponent's argument sound ridiculous."

When the day comes for my speech I begin by showing deference to the bill's author.

It is not without considerable apprehension that I venture to cross tracks with the gentleman from Coles County, Mr. Linder.

I do not believe I could muster sufficient courage to come in contact with the gentleman, were it not for the fact that some days ago he graciously condescended to assure us he would never be found wasting ammunition on small game.

Linder forces a smile.

On the same fortunate occasion, he also gave us to understand that he is decidedly the superior of our friend from Randolph, Mr. James Shields. Feeling as I do that I am nothing more than the peer of our friend from Randolph, I shall regard the gentleman from Coles as decidedly my superior also.

Consequently, in the course of what I have to say, whenever I allude to the gentleman, I shall endeavor to adopt the kind of court language which I understand to be due to decided superiority.

Seated in front of me near a spittoon, Linder leans back in his seat, his mouth drawn tight, arms folded across his chest. In the gallery, Stuart is grinning.

In one faculty there is no dispute of the gentleman's superiority; that is, his ability to entangle a subject so that neither he, nor any other man, can find head or tail to it.

Cheers and laughter erupt from the anti-Jackson men. Linder leans forward, scowling.

Here he has introduced a resolution, containing ninety-nine printed lines, yet more than half of his opening speech addressed the constitutionality of the Bank, about which there is not one word in his resolution.

*Although I am satisfied that small game could find
ample fodder for debate within the resolution itself,
since the gentleman has travelled outside of it, I feel
that I may, with all due humility, venture to follow
him.*

Linder turns to his left and whispers to Douglas.

*In such respect, I simply point out that our Supreme
Court has decided in favor of the constitutionality of
the Bank, and this is a sufficient answer to his
argument.*

The anti-Jackson men applaud.

Linder slams his hand on his desk and verbally
accosts Douglas. Then he turns and jaws at one of the
lesser Democrats.

*Now addressing the resolution, there are several
insinuations which are too silly to require notice,
except that they conclude by saying, "to the great
injury of the people."*

*The truth is no such oppression exists. If it did, our
table would groan with memorials and petitions.
The people know their rights; and they are never
slow to assert and maintain them, when they are
invaded.*

While the anti-Jackson men hoot their approval, the
Democrats murmur among themselves. I look at Stuart. He
clasps his hands together then shows his approval,
pointing his thumb straight up in the air. When I turn to
face Linder he's shaking his fist at me.

I continue my speech.

*It appears that a principal object of the proposed
committee is to ferret out a mass of corruption
supposed to have been committed by the
commissioners. I believe it is universally
acknowledged that men will act correctly, unless
they have a motive to do otherwise. If this be true,*

we can only suppose that the commissioners acted corruptly if we also suppose they were bribed. Now, I would ask if the Bank will find it more difficult to bribe a committee of seven politicians than it might have encountered if it had bribed the twenty-four commissioners.

Linder jumps to his feet and shouts, "Point of Order." The Speaker denies his plea. Linder shakes his head and says, "Let him go on then. He'll wind up breaking his own neck." I stifle a grin.

Thank you, Mr. Chairman. That's another gracious condescension by 'decided superiority.' I acknowledge it with gratitude. I was not saying that the gentleman from Coles could not be bribed, nor, on the other hand, will I say he could. In that particular, I leave him where I found him.

The Bank's commissioners are twenty-four of the most respectable men in the State. Probably no twenty-four men could be selected in whom the people would more readily place their confidence. So, there is less probability that those men have been bribed and corrupted, than might be the case for any seven men headed by 'decided superiority' himself.

The anti-Jackson men shout in unison, "Hear! Hear!" My chest swells.

In point of fact, the common people of our State have benefited greatly by the Bank, and they would be devastated financially by its demise. Any unwarranted blemish on the Bank's good name would by large measure diminish the value of its notes held by our farmers, shopkeepers and common people.

I have said that cases might occur, when an examination of the Bank might be proper; but I am opposed to encouraging that lawless and

*mobocratic spirit which is already abroad in the
land, and is spreading with rapid and fearful
impetuosity to the ultimate overthrow of every
institution, or even moral principle, in which
persons and property have hitherto found security.*

As I take my seat, the anti-Jackson men are
cheering, and Douglas shaking his head. I have offended
his pet notions that institutions and moral principles are
flexible, that out of necessity they must bend to the whims
of progress.

Once I'm seated, Linder moves for a vote on the
measure. It passes 55-21. Nonetheless, the Whigs
congratulate me and say they anticipate more of my speech
making. I sit taller and soak in their accolades.

Stuart insists I attend meetings of the Internal
Improvements Committee as an observer. The dog fight
over who gets to spend ten million dollars in their counties
puts a sour taste in my mouth. The project I find the most
distasteful is the central railroad line. Galena is the only
town on the whole route which is more than a mere name,
and it sits on a navigable branch of the Mississippi. I ask
Stone why anyone would favor such a waste of public
money. He says we must support the line to earn favors
from legislators in those counties. Their votes will come in
handy when we try to move the state capital to Springfield.

When the Senate bill for relocating the capital finally
comes before the House, the Sangamon members look to
me for leadership. If we succeed at putting the new capitol
in Springfield, we will be welcomed home as heroes.
Otherwise we won't likely be returned here by the voters.

Alton, Vandalia, and Jacksonville are Springfield's
chief competitors, while another sixteen communities find
their way into the debate. Most of the sixteen are entered
into the record to appease local constituents.

The Senate bill only provides for relocating the
capital; the location will be chosen in a joint session of the
House and Senate. John Dement of Vandalia, the mousey
former State Treasurer who went behind our backs to fund
construction of this hastily cobbled structure, tries to
prevent a reading of the Senate bill. He makes a motion to

lay it on the table until December, 1839—nearly three years from now. His maneuver would kill the bill. It's defeated by a slim margin of 42-38. We have our work cut out for us.

Three days later during intense debate, various amendments are offered, slowing our progress. One amendment is introduced by Benjamin Enloe of Johnson. We share similar physical attributes; he is tall and angular with dark hair, dull skin, and deep set grey eyes; however, he's better attired. Since the first time I saw him, I've wanted to ask whether he is one of the Kentucky Enlows whose blood is rumored to course through my veins.

By the end of the afternoon, members are gazing outside through windows crosshatched by blowing snow. Some scurry out of the chamber, hoping to avoid being trapped by the storm, but most stay put. Enloe offers a new motion to lay the bill on the table until July 4—four months after this session will be adjourning—effectively killing the measure. His motion prevails by 39-38. Almost at once, the hall empties. Only the seven of us from Sangamon County remain.

I gather my six colleagues and propose a plan. Despite the blizzard, we agree to fan out across Vandalia to pressure those who support relocation to brave the bitter weather for a vote the next morning. We also set up two teams to call on several members whose friendship failed us on the motion to table the bill—one team will call on Thomas Atwater of Putnam and Thomas Hunt of Edwards, the other is assigned to Edward Smith of Wabash and Francis Voris of Peoria. These men will be confronted over their lack of gratitude for our support for running the railroad through their districts.

I set out on my own to visit another defector, Benjamin Enloe. When he answers the door my throat is tight. Part of me wants to seize the chance and ask him if he's one of the Kentucky Enlows, but I bite my tongue.

After we're seated across from each other at his small dining table I say, "Enloe, the longest railroad in the state will run along the western boundary of your county. You wouldn't have won that plum without support from the Sangamon delegation."

He strokes his chin. "You folks opposed me for Warden of the State Penitentiary. Douglas got me the votes."

"Did Douglas lobby you to table the Senate bill?"

"We Democrats like to take care of our own."

I knead my forehead, wanting to appeal to the rightness of my cause, or even a family bond we might share. Instead, I say, "The Senate hasn't voted your railroad yet. You may have forgotten that we Whigs have control over there, and the Sangamon members could call in some favors to direct the route elsewhere."

He slams his fist on the table. "Our railroad is a good thing for the whole state."

I rise to my full height and look down at him. "Relocating the capital to Springfield is good for everyone as well. Yet you and Douglas are trying to stop it."

He jumps to his feet. "I never said I'd vote against it when the time comes."

"Very well, then." I put my hand on his shoulder. "It's time. Since you voted to put the bill on the table, you're allowed to move to take it off. We need your help."

He glances at my hand, still on his shoulder. "Douglas won't like it."

"You should worry more about the folks at home and what they'll say when there's no money for the railroad they think they ought to have."

"You drive a hard bargain, Lincoln."

"I'm not bargaining. Only pointing out what some men might do if they take offense over you doing Douglas' bidding. It's not something I would have them do, nor is it something they can be stopped from doing."

"So, you're saying I have little choice."

"You certainly have a choice ... but your choice may have consequences."

He grimaces. "I'll be on the floor in the morning to make your motion."

We shake hands, and I leave. As I plow my way back to my room through drifting snow, I try to imagine what relationship I might have to Benjamin Enloe.

The following morning the Senate bill is taken off the table by a vote of 42-40.

Stephen Douglas demands a roll call. He doesn't oppose relocating from Vandalia, but his pride is wounded by the defection of a handful of Democrats and the success of a small band of Whigs. The vote holds as the roll is called, and the bill moves forward.

That victory is met with another motion to table the bill. I hold my breath as the roll is called once more, and we win by a margin of nine. Momentum has turned in our favor. Nonetheless, when the amending game begins anew, I begin to fear our margin might collapse. I leap to my feet and move to table the bill until Monday, giving us time to shore up our support.

Additional attempts to amend the bill are made when it comes up again, but those efforts are defeated by comfortable margins. On the final vote, we prevail 46-37. The capital will be relocated, but a joint session with the Senate is needed to determine where.

When the Senate joins us to select the city for the new capital, Springfield heads the pack on the first ballot with thirty-five votes out of seventy-three needed. Vandalia and Peoria follow with sixteen each, Alton with fifteen, Jacksonville fourteen, and Decatur four. Five towns garner two or three votes each and nine get one. A quarter of Springfield's votes come from counties that gained railroads in the internal improvements bill.

On the second ballot, Springfield gains nine more votes, all of the new support coming from members who won railroads. The third ballot adds five more railroad votes to Springfield's tally, and on the fourth ballot we reach the seventy-three needed to win.

Ninian Edwards, the aristocratic Springfield legislator, hosts a celebration at Ebenezer Capps' tavern near the State House. The tab totals $223.50, and the fare includes cigars, smoked and canned oysters, almonds, raisins, and fruit. Eighty-one bottles of champagne are consumed, as well. As a temperance man, I don't participate in libations. I nibble on popcorn, peaches, apples, and bread. Stuart draws a round of laughter imitating my way of savoring apples. He clasps his forefinger and thumb around the equatorial part, points the stem toward his mouth, and bites.

Edwards toasts my leadership in the successful endeavor. What began as a dull session gives me hope I may yet do something to leave my mark on the world.

Despite the celebratory mood my thoughts turn to the resolution passed early in the session condemning abolitionist activities. My stomach knots whenever I consider its assertion that—*the right to hold slaves as property is sacred to the slave-holding states.* Having been little more than property once myself, the memories of injustice sting my back and pinch my flanks. Slavery sickens me, yet the Federal Constitution protects it, and nothing can be done except let it gradually die out. Even if my effort is little more than a token, I cannot say nothing.

Before returning home, I seek out the other five House members who opposed the measure and ask them to join in a small protest—a letter dissenting to the resolution's passage. Only Dan Stone agrees. We assert that "... the institution of slavery is founded on both injustice and bad policy; but the promulgation of radical abolitionist doctrines tends to increase rather than abate its evils ...."

Our letter is entered into the record on March 5, the closing day of the legislative session—too late for anyone to take retribution against us by rescinding their votes naming Springfield as the new capital.

Chapter Seventeen

The heartache that consumed me on my departure for Vandalia last December has succumbed to numbness as I kneel at Annie's grave in early March. "My dear Annie, John Stuart has offered me a partnership in his law office in Springfield." Tears trickle down my cheeks. "It's not that far away."

I recall the sweetness of her voice. She's proud.

A few weeks later I tie up Bill Butler's horse to a post outside Springfield's general store—Butler has loaned me the horse until I get settled. I step onto the wooden porch and stomp my feet to knock the dust off my boots. These streets probably get just as muddy as New Salem's in winter.

On entering the store, I'm greeted by a set of cordial blue eyes belonging to the man behind the counter. The young dandy asks, "Can I help you?"

"I'm likely a hopeless case, but I'd be obliged for any help you can offer."

"New in town?"

"From New Salem ... but this is home now."

He takes out a quill and paper. "What can I do for you?"

I set my saddle bags on the counter. "How much would a single bedstead cost?"

He jots down a list. "You'll need a bedstead, mattress, linens ... that'll be ... seventeen dollars."

I scratch my head. "It's probably cheap enough, but as cheap as it is, I have no money to pay you right now. You see, I came to town on a borrowed horse, and my only possessions are the clothes here in my saddle bags and a few law books."

He straightens up.

My back tightens. "If you'll credit me until Christmas ... and my ... my experiment here as a lawyer succeeds ... I can pay you then." I hang my head. "But if I fail in that ... I'll probably never be able to pay you."

"Joshua Speed," he says, extending his hand.

"Lincoln. Abraham Lincoln."

"Yes, I recognized you when you came through the door. Heard you give a speech when you were canvassing for votes."

"Was it a good one?"

He rubs the back of his neck. "It seems that taking on a small debt would be a hard pill for you. Here's a suggestion that won't cost you anything. There's a room above with a large double bed. You're perfectly welcome to share it with me, if you like."

I take my saddle bags and go up the narrow stairs where I find the room is exactly as he described. After dropping my things on the floor, I bound down the steps. "Well, Speed, I'm moved in."

He gives me a hardy handshake. "Whatever you need, just ask."

"There is one thing. I'm looking for a fellow I once met back in New Salem—a Negro man from the Caribbean Islands named Billy Florville. He's a barber. Said he planned to settle here."

"Sure. Everyone knows Billy. You'll find his shop across the square from where they're building the new capitol."

A few minutes later I walk into Billy's barbershop. On seeing me, he tosses the razor he's been using into a bowl and plants his hands on his hips. "Well, if it isn't the honorable Mr. Lincoln!"

"Hello, Billy."

"Don't tell me you come all the way from New Salem to get that matt of hair tamed?"

I run my fingers through my tangled hair. "A haircut would be nice, but came mostly to say hello. Just moved to town. Got a room over the general store with a nice fellow named Speed."

Billy turns to his customer. "Mr. Lincoln is the best man I've ever known. Late one evening back in '31 I'm approaching the little village of New Salem on foot when I run into this gangly fellow returning from a day of labor in the woods, carrying an axe on his shoulder. This being almost slave territory, I'm skittish at first. Before I know it, though, we fall into easy conversation—him being almost as good a storyteller as me."

I laugh. "Since I tell a few of your stories now, that puts us on level ground."

The customer laughs.

"Anyways," Billy continues, "when he finds out I'm a barber and about out of money, he takes me over to the tavern to cut hair for all the men boarding there. Next morn, with my pockets full of money, I set out for Springfield. Been here ever since."

When Billy finishes with his customer, he gives me a haircut and a steaming hot shave for free. "When you get to be a rich lawyer," he says, "you start paying regular fare."

After leaving Billy's place, I call on my new law partner John Todd Stuart. His office, an upstairs room less than a block from Speed's store, is furnished with a small bed, a buffalo robe, a chair, a bench, and a shelf for books. When Stuart explains that our cases are mostly related to debts, I tell him, "I know a great deal about the subject."

He cocks his head. "If memory serves me, you certainly do. Calamities such as yours are the reason we fight against the Jackson men who want to kill the Bank."

"You're right. The frontier customs must be changed for our state to grow. Both Billie Greene and Radford used the notes Berry and I gave them as currency. Back in New Salem, a good many folks exchanged notes that were made payable to the bearer. That way the notes could pass through several hands the same as money before they landed with someone substantial enough to convert them into bank notes. Since we were a good distance from the

State Bank offices, only the wealthiest men in the county did so."

Stuart nods. "That's exactly how you wound up encumbered to Van Bergen who sued you for your horse and surveying tools. He became the bearer of your notes, and your horse was a suitable substitute for cash."

I spend a few weeks poring over cases to learn court procedures and applications of the law—what makes debts collectible or not. One well known law is that promises lightly made can become heavy burdens. I decide to deal with one such promise by writing Mary Owens. My first two attempts are only good for stoking the fire. One is too serious, the other not serious enough, and both are discarded before I'm half done.

On the third try, I ask Speed to help me. He has a silver tongue when it comes to the ladies and tells me to play on her sympathies.

I begin,

> *Springfield is a rather dull place. I am quite as lonesome here as I ever have been anywhere.*

Speed reminds me that women like to treat their men as if they were children. I add,

> *I have not yet been to church. I stay away because I do not know how to behave.*

He says, "That's good. She'll feel your very soul is at stake."

We laugh.

I don't discuss the next part with Speed. If I don't give her an excuse for backing out, I'll be honor bound to keep my promise. I must discourage her from coming—such as,

> *Nothing would make me unhappier than failing to assure your happiness.*

He demands to see my letter, and I hand it to him.

I know I would be much happier with you than without you, provided I saw no signs of discontent in you. What you have said to me about our future may have been in jest, or I may have misunderstood it. If so, then let it be forgotten; if otherwise, I much wish you would think seriously before you decide.

For my part I have already decided. What I have said I will most positively abide by provided you wish it. My opinion is that you had better not do it. You have not been accustomed to hardship, and it may be more severe than you now imagine.

He says she'll be insulted, so I add:

I know you are capable of thinking correctly on any subject; and if you deliberate maturely upon this, before you decide, then I am willing to abide your decision.

I close by asking her to write me a good long letter and sign it:

Yours, &c.
LINCOLN.

A few days after I post Mary's letter, the Bank of Springfield runs out of gold and silver. My Whig friends and I are in a panic. People can no longer exchange their bank notes for coins. This puts the Bank in violation of its charter and means it must close down unless a remedy is found. If that happens, the bank notes folks use for currency will become worthless, and commerce will come to a halt. Internal improvement projects will be abandoned and our State's growth will be jeopardized. Illinois' Whigs have fought long against the Democrats whose chief aim has been to dissolve the Bank.

That evening, Speed invites me to join him after hours at his store to discuss the matter with a handful of young men. When I walk in and see the chief Democrat, Stephen Douglas, sitting in the corner nursing a liberal pour of whiskey I glare at Speed. "How can we have an intelligent exchange with that bantam rooster strutting about, crowing?"

Speed smirks. "At least he's outnumbered."

His count is accurate. Besides Speed and me there are two other Whigs—a charismatic, London born orator Ned Baker, and Dr. Anson Henry who's renowned for his ability to make bitter enemies more readily than warm friends. Douglas' lone Democrat ally is John Calhoun—my old employer who consistently maintains the appearance of a man sucking on sour apples.

Douglas knocks back a gulp of whiskey and takes the first swipe. "Well, gentlemen," he says. "Your Bank's foolishness has sealed its fate. After sixty days its charter will be suspended automatically. It's as good as dead."

Douglas gloats while Baker counters. "You and your traitor friend, General Jackson, will boast with your dying breaths that you killed the Bank—him, the United States Bank, you, the State Bank. But just like he's killing the country with his half-witted crusade, you'll have killed the State of Illinois."

Calhoun, a calculating man, leans forward on his stool. "If the country dies, it will be because we didn't end this paper money scheme long ago."

I unfold myself from my seat and loop my thumbs under my hand-knit suspenders. Douglas tries to mock me, but his body is so compact it hinges into only two pieces, while mine is said to fold in at least half-a-dozen places.

I shake my head and rebut him as he sits back down. "Until little more than a month ago, tariffs and monies from land sales were flowing into the federal treasury like a springtime flood. Along with those revenues silver was coming into the country from Mexico and China in copious amounts. But suddenly cotton prices plummeted, and the flow of metals dried up."

Douglas leans back, holding his hands up as if surrendering. "So what happened?"

I continue. "All was well until Jackson vetoed the National Bank's charter and demanded people pay for land purchases in gold and silver. There was no money to fuel commerce. Now granted, he tried to fix the problem by taking the national bank's capital and spreading it across the frontier—"

Douglas bounds to his feet. "Where it did more good than it would have on Wall Street."

Baker leans forward, teetering on the edge of his seat. "How much of the gold and silver made it into the State Bank in Springfield?"

Douglas laughs. "Jackson did right not sending it here. The Bank's charter is unconstitutional."

Baker's face reddens. "Jackson men favor state banks everywhere else in the country. Why is it that you Democrats here in Illinois want to kill our bank? The only reason is that its board is made up of Whigs."

Douglas laughs, "But, now that's all moot, isn't it? Without sufficient gold and silver in its vaults to redeem its notes, the bank's charter is doomed."

Dr. Henry draws his deep-set eyes into narrow slits. "As is our state and its internal improvements."

"Jackson was a fool," I say. "Britain's bankers saw what was happening, so they raised their interest rates on loans to our eastern banks. Our banks in turn raised their rates, and merchants slowed their borrowing. Commerce came to a near halt."

Douglas jumps to his feet. "Thank you, Lincoln. You have made an argument in favor of the slave system. Now perhaps you will stop opposing it."

"I did no such thing."

He puffs out his chest. "Yes, cotton prices dropped because money became too expensive to borrow. Can you imagine how much worse things would be if planters had to pay wages for labor on top of everything else?"

I glare at him. "That's a different matter entirely. In the early days of the world, the Almighty said to the first of our race, *In the sweat of thy face shalt thou eat bread*. But to eat bread from the sweat of another man's brow is a sin. It can never be justified—at any cost."

Calhoun finally joins the fray. "Argue over your slavery differences some other time. The pertinent question is—what do you propose to do about this damned banking mess?"

Douglas adds, "I hope you aren't going to say President Van Buren should rescue the bankers who caused the problem by their imprudent and inflationary speculations."

Our debate rages into the night with no resolution, as if any should be expected. In arguing with Douglas, logic is as useless as casting pearls before swine.

With the State Bank in jeopardy of losing its charter, the Bank commissioners ask the governor to convene a special session of the legislature. He responds by calling us into session on July 10. We're to convene in Vandalia since the new capitol in Springfield is still being constructed.

Chapter Eighteen

Vandalia, in spite of being in its final days as our state capital, displays confidence in every fashion when the coachman's horn signals our arrival for the special legislative session in July 1837. The Cumberland Road is nearing completion, and surveying has begun on a new railroad line heading south to Jacksonville. Merchants are standing pat, giving no sign of quitting their posts, while builders work to complete the soon to be abandoned State House. Construction was in progress in March when the previous session ended.

I turn to Ned Baker who's replaced Dan Stone on the Sangamon County delegation. "This place reminds me of a condemned prisoner expecting the hangman's noose will be cut from his throat at the last moment."

He shakes his head. "If you knew you were going to die at this time tomorrow, what would you do?"

I stroke my chin. "Nothing different."

We overhear chatter in the hotel lobby that a handful of legislators, spurred by biting editorials in Vandalia's newspapers, intend to repeal the relocation of our capital to Springfield. They are led on the floor by the aging former governor and United States Senator, William Ewing. Even though Douglas resigned from the legislature to take a plum job as Register of the Federal Land Office, he's on hand to help marshal the Democrats in support of the repeal if the battle gets close.

While Sangamon County's delegation is slightly reconfigured, we have the same focus as always; save the Bank and cede no ground on relocation. If a skirmish arises on the relocation issue, we hope it comes early and we're able to keep enough powder in reserve to fight a vigorous battle over the Bank. If the capital question comes up at the end of the session, however, we run the risk of having expended all of our goodwill while saving the Bank.

We're relieved, therefore, when Ewing's bill comes up early: *An Act to Repeal Certain Laws Relative to the Permanent Location of the Seat of Government of the State of Illinois*. Then amendments are added to render the bill toothless, and we're delighted. The bill's passage has no effect, and we are fully armed for the Bank fight.

When a bill is put before us to allow the Bank to suspend redeeming bank notes until the end of the next session, I glance into the gallery and my eyes meet those of an old foe. Usher Linder, the decidedly superior whom I skinned in my big speech last session, is our new State Attorney General and no longer a member of the legislature. Nonetheless, he's in the hall for the debate. Douglas is seated next to him, his arms folded across his chest in the imperial fashion.

On the House floor, Ewing rises on behalf of the Democrats to argue that the Bank is at the heart of our state's economic crisis. After an aristocratic pause, he adds that the meager confidence the Bank commissioners may have once enjoyed has been squandered by their corruption and inability to redeem its notes with gold and silver.

When he finishes, I take the floor. "Mr. Chairman, in our previous session, one decidedly superior gentleman from Coles County made similar arguments." I gesture toward the gallery where Linder is seated. "These arguments were rebutted at that time and facts have not changed in the intervening months."

I glance back at Linder and Douglas who are engaged in agitated, though hushed, conversation. Then I turn back to face the members and continue, "I will repeat what I have said before, that there has been no corruption shown on the part of the Bank's commissioners. Were they guilty of such, the offended parties would have come forward to make their claims—but no one has done so, except the politicians who only desire to stir the pot for their own selfish gain."

The other Whigs applaud and shout their agreement, encouraging me to continue. "On the matter of our economy's sad state, let it be understood that the fault lies squarely with those who support Jackson and Van Buren."

The Democrats hiss. Their disapproval spurs me on. "Jackson killed the United States Bank, stripping the economy of paper currency which is essential to the rapid growth and maintenance of frontier commerce. Mr. Van Buren has maintained the venerated general's disastrous course."

Ewing jumps to his feet and accuses the Sangamon County legislators of chicanery, selling our votes on internal improvements to gain support for Springfield's selection as the state's permanent capital. Pointing to me he says, "Lincoln, here, is chief among the miscreants. He is a statesman of no account."

I gesture toward Ewing and grin. "It's an honor to be promoted from small game to statesman by the successor to decided superiority, himself." Before he can respond, I turn to the chairman and ask for a vote on the question before the House. He grants my motion, and the members pass a resolution to allow the Bank to suspend redeeming paper money with gold and silver until the end of the next session.

Several weeks later, I sit with Speed on our bed and hand him Mary Owens' letter. On reading it, he slaps my knee, "So she's declined your marriage overture."

I cross my arms over my chest. "It seems so."

"Maybe you shouldn't have pressed the matter."

"I had to. I told her sister that I would take her for better or for worse. It was a point of honor and conscience, and I'm fairly convinced that no other man on earth would have her."

He grins. "She should have been deeply indebted to you for asking."

"She and her sister ... well, at least her sister was bent on holding me to my end of the bargain. So I thought, I have said it, therefore I will not fail to do it, unless of course, she backs out."

He folds the letter and hands it back. "Fine, you did the right thing in pressing the matter."

"She had already replied 'no' the first time I wrote."

He furrows his brow. "Wait. She turned you down more than once?"

"I'm ashamed to say, yes. At first, I thought she declined out of modesty, but when she rejected me again, with more resolve, I was mortified and too stupid to discern her intentions. I tried again and again, but with the same want of success."

He laughs. "Isn't that what you wanted—to have her turn you down?"

I hang my head. "Yes, but after convincing myself nobody else would have her, and then having her throw me over, I realized I was a little bit in love with her."

He lies down and rolls to his side with his back to me. "Lincoln," he mutters. "You are the most hopeless case I've ever known."

One evening in late October, several of us have gathered around the stove in Speed's store to gab. Just as Stephen Douglas coaxes the last drop of whiskey from the cask behind the counter, Ned Baker shows up. A moment later, Speed comes out of the back room carrying a tub of corn and sets it on a shelf.

Speed studies Baker. "Sounds like there was quite a fracas at First Presbyterian this afternoon. Heard you were in the middle of it, Ned."

Baker grabs a couple sticks of wood to stoke the fire. "It all started on the square just past noon. Word had spread that one of the preachers at the Synod meeting was to give a speech denouncing slavery."

I lean back in my chair. "Heard about it, but I'm not one for church meetings."

"Well," Baker continues, "someone rang a bell, and a mob gathered in the square, intent on putting a stop to the meeting. Suppose if it had been the local pastor, the crowd wouldn't have been so agitated."

Speed asks, "Who was the speaker?"

Baker says, "Jeremiah Porter from up in Peoria. Was from Chicago before that. The boys weren't pleased about an outsider coming to town to stir up trouble. So, some of them went over to the church to work him over."

Douglas takes a sip of whiskey. "Why does religion come up every time anyone mentions the word slavery?"

My back twitches. I grit my teeth. "Because it's evil."

Douglas dismisses me with a wave of his hand. "Slavery's neither good nor bad. It just is."

I fold my arms across my chest. "When did you ever pretend to know the difference between good and evil?"

Douglas shrugs. "Anyway, thought about joining them, but I was otherwise occupied."

I snicker. "What? Your lips won't let go of the bottle?"

We all laugh, except Douglas. He knocks back a gulp of whiskey and says, "What's next for you, Lincoln. You going to be joining the Temperance movement?"

I shake my head. "I don't go for vilifying men over their whiskey any more than I favor the bondage it puts them in."

Douglas laughs. "You jealous my lips have more to keep themselves occupied than a bunch of words?"

"Ooh," Speed teases.

"Settle down," Baker warns. "We've had enough excitement for one day. Don't want another brawl."

I bite my tongue while Douglas taps a fresh cask and draws another mug full.

Speed gestures to Baker. "Go on."

"Well, I stepped into the middle of the fellows and told them they should go hear what the preacher had to say before they assailed him."

"Did they?" I ask.

"They did."

"Mighty bold for a fancy fellow like you," I say. "Though, it would have been a better show if little Douglas over here had taken on a mob like that. Except, he'd have been one of them wanting to ride the abolitionist out of town on a rail. Maybe I should have been there."

Douglas wags his finger at me.

Baker shakes his head. "Would have paid admission to see that."

Speed gestures to Baker. "And?"

Baker continues. "The mob sent a delegation to the church to hear Porter out. When one of the delegates read the animosity on their faces, he stood and tried to temper Porter's denunciation. Another minister interrupted him and attacked slavery with fire equal to Porter's. He pointed to the fellows seated in the back and said, 'These men have dared come into the House of God to intimidate a Christian minister speaking the truth.'"

I ask, "What happened next?"

"The men slinked out," says Baker with a grin.

Two weeks later in early November, Baker bursts into my office. "Elijah Lovejoy was attacked by an anti-abolitionist mob in Alton."

I look up, unable to form any of the words that are swirling in my head. Lovejoy was an abolitionist editor who recently started up a newspaper in Alton. Before that he'd run an anti-slavery paper in St. Louis and was chased out of town by mobs that ransacked his offices three times.

He goes on. "After the mob destroyed his printing presses, there was an exchange of gunfire, and Lovejoy was killed."

Finally my words spill out. "Why would they do such a thing?"

When no one answers, I say, "Radicalism only invites trouble. Just the same, these lawless mobs must be stopped."

Baker pounds his hand on my desk. "Are you saying Lovejoy deserved what he got?"

"No one deserves that," I say, "but he's partly responsible for what happened."

"Do you hear what you're saying?"

"I'm saying that each side is pushing the other to become more radical with every passing day. Slavery will die out in time if we don't let it spread any farther and we just leave it alone where it's protected under the Constitution."

Baker's face reddens, and his veins bulge under his

collar. "Wait. You've said yourself that slavery is a great evil. Evil ought to be stamped out."

I lean back. "It may be evil, but it's still the law."

For weeks, a war wages in my head between anger at the mob for its lawlessness and despair over the treachery radicalism invites on itself. Not until late January of the following year do I find the words to express what's in my heart. I make a speech entitled *The Perpetuation of our Political Institutions* at the Young Men's Lyceum meeting held in Springfield's Baptist Church.

There is even now, something of an ill-omen amongst us. I mean the increasing disregard for law which pervades the country. The growing disposition to substitute wild and furious passions in lieu of the sober judgment of Courts, and worse supplanting the executive ministers of justice with the rule of savage mobs...

The question recurs, 'how shall we fortify against it?' The answer is simple. Let every American, every lover of liberty, every well wisher to his posterity swear by the blood of the Revolution never to violate in the least particular the laws of the country, and never tolerate their violation by others...

Let every American mother breathe reverence for the laws to the lisping babe that prattles on her lap....

A few weeks later, as several of us are huddled around the fire at Speed's general store, Douglas chides me about my speech. He says the law should always bend with the times.

Billy Herndon, who's recently begun clerking for Speed, casts him a sideways glance from behind the counter. Billy, a young college man, with his mouth perpetually drawn in a puckering frown, is staunchly anti-slavery, though his father is the opposite. When Illinois College was swept up in the abolitionist sentiment after Elijah Lovejoy's murder, Billy's father forced him to return home.

Billy scolds Douglas. "The only way to rid the country of slavery is through bloody revolution."

I lean back in my chair. "Well, Billy, we've seen where that gets us. Nothing will destroy this country faster than disregard for the law. It's the law that keeps the world in order. Tear it down, and everything falls apart."

Douglas guzzles a dram of whiskey and heaves a sigh. "The law is not a fixed thing. The system of Common Law, just like the people it ruled and protected, was simple and crude in its infancy. Then it grew, improved, and became polished as the nation advanced in civilization, virtue, and intelligence."

Billy scowls. "Intelligence?"

Douglas shrugs. "It adapted to the condition and circumstances of the people. But as for Billy's abolitionism, that is not a refinement. It proposes to destroy the law and extinguish the principle of self-government for which our forefathers fought, and upon which our whole system of free government is founded."

Billy's eyes grow wider. "Slavery is an abomination. It goes against everything our forefathers fought for, and Lovejoy's murder makes me all the more determined to see its evil wiped off the face of the earth."

"Fellows," I say, grabbing a log for the fire, "Let's move on. These claims that our Founders were in one accord either for or against slavery only serve to whip folks into frenzy. They're contrivances manufactured by self-serving politicians."

Billy turns his back to us and begins rearranging merchandise on the shelf.

Douglas smirks, the same expression Father wore each time he abused me over my excess of 'eddication.'

Speed comes out of the storage room in back of the store carrying a sack of cornmeal.

I ask, "So, Speed, are you getting any these days?"

He laughs. "I'm getting enough these days that I'm willing to share my leftovers. Why just the other night, Douglas was pawing a pretty little brunette I'd recently thrown over."

Douglas leaps off his stool and shakes his fists at Speed, as if challenging him to fight.

"Settle down, boys," I say, picking up a book of Byron's verse to read aloud.

Conqueror and captive of the earth art thou!
She trembles at thee still, and thy wild name
Was ne'er more bruited in men's minds than now
That thou art nothing, save the jest of Fame,
Who wooed thee once, thy vassal, and became
The flatterer of thy fierceness, till thou wert
A god unto thyself; nor less the same
To the astounded kingdoms all inert,
Who deem'd thee for a time whate'er thou didst assert.

Chapter Nineteen

I n March of the following year, Ned Baker rushes into my office with news that Henry Truett, a small, passive man, shot Dr. Jacob Early the previous night at the Spottswood's Hotel. Truett went there to confront Dr. Early, a fellow Democrat much larger and more temperamental than himself, over a political matter. Truett had lost his post as Register of the Land Office at Galena, and friends told him Dr. Early was the cause.

Baker's partner Judge Stephen Logan, the stern-faced dean of Sangamon County's Bar, will lead the defense while Stephen Douglas takes charge of the prosecution. Logan wants me to assist in the defense.

When the case comes to trial in October 1838, Douglas' mood is as foul as I've ever seen. He's still fuming over losing to my law partner John Stuart in the August Congressional election. The two of them debated six days a week for three months—except for the month of May when Stuart was too ill to campaign, and I stood in for him. Douglas and I haven't exchanged cordial words since.

On the witness stand, Truett testifies that he lingered by the fireplace in the hotel bar while Dr. Early sat nearby in a chair, reading quietly. After everyone else went home he verbally accosted Early, demanding to know whether the doctor was the cause of his misfortune. He claims Early replied, he was. Then Early demanded the name of his informant."

Truett refused to identify his source, after which Early called him a "damned liar." The ensuing argument grew heated, and Truett says he drew a pistol; though, he did so in response to Early picking up a chair and wielding it in a threatening manner.

Under cross-examination, Douglas presses Truett to admit he'd drawn his weapon before Early raised the chair. Truett remains resolute, just as we counseled him. He insists he retreated—fearful that Early might crush his skull with the chair—then he fired a single shot without aiming in hopes of disarming his attacker.

Douglas' three witnesses claim, with varying degrees of certainty, that Truett drew his weapon before Dr. Early lifted the chair as a shield. Logan and Baker question one witness each before I cross-examine the third, a handsome, bearded young man who was cock-sure of his answers.

"What was your name, again?"

He answers in a strong voice. "James Reed."

I smile. "Well Jimmy, I have a dear friend up near Petersburg named Jimmy."

He grins.

"It's a very good name, and a good name is something you want to protect. Take Mr. Alexander Trent over there in the jury, for example." I glance over at Trent; he squirms in his seat and looks away. "When I was a young man, I sold a general store to Mr. Trent and his brother Billy."

I turn back to the witness. "You see, the two of them skipped town after a month, making off with all the inventory, and they never did pay me. Reckon there are still some folks out New Salem way who don't think highly of the Trent name."

Folks in the courtroom murmur.

I point to my client. "Jimmy, you don't mind if I call you Jimmy, do you?" I don't pause for his answer. "Do you know my client here, Mr. Truett?"

He looks at my client. "I know of him, but don't have a personal acquaintance."

I stroke my chin. "Very well. Did you know the deceased, Dr. Early?"

He raises his chin. "We were acquainted."

"Did you know him to be a good man?"

Jimmy leans forward, studying the jury. "What I knew of him was good."

"Reckon that would be so." I pull back my shoulders. "I knew him quite well for many years. Served under his command in the Black Hawk War and have, of late, been connected with him in politics. Even though he was a bit hot-tempered as well as a Democrat, and me a Whig, I liked the man. Now, with his untimely demise, I watch after the welfare of his children. I'm what's called their guardian ad litem."

Jimmy slumps back in the witness chair and says in a quiet voice, "Suppose he'll be missed."

"Yes...." I turn and survey the jurymen then look back at the witness. "So, tell me Jimmy, you have pretty good eyesight?"

He nods. "Yes."

I smile. "Good. Do you have a decent memory?"

He straightens himself. "More than decent."

"I'm sure that must be. So, reckon everything was just the way you have said."

"Yes sir, exactly."

"You were in the room when my client shot Dr. Early?"

His eyes widen. "Yes."

"Likewise you were present when the accused man, here, first spoke to the doctor and for the duration of their argument?"

Jimmy shakes his head. "No ... not from the beginning."

I look to the jurymen. "Oh ... but you were there when Dr. Early rose out of his chair and picked it up?"

"I was there when he picked it up, but not when he rose."

My eyes remain locked on the jurymen. "Reckon you saw everything pretty clearly from that point on?"

"Yes sir." There's a hint of doubt in his voice.

I turn and stare at him. "But not before?"

His voice cracks. "Not before what?"

"You didn't see whether Dr. Early picked up the

chair in a menacing way then set it down and picked it up again? Nor did you see Mr. Truett draw his pistol?"

Jimmy glances at the jurymen, at the judge, then at me. "No, suppose not."

"Thank you, Jimmy."

On the third day of trial Judge Jesse B. Thomas, Jr.—a round-faced aristocrat with whimsical eyes— announces he's ready for our summations. Douglas pops to his feet, slicking back his long, wavy mane, and puffing out his chest as if to accentuate his newly tailored black suit and the buttons on his brocaded silk vest. Strutting to a spot in front of the witness chair where his short frame is fully visible to the court, he pauses. His face is stern as he gazes at the jury.

I glance down at my soiled shirt with frayed cuffs that protrude several inches beyond the sleeves of my faded jeans jacket.

"Members of the jury," Douglas says, his voice filling the room, "I'm honored to stand before you today to plead for justice on behalf of an American patriot—Captain Jacob Early, hero of the Black Hawk War."

He shakes his head. "Yes. Justice is what we seek here. Captain Jacob Early was gallant in battle. The bravest of the brave. A warrior. Defender of the weak. He answered duty's call to protect our homes, our wives, and our children from a marauding band of savages. God preserved him on the field of battle."

He points to Truett. "However, this man put himself above the law, even above the will of the Almighty, and stole from us a dedicated servant, a physician, a healer. That man did wrong. He was merciless ... and why?" He spreads his arms wide like a shepherd gathering his flock. "Over a petty argument. Out of resentment toward the Honorable Jacob Early who, in his best conscience, had discharged his duty as a public servant."

I survey the jurymen. Every eye is fixed on Douglas.

Douglas points once more at my client. "Justice, good men of the jury, requires that this man Truett should be condemned in all righteousness to the same sentence he wrongly laid upon the head of our friend, our neighbor, our servant, Dr. Jacob Early."

At Douglas' conclusion, I rise deliberately, but not so slowly that the jurymen miss seeing his dark mane flow below the plane of my shoulder before he takes his seat. Then I proceed to the short riser where the jury is seated and stop in front of Alex Trent. With one foot up on the edge of the platform, I lean forward, smiling, and gaze over the faces of the jurymen. "How do, folks?"

Besides Alex Trent, four other jurymen are acquaintances of mine. The four smile back and nod.

"Thank you, gentlemen. You're what the old farmer calls the cream of the crop. More than twenty prospects were challenged peremptorily, and three-hundred were dismissed for cause." I stand up straight and grin at Trent. "We were so short at the end that we had to take old Trent here."

Noticing that Trent's face is a bit flushed I put my hand on his shoulder. "Don't mean to embarrass you. If I have, I beg your forgiveness."

Trent nods.

Stepping back I say, "Now fellows, as I've already said, I knew Dr. Early quite well. Not at a distance like Douglas there. Captain Early and I wandered through the woods together for about a month, hunting for Indians." I chuckle. "Of course, I think old Captain Early would be amused hearing Douglas make the whole thing sound like a lot of gallantry. See, truth is, we never saw even one Indian the whole time. Closest any of us got to getting wounded was accidentally shooting ourselves cleaning a musket."

The jurymen snicker, nodding to one another.

"Now, I'm sure if the need had arisen, Captain Early would have been the bravest of the bunch, just as Douglas speculates. Kind of the way he speculates about the kind of man my client is.

"By the way," I say, turning and eyeing Douglas, "that was a fine speech he gave us, don't you think? It's one of the finest speeches I've heard him give, and I've heard quite a bit from him. He's a dandy performer in the court room, and I've heard him make some impassioned pleas in the state legislature. Earlier this year, I got a healthy dose of his speech making when he was running against my partner John Stuart for the Congressional seat being vacated by Mr. Truett's father-in-law."

I wink at the jurymen. "By the way, my partner won the contest by thirty-six votes out of thirty-six thousand."

George Tinsley, a juryman who campaigned for Stuart, grins back at me.

"Douglas, here, sits around Speed's General Store with a few of us most evenings trying to help us make sense of politics." I snicker. "He hopes us knuckleheaded Whigs can be elevated to his higher way of thinking. In fact, there may not be another man in the State of Illinois who's better at switching one principle for another or rearranging facts to fit his argument." I shake my head, "I'm still trying to sort out this business of his that the law must bend with the times."

Douglas leaps to his feet. "Your honor," he shouts.

I wave to the judge. "Sorry for wandering off track."

Turning again to the jurymen, I continue. "Now, where were we? Oh yes. We were speaking of speculation. Well, what do you speculate was the reason Mr. Truett shot Dr. Early? Did he go to the Spottswood's Hotel plotting to murder a man with whom he was quarrelling? If so, why would he do such a sinister deed in a public place? Why not lie in wait for him in some dark alley? Or, did his senses flee him in a moment of passion? I think not."

I take my time gazing at Truett, hoping the jurymen will consider him at length, as well. "Truett is a Democrat like Dr. Early was, and I might hold that against either of them, but I don't. I know both well. If anyone was prone to losing his temper or capable of a brash act, it would be Dr. Early. Anyone who knew him would agree. Truett, though, is a principled man."

I hook my thumbs under my fraying suspenders. "I submit to you that Henry Truett, a gentle man, was afraid for his life. Dr. Early was much larger and certainly capable of crushing another man's skull with the chair that he had lifted high in the air in a threatening manner." I raise my hands over my head as if gripping a chair and bringing it down forcefully in front of me.

Peering up at the jurymen I say, "Now I ask you to put yourselves in Henry Truett's shoes. He'd been slighted, and according to good references, the deceased had been the author of his abuse. Dr. Early admitted his offense then demanded to know who had betrayed him. When Mr. Truett refused to name the traitor, the doctor became belligerent, picked up a heavy chair, and wielded it in a manner which instilled in Truett genuine mortal fear."

I point to my client. "Henry Truett did what any logical man would do. Fearing for his life, he drew his pistol and fired a single shot to stop—not to kill—his assailant. Unfortunately, Mr. Truett missed his intended target—the victim's shoulder—and the ball pierced a lung instead."

I look into each juryman's eyes. "If you were in the same circumstance as Mr. Truett, here, what would you have done? Or, if you came upon a loved one under attack, in mortal jeopardy ..." I hold out my hand, imitating a pistol "... would you not draw any weapon at your disposal in their defense?"

After my summation, the twelve men of the jury deliberate for forty minutes before returning a verdict of "Not Guilty."

I slough off praise from Truett and Logan for my "brilliant" summation, telling them, "It was merely simple logic given to simple folks who knew the right thing when it was laid before them."

Douglas walks up behind me and snarls, "Defending oneself as a justification for murder? Sounds like bending the law to suit your whims, if you ask me."

Logan scowls. "No one asked you."

Chapter Twenty

I n December 1838, the legislature convenes at Vandalia for the last time before the capital moves to Springfield. I still miss Annie. One person I don't miss though is Stephen Douglas. He left the legislature a year ago to become Register of the Springfield Land Office, earning a handsome salary while still maintaining his law practice.

Most evenings after supper, I hang out around Vandalia's taverns, swapping stories and jokes with anyone who will indulge me. Laughing distracts me from a small voice in my head. Later, when I lie in my too-short bed, unable to sleep, the voice comes at me like a gale, howling "Your foolishness drove her to the fever." When I hide my head under the pillow it murmurs, "Your love doomed her, just like the others." Then it scolds, "You'll never amount to anything special."

As much as possible I let busyness numb me so the voice is little more than a rustling in my ears.

John Calhoun, my former employer when I was a surveyor, puts a resolution before the House which has three parts—the first advises the Federal Congress that slavery should not be abolished in the nation's capital, the second expresses the sentiment that new slave states ought to be admitted, and the third declares measures that grant equal rights to Negroes "unconstitutional." I join with the majority in opposing his motion.

Another resolution advises Congress that the abolition of slavery in Washington City is unwise, unconstitutional, and inexpedient. I vote for the measure, which passes after an amendment to strike the word "unconstitutional" is adopted.

I also support a bill levying taxes on the property of Illinois citizens. The old law taxes only citizens of other states who own property within our borders. However, when those aliens sell their properties to our own citizens, our revenues decline. We cannot afford to lose those funds. The new law also extends the definition of property to include slaves and servants of color.

After we vote on the taxation measure, a novice legislator from the southern part of the state sits next to me at supper. He suggests I must chafe over the idea of labeling slaves as property.

I furrow my brow. "Why would you say such?"

"Because you're reputed to be a rabid abolitionist."

"Reputed by whom?"

"Why, nearly everybody in my county."

I stand to my full height and stare down at him. "I consider myself a man of moderation, which means abolitionists count me as an enemy. They can't abide the truth that the Constitution protects the rights of slave owners to own slaves."

"So you approve of slavery?"

"I think not. When I was a boy, my father sent me out to labor in the fields for anyone who'd pay as much as ten-cents a day. Only thing was, Father kept all my wages. It's unjust for a man to feed from the sweat of another man's brow ... and Negroes are men."

He hooks his suspenders with his thumbs. "Our forefathers owned slaves. Are you saying Washington and Jefferson, as well as others, were unjust men?"

I scratch my head. "You ask a knotty question. Reckon it's one I shall have to work on unraveling." It's a question that's perplexed me for a long time.

At the conclusion of the session in early May, I'm handed a letter from a constituent protesting my vote supporting the property tax measure. Before boarding the coach for Springfield I write a quick reply.

*The passage of a Revenue law at this session is
right within itself. It does not increase the tax on the
"many poor" but upon the "wealthy few" by taxing
only land that is worth $50 or $100 per acre. This
valuable land belongs, not to the poor, but to the
wealthy citizen.*

*If the wealthy should, regardless of the justness of
the law, complain, it should be remembered that
they are not sufficiently numerous to carry the
election.*

My hasty departure from Vandalia is on account of
four cases that demand my presence at the Sangamon
County Circuit Court in Springfield in the morning.

In late September I ride my horse "Old Tom" out onto the
newly formed Eighth Judicial Circuit. Along the trail, I plod
through lonely prairies and woods with little to occupy my
mind except lamenting over Annie's death. I often take off
my hat and pull out a copy of Shakespeare's *Richard III*
that I always carry with me. The opening soliloquy always
captures my attention.

*But I, that am not shaped for sportive tricks,
Nor made to court an amorous looking-glass;
I, that am rudely stamp'd, and want love's majesty
To strut before a wanton ambling nymph;
I, that am curtail'd of this fair proportion,
Cheated of feature by dissembling nature,
Deformed, unfinish'd, sent before my time
Into this breathing world, scarce half made up,
And that so lamely and unfashionable
That dogs bark at me as I halt by them;
Why, I, in this weak piping time of peace,
Have no delight to pass away the time,
Unless to spy my shadow in the sun
And descant on mine own deformity:
And therefore, since I cannot prove a lover,
To entertain these fair well-spoken days,*

I am determined to prove a villain
And hate the idle pleasures of these days.

I take leave from the Circuit in early November to tend the office in Springfield while Stuart is away for the Congressional session in Washington City. I make an entry in our ledger book, *Beginning of Lincoln's Administration*. A month later I'm admitted to practice before the United States Circuit Court. All the extra work keeps my mind off matters that would otherwise oppress me.

One night during the first week of December, our regular gathering around the stove at Speed's store turns ugly. Billy Herndon breaches the political boundary once more. He accuses Democrats and the Governor of trying to kill both the State Bank and the Internal Improvements Program. Gossip coming out of the recently adjourned Democrat's state-wide convention and the governor's call for a special session are the bases for his charges.

When Ned Baker takes Billy's side, Stephen Douglas, still sour over his loss to Stuart, challenges the lot of us to three days of public debates. Of course, he doesn't take us on single-handed. He's reinforced by the best of the Democratic Party's orators.

I make the opening speech, and my friend John Calhoun is chosen by the Democrats to rebut me on the following Saturday. I'm at the podium again the day after Christmas to offer the Whig summation. When I attack the astounding expenses amassed under the alleged fiscal conservatism of General Jackson's and Mr. Van Buren's administrations, Douglas and his friends squirm in their seats. A chorus of boos erupts when I point out that during the last ten years the federal government has spent more money than it did the first twenty-seven.

I also take aim at the Democrats' proposed Sub-Treasury system under which the government's hard currency and notes would be kept in the Treasury Building in Washington City, though some would be doled out to sub-treasurers at branch offices located in various cities around the country.

Douglas and his men begin murmuring when I complain the system will reduce the quantity of money in general circulation, greatly increasing the troubles faced by merchants and the poor. "Giving money over to the Sub-Treasurer would be like asking Judas to carry the purse for the Savior and his disciples. If we know anything about human nature, we must consider that self interest will often prevail over duty, and that the Sub-Treasurer might well prefer opulent knavery in a foreign land to honest poverty at home."

I hope a stylish young lady who's seated in the second row of the auditorium is as impressed as the gleam in her eye suggests. Her apparent interest in politics is somewhat out of the ordinary, since women don't have the privilege of voting. Afterward when I inquire of Speed whether he knows the girl, he tells me her name is Mary Todd, called Molly by her family. She has recently left her father's home in Lexington to live with her sister Lizzie Edwards, wife of the aristocratic Whig Ninian Edwards. She is also a cousin to my law partner John Todd Stuart.

A few evenings later, Speed insists I go along with him to a Christmas dance. He says all the eligible girls will be attending. I argue that no self-respecting girl would have a second glance at me, and if she did I would be inclined to question her judgment. He presses me nonetheless, and I eventually agree, but with trepidation.

Near the end of the dance, Speed drags me to a circle of girls to introduce me to Miss Todd. As we navigate the waltzing couples, he warns me that behind her vivacious, society girl charm lurks a temperamental streak. My mouth is dry as I rehearse in my head what I should say to her.

By the time Speed whispers in her ear and they glance in my direction, perspiration dampens my collar as well as the rest of my shirt. Her blue-gray eyes and short stature remind me of my sister Sally, though her frame is slightly plump, rather than muscular.

She smiles ... then greets me in French.

I stutter, "Miss Todd, I want ... to dance ... with you in the worst way."

When she consents, delight and fright collide within me, and as the dance ensues, my delight gives way to embarrassment, and my fright stumbles into horror. I teeter with each step, and my foot lands on hers so often my face grows hot. By the end of our waltz, my shirt sticks to my skin. My only salvation is that it's covered by my black suit coat.

Miss Todd looks up at me and wrinkles her nose. "Why Mr. Lincoln, it seems you have succeeded."

I raise an eyebrow. "Succeeded?"

She giggles. "Why, yes. You've danced with me in the worst possible way."

My shoulders droop. "I'm sorry."

She comes close and peers up into my eyes, smiling. "Don't let it bother you. It didn't bother me."

"Sorry, dances make me nervous."

"Mr. Lincoln," she says. "There are more important things in this world than dancing. I hope to have the pleasure of seeing you again."

My throat tightens. "Thank you, Miss Todd."

"Please, call me Molly. All my friends do."

My heart races. "Yes, Molly. May I call on you this Saturday?"

She curtsies. "Saturday will be fine."

I nod. "Best be going, now."

She frowns. "Must you?"

Shadows of past heartaches warn me not to linger. "Yes, I truly must."

When Speed returns from the party, he rustles me awake. "Tell me. How did it go with Molly?"

I rub the sleep from my eyes. "Uh ... let me sleep. I'll tell you in the morning."

He shakes me harder. "No. You'll tell me now."

I sit up and rake my fingers through my hair.

Speed plants his hands on his hips. "Well?"

"She said I danced in the worst possible way."

He laughs. "Is that all?"

"No," I draw my knees up to my chest. "She said I can call on her this Saturday."

"Good job." He clutches my shoulder. "So we'll have to get your suit spruced up ... and you'll need to get her some kind of winter nosegay ...."

I rest my chin on my knees, frowning. "I'm not sure this is all such a good idea."

Speed sits on the bed, crossing his legs in front of him. "You're kidding, right?"

"What could she possibly see in me?"

"True," he says. "You're not much to look at. Maybe she's desperate."

"Exactly right."

"Is she pregnant?"

I glare at him. "Another fella's child could never be ugly enough to fool anyone."

He puts his hand on my shoulder. "Look. You're not so ugly as you think—and you have great qualities. You're funny, clever, and most of all, there's not a man alive who can match your intelligence."

I look down. "You forget one big problem."

"What's that?"

My eyes mist over. "Supposing she loves me, and I love her. She'll likely die and break my heart."

He rubs my head. "You've had some bad knocks, but that doesn't mean life is always going to bite you."

"I want to believe that ... but I'm afraid to."

Speed gets up and starts changing into his bedclothes. "Let's get some sleep. Maybe things will look better to you in the morning."

The following Saturday I walk over to Ninian Edwards' two-story brick mansion. A dozen frontier cabins could fit comfortably within its interior. When I first came to live in Springfield, Speed would bring me here for Sunday afternoon soirees. Later, Ninian sought appointment by the State Assembly as Attorney General, and I voted for him. Two years after that he showed up in Vandalia as part of Sangamon County's delegation; he was a dutiful Whig.

Reputed for his vanity and hot temper, he's not well liked. However, his father, a former governor, wielded a great deal of power that he passed on to his son. Most men tolerate Ninian's arrogance in hopes of tapping into the Edwards' wealth and influence. The womenfolk swarm over him, attracted by his dashing figure and social position. He's quick at reminding me he's my elder by two months.

Andy, the Edwards' Negro butler, answers the door and ushers me to the parlor. After a few moments, Ninian's wife Lizzie, a dainty, well-bred young woman, joins me in the parlor. "I'm sorry, Mr. Lincoln, but my husband isn't home."

"That's quite all right," I fidget with the brim of my hat. "I told your fellow, Andy, I came ... to call on ... uh ... Miss Todd."

She screws up her face. "Molly?"

"Yes, Miss Molly."

She gestures to the black horse-hair sofa. "I'll be just a minute."

I remain standing as she walks off.

While I'm left waiting, a tickle irritates my throat. It won't go away. I glance around for something that might help. A small table across the room holds a vase with a nosegay of evergreens. I stare at it for a moment, mulling whether a sip of water might offer some relief. Before I can make up my mind to do so, Miss Todd and her sister Lizzie appear at the doorway. I let out an unrestrained cough. "Excuse me."

Lizzie scowls.

Molly's lips curl into a coy smile.

Chapter Twenty One

U ntil the legislative session adjourns in late January, Molly and I spend little time together. It's probably for the better. Melancholy has been my constant companion for weeks, and if she saw that side of me, I'm sure she wouldn't fancy me as much as I'm told she does.

The Democrats buried the program of internal improvements—passing a resolution to suspend construction of new bridges, railroads, dams, and canals. Even those projects which have been completed are required to halt operations until more capital is available. Nothing can be done about it until we reconvene, so I'll try to put the dreary business out of my mind and put on a more cheerful face.

I walk six long blocks to the Edwards' mansion, bracing against a bitter wind. The butler answers the door, and Lizzie, standing behind him, rolls her eyes. She calls over her shoulder in an icy tone, "Molly, it's Mr. Lincoln."

"Good day, Lizzie," I say.

She says nothing and points to the parlor.

It takes Molly only a minute to join me on the horse-hair sofa. We both look over at Lizzie standing in the hallway.

Lizzie scowls back at us, her hands on her hips. I turn to Molly with a quizzical look. Lizzie tosses her head back and walks away.

I say to Molly. "What's your sister in a huff about?"

"My high-and-mighty brother-in-law lectured me after you came calling. He doesn't want me to give my attentions to the likes of a fellow so 'rough cut.'" She looks down. "He'd rather see me keeping company with the 'Little Giant' Douglas."

"I see."

"You know, he's quite incensed about not being re-nominated by the Whigs for a seat in the legislature. He's talking about joining the Democrats."

I look out the window beyond the snow covered lawn. A bank of storm clouds is gathering on the horizon. "It seems he's intent now on carrying a grudge against all of us Whigs."

She takes my hand. "Maybe we should tread lightly. We can exchange letters, and when you have time to call on me, we can meet somewhere private."

I squeeze her hand. "I'm sorry I've been scarce lately. The session got brutal toward the end."

"I understand."

"You know, I'm going to be away an awful lot. There's the Circuit coming up, the law office where I'm canoeing up river without a paddle thanks to your cousin Stuart's re-election campaign, and the national campaign coming up in the fall."

She gazes out the window. "You're worth waiting for."

I shake my head. "Why is that?"

She beams. "Why, haven't I told you? You're going to make me Mrs. President some day."

I laugh. "You have quite an imagination."

In early April, Speed and I are preparing to turn in for the night when we hear a loud, persistent knocking on the store's front door. We pull on our trousers and scramble downstairs.

On opening the front door, we find Speed's older brother James, his face drawn, eyes sagging and bloodshot. He's travelled all the way from Louisville.

Speed grabs his brother's arm. His voice is pitched as he says, "What is it?"

I can't imagine the news is anything good.

James clutches Speed's shoulder. "It's Father."

Speed's eyes widen. "What of Father?"

"He's dead," James whispers.

Speed shrinks back. "Dead? How?"

James shakes his head. "Fever."

Speed throws his arms around James and buries his face in his brother's chest. Both men sob.

After their sobbing subsides, I guide James inside and find both of them chairs to sit in. Then I stand away from them to give them space to grieve.

After James explains the sudden illness that took their father, he helps his brother pack to leave for the family's Farmington estate near Louisville. Speed wants to start out right away.

As they climb in James' buggy I ask Speed, "How long will you be gone?"

He glances at his brother.

James looks at me. "That's hard to say. We'll be talking about that along the way."

During Speed's absence, my mood is dark, and memories of winter chills riddle my bones, despite the warming weather. I bury myself in work.

Weeks later, when Speed returns, his normally bright eyes are dull, and his face is drawn. His countenance is not solely from mourning.

My chest tightens. "It's good to have you back."

He stares blankly into the horizon. "They want me to move back. To take over the plantation."

"What about James? He's the elder."

"His law practice is too lucrative to abandon. They say it's time for my frontier adventure to come to an end. My place is Farmington."

My heart races. "You don't want to go, do you? You'd be a slave master."

"Not sure it's about what I want. I'm about duty."

"There has to be another way. You don't have any duty to become a slave master."

"It's my father's legacy."

Welts rise on my back where Father used to whip me. I mutter under my breath, "Damn our fathers. Why are we bound to their legacies?"

"What did you say?"

"Nothing worth repeating,"

We stand in silence for a moment, then I ask, "How long before you leave?"

"Don't know."

"What'll you do with the store?"

"Sell it, I guess."

I gaze at him. He shakes his head. "I'm not even sure I'm going back."

"Do you have to decide right away?"

He furrows his brow. "Don't know. Need to go upstairs—I'm tired."

I don't wait long for Speed to make up his mind about leaving before I seek out new lodging. William Butler, an old friend from New Salem who loaned me his horse when I removed to Springfield, is now Clerk of the Sangamon County Court. Speed and I have taken meals with him and his family most evenings since they moved here, and now he offers to rent me a large room in his spacious home.

When I tell Speed of my plans to move in with the Butlers, he insists on joining me. My room will be bigger than the loft we've been sharing. On top of that, he'll be able to tout our old living quarters as extra storage space. I agree, though a twinge in my chest complains that I'll be abetting his plans to return to Farmington.

On a sweltering July evening the Courthouse in Springfield is packed with folks who've come to hear candidates make pitches for votes. Judge Jesse B. Thomas, Jr., who presided over the Truett murder trial, is one of the Democrats running for the legislature.

In an eloquent fashion fitting his refined manners, Thomas accuses members of the Sangamon delegation of chicanery and swapping votes for favors. When he finishes, I take the podium and exaggerate his voice and gestures, caricaturing his walk as I pace the stage.

I point to Thomas. "He says Sangamon County men are *devious, underhanded.*"

Whigs in the audience snicker.

I spit out seemingly odious words as if they have a bitter taste. "They *compromise.* Vote for *railroads* and *canals* that are certain to bring greater prosperity to our state. What do they receive in *exchange?*" I wag my finger in the air. "*Votes*—votes to make *Sangamon* County the *center* of *banking* and *power.*" I turn my thumbs down.

Others join the Whigs, roaring their approval.

Pointing to Thomas again, I mimic his voice, chanting, "Shame. Shame. Shame."

Many in the crowd look at Thomas and echo, "Shame. Shame. Shame."

I say, "Thomas, here, has been soft on the scoundrels. Surely he should have turned them over to the sheriff as thieves. After all, they must have robbed the other politicians of their votes. How else would our legislators have voted for the Internal Improvements bill? Surely, no honest politician would have supported better transportation systems, more efficient commerce, and prosperity for the average man."

With a host of folks laughing, heckling him, and calling him names, Thomas bolts from the arena. Someone calls out from the back of the hall, "Lincoln's made the old fellow cry." Hearing that, I chase down Thomas to make my apologies. Of late, my head is ruled by gloom, jealousy, and resentment. It is I who should be ashamed. I shall never again go to such an extreme in attacking an opponent.

The next day, after winning re-election, melancholy continues to taunt me. It would overwhelm me except for nine cases pending before the Illinois Supreme Court that require my attention. The national election three months hence also occupies me.

I'd rather the Whigs had nominated Henry Clay, the Senator from Kentucky for president. He's my ideal candidate. Every Whig heart should burn with the same zeal that he has for our country's prosperity and glory. We are proof to the world that free men can prosper.

Mr. Clay's predominant sentiment, from first to last, is a deep devotion for the cause of human liberty, a strong sympathy with the oppressed everywhere, and an ardent wish for their elevation. He believes the elevation of the oppressed must be gradual. Otherwise freedom, if not all of civilization, would be crushed by the force of such drastic change. I concur.

Instead of Clay, we nominate William Henry Harrison to block Democrat Martin Van Buren from winning a second term as president. I crisscross the state making speeches on Harrison's behalf. In my speeches, I try to turn Illinois voters against Van Buren by criticizing his advocacy of reckless polices being debated in his home state of New York. He supports laws allowing free Negroes to vote and slaves to testify against white men in court.

Upstate abolitionists accuse me of being pro-slavery. I reply, "I am by nature opposed to slavery, but I agree with Senator Clay. Equality of the races is too abrupt of a change."

The down-state slavery sympathizers complain I'm a friend of abolition. I try to reassure them that the slave system is safe, though wrong. "It is protected by the Constitution which makes the Negro lesser than the White in terms of franchise."

Neither side is appeased, nor do my efforts have much effect on the outcome. The Democrat Van Buren wins our state's Electors, but Harrison becomes the first Whig to be elected president.

In late November, when I return from campaigning for the national ticket and traveling the judicial Circuit, I call on Molly. Her face is aglow when she comes into the Edwards' parlor to greet me. Lizzie hovers out in the hallway, pursing her lips and glaring at the bouquet of flowers in my hand. She's shadowed by a willowy, blue-eyed girl, whose golden hair reminds me of Annie. Her features, though, are more like those of a goddess than a frontier girl.

"Mr. Lincoln," Molly says. "I'm so delighted you've come. Won't you have a seat?" She leads me to the sofa.

"Oh ... yes, thank you." I take my seat and glance at the girl. Her beauty captivates me.

Molly puts one hand to her mouth. "My goodness, pardon my rudeness." She motions for the girl to join us in the parlor. "Mr. Lincoln," Molly says, "this is my cousin, Matilda. Her father is Cyrus Edwards. I'm sure you know him; he's a Senator from Alton, and young Mattie has come along with him for the legislative session."

I stand and nod. "Miss Edwards, it's a pleasure to make your acquaintance."

Mattie curtsies and smiles. "Call me Mattie. Everyone else does."

I look down at the flowers in my hand. "Oh, Molly." My face warm with embarrassment. "These are for you."

She touches my hand as she takes the bouquet. "Why, thank you. You shouldn't have."

Molly smiles at Lizzie. "Thank you for showing Mr. Lincoln in. I'm sure he has many things to tell me about his exploits on the campaign trail and the Circuit."

My eyes are drawn again to Miss Mattie, her supple figure swaying as she follows Lizzie into the hallway.

Molly sits next to me, folding her hands in her lap. "I enjoyed every one of your letters while you were away."

I look down and pinch the creases in my trousers. "I enjoyed yours as well."

"Did you mean what you said about making future plans?"

"Oh ..." I glance toward the hallway, then look back at Molly. "Yes. It seems to me the right thing to do."

"The right thing?" she says, pursing her lips.

"Yes, the right thing because of our feelings."

"Precisely what feelings are you referring to?"

I press my palms onto my legs. "Why ... uh ... feelings of love, I reckon."

She raises her voice. "You reckon?"

"I reckon for sure."

"Then you mean you love me?"

"Yes, I love you."

A smile unfolds across her face. "And I love you, Mr. Lincoln."

I slide off the sofa and kneel in front of her. "Molly, will you marry a poor, homely fellow such as me?"

She takes my hands in both of hers. "Why Mr.

Lincoln, I'd be proud to be the wife of such a bright, enterprising, clever man as yourself."

We both stand, and I gather her into my arms. She clutches me tight around the waist. Just as I lean down to kiss her, a loud "Humph," from the hallway stops me.

I turn to find Lizzie again standing in the doorway. "Mr. Lincoln," she says, her eyes narrowed. "In this house we have certain protocols. Springfield is not some backwoods village."

Molly steps back and glares at her sister. "Mr. Lincoln has just proposed marriage."

Lizzie plants her hands on her hips. "As your guardians, I'm sure Ninian and I will want to discuss the matter when he comes home."

Molly presses the back of her hand to her forehead.

Lizzie glares up at me. "And, as for you Mr. Lincoln, I imagine my husband will have a word with you, as well."

"Yes, Ma'am."

Her face hardens and she points to the door. "It would be best if you took your leave ... now."

As I stand and tread lightly into the hallway, she stares in the opposite direction. When I pause at the front door and glance to the top of the stairway, Miss Mattie smiles down at me. Her image prompts me to ponder Shakespeare's verse.

From fairest creatures we desire increase,
That thereby beauty's rose might never die

More of the bard's verse taunts me as I walk back to the office.

Music to hear, why hear'st thou music sadly?
Sweets with sweets war not, joy delights in joy.
Why lov'st thou that which thou receiv'st not gladly'
Or else receiv'st with pleasure thine annoy?

At my desk, I stare at a stack of promissory notes our firm has been hired to collect. My mind stays fixed on the memory of Mattie's alluring smile and striking features. The sheen of her hair gives it a near halo appearance. Her shapely curves and alabaster skin can only belong to some heavenly being. No woman has consumed my thoughts this way since Annie.

The next morning, I'm awakened by pounding on my office door. "Lincoln," a man shouts. "Are you in there?"

I roll off the sofa and spring to my feet.

He bangs again. "Lincoln! It's Ninian Edwards."

I tuck in my shirt and rub the wrinkles out of my suit. "Coming."

When I open the door, Edwards pushes his way past me and stops in the middle of the room. He turns and surveys me, sneering.

"Can I help you?" I ask.

"Lincoln, I'll be direct. You're to stop seeing Molly."

"But —"

He raises his hand. "No buts. I heard about your ridiculous proposal. This thing must stop, now."

"I intend to make her a fine husband."

"Look." He juts out his jaw. "I'm sure your intentions are honorable. You're a popular young man, but your future is nebulous at best. You two are the wrong match."

"Isn't that for her to say?"

"No. As her guardian, this matter is my responsibility. You don't appreciate the demands that society puts on families like ours. She comes from a well-bred home." He glares at me. "Lincoln, you're beneath our station. You are destitute, your education is desultory, you have no culture, no command of social forms and customs."

"My promise to marry her is a contract. She accepted. Even if I wanted to back out, she must agree. Have you spoken with her?"

"I came here this morning hoping you'd have the good sense to let her down—gently. It's not my intent to break the girl's heart."

"So you want me to break her heart, to break a sacred promise?"

"It is for the best, Lincoln. You need to exercise good judgment and consider Molly's best interests."

I walk to the door and hold it open, glaring at him. "Good day, Ninian."

He glares back at me. "I will amend my statement. You show good judgment and do what's in *your* interest, as well. In addition to my family being above your station, we also wield a goodly amount of power."

After he leaves, I rush over to the store and find Speed displaying the day's goods. "Speed, I need your advice."

"Where did you sleep last night?" he asks.

"Oh ... at the office. Had things on my mind."

He unrolls a new bolt of fabric. "That makes two of us who slept alone ... and on such a cool night."

"Sorry. Didn't think about ...."

He laughs. "Frankly, I was hoping for someone a bit daintier, someone who wouldn't take up so much of the bed."

I cock my head. "Anyone in particular?"

"Maybe."

"Thought you were planning to sell the store and go back to Farmington. You were going to court a girl back there."

He rubs his forehead. "Still haven't made up my mind to leave. Been thinking a lot about a local belle."

"Who is it this time?"

A customer comes through the door, and Speed motions for me to have some coffee and wait while he attends to business. When he finishes he says, "I met the most exquisite beauty the other day. She's just come to town with her father and will be staying through the legislature's special session."

"What's she like?"

He gazes out the door. "Clear blue eyes, a brow as fair as Palmyra marble touched by the chisel of Praxilites. Lips so sweet, fair, and lovely that I'm jealous even of the minds that kiss them. A form as perfect as Venus de Medici's. Her mind is clear as a bell, and her voice bewitching, soft, and sonorous. She smiles so sweetly, playfully, that her soul shines through it. All these charms combined in one young lady."

"Who is she?" I take a sip of coffee.

"Matilda Edwards. Her father is a Senator from Alton."

I choke on the coffee.

He tosses me a rag. "Aren't you happy for me?"

"Of course I am." I look toward the doorway. "Does this mean you might be staying?"

He looks away. "That's another matter. If I can capture her heart, I will take her wherever I go."

I fidget with the coffee mug. My chest tightens. "What about the girl you've talked about over in Louisville?"

He looks down. "Choices. Indeed it seems I'm cursed with an abundance of them lately."

I hang my head.

He looks up. "Oh ... but you wanted to ask me something?"

"No ... it can wait." I force a smile and leave. I could never compete with my dearest friend.

Chapter Twenty Two

T he two-week special legislative session convenes on November 23, and I use it as a pretense for avoiding Molly, as well as other members of the Edwards family. Since the capitol is still not completed, the House meets again in the spacious Second Presbyterian Church, and the Senate conducts business in the Methodist Church.

The session is uneventful—until the Thursday evening before we're scheduled to adjourn. Ned Baker storms into my office and announces he has uncovered a plot hatched by the Democrats to kill the Bank.

He says, "They plan to take a vote tomorrow to adjourn the special session without extending the Bank's ability to suspend payments in gold and silver."

I send out a call for several key Whigs to gather in my office at once so Baker can fill them in on his news. When they arrive, he briefs them, and I add, "This isn't supposed to come up until the regular session. The bill we passed last session gives us until the end of the next session to pump more money into the Bank to fix the problem."

Baker throws up his hands. "Apparently, this special session is considered to be the 'next' session."

Joseph Gillespie, a tall, hardy man from Madison County, pounds his fist on the wall. "That means the Bank will be in violation of its charter and it will be revoked automatically."

Baker shakes his head. "They're trying to sneak one past us. What can we do?"

I grin. "If we don't adjourn, unfinished business—including the Bank issue—gets carried into the regular session that starts Monday."

We agree to round up all the Whigs and boycott the final day of the session. No quorum, no vote, no adjournment. Two of us must remain in the hall to demand a roll call vote on the adjournment motion. The roll call is necessary to provide a record that a quorum is not present.

The next morning Gillespie and I sit in the back of the hall swapping stories and laughing while the Sergeant-at-Arms is out hunting down the absent legislators. A couple of hours later our laughter ends when he returns, having rounded up enough Whigs for a quorum. Turning to Gillespie, I point to a window, the only possible exit that isn't blocked, and motion to the other Whigs who've just been rounded up. As the Democrats rejoice at having spoiled our scheme, we make a dash for the window. I throw it open and jump out. The others follow. The drop from the sill to the ground is nearly five feet.

A short time later, we learn that our plan failed. The Speaker ruled that not enough of us made it out the window before the vote was taken. In the space of a few seconds, most of what I achieved in four terms as a legislator is undone, and all anyone will remember of me is the gangly buffoon who jumped out a window. I retreat to my room and cover myself with a blanket, trying to block out the world around me.

After sulking for the entire weekend, I clean up and call on Molly. Miss Mattie answers the door. My heart jumps. She giggles. I can only imagine the awkward expression on my face.

"Will you please tell Molly I'm here?"

She smiles. "Certainly."

She sways supple grace as she walks away. I follow her, almost forgetting to turn into the parlor.

Nearly a half an hour later, Molly appears at the doorway, unsmiling.

I stand to greet her. "How are you, Molly?"

She sits down, crosses her arms, and stares straight ahead.

I sit next to her and repeat. "How are you?"

"I am fine, and you?"

"Fine."

She still doesn't look at me. "Have you been waiting long?"

"No. Not too long."

She turns and glares at me. "Well, I hoped I wasn't making you wait long. After all, one never knows if a person as important as you has the time to wait for anyone."

I hang my head. "It's been a grueling session."

She looks away again. "Yes, and I understand your duties even involve acrobatics."

I study her face for a hint of sympathy, but find none. "Molly, I'm sorry I've neglected you."

"Not at all, Mr. Lincoln." Her eyes are uncommonly dark. "You've shown up just in time to escort me to a dance tonight."

"With my two left feet?"

"If you don't care to go along, I'm sure there are other willing escorts." She purses her lips. "Or maybe Mattie will join me."

"No, Molly. I'll go. What time shall I call?"

"Eight o'clock will be fine." Her smile is more calculated than pleasant.

"Yes. Eight."

She stands. "I'd best get myself ready."

By the time I'm on my feet, she's already in the hallway. I go after her, but stop at the parlor doorway. My gaze follows Molly to the top of the staircase where Mattie is leaning against the banister with a coy smile.

Mattie's image stays with me all the way to Speed's store where I find him busy putting out some new merchandise. I stare at him. "Speed, we need to talk."

He closes the door and puts up the *Closed* sign.

"What's up," he says.

I rake my fingers through my hair. "Have I incurred an obligation to marry that woman?"

"You're engaged, aren't you?"

"Reckon so, but her guardian hasn't given consent."

He grins. "That sounds like a fine line you're trying to draw, Councilor."

"The fact is he disapproves. He told me so."

"That helps."

I bite my lip. "Speed, how do I dodge this thing?"

He scratches his head. "Why is it you all of a sudden don't want to marry her?"

"That's the hard part."

He raises an eyebrow. "Well ...."

"Maybe you're not the one to talk to."

"Look, I know things have been strained between us since my family asked me to come back to the plantation."

I sigh. "I'm in love with her cousin."

"Her cousin?"

"Yes. Mattie. Her cousin."

He tilts his head and his eyes narrow. "Suppose I can understand how that could happen."

I swallow. "That's for sure."

We're silent for a moment.

I rub my knuckles. "Speed, I'm not going to compete with you for Mattie. Even so, it's just wrong for me to marry Molly if I have feelings so easily for someone else."

I reach into my hat and pull out a letter.

Speed stares at it and says, "What's that?"

"I've agonized over this for weeks. There have been times of late when I couldn't drag myself out of bed even to cast votes in the legislature."

He takes the letter. "I've sensed you have been out of sorts, but just chalked it up to my plans to go back to Farmington."

When he finishes reading, I say, "I can't bear to face her. Will you deliver it for me?"

"No."

My pulse races. "I'll get someone else, then."

He waves the letter over his head. "No, you won't because I'm not giving it back."

I reach for the letter.

He ducks under my arms and lunges toward the stove, clutching the letter to his chest.

I wheel around and glare at him.

He stands in front of the stove, facing me. "Look, this letter is a bad idea. In private conversation words are forgotten ... misunderstood ... passed by. But once you put them in writing, they stand as an eternal monument. A letter shuts off any hope for a second chance if you change your mind."

I slump into a chair and lower my head. "What should I do?"

"Go see her and lay out your heart. It's the honorable thing."

I look up at him. "What are you going to do about Mattie?"

"Oh ...." He combs his fingers through his hair. "I've been holding off letting people know until I told you first."

I search his eyes. They're as soft as I've ever seen them.

He puts his hand on my shoulder. "I'm selling the store and going back to Kentucky. The matter should be settled at supper tonight."

I stare out the window. My heart aches. Pain rises from my chest and pinches my throat. "Speed, you can't leave me."

"I will miss you," he says.

I search his eyes. "We can't let this affection we have for each other die out."

He looks away. "We'll write ... often ... and I'll let you know how things go with Fanny."

"So you're not going for Mattie?"

He flinches. "No. I'm done with that."

His words are bittersweet.

He shakes his head. "Can you imagine a girl so consumed by her own beauty that she boasts, 'Well, if all the young men like me, it is of no fault of mine?'"

My jaw drops. "She said that?"

"Yes, can you believe it?"

I rub the back of my neck. "So, she's just a tease."

"She's a goddess, but she prefers eating a man's heart to holding onto it."

"Thanks for the warning."

We embrace and promise to keep our friendship

alive. On my way out, I stop at the door and ask when he'll be home.

He shakes his head, "I'll be late. Will try not to disturb you."

I trudge back to the Butlers', dragging my feet; my shoulders droop. If only the earth would swallow me up and end my pain. Back in our room, I sit in a chair in the corner, pull my hat down over my eyes, and escape into melancholy.

Sometime later, I wake from my trance and bolt from my seat. I'm late to pick up Molly for the dance. I dart out the door without changing clothes and hurry to the Edwards' mansion. On arriving there, Lizzie greets me with her usual chill. She sneers, assessing my appearance, and her face betrays no small amount of satisfaction in telling me Molly has already gone to the dance on her own.

I rush over to the Leverings' home where the affair is under way, and survey the single ladies seated in the parlor; Molly is not among them. I make my way to the dining hall, hoping to find her dancing there with Mattie. As I'm scanning the room her cousin steps up to me.

"Looking for Molly?" she asks.

"Why, yes. Have you seen her?"

She points and says. "Over there."

I trace the path she indicates with her dainty finger, taking note of each couple as my gaze travels across the room. Then there ... in the middle of the dance floor ... is Molly ... with the little bantam, Stephen Douglas. My blood turns hot.

Mattie giggles.

I straighten my coat, pull back my shoulders and stride past several couples in Molly's direction. I circle behind Douglas and tap his shoulder, staring into my fiancé's eyes. "May I?"

He glances at her then back at me. "Be my guest."

I nod and take her hand.

She stares away. "So you decided to come."

"I'm sorry ...."

"It doesn't matter," she says, still looking away.

"Molly?"

"I came here to dance," she says. "Not to converse."

We stumble through the dance, and at the end of the music I follow her to her seat.

I take her hand. "Molly..."

She pulls it away and glares at me.

"Can we go some place and talk in private?"

She stands without giving a reply, and leads me out onto a side porch.

I study her for a few moments as she stares into the night.

She turns to me, unsmiling. "You wanted to talk, so talk."

"I've been greatly distressed of late."

She sneers. "Yes, Ninian told me about your window jumping escapade. Quite dignified."

"Nearly everything I've ever wanted has fallen apart."

"Nearly, you say?"

I lower my head. "Maybe more than nearly."

She glares at me. "What are you saying, Mr. Lincoln?"

I stare into the black sky, dotted with tiny pins of light. "Providence is a fickle master, don't you think?"

"No. Providence is resolute. Its servants are the ones who vacillate." The edge in her voice softens. "Fate brought us together. Are you wavering, Mr. Lincoln?"

I wince. "Molly, I'm not sure I love you enough to be a faithful husband."

Tears trace the edges of her eyes. "What are you saying?"

"Ever since I met your young cousin I've not been able to get her out of my mind."

"That little witch!" She purses her lips.

"Don't blame her. I'm the one ...."

Her round face grows taut, and her voice turns hoarse. "You're the one who what?"

"I did nothing, but I'm afraid of the things I imagine doing...."

She throws herself at me, pounding my chest with her fists. Tears cascade down her cheeks.

I grab her wrists and pull her into my arms. "Molly, please don't cry. I never wanted to hurt you."

She buries her face in my shirt, sobbing.

"Molly dearest, I'm so sorry."

Her heaving relents, and she gazes up at me. "Do you love me at all?"

I wince. "Yes Molly, of course."

"You know that evil little girl makes a sport of crushing every young man's heart she captures."

"Yes. Reckon she does."

Molly's doe eyes brighten. "Do you suppose we can make another go of it?" She rises on her tip toes, stretching to bring her lips close to mine.

I gaze into her blue-gray eyes, still moistened by tears, wondering if she is right. Maybe I've been too quick to let go. How was it so easy to forget what a magnificent woman she is?

She closes her eyes, and I lean down; my lips meet hers. She wraps her hands around the back of my neck and draws me closer. We kiss the way lovers kiss. When our lips separate she leans her head back and smiles.

"Your brother-in-law doesn't want us to marry." I bite my lip.

Her nostrils flare. "My brother-in-law and little cousin be damned."

After walking Molly home, I go to Speed's store and plop myself on the stoop until he returns. When he arrives, his grin is as wide as the Mississippi, but on surveying my countenance, he turns somber.

"What went wrong?" he says.

I tell him about my talk with Molly, unable to explain how it happened that the engagement is still on.

He furrows his brow. "If you ask me, that kiss of yours was a bad lick ... but it can't be helped now."

I knead my knuckles. "What should I do?"

"Suppose you'll have to give it a try for now."

I hang my head. "That's not how things were supposed to turn out."

He clutches my shoulder. "She's not going to let you off easy, friend. You'll just have to be more resolute than she is."

For a moment, I'm lost in thought, imagining how to get loose from her grip. Then I look up at Speed. "How did your business go tonight?"

He looks away. "I'll know soon."

Silence fills the space between us for a long moment.

After a while, Speed sits next to me. "Say, I have an idea."

I cock my head. "Okay."

"You want to get some?"

"What?" I stare at him in disbelief.

He digs into his pocket and pulls out his card and a pen. Scribbling a note on the back of it he says, "Here. There's a girl who can take care of you. This is where you can find her. If you give her my card she'll see you."

I shake my head. "Are you sure about this?"

"Yes," he says. "This is the perfect thing."

"Last time it ended in disaster."

"Hey, this girl knows how to take your mind off your troubles. Besides, what better way to prove to yourself you don't love Molly?"

I trudge over to the inn, following Speed's directions; my shoulders sag and my feet weigh like anchors. When I stand at the door to her room, my face turns hot and my palms sweat. My balled up hand is poised next to my ear, waiting to knock.

After a seeming eternity, I rap on the door. Another eternity passes before she answers. Had she waited one more second, she wouldn't have found me there.

She studies Speed's card. A smile unfolds across her face, and softly she says, "Come on in."

I stand just inside the closed door and watch her disrobe, a war waging in my head. My hands hang at my sides as if pinned in place. Am I so determined to prove I'm unfit to marry?

The girl turns, displaying two twists of chestnut hair cascading over her pale shoulders.

My gaze stops at the base of her throat.

She glides up to me, gently manipulating the buttons on my shirt. My breath weakens to a mere whisper as she unfastens my frayed suspenders and guides my trousers to the floor. She takes my hand and leads me to the bed where we lie beside each other.

After a moment of silence I turn to her and say, "How much do you charge?"

She laughs. "How much …?"

My face turns hot from embarrassment.

"Five dollars."

My throat is dry. "I only have three."

She laughs again. "You can owe me the two. If you don't pay, I'll take it out of Speed's hide."

"I can't."

She rolls over and glares at me. "Why not?"

"I just can't." My skin itches. I get out of the bed and start to dress.

She furrows her brow. "I can't believe this."

My fingers fumble with the buttons on my trousers. "I'm sorry, I'm too much in debt already."

I let myself out.

On my return to the Butlers, I sit quietly in my room—my hat pulled down over my eyes—and enter that dark space that's become so familiar to me of late.

A few days later, on the eve of the New Year, I stand at the basin in my room, washing. Welts cover my body. My heart freezes. Is the syphilis returning to take its vengeance? I stare in the mirror. Tonight ends a leap year, and according to the customs of society, I must declare my intentions for Molly before the midnight hour.

On the way to the Edwards' mansion I labor over each step, no different from a condemned man climbing the gallows steps. Turning the corner past Speed's store, I find him locking the front door.

I ask him if all is well.

He replies, "Yes, but probably too well."

"What does that mean?"

"The store sold. I leave in the morning."

My breath catches in my chest. I can't swallow. The world around me begins to spin.

Speed grabs me, steadies me. "Are you all right?"

"Just give me a minute."

He guides me to a chair he keeps on the porch.

I take slow, deep breaths. My shoulders relax.

He lays his hand on my shoulder. "This isn't the end, you know. A friendship like ours can never die."

"But it will never be the same."

Silence fills the space between us.

After a few moments I stand and ask, "Will you be sleeping at the Butler's tonight?"

"No," he says. Have some other goodbyes to say.

We embrace without saying another word. What good are words anyway?

Later in the evening when I arrive at the Edwards' mansion, Molly is in a gay mood dancing with Edwin Webb, a stylish widower who's much older than she. Lizzie walks up beside me, smiling. "They make a fine couple, don't you think?"

My mouth hangs open. I turn and rush outside, down the pathway, onto the street.

Just after midnight, after hours of wandering the streets, I return to the Edwards' to have words with Molly. Lizzie shows me to the parlor where I wait for hours, seated on the sofa, seething. When the last of the holiday guests leave, Molly appears. Her lips are drawn tight, her nostrils flared.

I stand. My jaw set. "We can't marry." My resolve is as strong with her as it was with Speed's girl.

Her face turns red. "Go," she shouts as she stamps her foot and points to the door.

I plod through the muddy streets for more than an hour before finding myself at the law office seated at my desk, staring at mounds of paper. If only Stuart was here.

The longer I stare at my desk, the darker my mood grows. In time I'm caught in a black whirlpool. It sucks me downward, just like the creek that nearly swallowed me when I was a boy. Days later I wake up in Dr. Anson Henry's infirmary. As he's my friend, I'm accustomed to the brusque manner in which the doctor tells me I suffer from hypochondria brought on by anxiety, overwork, and exhaustion.

I tell him, "I am now the most miserable man living. If what I feel were equally distributed to all of humanity, there would not be a single cheerful face on the earth. To remain as I am is impossible; I must die or get better."

Speed comes to visit, having postponed his departure until I could see him. He tells me they have removed all the knives and razors from my room. I'll be in good hands with the Butlers and Dr. Henry, he says. The nurse interrupts us, handing me a cup of dark peppery water. "Here, take this," she says. Almost instantly my stomach wrenches into knots.

Later, Dr. Henry applies heated glass cups on my temples and behind my ears, drawing blood to the surface. Then he applies leeches to suck out the blood. Over the ensuing days, he feeds me arsenic, strychnine, and little blue mercury pills. My puking is interrupted only when a soupy discharge rushes out of my bowels.

He says, "You'll feel weaker, but once we force out the black bile from your entrails, you'll be on the mend."

By week's end I'm emaciated—dehydrated and malnourished. My stools turn green, and the doctor is pleased. I would pay a king's ransom for a little sleep.

I regain enough strength in late January to return to the legislature for an important vote. Though my body is present, my spirit teeters at the edge of a dark abyss. My evenings are made passable by joining friends around the fireplace in the Butlers' parlor, telling stories and reading poetry. Often, I recite my favorite poem:

> *Oh! why should the spirit of mortal be proud?*
> *Like a swift-fleeting meteor, a fast-flying cloud*
> *A flash of the lightning, a break of the wave*
> *He passeth from life to his rest in the grave.*
> *The leaves of the oak and the willow shall fade,*
> *Be scattered around, and together be laid;*
> *And the young and the old, and the low and the high,*
> *Shall moulder to dust, and together shall lie.*
> *...*
> *Yea! hope and despondency, pleasure and pain,*
> *Are mingled together in sunshine and rain;*
> *And the smile and the tear, the song and the dirge,*
> *Still follow each other, like surge upon surge.*
> *'Tis the wink of an eye -- 'tis the draught of a breath—*
> *From the blossom of health to the paleness of death,*
> *From the gilded saloon to the bier and the shroud:—*
> *Oh! why should the spirit of mortal be proud?*

On mornings when I can't drag my body down to the legislature, I'm in my room dressed in bedclothes with the window coverings drawn, writing verse. Stories and poetry are better medicine than the little blue doses of mercury Dr. Henry prescribes to subdue my "hypos"—his pet name for my condition.

The pills make me irritable, as if seeing Molly strolling on Douglas' arm isn't unsettling enough. My failures in the legislature haunt me as well. When I think of Speed leaving for Farmington, a dull pain pinches my heart. I would bury myself in legislative work to keep my mind off those things, but I'm lost this session without Stuart's guidance.

At Dr. Henry's urging I write to Dr. Daniel Drake, a renowned physician who resides in Louisville. I describe my condition as well as the brutal treatment I've recently survived, telling him I'd rather die than endure the likes of it again. I add a note about my fears over the syphilis I may have contracted due to a devilish passion in Beardstown. My hopes are not high that he'll have good news for me. In his response, he invites me to pay him a visit.

In early March, Stuart returns from Washington and begins reciting a tedious litany of details regarding the recent Congressional session.

I swallow hard. "Stuart, I cannot continue as your partner. I'm only a little better off now than I was as my father's hireling. I make the bread, but you get to eat most of it."

"Be patient," he says. "Your time will come."

"That's not all. Even when you're not away, you're always preoccupied. I can never amount to much of a lawyer without someone to tutor me."

He puffs out his chest. "You're doing your country a service by making it possible for me to continue in Congress."

"If I work on improving myself, I can go to Congress someday and do greater good."

He folds his arms across his chest. "Since it seems you're determined to leave, I hope we can still be friends."

"Yes. I would like to remain friends."

As I'm packing my few belongings, Ned Baker drops in to be sure I'm well. I tell him I'm leaving Stuart. He says he's dissolving his partnership with Stephen Logan, and the Judge would like for me to take his place. Logan's invitation is a great compliment as I have tried cases before him when he was a judge on the Circuit. I've also argued against him a few times since he re-entered private practice. He's a hot tempered old prune, but a master lawyer and the leader of the Springfield Bar.

When my things are packed, I visit Judge Logan. He makes an offer, and I readily accept. Whereas Stuart was always absent, Logan hovers over me as I work, always poised to correct me. Even when his manner is callous, his criticism inspires me to become a better lawyer. His chief aims are succinctness, clarity, and avoiding technicalities which clutter up the salient points of a case. When examining my briefs he crosses out page after page of nonsense, legal formalities, and the like, saying, "This is what we want to say, just these twelve lines, not these fourteen pages."

By keeping me focused on work, Logan distracts me from miseries that besiege me—seeing Molly in the company of other men, knowing my word and my honor were spoiled by my broken promise, imagining Speed lording over his slaves, Dr. Henry's medical persecution. All of it haunts me, even in my dreams. The law becomes my refuge.

In the July term of the State Supreme Court, although we're partners, Logan and I argue opposite sides of a case under appeal. The suit involves collection of a promissory note given in exchange for the sale of a slave girl. The trial court in Tazewell County found in favor of Logan's client, the creditor. I represent the debtor on appeal.

In my summation I say, "Under the Ordinance of 1787 and the Constitution of this state, the presumption of the law is that every person is free without regard to color. Accordingly, the sale of a free person is illegal, and any debt given in exchange for such purchase is void."

The judges agree, and my client is absolved of the debt. Logan's mentoring has cost him dearly. In a small measure, the court's decision salves the lingering injury I bear from times when Father hired me out as a laborer and kept my wages to pay off his imprudent debts. The case also fuels my resentment over his indolence, which led him to drive us into the wilderness where my angel mother withered and died.

Chapter Twenty Three

One afternoon in early August, Molly and Douglas are strolling down the street, arm-in-arm. A punishment I deserve. My pulse runs wild. I hurry to my room at the Butlers' and plop in my chair, pulling my hat down over my eyes. If only Speed were here to lift me out of the mire.

Sometime later, Mrs. Butler knocks on my door, calling me to supper. After joining the family at the dining table, I announce, "I have a mind to leave tomorrow for a visit with Speed in Kentucky."

Farmington. The Speed family plantation is a place I've not wanted to believe exists, but now I'm almost there.

Along the five mile carriage ride to Farmington from the Louisville steamboat dock, Speed attempts, with little success, to coach me on the etiquette of fine living. As the carriage turns down a dusty lane bordered by lush gardens he says, "Just follow my lead. Whatever you see me do, copy it." The elegant two story brick mansion looms before us. He tells me there are fourteen rooms, and the estate was built by his father on a plan laid out by Thomas Jefferson.

When the Negro driver pulls to a stop in front of the mansion, Speed's mother, his twelve siblings, and an aunt are lined up to welcome us. A battery of household slaves flanks them on either side. I poke Speed. "Are they expecting a crowned prince?"

After greeting each member of the family, I follow Speed inside where embroidered fabrics cover plush furniture, elegant tapestries hang the entire length of walls, and lavish draperies frame massive windows. Strategically arranged around the entry and down the great hallway is an assortment of polished wooden tables, each bearing a large porcelain vase stuffed with flowers. I nearly trip over my feet while gawking.

My room—to the left as we enter the hallway—is larger than my boyhood home. Waiting for us in the room is a Negro who will serve as my valet. I argue that I'd feel more comfortable dressing myself, but Speed silences me. He goes on to apologize for being unable to provide me with a formal jacket as there are no men in the family with a frame as long as mine.

Later that evening when the dinner bell is rung, I put on my jeans suit according to Speed's instruction. On entering the colossal dining room, I survey his family, all clad in their finery. An ornate table stands in the center of the room bearing gleaming silver and settings of fine bone china. Even the slaves are better dressed than me. I step quickly to Speed's side and say, "I'm out of place here."

He pats me on the shoulder and whispers, "Just follow my lead. When we take our seats, you'll be sitting next to my half-sister, Mary."

I peek over at Mary. She's noticeably older than Speed and me. The aunt whispers something to her, and both women glance sideways at me.

I avoid their stares and scan the table. My stomach tightens at the array of implements lined up on either side of each plate. I whisper to Speed, "Why would a person require all of those to eat a single meal?"

He shrugs.

My temples begin to ache.

During the meal, I mimic Speed's every movement. I don't as much as touch a fork or knife without noting which utensil he chooses and the precise manner in which he holds it. When he stops eating a portion, I lay my utensil aside and wait for the next to be served. Even when

Mary or Mrs. Speed attempt to engage me in conversation, my eyes don't wander far from their focus on Speed.

After supper we take seats in the living room where Mary will entertain us playing the piano. Before Mary starts, Mrs. Speed comes beside me and puts a copy of the *Oxford Bible* into my hands. She expresses the pain she feels for my "extreme melancholy" and says, "Read it and you shall find all you need to bring happiness into your life. Adopt its precepts and pray for its promises."

I thank her and assure her I will do as she says.

As Mary plays, my headache subsides.

Speed leans toward me and whispers, "She composed that piece herself."

I turn to him and stare wide-eyed.

He says that for many years his father sponsored a Bohemian composer named Anton Phillip Heinrich. At one point the musician lived at Farmington and worked on a collection of compositions; he made a great impression on Mary.

I say quietly, "So that's why she never married?"

He nods. "She lost faith that anyone could fulfill her."

Will Molly lose faith in finding a suitable husband, as well? Have I proven that even a man who cherishes truth cannot be counted on to keep his word?

When the music is over, Speed and I talk late into the night about his new life and love, and about my disastrous courtship of Molly. His side of our conversation is animated, full of hope. Mine is gloomy, dull. It's a familiar pattern for us. One of us has always been lifting the other out of the depths of despair.

At some point I say, "Doesn't it bother you that this house was built on the backs of slaves who are not permitted to enjoy it? Even the draperies and tapestries—your fine clothes, as well—are stained by the sweat of those less fortunate than you."

He looks away. After a long silence he says, "I should be off to bed."

The next morning Speed and I go into the hemp fields to view his great economic machine at work. He tells me that at harvest time there are over a dozen plants per square foot, each more than twice a man's height. He often gets three crops a year, sometimes four. Not much hoeing is needed either, since the plants are packed so tightly together they crowd out any weeds that might want to spring up.

"So," I say, pointing to a band of slaves who are singing as they roll up bales of hemp stalks. "Your 'machinery' down there doesn't have to work as hard as it might if you were growing cotton or tobacco."

He shakes his head. "We treat our slaves better than most. They're far better off here than they would be if they were trying to make it in a white man's world."

"It's still like eating bread from the sweat of another man's brow."

He shakes his head. "Friend, I invited you here to lift you out of your misery. Why don't you forget about everything else and try to have some fun?"

I shrug. "It's hard to have fun while you're watching men in a worse state than yourself."

He points to the field below at a chorus of dark-skinned men singing what sounds to be a merry tune. "Do they sound miserable to you?"

I study the Negroes as they bind up the bales. After a moment I say, "Your brother said I could borrow some law books. Why don't we go into town?"

"If that's what you want to do, certainly."

On our walk back to the house he adds, "Anytime you want, you're welcome to talk to our slaves. Ask them for yourself whether they are happy here."

My trips to town to visit James Speed's library become a regular affair. On one occasion, about two weeks after my arrival at Farmington, I look up Dr. Drake who gives me the interview he offered in his letter. He confirms my suspicion, the "little blue masses" of mercury relieve my "hypos" but they make me irritable. I should be more discreet in taking them.

"The first step to happiness," the doctor says "is simply getting out of bed each day, even if it is only out of an instinct to survive or out of a sense of duty. After that, one must keep sight of some great potential that lies in the distance and strive toward it as if little else matters."

"So there is hope that one day I shall be happy."

"That's difficult to say. For some people happiness is not possible."

"Not possible?"

"Happiness isn't the only goal of existence. Pain can be a precious gift. It may enable you to see the world as it truly is. If you don't allow it to oppress you, you can use pain as a stepping stone to a degree of success that few are able to achieve. Even without happiness, you can still find fulfillment."

I hang my head. "One of the great frustrations of my life is that I haven't yet discerned any great purpose to which I've been called."

"Relax," he says. "That will come to you when the time is right. Until then, keep busy as much as Providence allows and take every opportunity to prepare for meeting the challenge when it comes."

I manage a faint smile. "I'll do my best."

"And one more thing ...."

I cock my head. "Yes."

"On this syphilis matter. If you did contract the disease, it seems that you passed the first phase without any difficulty."

I swallow. "I figured so much, but—"

"You said the incident was a few years ago?"

"Yes, about five." I try to read his face.

"You've had no other symptoms?"

"Welts ... a rash ..."

"Where?"

I rub the backs of my hands and arms. "Here ... and sometimes all over my back and down my legs."

He shrugs. "If it had been on your palms, you'd have reason to be concerned. What you had was likely an irritation of the skin from nerves, or from some external source."

When I leave, my step is more buoyant, as if a yoke has been lifted from my shoulders.

That evening at supper another burden is lightened. For the first time, I use the silverware in the correct order, and don't tip my soup bowl to scoop out the last drop of broth. My mood is so gay that while playing a game of hide-and-seek with Mary, I shut her in a closet to keep her from assaulting me. She scoffs at my complaint that she's acting like a child rather than an adult woman of breeding.

When at last I release her from "jail," we laugh together, me harder than I have in a long time.

A few days afterward, Speed takes me along with him to Lexington to meet Miss Fanny Henning, the sweet, raven-haired beauty he hopes to marry—even more beautiful than Mattie Edwards. Fanny is an orphan living with her uncle, John Williamson, an ardent Whig. Speed, now a Democrat, tries to tread lightly so as not to offend the old man, but the uncle nonetheless insists on talking politics. Their conversations become so lengthy that Speed never has enough private time with Fanny to propose marriage.

During our visit, I wink at Speed and begin to engage Fanny's uncle in political banter, pretending to be a Democrat. Our argument becomes so heated that the old man doesn't notice Speed and Fanny slip away to be alone. An hour or so later when they return, the happy couple announces they are now engaged.

I cannot say that the remainder of my days at Farmington are filled with fun and hilarity. In the final week of my holiday, after spending the morning with James in his office discussing slavery issues, I see a local dentist to have a tooth extracted. The operation is a failure; the tooth's nuisance is transformed into a debilitating pain. I can neither talk nor eat. Fortunately, Speed's mother rescues me from my misery by serving me dishes of peaches and cream.

After nearly four weeks at Farmington, Joshua and I leave together; he accompanies me as far as St. Louis. At about noon we board the steamboat *Lebanon* in the locks of the canal that I helped build over a decade ago. Aboard ship, a gentleman who has purchased twelve Negroes in different parts of Kentucky is transporting them to a farm in the South. They are chained together six and six.

A small iron clevis is around the left wrist of each slave, and this is fastened to the main chain by a shorter one at a convenient distance from the others. The Negroes are strung together precisely like so many fish upon a trot-line. In this condition they are being separated forever from the scenes of their childhood, their friends, their fathers and mothers, and brothers and sisters. Many are being torn from their wives and children, going into perpetual slavery in a region where it's said the lash of the master is more ruthless and unrelenting than any other place.

Yet amid all these distressing circumstances, they are the most cheerful and happy creatures on board. One, who was sold as punishment for having an over-fondness for his own wife, plays the fiddle almost continually while the others dance, sing, crack jokes, and play various games of cards. This they do all along as we steam southward. How true it is that "God tempers the wind to the shorn lamb," that He renders the worst of human conditions tolerable while He permits the best conditions to be nothing better than bearable.

Two months later my step-brother John chastises me by letter for failing to aid Father, who's experiencing financial distress. Presumably, he addresses only the immediate case. Otherwise, he proves the point I often make when such requests are made, that Father's suffering is a permanent condition arising out of the old man's indolence. Of course, John always meets my objection by telling me, in all honesty, he is pleading on Mama's behalf. He insists that I should be eager to help, considering all she has done for me.

I argue with myself that my debts are too large to allow me to be of any help. Besides, I have already given him twenty-one years of indenture, which should have been enough. Nonetheless, I saddle up Old Tom and ride off to Coles County for—as everyone will say—a long overdue trip. I resolve along the way not to spend a single night under Father's roof.

Before going inside to greet Father, Mama and I visit in the yard, catching up on news and reminding her of how deeply I love her. She tells me that Father's health and strength are failing and that I should "treat him gently." My memory wanders back to the iron hand with which he beat me and took my wages during my boyhood.

When Mama and I step inside, Father's advanced years are evident in his slouched posture and drawn face, but he's far from death's door. He greets me with his usual scowl. "Was beginnin' to think I'd never see you again."

I clench my teeth, refusing to argue with him.

He stays seated at the table. "Hope yer not plannin' on givin' me one of your speeches."

I furrow my brow. "Wouldn't think of it."

"Why's ya come?" He shifts in his seat.

"John said you have a proposition."

He looks away. "You could say that."

I cock my head. "Well?"

"Git right to the point, huh?"

"Don't see any reason not to."

He looks up at me. "Don't want no charity."

I look away. "None offered."

"Want ya to buy the farm."

I laugh. "What do you expect me to do with it?"

"Nothin'. Just buy it. It's yours for two hundred."

I pull out a chair and sit. "On one condition."

He looks down at the table and mutters, "I'm no child. Don't need to be told how to run my life."

"The condition is that you and Mama will have the privilege of staying here as long as one of you is alive. We'll put it in writing so there's no chance anyone can kick you off if something happens to me."

He looks at Mama. "Fine."

"Fine, then." I reach into my satchel for my writing implements. "I'll draw up the document. We can sign it now, and I'll send the money as soon as I get back to Springfield."

Chapter Twenty Four

S peed marries Fanny on February 15, 1842, the same day Judge Bowling Green dies. Several days later, I step forward at the Judge's Masonic burial to say the eulogy. Among those gathered are many friends he won with his jolly hospitality and good natured ways. My lips quiver, and tears roll down my cheeks. Others in attendance join in a sorrowful chorus as I stand silent, quaking. I loved him like a father.

At the end of the singing, all is quiet. The only words I manage are, "I'm unmanned." Still sobbing, I lumber away from the gravesite and make my way to Mrs. Green's carriage.

Memories of Judge Green's funeral hang over me during the ensuing days as I prepare a speech for the Washington Society of Springfield. They'll be gathering on the one-hundred and tenth anniversary of General Washington's birth to celebrate recent progress in the Temperance movement. The opening portion of my speech is inspired by memories of the kind and unassuming persuasion by which Judge Green drew in and guided the most down-trodden and desperate men—especially young men like myself.

Ned Baker, the London-trained orator, insists on hearing me read my speech the morning before the meeting. He leans back in his chair.

My speech begins,

In the recent past, the warfare against
Intemperance has been erroneous. Its champions
have been Preachers, Lawyers, and hired agents
who suffer from a want of approachability.

"Wait," he says. "You'll lose them at the very start. You can't tell them they've done it all wrong. They're celebrating achievements."

I shake my head. "These Washington Society men are different. Many are reformed drunkards, folks who acknowledge the old ways did not work. They embrace the same principles that Judge Green practiced."

Baker leans forward in his chair. "Surely, there'll be some preachers, lawyers, and agents in the audience wanting to have their feathers stroked."

"Drunkards and dram-sellers don't listen to the old champions. They know preachers advocate temperance because they're fanatics, wanting a union of the Church and State. Lawyers argue for it out of pride and vanity, caring only to hear their own voices. Hired agents are concerned about their own salaries. But when a victim of intemperance appears before his neighbors, "clothed and in his right mind," with tears of joy in his eyes, telling of the miseries once endured, his language is simple and logical. Few can resist him."

I start to pace. "Though I rarely tasted whiskey at all in my youth, I saw how Judge Green dealt with dram-sellers and drinkers. He knew they would shrink away from thundering accusations that they were the authors of all the vice and misery and crime in the land. Judge Green never shunned them."

Baker nods. "You have a point, but you'll be giving this speech in a church. Not everyone is going to like it."

I stop pacing. "It is a reversal of human nature to do other than meet denunciation with denunciation. A drop of honey catches more flies than a gallon of gall. So it is with men. If you would win a man to your cause, first convince him you are his sincere friend."

He smirks. "You should take to your own counsel."

I wave off his criticism. "There's a difference. The preacher, lawyer, and hired agent are free men who go about as they please without anyone's help, while the drinker and the dram-seller are in self-imposed bondage. If we assume to dictate to their judgment, or command their actions, or mark them as ones to be shunned and despised, they will retreat deeper within their inner prisons, closing all the avenues to their heads and hearts. Though your cause be the naked truth itself, even if it were as the heaviest lance—harder and sharper than steel can be made—and you throw it with more than Herculean force and precision, you shall no more be able to pierce them than to penetrate the hard shell of a tortoise with a rye straw."

Baker shakes his head. "I still think you're going about this the wrong way."

Nonetheless, I deliver my address that evening pretty much as I have written it. I conclude by saying,

> *In the temperance revolution, we shall find a*
> *stronger bondage broken, a viler slavery*
> *manumitted, a greater tyrant deposed than we did*
> *in that glorious Revolution of '76. And, what a noble*
> *ally Temperance can be to the cause of political*
> *freedom. With such an aid, freedom's march cannot*
> *fail to go on and on until every son of earth shall*
> *enjoy perfect liberty. When the victory shall be*
> *complete—when there shall be neither a slave nor a*
> *drunkard on the earth—how proud will be*
> *that Land which may claim to be the birth-place*
> *and the cradle of both those revolutions.*

As I'm walking home after the meeting, an old preacher accosts me over my speech. "It is a shame," he scolds, "that you should be allowed to abuse us so in the House of the Lord."

Despite the parson's disapproval, I pull back my shoulders and lengthen my stride. Judge Green would have been proud of my speech.

About late August, James Shields—a scrappy little Irishman noted for his arrogance and self-importance, who once was my peer in the legislature, and who is now Illinois' State Auditor—institutes measures that prohibit the State from accepting its own paper money for the payment of taxes and other debts.

In response I publish an anonymous letter in *The Sangamo Journal* under the name of "Rebecca," lampooning Shields as:

> *... a ballroom dandy, floatin' about on the earth without heft or substance, just like a lot of cat-fur after a cat fight.*

I also poke fun at his vanity, an air which puts off many of the young ladies, and quote him as saying,

> *Dear girls, it is distressing, but I cannot marry you all. It is not my fault that I am so handsome and so interesting.*

My letter creates a stir across the county, sending Shields into near apoplexy. It also prompts an unknown contributor to join in on the fun and write Aunt Rebecca's humble apology for my first letter. In the "apology," which is published in the next edition of the *Journal*, Aunt Rebecca offers to let Shields squeeze her hand for satisfaction. She goes on to say,

> *If the offense against Mr. Shields cannot be resolved so easily, I expect to take a lickin'.*
>
> *Now, I have all along expected to die a widow; but, as Mr. Shields is rather good-looking than otherwise, I must say I don't care if we compromise the matter by—I can't help blushin'—but I must come out with it—well, if I must, wouldn't he— maybe sorter—let the old grudge drap if I was to consent to be his wife?*
>
> *I know he is a fightin' man and would rather fight than eat; but isn't marryin' better than fightin',*

though the two sometimes run together. And, I don't think I'd be sich a bad match; I'm not over sixty, and am just four feet three in my bare feet, and not much more around the gerth.

Maybe I'm countin' my chickens before they're hatched, and dreamin' of matrimonial bliss when the only alternative reserved for me may be to take a lickin'.

I'm told the way these fire-eaters do it is to give the challenged party the choice of weapons. Well if given that choice, I'll tell you now, I never fight with anything but broomsticks or hot water, or a shovelful of coals or some such thing.

I will give him a choice in one thing, though, and that is whether I shall wear breeches or he petticoats, for I presume this challenge is sufficient to place us on an equality.

Shields brandishes a pistol, threatening the *Journal's* bespectacled publisher, Simeon Francis, and demands to know who authored the letters. Francis, who regards me as family, asks Shields for a day to sort out the matter. When Shields agrees, Francis rides out to Alton where I'm on the Circuit to ask what he should do.

"You know full well that this is none of my doing," I say.

He hesitates. "Yes, but here's the sticky thing."

"What?"

"It's Molly."

"Molly? What about Molly?"

"She's the one who wrote it."

I clutch my forehead. "Molly?"

"Yes, Molly."

"What do you expect me to do? We haven't spoken for a year."

"Just thought you should know ... in case...."

I pinch the bridge of my nose. "Did she send you?"

"No. Thought you might want to do something, though."

I shake my head. "You did the right thing."

He wipes his spectacles with a kerchief.

"Look. Here's what we should do. Tell Shields it was me, but say nothing to Molly. Do you understand?"

"I will do that, but Shields is furious."

"Well, reckon I owe it to Molly. After all, it was rotten of me to go back on my word. I feel as though I've lost the best part of my character. Maybe taking the blame for her will help me gain part of that back."

The next day when Shields hears from Francis, he makes tracks to Alton and hands me a written challenge to a duel.

After reading his complaint, I apologize.

He wags his finger up in my face and complains of the great personal injury I've caused him.

I say, "What I wrote was purely for political effect and meant nothing personal."

"You insulted my character as a man," he insists.

"I intended no such thing." I write out my apology and give him permission to publish it in any manner he chooses.

He crumples the paper and throws it to the ground then grinds it with the heel of his boot. "I have challenged you to a duel to the death, and I intend to defend my honor as a man."

"If you wish, but it is my prerogative to set the conditions for our fight."

He folds his arms across his chest. "I have no mind to tinker with such customs."

"Very well." "When I have written my terms, they will be delivered by my second."

Shields raises his chin. "He can give them to General Whiteside on my behalf."

Later in the evening, I write out the instructions for our duel. We will use cavalry broad swords. A line will be drawn between us, and if either of us should pass a foot over it, he shall forfeit his life. A boundary will also be drawn behind each of us, exactly the length of the broad sword plus three feet, giving me the advantage of my superior reach. Finally, Shields shall choose a time and place which is to be on the Missouri side of the river.

Even though Shields is given one more chance to

accept my apology, he declines. Consequently, on the appointed day we meet on Sunflower Island on the Missouri side of the river.

As I stand back from the center line, my mouth is parched. The guilt I will bear for taking a man's life already weighs on me. I pray that Providence chooses to take me instead, even though I have made it impossible for the fates to intervene.

Looking up toward the heavens, I see above Shields' head, out of his weapon's reach, a drooping sycamore limb. I take a practice slice with my blade and lop off the branch. It falls at his feet. Although he doesn't immediately see that he is doomed by the superior length of my reach, his second, General Whiteside, rushes forward and convinces him to withdraw.

Days after the aborted duel, Simeon Francis and his wife invite me to supper, a familiar custom so it gives me no cause for suspicion. Their ulterior motive becomes clear, however, when I enter the dining room and Molly looks up at me, smiling—just the way Father used to do when he found a fox in one of his traps.

After a brief silence I say, "How do, Miss Molly?"

"Quite well, Mr. Lincoln ... and how are you?"

"Reckon I'm more alive than I might have been."

She pats the empty seat beside her. "Please do sit. I'm so glad to have a chance to thank you for rescuing me from that pompous Mr. Shields."

I scratch my head. "After my bad manners on our last encounter, it was the least I could do."

Her smile dissolves. "Why Mr. Lincoln, you don't *owe* me anything."

Before she can say more, Simeon breaks in. "We're pleased to see you two on cordial terms again ... and since we were in the middle of this Shields affair, so to speak, we thought, what better place than around our table for Miss Todd to express her gratitude?"

"Thank you," I say nodding to our hosts.

The next two hours we engage in civil, at times pleasant, conversation. Molly's charm is beguiling, and my only moment of ill ease comes when she reminisces about some of the gay time we enjoyed together.

After Molly leaves I confide in Simeon that I have lost faith in my ability to keep the resolves I make. The manner in which I ended my engagement with Molly demonstrates I have lost the chief gem of my character. Until I regain it, I cannot trust myself in any matter of much importance.

He encourages me to meet with her privately in their home where we can work on mending our relationship undisturbed by Molly's meddlesome sister and brother-in-law. In fact, we meet several times in the weeks that follow, and while alone on a Wednesday evening in early November, we find ourselves entangled in a passionate romp.

At the conclusion of the affair, she clutches me tight and whispers, "Tomorrow night. Yes, tomorrow night we shall marry."

I snap my head around and study her expression. "Shouldn't we make some kind of arrangements first?"

She claps her hands; her face is flushed with delight. "Rev. Dresser can do the ceremony at his home. You'll go to him first thing tomorrow."

I raise an eyebrow. "First thing?"

She bats her eyes. "Before breakfast."

I swallow. "Yes."

My shoulders droop on my way back the Butlers after saying goodnight to her. If Speed were here, I could complain to him about the soup I'm in; once again, passion has led me to the brink of a dreadful consequence. Of course, his answer would be the same as he has written in his letters for nearly a year now. Molly and I make a perfect couple—I should grab her before the likes of Douglas snatches her away.

The next morning I rap on the door of Rev. Dresser's modest home. When he answers I peer into the kitchen and notice his family is still eating breakfast.

"How can I help you?" he asks.

I fidget with my hat. "Molly wants to get married."

"Excellent," he says folding his hands as if in prayer. "Where?"

"It's to be a quiet affair. Miss Molly would like to do it here … tonight … without any public notice … if it's not inconvenient."

He agrees. My fate is sealed.

Moments later on my way to the courthouse, I cross paths with Ninian Edwards. After exchanging pleasantries, I tell him Molly and I will be married in the evening at Reverend Dresser's home. A piece of me hopes he'll object.

"No," he says.

I cock my head.

He pulls back his shoulders. "I am Molly's guardian, and if she's going to get married, no matter to whom, it will be done at my house. I shall go talk with Mrs. Edwards right away and make proper arrangements."

I force a smile. "Thank you. That'll make the girl quite happy."

Later that morning, Molly comes to my office with the news that the Edwards have agreed to host the wedding in their home, but it must be postponed until the next evening.

I put down the papers I've been studying. "What's wrong with tonight?"

"After Lizzie berated me for thrusting the wedding on her without enough notice to make the customary preparations, she snickered and said it was just as well— the Episcopal Sewing Society is meeting for supper in their home tonight. She said it is a convenience that dinner is already made."

Molly shakes her head. "I stamped my foot and said the arrangement is too cozy and entirely unsuitable. So the sewing society meeting will go on as planned, and the wedding is postponed until tomorrow night."

I glance at my papers. "Whatever you wish."

"Did you order the rings?"

I look up at her. "I intend to do that shortly."

She folds her arms across her chest. "It would make me happy if you attended to it now."

I lay aside the papers and stand, offering her my arm. "Shall we?"

At the Chatteron's jewelry shop we order two gold bands. I ask the jeweler to inscribe hers with *A.L. to Mary, Nov 4 1842. Love is Eternal.*

On Friday evening, November 4, 1842, as a few close friends and Molly's family arrive at the Edwards' mansion, black clouds send down a torrent of rain. The ensuing thunder rattles the doors and windows, and the storm reaches its crescendo at the precise moment we become husband and wife.

Our first home is a two room apartment over the Glove Tavern. Soon after we move in, I strut around like a peacock, broadcasting the news that Molly is expecting our first child. It doesn't take long for my pride to dissipate. Molly, who isn't easy to live with on a good day, becomes a tyrant. In the midst of one of our rows, she throws hot coffee in my face. Our neighbor Mrs. Early—the wife of Captain Early from the Black Hawk War—helps me clean up before I go to work.

On August 1, 1843, in this tiny abode—just shy of nine months after our marriage—Molly gives birth to our son. We name him Robert Todd Lincoln after her father. Memories of the lesson I learned on Annie's death come over me in a wave; I'm possessed by an evil fate. I shall lose those whom I hold dear. First Mother, then sister, and lastly Annie. At least now, Providence has matched me with a woman who is not so easy to love. Though, the thought of losing little Bobby makes me quake.

Dr. Drake's recipe for warding off bouts of melancholy is helpful. I keep busy, even when it means burying myself in mundane legal affairs—collecting debts, defending misdemeanors, or litigating slanders. Most evenings after working late, I come home to find Molly sitting by the fire, nursing little Bobby. I kiss her forehead, pat the baby's head, and sit down at the opposite side of the hearth to read. I glance at them, wanting to take my little boy to rock him, but judgment warns me he's safer in his mother's arms.

In the beginning of September, when court begins on the Eighth Judicial Circuit, I hook up our rickety carriage behind Old Tom and set out for the six week journey, covering more than four-hundred miles and fourteen counties. Not only do the cases keep me busy, but my absence spares me Molly's tyranny.

In Urbana I defend members of the Spurgeon family against an assault complaint by the State's Attorney. The trial jury finds three of them not-guilty and convicts two.

I'm successful in pleading for a new trial on behalf of one of the two, but the other guilty verdict is sustained, costing my client $20 in fines. When he complains of the fine, I tell him to be grateful the judge didn't throw him in jail.

In Charleston, Coles County, I assist Usher Linder, a former adversary in the state legislature, in defending James Bagley against accusations of slander. Isaac Vanmeter claims that Bagley "swore a damned lie," but when Vanmeter is unable to prove it, our client wins.

Before leaving Coles County, I visit Mama and Father who live a short ride outside of Charleston. Mama begs me to bring Molly and Bobby on my next trip. I promise to try, although Molly will never darken the door of Father's home. Neither do I wish for Bobby to suffer the old man's temper.

Later, in Petersburg, my client Eliza Cabot sues Francis Regnier for saying that Elijah Taylor was "after skin and he has got it with Cabot." A local newspaper compares my summation speech to the great Cicero's attacks on Mark Anthony. It's clear of course, that the editor never heard the ancient Roman give a speech.

I make a couple of brief trips back to Springfield during October for political events, and, in mid-November, I return home and remain until spring. Days before Christmas, we move into a three room cottage on Fourth Street. Molly is delighted. I scrounge up more cases to cover the added rent.

The following February, I go out on the Spring Circuit, returning home in mid-April. On my return, Mother—it's now my pet name for her—meets me at the door with pursed lips that aren't intended for kissing. "If you're to leave me all alone here for such long spates, I insist on a proper house."

I lay down my saddlebags. "Mother, how are we to buy a house? The rent here is all we can afford."

"As hard as you work, we can certainly afford it."

I drop my coat on a chair.

She scoops it up and wags her finger at me. "I will not have my son growing to be so ill-mannered. You need to start setting a better example."

I take my coat from her and hang in on a wall peg.

"A proper house has closets. I'm tired of living in this ... this coop."

"What are we to do?"

"Reverend Dresser is selling his home."

"How will we pay for it? I shall not endure another dollar of debt."

"We don't have to. Father has offered help."

"I'm going to bed."

She points to the sofa. "I'll get a blanket."

I furrow my brow. "What's wrong with the bed?"

"I'm not feeling well. You can sleep here. Besides I'm sure it's more comfortable than where you sleep out on the Circuit." As she walks away she adds, "At least you won't be sharing it with another snoring lawyer."

I shake my head.

On May 2, we move to our new home, three rooms downstairs and two sleeping lofts above in the half-story. Mr. Todd provided a modest contribution, but I foot most of the fifteen-hundred dollar purchase price myself. That's just the beginning of the financial burden. Mother immediately begins talking of servants and renovations.

"I'll chop my own wood and open my own door."

"How will I ever make a gentleman out of you if you resist every means of culture?"

I examine my hands, front and back. "What shame is there in a man using his own two hands?"

"Abe ...."

"Please don't call me that. You know I hate it."

"Father, I cannot go about in society as the wife of a leading citizen if I'm to spend my whole day cooking, cleaning, and tending a child. It's not practical."

I take both her hands in mine. "After the national election, I have a mind to strike out on my own in practice. If I take on a junior partner, I should still keep a full half of the fees. Maybe then we can afford to hire a little help."

She shakes her head. "I suppose I can tolerate it for another few months, but you must promise ...."

"You have my word. When we've finished campaigning for Mr. Clay, I'll set our financial house in order, and we can bring on some help."

The next morning I leave to make a series of

speeches across the state and in Indiana. While visiting my old home in Little Pigeon Creek where my mother and sister are buried, I choke back tears. Though it is an unpoetic place, my visit inspires me to pen some reflections of my boyhood.

My child-hood home I see again,
And gladden with the view;
Still, as mem'ries crowd my brain,
There's sadness in it too—
O memory! thou mid-way world
'Twixt Earth and Paradise;
Where things decayed, and loved ones lost
In dreamy shadows rise—
Freed from all that's gross or vile,
Seem hallowed, pure, and bright,
Like scenes in some enchanted isle,
All bathed in liquid light—
As distant mountains please the eye,
When twilight chases day —
As bugle-tones, that, passing by,
In distance die away —
As leaving some grand water-fall
We ling'ring list its roar,
So memory will hallow all we've known,
But, know no more—
Now twenty years have passed away,
Since here I bid farewell
To woods, and fields, and scenes of play
And school-mates loved so well—
Where many were, how few remain
Of old familiar things!
But seeing these to mind again
The lost and absent brings—
The friends I left that parting day —
How changed as time has sped!
Young childhood grown, strong manhood grey,
And half of all are dead—
I hear the lone survivors tell
How nought from death could save,
Till every sound appears a knell

And every spot a grave—
I range the fields with pensive tread,
I pace the hollow rooms;
And feel (companion of the dead)
I'm living in the tombs—
All mental pangs, by time's kind laws,
Hast lost the power to know—
The very spot where grew the bread,
That formed my bones, I see
How strange, old field, on thee to tread
And feel I'm part of thee!

On my return home, I keep my promise to Mother and dissolve my partnership with Logan. Billy Herndon agrees to come on as my junior partner; we will split the firm's fees equally. Mother hires a cook who also helps with other chores, and when I am not away on the Circuit or busy with legal cases, I work on expanding our house.

Chapter Twenty Five

I n early March of 1846, I rush home from the Circuit on receiving news our second son is born. I want to see for myself that our little family is well.

We name the boy Edward Baker Lincoln after my good friend, Ned Baker, who served alongside me in the state legislature and who was quick to join in on the lively conversations around the stove at Speed's store. Unlike his stocky big brother Bobby, who bounds with energy and curiosity, young Eddy is frail and lethargic. His delicate little body pulls at my heart.

Mother withdraws to the new bedroom I've installed at the back of the house, turning it into a maternal lair where she nurses her newborn cub. She takes her meals there as well, and Bobby and I get to see his little brother when we take in her tray.

One afternoon, I'm home tending Bobby as he plays with a toy wagon on the floor while I sit by the fire reading. I glance at him a few times, wondering if he truly understands I'm his father.

When he begins crying, Mother flies out of her room like a hornet stirred from its nest, little Eddy cradled in one arm. She shrieks, "Why haven't you picked him up?"

I look up from my newspaper. "It's not even been a minute."

She eyes a pile of unfolded laundry, walks over to it and holds up my cotton shirt. "What's this rag doing here?"

Bobby is still crying.

I lay down my paper and get up from the chair. "I was about to put those away."

She waves her hand around the room. "Must I do all of the work around here? Where are the servants?"

Bobby wails louder.

"I sent them home."

"Then you should do their jobs. The nanny wouldn't let him just sit there and cry." She throws up her hands. "Why does everything fall on me? What would my father say if he saw me doing this kind of work?"

"I'll take care of it straight away." I pick up Bobby, his little red face contorted.

"No. I've had my fill. Get out of this house. Now."

As she goes for the broom she often uses to chase me, I grab my coat and head for the door, Bobby tucked under one arm."

"Good, take him with you. I need peace and quiet."

Once outside, Bobby ends his tantrum, and I carry him to the office. He plays on the floor for a with his toy wagon while I work, but soon begins whining from hunger. I get him some crackers and promise to fix supper when we go home. After a while, I put down my work and sprawl out on the floor to join him in play. As the night drags on, he tires enough to curl up and go to sleep, laying his head on my lap for a pillow. I pat his head.

Later, we steal back into the house, and I get Bobby something to eat before carrying him up to the loft to sleep. We slip back out just before sunrise while Mother is still sleeping and go to a restaurant for breakfast. I say to Bobby, "This ain't so bad after all, is it? If your ma don't conclude to let us come back, Reckon we can board here all summer."

Mother takes us back that very evening, but her tyranny does not diminish.

Five months later I'm elected to serve in the United States House of Representatives. Since it's more than a year until my term begins, the law business consumes my full attention. I spend three, ten-week terms on the Circuit, riding through forest and prairie, fording swollen streams, and trying cases in the various county seats. I love the solitude of the countryside and cherish friendships I make with the curious assortment of people.

In October of 1847, Usher Lindner calls me out to Coles County where a slavery case has drawn a good amount of attention from across the state. In my early days in the state legislature, Lindner fell victim to one of my "skinning." On this occasion he asks my help in arguing a case on behalf of a slave owner trying to regain possession of his "property."

Robert Matson, a resolute Kentucky planter, has filed for a writ to recover five slaves. The family of slaves—a woman named Jane Bryant and her four children— escaped his farm. They were taken into custody by the sheriff when they failed to produce "letters of freedom" which are required under the law.

The local justice of the peace would not give the sheriff the writ as requested, fearing violence from a small band of abolitionists. One of the abolitionists, Gideon M. Ashmore—a middle-aged hotel keeper who harbored the slaves for several days when they first ran away—has now filed for a writ of habeas corpus to free the slaves. He's represented by Orlando Fricklin, a locally renowned lawyer and modestly successful politician.

Under the law of Illinois, slaves can be brought up from slave states to work seasonally, as long as they do not stay here year-round. Matson owns a plantation in Kentucky where he domiciles his slaves. He brings slaves up from there to his Coles County farm at harvest time and returns them across the border when their work is done. The mistress he keeps in Coles County became jealous of Jane, the slave mother, and Matson vowed to sell the whole family down South to work on cotton plantations.

The local sentiment favoring freedom for the slaves stems from the situation of the oldest daughter, Mary Catherine—age 14. She's as fair skinned as any white girl, with red hair and blue eyes. It escapes no one's imagination that she'll be forced into sexual service as a "fancy piece" once she's sold at auction. My stomach knots up at the thought of it.

The case is now before Judge William Wilson of the Supreme Court, a distinguished justice nearing the end of his career. He has Whig leanings, but no political ambitions. At his request, he's joined on the bench by my friend Judge Samuel Treat. The afternoon before the trial begins, I'm telling stories to a crowd at a local tavern when a young, boyish-faced, abolitionist physician by the name of Hiram Rutherford interrupts me. He insists I should take the case on the side of the slaves.

When I tell him of my obligation to Mr. Matson he berates me and storms away. I follow after him and even offer to try freeing myself from Matson's cause, but Rutherford will have nothing more to do with me. Instead, he hires Charles Constable, a classically educated lawyer and capable debater, tall with chiseled features and an air of confidence.

Several years earlier, when opposing my partner Judge Logan in the Bailey case, I successfully obtained a writ to free slaves. My argument was that slavery does not exist in Illinois under the state Constitution and the Northwest Ordinance, a statute passed by the first United States Congress. In the present matter, I'm expecting the opposing lawyers to use my own precedent against me. By doing so they could easily disarm me in front of the judges, leaving me floundering in a vain effort to defeat the very arguments that served me well in a similar trial.

Fricklin and Constable take a different tact. They anchor their cause on the notion that slavery does not exist under British law or any system of law derived from it. Fricklin makes me wince when he asserts, "I speak in the spirit of British law which makes liberty commensurate with and inseparable from British soil."

Doesn't he realize we fought the Revolution of '76 to be free of British tyranny, and this is no longer British soil?

I rise and make the case against the writ, arguing that slave property is protected wherever the Constitution of our country holds force. I say on summation, "The existence of slavery or the lack thereof is solely under the jurisdiction of each state. This is a sacred, though regrettable, pact entered into at our nation's inception. Illinois cannot undo Kentucky's laws."

When the court rules against Matson, freeing the slaves, I toss my saddlebags onto Old Tom and head off to the next stop on the Circuit, not taking time to speak to any of the parties. I breathe a sigh of relief for the Bryant family and grieve over the abuse our Constitution suffered at the hands of the court. It is a knotty problem that our Founders sacrificed for liberty on one hand, and on the other, took measures to protect slavery where it existed when the nation was formed.

In early November, I pack up the family for my single term in Congress. Since I've agreed to serve only one term, we'll live as vagabonds in the nation's capital for the duration of the session. On the way to Washington City, we make a long visit with Mother's family in Lexington. She idolizes her father, and he dotes on her. On the other hand, relations between Molly and her step-mother are strained. Their acrimony prompted Molly to leave home for Springfield where we met.

We travel by boat to Frankfort, Kentucky where we board a train to Lexington. Little Bobby and I romp through the rail cars, collecting smiles from some passengers, stares from others. One studious young man looks up from his book with a scowl each time we dash past his seat. When we return to our compartment I whisper to Mother, "Our boys are going to have fond memories of childhood. I'm determined to see it so."

As the carriage that Molly's father sent to pick us up turns onto Main Street, the icy wind that had cut across our faces in the countryside is tamed by rows of grand houses. Molly tells me to make good notes about the style of her family home. In her mind, it's the model for how ours shall look someday.

I wince. "You've always said your father's house is a mansion."

She blows on her mittened hands, warming them. "It's only fourteen rooms—if you don't count the carriage house, outdoor kitchen, wash house, and slaves' quarters. Of course *we'll* never own slaves—I could never tolerate such a thing in my own home."

I glance at her. "Which part of the house do you want ours to look like?"

She folds her hands on her lap and stares straight ahead. "You'll be pleased to know that your hero Henry Clay lives in Ashland, only two miles away."

A short time later, we pull up in front of a magnificent brick house. The entire family, dressed in finery despite the weather, is standing at the open front door in the same welcoming style I had witnessed at Speed's estate in Farmington. A Negro footman helps Mother out of the carriage as she cradles little Eddy who's wrapped in a wool blanket in her arms. She wastes no time greeting her father. I follow her into the hall toting young Bobby, swimming in his long winter coat. Once inside, I put the little fellow on the floor and spot the Colored contingent gathered at the rear of the hall. They're eager to greet Molly and dote on the babies.

The wide hall is chilly with the door thrown open. I keep on my long cloak and the fur cap with its ear flaps still covering the sides of my face. After shaking hands with all the grown-ups, I lift Emilie—Molly's pretty, eleven year-old half-sister—and say, "So this is little sister." Thereafter, I make a habit of calling her "Little Sister" although her family's pet name for her is Pariet. By every measure she's the beauty of the Todd clan.

Molly's younger brother Sam, who attends college at Danville, is home to see his sister and little nephews. He swaggers around reminding everyone of the importance of being an uncle and teaches Bobby to call him "Uncle Sam."

Molly stands back surveying her brother and broadcasts to everyone, "What a big handsome boy Sam has grown to be. He was such a little scrap of a baby."

Sam strikes a superior pose. "At least I had the grace to grow up. You're still but a tiny piece, hardly reaching my shoulder. I hope your boys inherit their father's length."

Her eyes sparkle. "And their mother's lovely disposition."

I hold my tongue. They all know her true nature.

During much of our stay, I sit inside at a window reading a book of poetry from Mr. Todd's library, watching Bobby with Little Sister play in the garden behind the house. If it were warmer, I'd be outside on the long veranda. I bracket some lines of William Cowper's poem *Slavery and the Slave Trade* and turn down the page in the book. Molly tells me Cowper's friend John Newton wrote the beautiful poem *Amazing Grace*.

It's no surprise to find writings of an English abolitionist and free-soiler in this slave owner's house. While handling legal work for Molly's father, I've learned that he's an admirer of Henry Clay. Mr. Todd opposes trading slaves among whites and hopes slavery will die out someday—views which have torn apart his family. Later, I find a book of William Cullen Bryant's verse and memorize *Thanatopsis*. Several lines capture my attention.

> *When thoughts of the last bitter hour come*
> *like a blight over thy spirit,*
> *and sad images of the stern agony, and shroud,*
> *and pall, and breathless darkness,*
> *and the narrow house make thee to shudder*
> *and grow sick at heart,*
> *Go forth under the open sky,*
> *and list to Nature's teachings,*
> *while from all around Earth and her waters,*
> *and the depths of air*
> *Comes a still voice ...*

During our time in Lexington, Molly and I attend an address given by Senator Clay. At the time the meeting is to begin, an overflow crowd stands outside on the street, braving a bitter storm. As a result, we're herded over to the Lower Market House on Water Street where a temporary platform has been cobbled together at one end of the building.

Once the meeting reconvenes, Judge George Robertson, the chairman, is seated on one side of Senator Clay, and Molly's father Robert Smith Todd is on the other—bright-eyed, balding, and erect—with a smile peeking through his greying beard.

The awe of the moment is dashed, however, when the Senator begins to read his speech. I have long heard of his oratory flair; though tonight, he's timid and dry. Over the course of two hours, he drones on about the illegitimacy of the war with Mexico. Then he touches on slavery, saying it's a great evil, an irremedial wrong to its unfortunate victims. His challenge—*to disavow in the most positive manner any desire on our part to acquire any foreign territory whatever for the purpose of introducing slavery into it*—is void of passion.

Later, we dine with the Senator at his Ashland estate, even a grander house than Speed's Farmington. As we enter, the man I've thought of as my ideal greets me with a feeble handshake, cold and empty of charm. His trembling weakness shocks me.

During dinner, served to us by household slaves, Senator Clay expounds on the necessity of leaving slavery alone where it was already in place when the nation was formed. He insists it was our Founders intention to do so. "Let it die a slow death," he says, "and we should not add any new territories where slavery will be allowed."

I pick at my food. Melancholy hovers over me, ready to swoop down and steal my mood. His words "die a slow death" ring in my ears. This man, whom I have esteemed as the savior of our land, is himself dying out, yet injustice lives on. The room grows dim, the faces around me seem ghostly, conversations become but a murmur. Then all is dark and silent.

When I'm jolted back to the present by a young mulatto who whisks away my plate, I look about the room. All eyes are fixed on me, except those of Senator Clay who is cutting a piece of meat on his plate. Without looking up he says, "It is good that young Mr. Lincoln has seen fit to rejoin us."

The chill and gloom of the evening stay with me for the remainder of our time in Lexington.

On November 25, Mother, the children, and I continue on to the nation's capital where we move into a boarding house. Mother is unhappy from the moment of our arrival.

No matter how hard I try, nothing improves her spirits. On the other hand, she's quite adept at dampening mine. Soon after Christmas, she and the children return to Lexington to stay with her family until my term ends. I breathe a sigh of relief on their departure even as my heart aches over being left behind.

Twice during my term, I strive to influence important questions of the day. On my arrival, I engage in a debate on tariffs and write an argument advocating free-labor which is widely ignored.

> *In the early days of the world, the Almighty said to the first of our race, "In the sweat of thy face shalt thou eat bread." Since then, no good thing has been enjoyed by us without the necessity of labor.*
>
> *But it has happened in all ages that some have labored and others have, without labor, enjoyed a large proportion of the fruits. This is wrong. To secure to each laborer the whole product of his labor is a most worthy object of any good government.*

In January I give a speech opposing the war with Mexico, of which my colleagues take little note. When my term ends in March 1849, I have accomplished nothing by which the world should take notice of me. My seat in Congress now belongs to the Democrat who defeated Judge Logan, and I resign myself to the belief that Providence has a different calling for me than politics. John Stuart's words to me several years ago have a hollow ring, "No defeat is ever as final as it seems."

A couple of months after settling into my quieter life back home in Springfield, business takes me to Coles County where I pay a visit to my parents. To protect myself from Father's tirades on politics and complaints about "wasting time on a career in the law," I stay overnight with my step-brother John Johnston. John tells me that Father's health is in steep decline and his eyesight is dwindling. It's not the first time I've heard this lament.

When I arrive at Father's farm the next morning, Mama greets me with a lingering embrace. She says her tears spring from a fountain of joy. When we go inside the cramped cabin, Father remains seated at the table. He glances at me, expressionless, and says, "You look like you're dressed for a funeral. Do I have to die for my only son to pay me a visit?"

I look over to Mama. "I've been away."

Father sneers. "That's right, I heared you went to Congress. No wonder my purse feels so much lighter."

I bite my lip. "You're safe now. I'm done with politics. It's time for me to stay at home with Molly and the boys. Besides, the law business keeps me plenty busy."

He shrugs. "Speaking of that fancy wife of yours and the little ones, did you bring them along this time?"

"No, they're home."

"Hope you ain't spoilin' 'em. Too much book learnin' and they'll be good for nothin'."

I glance at the doorway. "Mama, why don't you show me around the farm?"

Father sneers. "How much farmin' do you s'pose goes on around here with a withered up old man handlin' all the chores by hisself?"

I shake my head.

Mama ushers me outside to a bench under an old oak tree. We sit, and she takes my hand in hers. "When do I get to meet Molly and those precious little boys?"

I pat her hand. "The youngest doesn't travel well. He's still ailing after the trip back from Washington."

"And little Bobby? He must be nearly six by now."

I laugh. "Standoffish like his father."

She looks away. "After seven years, I still haven't met Molly or seen my grandbabies."

I pat her hand again. "Someday, Mama ...."

Chapter Twenty Six

S weat drips from my brow under the harsh July sun. The patch of shade in the front yard under an old oak is mighty inviting. Just one more row of bricks to lay, and I can take a break. Mother insists a retaining wall would dress up the street-side of our home. To make her happy, I'm neglecting clients—most of whom will set about making me miserable when I return to the office. As for myself, a spot of shade and a draw of cool water from the well out back will bring pleasure enough.

As I bend over to pick up another brick, Molly's brother Levi rides up and dismounts in front of me, handing me his reins. He's come all the way from Lexington, unannounced, trouble etched on his face.

"What's up?" I say.

He takes off his hat and fidgets with the brim. "I need to see Molly."

I take off my hat and wipe my brow.

What's happened?"

"Our father is dead."

I tip back my hat to wipe my brow. "What? How?"

He looks down. "There's been an epidemic of cholera."

"How are the others?" I search his face for a hopeful sign.

He sighs. "So far, everyone else is fine."

I lay my hand on his shoulder. "You'd best go in and tell Molly. I'll occupy the boys."

As soon as we come through the door Molly smells calamity. I gather up the boys to take them into the bedroom in the back of the house, leaving her alone with Levi. Just when I start to tell the boys about their grandfather's death, wails erupt from the other room.

Bobby looks up at me. "Is Mother all right?"

For a few days, Mother holes up in her bedroom cuddling little Eddy, sobbing off and on. I've sent the cook home while I take time off from work to tend to Bobby and fix meals. Mother only picks at her portions. One morning, after nearly a week, I climb down from the sleeping loft to find Mother bustling about the kitchen, barking at the cook, whom I reckon she summoned to make breakfast. I wish Mother a good morning, but she continues her busyness without a word. It's as though I'm not present. I pack up my files and take Bobby by the hand. He tags along with me to the office. As the weeks pass with Mother keeping her distance from us, Bobby becomes withdrawn, eventually refusing my attentions all together.

When the chill of autumn invades the Illinois prairie, we learn that her father's home and all its belongings are to be sold at public auction. There are deficiencies in her father's will, and Molly will inherit nothing.

She looks up at me with the fiercest eyes. "I have no intentions of going back there, anyway," she says.

In early December, little Eddy is lethargic and wracked by persistent coughing. Mother and I spell each other hovering at his bedside, daubing his forehead with cold, damp cloths, and praying for him. Of course, prayers are useless in changing the course of events, but they bring me comfort.

At the start of the New Year, his cough produces bloody phlegm. Night sweats and chills soon progress into an unrelenting fever. His appetite evaporates along with the remainder of his strength. On February 1, 1850, just before his fourth birthday, Eddy's frail lungs draw their last raspy breath. Choking back tears, I pry Mother away from his limp body. As I hold her close, she wails through clenched teeth and pounds my chest with her fists. Death took Molly's mother at an early age, her father much too soon, and now it takes a child whom she bore. The greatest thing we have in common is the deaths of those we love.

When her grief is spent, at least for the moment, I lay her on the sofa and climb up to the loft to give Bobby our sorrowful news. I find him there, staring at the ceiling, his eyes blank and misty.

"Your brother ...."

He turns and looks at me. "I know. He's dead."

"I'm sorry."

He says nothing more and begins weeping.

I want to reach out and draw him near, but a small voice inside me warns, *What you hold close will be ripped away.*

I save my own tears for when I'm alone.

During the weeks that follow, Molly writes a verse that we publish in *The Sangamo Journal.*

Those midnight stars are sadly dimmed,
That late so brilliantly shone,
And the crimson tinge from cheek and lip,
With the heart's warm life has flown—
The angel of Death was hovering nigh,
And the lovely boy was called to die.
The silken waves of his glossy hair
Lie still over his marble brow,
And the pallid lip and pearly cheek
The presence of Death avow.
Pure little bud in kindness given,
In mercy taken to bloom in heaven.
Happier far is the angel child
With the harp and the crown of gold,
Who warbles now at the Savior's feet
The glories to us untold.
Eddie, meet blossom of heavenly love,
Dwells in the spirit-world above.
Angel Boy - fare thee well, farewell
Sweet Eddie, We bid thee adieu!
Affection's wail cannot reach thee now

Deep though it be, and true.
Bright is the home to him now given
For 'of such is the Kingdom of Heaven.'

In late March, shortly before I take to the Circuit again, Mother begs me for another child. I search her face for some hint it's just a whim. She nuzzles up to me, her sparkling eyes luring me closer. Her touch radiates warmth through my body. Before I grasp hold of my senses, she leads me to her bedroom, relieves me of my clothing, and we share a night of bliss so rare in our marriage. The next morning, out of duty or in search of escape, I saddle my new horse, Old Buck, and ride off to meet up with Judge David Davis and the other lawyers on the circuit.

Davis took over for Sam Treat as Circuit Judge while I was serving in Congress. At three-hundred pounds, he's too large to ride on horseback over the four-hundred mile circuit, so he drives a two-horse which often gets stuck when the roads turn muddy. Swollen streams can also present problems. To help him across fast flowing currents, I dismount Old Tom, tuck my papers under my hat, and, disposing of my pants, I wade into the water to scout for the shallowest crossing. I'm the logical man for the task, since my legs are so long.

When we arrive in each town for the two or three day court sessions, accommodations are made for us in local taverns. Two or three lawyers share a bed, but Judge Davis gets his own. No one wants to risk getting crushed during the night. In the mornings we find a pitcher of cold water and a towel to share.

As someone once described our fare, "… the food is greasy, the floor is greasy, the table cloth likewise, and the waitress greasier than all the rest together." Some of the fellows complain, but I find the Circuit a welcome refuge from home. I suppose it's my fondness for these good frontier people that draws Judge Davis' rebuke. "You should go home to your family on weekends as the rest of us do."

His words pinch at my throat. "Yes, reckon you're right. Mother tells me if I stayed home as I ought to, she'd love me more."

"Well, there you are," he says.

I cock my head. "If she loved me more, I might stay home. Besides, I need the extra fees from working weekends to keep her in the finery she demands."

Judge Davis looks at me as if he's interrogating a witness. "Are you sure?"

"When I'm home she complains if I open the front door instead of having a servant do it. If I do something she thinks is uncouth, like eating butter, she throws coffee at me or chases me out of the house with a broomstick or pelts me with potatoes. Once she came at me with a long kitchen knife."

"Maybe it's her way of saying she misses you."

"Maybe so, but in the last seven weeks since we've been out on the Circuit, she hasn't written once."

He scowls. "If not for her, then go home and be with your boy."

When the Circuit ends in June, Mother is pregnant, and Bobby accompanies me to the office most days so she can rest. He often whines that he misses "Mama." On those occasions, I put down my work and join him on the floor to play. It doesn't take me long to understand that my attention is a poor substitute for Mother's. After taking him home for supper, I go back to the office alone and work late into the night to keep up on cases.

When September arrives, the Circuit's gaiety is a welcome refuge once again, and my story telling has won Judge Davis' favor. His appetite for merriment is as large as his frame, and he often calls on me to deliver a joke at the snap of his fingers. He even invites me to share his room, usually the largest in the tavern. I insist on my own bed.

Most of the cases we try deal with mundane issues of frontier life—figuring out who owns a litter of pigs, or who's to blame for an epidemic of foot rot that wipes out a flock of sheep. Each case presents the inevitable question of sorting out truthful testimony from false swearing. When I catch my client or his witness in a lie, I call the court's attention to the perjury, even if no one else knows of the offense.

On one such occasion, I rise and inform the jury, "Gentlemen, I depended on this witness to clear my client. He has lied. I ask that no attention be paid to his testimony. Let his words be stricken out. If my case fails, so be it. I do not wish to win in this way."

That's not to say I'm opposed to exciting the jurymen's emotions to steer them away from cold facts. During a luncheon recess, I overhear the opposing lawyer tell his client, "Our case is gone; when Lincoln quit he was crying, the jurymen were crying, the judge was crying, and I was a little damp about the lashes myself. We might as well give the case up."

Not all sympathies are won so easily. On returning home from the Circuit in December, I open a letter from my step-brother John Johnston who implores me to visit Father. The old man's days appear to be numbered. I steel myself and write back.

> *Say to him that if we could meet now, it is doubtful that it would be more pleasant than painful. But if it is his lot to go now, he will soon have a joyous meeting with many loved ones gone before; and the rest of us, through the help of God, hope ere-long to join them.*

A few days later, Mother gives birth to little William Wallace Lincoln, named after her brother-in-law, who is also our family doctor. We call the boy Willy. At the very first sight of him—those little gray eyes, a curly tuft of black hair, and his wrinkly skin—a magical bond forms between us, the kind that fathers and sons are meant to share. Beginning that day, whenever I'm away, there's a constant tugging, drawing me home.

Nearly a month afterward, Johnston writes again, this time telling me Father is dead. He asks that I pay for a headstone and give a eulogy at the funeral. I crumple up the letter and toss it into the stove, making no excuse for denying his pleas or staying away. My eyes are as dry as a summer wind.

More than a year later, word comes that Senator Henry Clay has died. The invitation to deliver his eulogy at a memorial service, to be held in Springfield, reminds me of the passion that coursed through my veins when he made his bid for the presidency. Other memories gnaw at me, as well—the letdown of his speech in Lexington and gripping his cold, limp hand at Ashland. Clay is the man after whom I have modeled my politics, and who showed me the emptiness of fame.

Standing before the assembly in Springfield I choke back tears.

Whatever he did, he did for the whole country. He believed with all his heart that the world's best hope depended on the continued Union of these States. He was ever jealous of and watchful for whatever might have the slightest tendency to separate us.

He loved his country because it is a free country. He burned with a zeal for its advancement, prosperity and glory, because he saw in our success the advancement, prosperity and glory of human liberty, human right and human nature. He desired the prosperity of his countrymen chiefly to show to the world that freemen could be prosperous.

As I step down from the rostrum, sadness consumes me, not only for his passing, but for my failure to have made something equally grand of my life.

While riding the fall circuit of the same year, I meet attorney Ward Hill Lamon. We are equal in height, but his girth out measures mine by a large degree. Hill is a genial type, much like Judge Davis, but unlike Davis, he's a hearty drinker and a minstrel of sorts. After the supper hour, Hill always comes to the room Davis and I share, leading a contingent of friends and carrying a pitcher or two of good liquor.

When Hill and the other imbibers are fully mellow, the judge calls out, "Now, Hill, let's have some music."

Hill cheerfully responds with a plaintive ballad like *The Blue-tailed Flay* or *Cousin Sally Downward.*

Chapter Twenty Seven

W hen our fourth boy is born on April 4, 1853, Mother insists we name him Thomas after my late father. On seeing him, though, I decide to call him Tad; his large head and wriggly little body remind me of a tadpole. I wonder if he'll be the hardest of our boys to tame. Of course, we don't make much of a fuss over their behavior, anyway, so it shouldn't be a problem.

Mother takes a couple weeks to regain her strength, while I do the best job of housekeeping I can. Mostly, I wrestle with little Willy and Bobby on the parlor floor. When Mother's on her feet again, and her cantankerousness becomes intolerable, I head out to join the other lawyers on the Circuit.

On August 24, Sheriff Robert Latham of Logan County appears in my office, joined by business associates Gillett and Hichox.

"What's up?" I say, standing to greet them.

Latham pushes a handful of his brown, wavy hair back behind his ear. "We've come to ask your permission for something."

I raise an eyebrow. "Reckon it's better to ask for permission than to come hat in hand begging forgiveness. What's on your mind?"

He looks up at me. "It's about that patch of land along the railroad extension near Postville."

"You mean the new town site your voters approved for the new county seat?"

Hichox nods. "Yes, we're mighty appreciative for the nice bill you wrote to get the legislature's approval so we could put the question to a vote."

I scratch my head. "You boys having any problems with those land sale contracts?"

Latham shakes his head. "No. That's not it at all. We came to ask your permission to name the new town after you. We want to call it Lincoln."

I laugh. "You have a good sense of humor."

"We're serious," Latham says, his eyes trained on me.

"Well, you'd better not do that. I never knew anything named Lincoln that amounted to much."

Latham smiles. "You're not just our lawyer, you're the best lawyer ever to set foot in Logan County. On top of that, folks think of you as their friend. You pushed the legislature to create our new county and you handle all its litigation. There's no one more fitting for the honor than you."

I hang my head. "If you can't be persuaded otherwise, reckon I'll have to grant my permission."

"And one more thing," says Latham.

I nod.

"You're the guest of honor at the town's christening three days from now."

On August 27, I stand under an increasingly hot summer sun and witness the sale of more than ninety lots at prices ranging from forty to one-hundred-fifty dollars each. My clients collect more than six thousand dollars, several times beyond what they paid for the land. After the sales are complete, I christen the town with watermelon juice from melons bought off a nearby wagon.

A couple of months later, I'm sitting by the fireplace at Mt. Pulaski House, a tavern where I stay while attending Circuit Court sessions at Logan County's soon-to-be-former county seat. I look up from staring into the fire and find my old friend Samuel Parks peering at me, his deep-set eyes perched above a long narrow nose.

"Lincoln," he says. "You've been looking into that fire for a very long time."

I turn to him. "Reckon so. Don't remember night falling. What can I do for you?"

"Saw you here and just wanted to say hello."

"Been sitting there long?"

"No, but I've passed by a few times wondering when you'd be back among the living."

I tilt my head side to side, loosening my neck. "Bet you're wondering what's gotten such a grip on my thoughts."

"Seen it happen too many times to bother asking."

I laugh. "You're right. Not even sure I can say precisely what it is. It's as if something unseen, far out in the cosmos, grabs hold of my mind and carries me off."

"What do you see out there?"

I shrug. "Darkness. Sometimes futility. Always an awareness of ultimacy."

After both of us fall silent for a moment, I ask, "Remember when we first met?"

"How could I forget? Was back in about '40 when I was studying law at Stuart's office." He chuckles. "Morose fellows such as you always draw attention. Never know what special gifts they might possess."

I laugh. "If you walked through life trailing a melancholy fog behind you, you might not think it so attractive."

"Ah, but to have your special insights ...."

I lean forward, resting my forearms on my knees. "You know, even back then I hated slavery every bit as much as any abolitionist."

He nods. "I remember. You hated oppression and wrong in all its forms. You said, 'it's unconstitutional.'"

"Reckon I can't take much credit for that. Somehow hatred for injustice made its way into my blood. It's not something I can help."

Late in the evening of June 1 the following year, I return home from the spring Circuit sooner than planned. I unsaddle and groom my horse before going inside through the back door. The boys are in the kitchen being tended to by a nanny.

The young woman looks up at me and says, "Mrs. Lincoln neglected to tell me she was expecting you."

I glance toward the parlor. "She wasn't."

"Shall I get supper for you?" she asks.

"No, thanks. I'll just sit and read the news." I kiss the boys and go into the parlor to take a seat by the fireplace. The news article that summoned me home absorbs my attention.

A few minutes later, Bobby peers around the paper. "Mamma's gone dancing," he says.

I laugh. "Grown people must play, too."

The nanny takes Bobby's hand. "Off to bed, now."

"Go on home when you're finished. I'll take care of them from here."

Their footsteps fade away as I stare into the fire. The room grows gradually darker until ....

I look up and blink. Mother is standing in front of me, scowling, her hands on her hips.

She shakes her head. "I knew you must be home. When I came in and saw the fire had died out, I figured you sent the help home and neglected to tend it."

"How was the dance?"

"Gay, as always." She kneels on the floor next to me and gazes at me, smiling. "They were all making bets on how long it would take you to make tracks for home once you saw the news."

I look down at the newspaper. "So who won?"

"No one. Everybody chose tonight."

I cock my head. "How long were you standing there?"

"I've been home more than an hour. I knew it would be useless trying to disturb you."

I smooth out the paper across my lap. "Mother, we have to stop this thing. Before we know it, the whole nation will become slave territory."

She nods. "Do you recall telling me about the woman in New Orleans who abused and mutilated her slaves?"

"Madame LaLaurie?"

"Yes."

"What about her?"

"When I was a young girl in Lexington, I was mortified at reading the accounts in the local papers."

My throat tightens. "You never told me."

Her eyes narrow. "From that moment to this, I've been resolved that everything which can be done to end the treachery of slavery must be done."

"You always complain you wish we lived in a slave state so you can live a pampered life."

She laughs. "Being pampered? Yes, but I couldn't abide owning slaves any more than you could."

We search each other's eyes for a moment then she asks, "What do you plan to do, Mr. Lincoln?"

I lean back. "I've decided to aim for Shields' U. S. Senate seat when the legislature votes this December."

"Don't expect him to run off with his tail between his legs like the time you almost dueled him on my account."

I take her hand. "You think it'll take more than lopping off a branch hanging above his head?"

After we share a good laugh, she says, "I can't wait to be sitting in the gallery watching you and Mr. Douglas dueling with words on the Senate floor."

I tap my finger on the newspaper headline *President Pierce Signs Kansas-Nebraska Act.* "It's not a game, Mother. Douglas means to use his new-fangled Popular Sovereignty idea to spread slavery into every corner of the continent. Hell, he won't stop until it's gotten all the way to the tip of South America. This Nebraska Act is just the beginning; mark my words."

After saying goodnight, I traipse over to the office. There's no use trying to sleep with the weight of the world on my shoulders. I must come up with a strategy for winning Shields' Senate seat. It won't be easy with the reapportionment of seats in the legislature tilting toward the Democrats' advantage. I pull out a map of the districts and begin a list of men in each part of the state who share my sentiments.

When Billy Herndon arrives in the morning, he stares and says, "You look like hell."

"So my countenance has improved."

"We all figured the Nebraska Act would get you riled. What are your plans?"

"I'm going after Shields' Senate seat. If we don't hit this slavery business in the head, and hit it hard, it'll swallow up the whole country. It'll be the end of free labor; every man will become a bondsman, unable to make a wage good enough to improve his condition."

"That should make for quite a show—you debating Douglas in front of the whole country."

My chest tightens. "Don't care about a show. The cause of liberty is at stake this very hour, and not just for the Negro. The whole nation will suffer for this evil."

He picks up the map of legislative districts. "How does Mrs. Lincoln feel about getting back into politics?"

I shake my head. "Her exact words were, 'I haven't given up on my hope of being Mrs. President someday.'"

"It's a long step from state legislator to president. You plan on using the Senate as a stepping stone?"

"Even with my long legs, that's quite a jump. Anyway, I can do a lot more good in the Senate than I could do as president."

He lays down the map and rubs his temples. "You know, if you're in the legislature when they vote on the Senate seat, you'll be in a good spot to influence the outcome."

I finger my watch fob. "I've been thinking the very same thing. On top of that, if I stump for anti-Nebraska men across the state, I'll be able to put some of them in debt to me."

Days later, I announce my run for the state legislature and learn that Douglas has the same notion. He sets out campaigning on behalf of Democratic candidates for the state legislature, at least those who take a pledge to support his Popular Sovereignty. I follow behind him bolstering the opposition candidates.

Early in September, before riding to Bloomington to address a German anti-Nebraska meeting, I take Billy to *The Sangamo Journal* office. Editor Simeon Francis has agreed to help us work up a new speech in response to Douglas' latest stump.

I tell them, "People say Douglas makes sense. They ask, 'Why shouldn't men be free to do whatever they have a mind to do with their own property?' If we can't wake them up, he's going to beat us."

Francis peers up at me. "You have to make Douglas' position on Nebraska sound ridiculous."

"What about, 'Judge Douglas says the principle of the Kansas-Nebraska Act originated when God made man and allowed him to choose between good and evil, making each man accountable only to the Almighty for his choices.'"

"That's not pointed enough," says Billy.

I rub the back of my neck. "His notion is similar to the old idea that a king can do whatever he chooses with his white subjects, being responsible to God alone for his actions."

Billy smirks. "Everyone knows we threw off that idea decades ago."

"That's my point exactly. Now Douglas wants to resurrect it by saying the white man can be left to do whatever he chooses with his black slaves, being responsible to God alone. We fought a bloody revolution in '76 to get rid of that principle, why should we bring it back now?"

Francis picks up a bodkin and toys with it. "All right. Hit that last part hard."

"What's next?" Billy asks.

I rake my fingers through my hair. "Something on the order of 'Slavery is founded on the selfishness of man's nature as opposed to his love of justice. The oldest laws concerning slavery are about regulating it where it already exists. There are no laws anywhere that permit it to be introduced as a new thing.'"

Francis asks, "What did our Founders intend?"

I wring my hands. "Slavery should not be extended beyond the original colonies."

Billy adds, "They were hostile to slavery in principle, but tolerated it only out of necessity. They conceded to demands by legislatures in the southern colonies because they knew a revolution fought by only half the colonies would have failed."

Francis nods. "Nearly eighty years ago we began by declaring all men are created equal; but from that beginning men like Douglas have run us down another path declaring that some men have a sacred right of self-government to enslave others."

I throw up my hands. "Some men now live in dread of absolute suffocation if they cannot exercise their 'sacred right' of taking slaves to Nebraska. That supposed right is something Jefferson never thought of."

Francis clenches his fists. "Slavery deprives our republican example of its just influence in the world. Our enemies taunt us as hypocrites, and our friends doubt our sincerity. We are the last civilized nation to tolerate it."

I pace the floor.

After a few moments I say, "There's something foul about this Nebraska Act. It breaks every compromise our government has made over the slavery business. It's as if two starving men divide their only loaf, then one hastily swallows his half and grabs the other half just as his companion is about to take a bite. How will we be able to trust them on any compromise, ever again?"

Billy bounces to his feet. "Each party is becoming increasingly bitter and more resolved against the other."

I scratch my head. "They must be made to see reason. They claim equal justice requires the extension of slavery—that inasmuch as they don't object to me taking my hog to Nebraska, I should not object to them taking their slave to Nebraska. That's perfectly logical if there is no difference between hogs and Negroes."

Billy laughs. "You're grasping for straws."

I shake my head. "No. Don't you see? In 1820 the South agreed it was wrong to buy slaves in Africa and sell them on our shores. They even agreed that such offense should be punished by hanging. Never did they say that a man should be hung for transporting a hog from Africa and selling it here. So they have already said that hogs and Negroes are not the same."

Francis grins. "You've got a point."

I stroke my chin. "On top of that, there are 433,643 free Blacks in the United States and Territories. At five-hundred dollars each, they are worth $200,000,000. Why does this vast amount of property run about without owners when we do not see horses or cattle or hogs running at large? Not even in the South do they believe that hogs and Negroes are the same. How is it they ask us to deny the humanity of slaves when they have never been willing to do so?"

Billy clasps Francis' shoulder. "You've got it. Tell them, 'If the Negro is a man, it is a total destruction of self-government to say that he shall not be allowed to govern himself. No man is good enough to govern another without his consent. That is the leading principle of American republicanism.'"

I follow Douglas to Springfield and Peoria, arriving shortly after he leaves each place, and deliver my new speech, making the points that Billy and Francis suggested. Then I conclude by saying,

> *I have no prejudice against the Southern people. They are just what we would be in their situation. If slavery did not now exist amongst them, they would not introduce it. If it did now exist amongst us, we would not instantly give it up.*
>
> *The question of the hour is whether slavery shall go into Nebraska or other new territories, and it is not a question of exclusive concern to the people who may go there. The whole nation is interested that the best use shall be made of these territories. New Free States are the places for poor people to go to and better their condition.*
>
> *The slavery question often bothered me as far back as 1836-40. I was troubled and grieved over it; but after the annexation of Texas I gave it up, believing as I now do, that God will settle it, and settle it right, and that he will, in some inscrutable way, restrict the spread of so great an evil; but for the present it is our duty to wait.*
>
> *I am not contending for the establishment of political and social equality between the whites and blacks. Neither am I combating the argument of NECESSITY, arising from the fact that the blacks*

are already amongst us; but I am combating what
is set up as a MORAL argument for allowing them to
be taken where they have never yet been. I am
arguing against the EXTENSION of a bad thing.

After winning my seat in the state legislature, the Secretary of State tells me I must resign in order to be a candidate for the U.S. Senate. My arms fall heavy to my sides. Under the new state constitution, senators continue to be elected by the legislature, but sitting legislators are prohibited from running for federal offices. I'm left to fight for the Senate seat as an outsider.

For the next several weeks, I sleep sparingly. Even as I attend to client business my mind wanders until it locks onto the list of incoming state legislators. I reshuffle their names between the columns for Shields, Lincoln, and "Undecided." With the "Undecided" legislators being too numerous to allow for a clear winner, I consider others who might also want to unseat Shields. Certainly, Douglas chafes at the prospect of an anti-Nebraska man from his own state challenging him in Washington. If Shields falters, he'll push for an ally who'll be an ardent defender of Popular Sovereignty.

Rumors persist that our Democratic Governor Joel Matteson, a balding, roman-nosed man, is buying votes to bolster his surreptitious candidacy, but he's staying out of the fray until the legislature is deadlocked. Another candidate is Lyman Trumbull, a slump-shoulder former school teacher turned lawyer. He's a Georgia-born Democrat, but he bolted from his party in protest over the Kansas-Nebraska Act. As a result, Douglas views Trumbull as a traitor to his party.

By custom, the State Senate and House convene together on the second day of the legislative session to elect the U.S. Senator. The voting usually occurs in early December, but a series of delays—orchestrated by the Democrats hoping to block me—has postponed the decision until February 8. I face another six weeks of restless nights and Mother's heightened irritability.

When the legislators finally assemble, Mother is in the balcony, anxious over a long-awaited step toward achieving a girlhood dream. Years ago, she spurned Stephen Douglas to marry me, and she told him her choice was because she wanted to marry a man who would become president.

I look up at her after the first ballot. The tally shows me 44, Shields has 41, Trumbull 5. She's beaming. I smile broadly.

Her countenance falls and my throat grows increasingly dry as ensuing ballots result in little change. After the seventh ballot, when Democrats begin switching from Shields to Matteson, her eyes narrow. On the ninth round of voting, I receive only 15 votes. Many of my supporters are going over to Trumbull's side. Sweat collects along my collar, in spite of a damp chill in the chamber. The contest is now between Trumbull and Governor Matteson.

During a recess, I overhear some of Trumbull's supporters speculating that Matteson might be a secret anti-Nebraska man. They say they could be swayed to vote for him, and it would be quite a coup to send a Democrat to Washington to stand up to Douglas. My throat tightens. Even if the gossip is true, rumors of Matteson buying votes are a bitter pill for me to swallow. I could not abide seeing him win this contest unfairly.

At the conclusion of the recess, I enter the House chamber and ask to be recognized by the Chairman. A hush falls over the assembly. My heart races.

"Mr. Chairman ... there are yet a handful of men in this hall who are full of faithful determination to see me join the United States Senate. I sincerely thank them for their steadfastness."

A cacophony of cheers and hisses fill the room. My ears are beset by ringing.

I swallow. "I release my supporters and urge them to vote for a man who will carry a strong anti-Nebraska message to Washington City. In my humble opinion, that man is Judge Lyman Trumbull."

On the tenth ballot, Trumbull wins. My body goes slack, weak. We succeed in sending an anti-Nebraska man to the Senate who will challenge Douglas at every turn. But once again, I fall short of my aim.

A wave of new energy washes over me, sparked by a fresh idea. I smooth the wrinkles from my suit, straighten my tie, and pull back my shoulders before walking over to Trumbull's office. I ask him and his supporters straight out whether they will support my effort to unseat Senator Douglas when he stands for re-election in 1858. They receive me warmly and assure me I'll have their votes in four years.

Later I find Mother seated in our carriage at the base of the Capitol steps with a blanket covering her legs. Her face is as stern as granite.

I climb aboard and sit next to her. "Mother," I say, taking her hand, "we'll make another go of it when Douglas' seat is up, and we will win."

She pulls her hand away. With her eyes still straight ahead she says, "I shall never speak another word to that Trumbull woman as long as I live."

In late August, I write a letter to Speed just before going on the Circuit. First, circumstances separated us; next, marriage widened the breach. Now, as the agitation over slavery threatens to rip our country apart, we face the death of our long, intimate friendship. He is dependent on slaves, while I bleed tears over the abuse of one human by another.

> *Dear Speed;*
>
> *You know I dislike slavery; and you admit the abstract wrong of it. So far there is no cause of difference. But you say that sooner than yield your right to the slave—especially at the bidding of those who are not themselves interested—you would see the Union dissolved. I am not bidding you to yield that right. I leave that matter entirely to yourself.*
>
> *I acknowledge your rights and my obligations under the Constitution in regard to your slaves. I confess I hate to see the poor creatures hunted down and caught and carried back to their stripes and unrewarded toils; but I bite my lip and keep quiet.*

In 1841 you and I made a tedious low-water trip by steamboat from Louisville to St. Louis. You may remember that from Louisville to the mouth of the Ohio there were on board a dozen slaves, shackled together with irons. That sight was a continual torment to me; and I see something like it every time I touch the Ohio, or any other slave-border.

It is hardly fair of you to assume that I have no interest in a thing which continually exercises the power of making me miserable. You ought rather to appreciate how much the great body of the Northern people crucify their feelings in order to maintain their loyalty to the Constitution and the Union.

I do oppose the extension of slavery, because my judgment and feelings so prompt me; and I am under no obligation to the contrary.

Your friend always,

A. Lincoln

Speed's private assurances that he prefers Kansas' admission as a free state bring me no consolation. I know he would vote for no man who publicly supports stopping the advance of slavery. The slave-breeders and slave-traders are as fully his masters as he is master to his own Negroes. My heart is as wounded now as it was a dozen years ago when he returned to Kentucky.

When the Circuit arrives in Bloomington in late September, I handle the case of a man named Jones who is being sued for damages by Phil Miller. Miller claims that Jones inflicted serious injury on him in a kind of running fight over a ten acre field. On cross examining Mr. Miller, I press him for minute details of the alleged assault and his injuries. On summation, I tell the jury, "I submit to you, that for a fight which spread all over a ten-acre field, this is about the smallest crop of a ten-acre fight you gentlemen ever saw." Jones is acquitted, but my tolerance for nonsense is reaching its limit.

The following week I leave the Circuit for a case in Cincinnati. A lawyer from Washington City named Peter Watson has hired me to serve as local counsel for a patent suit that was supposed to be tried in Chicago, but got moved on account of the defendant's illness. The suit against John Manny, our client who is a manufacturer of reapers, is being brought by Cyrus McCormick, whose reputation as an aggressive businessman is well known from one end of the country to the next.

Mr. Manny became the target of McCormick's wrath after the Manny Reaper bested the McCormick machinery at the Paris Exposition of 1855. In researching the case, I discover that McCormick lost an earlier patent challenge, so our chances of success are good. However, if Mr. Manny loses, he will have to cease production and pay McCormick four-hundred thousand dollars.

On arriving in Cincinnati, I stop in at the hotel where the distinguished cast of lawyers who are defending Manny are lodging. I stride up to Watson in the lobby, and he introduces me to George Harding from Philadelphia, a bookish, wispy-haired fellow, only twenty-eight but already reputed as one of the best patent lawyers in the country. After Harding greets me, Watson gestures to a pudgy, impeccably dressed lawyer named Edwin Stanton of Pittsburg. Stanton glares at me, his full lips puckered as if he's aiming for a spittoon, and refuses my handshake.

Turning to his partner, Stanton says, "Why did you bring that damned long-armed ape here? He does not know anything and can do no good ... If that giraffe appears in the case I will throw up my brief and leave."

I jerk back and stare at him. After a pause, I calm myself and choose to ignore his insult. I offer him the papers I've prepared on the case and insist I'm quite ready to make oral arguments.

Stanton refuses to take the papers.

I look at Harding and offer my papers to him. He takes them and nods.

Without looking at Stanton again, I turn to leave, rage rippling down my spine. When I'm a few steps away, Stanton tells the others in an unrestrained voice, "I can't imagine how they let that long, lank creature from Illinois enter a courtroom with his dirty linen duster for a coat. Did you see the back of it? It's splotched with perspiration stains that spread from one armpit to the next. The stain looks like a dirty map of the continent."

I slow my gait and consider turning back to abuse his ego with ridicule and insults. I decide otherwise and stride away at a quickened pace, imagining someday I'll show him who's the better man.

When court convenes, I'm not allowed at the counsel's table, but I attend sessions anyway, sitting in the back row taking notes. In the end, the judge finds for our client. Later, after my return home, Watson sends me two-thousand dollars in payment for my services on the case. He confesses they did not use my case notes. I return the fee with an explanation that my services did not warrant payment. He sends the money again, expressing his deep regret for the manner in which Stanton treated me. I give one half of it to Billy Herndon, according to our partnership arrangement, and use the remainder to pay off debts.

On the Circuit, still brooding over the Manny affair, I tell Judge Davis, "These eastern lawyers have got as far as Cincinnati now, and they'll be in Illinois soon. When they come, I will be ready for them."

Chapter Twenty Eight

I n May 1856, Billy Herndon slams *The Sangamo Journal* down on my desk. "Did you see this?"

I read the headline. *President Pierce Gives Recognition to Walker's Nicaragua Filibuster Regime!*

I look up from studying the paper. "It says Walker has called an election for July to set himself up as Nicaragua's president. He plans to reinstate Black slavery there and encourage southern plantation owners to immigrate so they can benefit from his government's new policies."

Billy's face is red. "Next he'll want his little kingdom to be annexed into the Union as a slave state."

I fold my arms across my chest. "Is that what Douglas is plotting? Mercenaries like William Walker carving new territories out of Central American nations and bringing them into the Union as slave states under Popular Sovereignty? He'll flood the Senate with pro-slavery men and outnumber us in the House as well."

Billy throws up his hands. "Why stop at Central America?"

I pound my fist on the desk. "It's no longer a fight to keep slavery out of Nebraska and Kansas. We must stop it from spreading over the entire hemisphere. As the soils continue to give out along the coastal plains, more eastern plantations will turn to breeding slaves for sale into new territories. After Nicaragua, they'll set out to conquer Mexico, Panama, Colombia, Argentina, and more. The demand for slaves will never die out."

At the end of the month, Billy and I go up to Bloomington for the first state convention of the fledgling Republican Party. Many old Whigs, principally abolitionists and anti-Nebraska men, have been lining up with free-soilers and anti-slavery Democrats to form the new party. Those who believe its platform is too radical have remained Whigs or declared themselves as independent. I've tried to walk a thin line, but with blood flowing over the slavery question in Kansas and elsewhere, even in Central America, it's time to act.

The first to address the convention is my friend O.H. Browning, whose speech fails to excite. When he's finished, the crowd begins calling out, "Lovejoy" and "Lincoln." My pulse quickens. Lovejoy glances over at me and I nod, deferring to him. Owen Lovejoy, the brother of the martyred abolitionist editor, is a popular politician throughout the state. He stirs the audience with his oratory, bringing them to their feet with applause.

At his conclusion, the delegates chant my name again. I steady my pulse, unfold myself from my chair, and amble up to the platform. I begin my speech standing at the back of the stage with my hands stuffed into my pockets. "I had picked up a speech in Springfield that I had intended to deliver here, but Browning and Lovejoy stole it from me. Now with what they have added, I give the whole thing when I get back to Springfield. Down there, they will think that it is a great speech."

Laughter erupts from the crowd.

Without consulting prepared notes, I move forward on the stage as I stress the logic of fighting slavery and declare the eternal rightness of our cause. I make a sweeping gesture with my hand to punctuate my insistence that we restore the Missouri Compromise because it embodies the great principles of American republicanism.

Delegates move from their seats, drawing closer to the platform, some standing at the foot of the stage. I urge the new party to bridle their emotions and fight with the ballot box, not with bullets. I demand that we keep slavery out of Kansas because human bondage is a great evil that is tearing our Union apart. Slapping my hand on the podium, I shout, "We will say to Southern disunionists: We won't go out of the Union, and you *Shan't.*"

My words are met with a thunderous ovation and later, Billy, who is often reserved in his assessment of my speeches, gives me unbridled praise. He tells me, "The flame that has been smoldering has finally broke out. You are now baptized, fresh born with the fervor of a new convert. You spoke with the force of a soul maddened by wrong. Now you have found the cross you've been seeking—your great purpose."

In the lobby, I'm congratulated for helping weld the discordant factions into a vigorous party. My face is warm, not from the fire on the hearth or from drink, but from pride. As we walk back to the inn after a night of celebrating, my steps are buoyant.

Weeks later, at the first national convention of the Republican Party, my name is put forward as a candidate for vice president. Though the honor doesn't fall on me, I join the national canvass, promoting General Fremont's presidential aspirations. On my return from a spate of out-of-town speeches, Mother is exceptionally cross with me. I also learn she unleashed her belligerence on our neighbor Jacob Taggart in my absence. When he comes to me and demands that I rebuke her, I say, "Friend, can't you endure this one wrong done to you without much complaint, for old friendship's sake? Why, I have had to bear it without complaint or murmur for lo these last fifteen years."

James Buchanan, a Democrat, is inaugurated president on March 4, 1857. His election is made possible by the disintegration of the old Whig Party, leaving only the nascent Republican movement to contest him.

I read Buchanan's Inaugural Address in *The Sangamo Journal* and say to Simeon Francis, the editor, "How does he plan to go about putting an end to the agitation over slavery, patching up the country's divisions, and beginning to heal the nation?"

Two days later, Francis bursts into my office with a dispatch. The Federal Supreme Court, led by Chief Justice Taney, has rendered a decision in the Dred Scott matter, saying Negroes do not, and cannot, have rights as citizens of the several states. They do not distinguish between free and slaves. Furthermore, Taney says neither Congress, nor any territorial legislature, may deprive its citizens of the right to hold slaves.

Francis shakes his head. "Buchanan says this is the final answer to the slavery question. But in truth, he's been handed a powder keg."

I press my palm to my forehead. "This so-called Dred Scott Decision will inflame even the most passive abolitionists. Their anger will sweep across the Northern region like a dry prairie wind fanning a wild fire."

In the fall, with the U.S. Senate contest still a year away, I succumb to personal and business pressures and return to the Circuit. In Danville one day during an afternoon court recess, Hill Lamon and a visiting lawyer remove their coats and agree to a wrestling match in the town square. After a time of pulling, grappling, and tearing up sod, Hill downs his opponent. Once he takes the top position, he strains to pin the visitor's shoulders to the ground, and the seam of his trousers gives way. At that very moment, Judge Davis calls us to the next case.

Given no time to change his pants, Hill dons his long-tailed coat and returns to the courtroom. All is well until Hill stoops over to recover a document he has dropped on the floor. His secret now being out, another attorney comes to his aid with a hastily prepared document soliciting funds to purchase a new pair of trousers.

Several other attorneys offer various exorbitant sums for Hill's relief before the document is laid before me. I wipe my spectacles and peruse its language in detail, as if studying an opposing attorney's brief. After I digest the matter with all due care, I scribble on it, "I can contribute nothing to the end in view." Laughter ripples through the courtroom as my reply is passed among the other lawyers.

One evening near the conclusion of our session in Danville, Judge Davis convenes what he calls an "Orgmathorial Court" to deal with my supposed breach of the Circuit code. The offense is charging too little in fees. Earlier in the day, Hill and I are representing a man named Scott, the guardian of a girl who suffers from persistent seizures. We win his case in twenty minutes, and he is so cheerful he pays up immediately. I watch as Hill accepts our fee, and my jaw nearly comes unhinged.

I ask, "How much did you charge that man?"

"Two-hundred and fifty," he says.

"Hill, that's all wrong. The service was not worth that sum. Give him back at least half of it."

"The fee was fixed in advance, and the man is happy."

"That may be so, but I am not satisfied. This is positively wrong. Go, call him back and return half the money at least, or I will not receive one cent of it for my share."

Hill follows my instructions, but our conversation doesn't escape Judge Davis' ears.

The Judge's voice booms from the bench. "Lincoln, I have been watching you and Lamon. You are impoverishing this Bar by your picayune charges of fees, and the lawyers have reason to complain of you. You are almost as poor as Lazarus, and if you don't make people pay you more for your services you will die as poor as Job's turkey!"

I glare at him. "That money comes out of the pocket of a poor, demented girl, and I would rather starve than swindle her in this manner."

When the Orgmathorial Court convenes, I am found guilty and fined for my offense against the pockets of my brethren of the Bar. Unshaken, I tell everyone, "Never during its life, or after its dissolution, shall my firm deserve the reputation enjoyed by those shining lights of the profession, 'Catch 'em and Cheat 'em.'"

On October 10, 1857, I'm at the Woodford County Courthouse in Metamora defending an elderly woman named Melissa Goings, who's charged with murdering her abusive husband. She has been free on bail since April;

even several of her dead husband's relatives contributed to the one-thousand dollar bond. The whole town believes she killed the old man in self defense. Her principal antagonist is Judge James Harriott.

When the trial commences, Harriott revokes her bond, making it clear he wants to get to the hanging straight away.

"Your Honor," I say, rising from my seat at a table provided for the parties at trial. "May I prevail on the court for a short recess to allow me to get acquainted with my client and the particulars of her case?"

"Granted," he says, glaring down from the bench.

I look over my shoulder as we leave the upstairs courtroom and notice the sheriff is lingering behind the bar rather than following us. Since Mrs. Goings is technically in the sheriff's custody, I consider we are liberated by his negligence. On reaching the front lobby I direct her out the door toward the large public square. We converse for a brief time, after which I return upstairs to the courtroom.

When Judge Harriott gavels the court back into session, Prosecutor Hugh Fullerton jumps to his feet. "Your Honor," he says pointing to the counsel's table where I'm seated with my co-counsel. "Where's the defendant?"

I rise and stare at the judge.

"Well, Lincoln," says Harriott.

"Sir?"

The judge's face is bright red, and his jugulars are bulging. "Where is Mrs. Goings?"

I look over to the sheriff. "As I last recall, she was in the sheriff's custody."

The sheriff bounces to his feet. "Your Honor, she was in Mr. Lincoln's charge, not mine."

Harriott asks again of Mrs. Goings' whereabouts.

"Your Honor, when she was last with me, she complained of being thirsty and asked where she could find some water. I told her I understand they have mighty fine drinking water down in Tennessee. What the sheriff did with his charge after that I am unaware."

The spectators in the courtroom begin hooting as they would at an Independence Day parade. Judge Harriott pounds his gavel and mutters, "Next case."

On accepting Fullerton's congratulations, I shake his hand and say, "Sometimes justice is a higher law than the statutes we make on its behalf."

During Congress' Christmas recess, Senator Trumbull travels back from Washington City and calls on me. Though our wives are still not cordial, we've enjoyed a collegial relationship since I paved the way for him to claim Shields' U.S. Senate seat in 1854.

"Lincoln," he says, "things might be looking in our favor, at least as far as the next Senate election is concerned. Douglas made a speech on the Senate floor defying President Buchanan on the Kansas Constitution. The Little Giant complains that accepting the LeCompton version, which Buchanan supports, goes against Popular Sovereignty; it was passed without support from a majority of voters. Douglas has spent years rallying his party around the Popular Sovereignty banner, and he's not going to let that ground slip away without a fight. Now Buchanan has little Douglas in his sights and means to take him out."

I hand him the *Chicago Tribune* and ask, "Have you seen this? The opinion page says that Douglas will gradually drift toward the Republican side and eventually join the party in 1860."

Trumbull clutches the back of his neck. "With this feud between Douglas and Buchanan, the Democrats are coming apart at the seams. I hear Douglas demanded that the national Republicans force you to stand down from challenging his re-election to the Senate. When word of a deal got out, the story changed. Now Douglas says he'll let you have the Senate if Republicans allow him to run unopposed for the House seat in his home district of Chicago."

I shake my head. "What's his angle? He must have some trick up his sleeve."

"Don't know. That's a mystery so far."

I pick up a copy of the *New York Tribune* laced with praise for Douglas. "This doesn't look like he has any plans to give me a clear path to the Senate seat."

Trumball takes the paper.

I don't wait for him to finish reading. "Shouldn't a Republican editor like Horace Greeley be on my side?"

He shrugs as he hands the paper back to me.

I throw the paper down on my desk and glare at him. "Does Greeley speak for the national Republicans? Have they concluded their cause can be best promoted by sacrificing us in Illinois? If that's so, I'd like to know it at once. It will save us a great deal of labor to surrender now."

Trumbull waves off my complaint. "Before coming down from Chicago, I met with Norman Judd, the Republican's state committee chairman. He agrees that Greeley has done us some injury, but he's not alarmed."

"Should I find solace in his lack of alarm?"

He shakes his head. "We should always be on guard, especially when it comes to Douglas."

"Will you take a message to Judd for me? Tell him I'm the only one who can beat Douglas."

"He already knows that, and he's more devoted to Illinois than he is to the national Republicans."

When Trumbull leaves, I send Billy Herndon to Washington to ask Douglas about his intentions with regard to the Senate.

Several days later, Billy returns and tells me the little bantam leaned back in his oversized chair, propped his feet on top of his massive desk and lit a cigar. With a grin stretching across his face he said, "Tell Lincoln I have crossed the river and burned my boat. I do not intend to oppose him."

While in Washington City, Billy also learned that Buchanan is pushing a candidate to oppose Douglas for their party's Senate nomination. The "Buchaneer" candidate, Judge Sidney Breese, feeds Billy a juicy morsel. He claims he was told by Senator George Jones of Iowa that Douglas has made a deal with the national Republicans. According to the deal, Seward will be the party's candidate for president in 1860, and Douglas will get the nomination in 1864. He'll be allowed to stay in the Senate in the meantime.

Billy reminds me of something I said during the Senate race I lost to Trumbull. "The race of ambition has been a failure for me—a flat failure. For Douglas it has been one splendid success after another. His name fills the nation and is not unknown even in foreign lands."

I could have added that Mother must regret that she did not choose Douglas as her husband when she had the chance.

Sweat runs down the back of my neck as I climb down off my horse in Beardstown. It's unseasonably hot and muggy for early May. That means the courthouse will be stifling for the trial of twenty-four-year-old Duff Armstrong who's accused of murder. Duff's sweet mother Hannah has asked me to defend him. She and his recently deceased father, my dear friend Jack, gave me shelter and fed me when I was a penniless lad in New Salem.

Judge Harriott, a "hanging judge" of mature years who attempted to try Mrs. Goings for murder in Metamora last fall, is to preside over the case. When I greet him in the lobby of Tom Beard's City Hotel, his hard, cold eyes have softened, and his beard is noticeably greyer than a few months ago. His recent trip to Iowa to recover the body of his own son—a young doctor who was killed by Dakota Indians during the Spirit Lake Massacre—has subdued his countenance.

I also find Hugh Fullerton, the slick-sure prosecutor, lounging by the empty fireplace. The fire in his eyes must account in small measure to the abnormal temperatures. I suppose he's still angry with me over Mrs. Goings slipping out of his clutches over in Metamora. Hugh tells me his key witness, Charles Allen, is missing, and the trial will not proceed without him. I want to tease him about losing a defendant and now a witness, but I bite my lip. Instead, I hurry off and locate Hannah to explain that Duff will remain in jail for another six months if Allen is not found and brought to testify.

Not wanting any more delays, she sends two of her nephews out to the town of Virginia where they have sequestered Allen in hopes his absence would avert Duff's conviction. By morning they return with Allen and the trial moves forward.

Allen, a rough-edged, middle-aged house painter from Petersburg, remains calm and confident as he gives testimony under questioning by Fullerton. Allen contends that Duff hit William Metzker in the head using a slung shot, a lead ball cradled in a leather thong. He says the blow killed Metzker. Allen claims he was able to see the weapon clearly in Duff's hand from a distance of around a hundred feet because the moon was almost directly overhead in the sky.

During his testimony, I sit back, staring at a fixed spot on the blank ceiling, only breaking my gaze a few times to stand and ask the witness to repeat the position of the moon at the time of the assault. The sweat Fullerton daubs off his forehead is only partly due to the weather. My interruptions bring him closer to a boiling point.

On cross examination, instead of haranguing Allen with the kind of invective I often use against opponents, I produce an almanac and turn to the page for the date of the assault.

"Charles," I say. "Can you read here where it tells us the time when the moon set that night?"

Allen reads the entry in the almanac and looks up at me, wide-eyed.

"Is something the matter?"

He looks down at the page. "It ... it says ... it says the moon was setting...."

"I'm sorry. Can you say that a little louder so that the jurymen can hear?"

He looks up. "It says the moon was setting when Metzker was killed."

Fullerton jumps to his feet. "Your Honor?"

Harriott calls us forward to the bench, asking to see the almanac. When he finishes reading it he hands it to the prosecutor.

Fullerton studies it, glares at me, and hands it back to the judge.

"Mr. Lincoln," says Harriott, glaring down at me. "You're mistaken. The moon was just coming up instead of going down."

"Your Honor, it serves my purpose nonetheless—just coming up, or just going down. It was not overhead as the witness swore it was. I would like the almanac entered into evidence."

Harriott looks at Fullerton. "Objections?"

"No, Sir."

After dismissing Allen, Fullerton rests his case.

I produce eight witnesses. One of them is a doctor who testifies that the wound above the victim's eye, which was allegedly made by a slung shot found near the scene of the fight, was not made by such a heavy object and couldn't have been fatal. Another witness claims that the slung shot in question belonged to him and was in his possession, not Duff's, at the time of the fight. The other witnesses say Duff hit Metzker with his fists after Metzker, the more powerful man, attacked him.

As I begin my closing argument, I remove my coat and vest. "Gentlemen, I admit that I have a personal investment in this case." I gaze into each of their faces. They are all young men, most of them not yet thirty. I have encountered many of them as children as they've grown up here in Cass County. Their parents are well known to me as well. Some of the older ones such as Milt Logan, a farmer and leading citizen, have either been clients or adversaries in this very courtroom; if not that, we've crossed paths in politics. To a man, their expressions are warm and attentive.

I turn and fix my eyes on Duff Armstrong. "When I was not much older than this boy, I often sat on the floor of his mother's home, rocking his cradle." I gesture toward Hannah sitting next to me, wearing a large sunbonnet covering her silvery hair. "On one such occasion, she was mending the only tattered suit of clothes I owned. I was penniless and alone in a strange village. They were one of many families that gave me shelter and fed me."

I turn back to the jurymen, removing my tie. "It would break his mother's heart, and mine as well, to see him hanged for defending himself." I dab tears with my tie and lay it on the witness chair. A juryman, Benjamin Eyre—the son of a plow and wagon manufacturer—swallows hard. Hannah begins to sob.

I take a kerchief from my trouser pocket and wipe my brow. I point to Duff; the suspender on my left shoulder slips off and hangs at my side. "This good boy is too bright to have attacked a man much larger than himself—Metzker weighing about two-hundred pounds while Duff is only one-hundred and forty. Had Duff done so, he would have armed himself first, even if under the influence of whiskey.

"Eight witnesses say Duff was unarmed. In fact, we are told that Metzker dragged Duff off of a bench, spat in his face and began to beat him. Only the witness Allen claims Duff was armed, but now he admits he could not have seen what he believes he saw due to darkness that evening. Furthermore, the alleged weapon was in someone else's possession at the time of the fight."

I step up to the jury box and lean in towards the twelve men seated there. One of them, a farmer's son who's no older than Duff, smiles. My voice cracks. "This boy's father was my dear friend. He died while Duff was in jail awaiting trial. Poor Jack never knew what his boy's fate would be, but he died knowing he'd raised a good boy who got caught up in circumstances that weren't of his own making. Circumstances that might have cost him his life if he hadn't defended himself. But in choosing to defend himself that night, he trusted his life would be safe in a courtroom in the hands of good men like yourselves."

Again, I gaze into each of the jurymen's faces. Not a single eye is dry. "I ask you, I plead with you to see the facts of this case clearly. If there be any doubt in your minds, consider a broken-hearted widow who needs her son back home to comfort her. Do not add the slightest blackness to her darkest hour."

Finally, I turn to Duff. "I can assure you on my own honor that this boy will go from here to make a good man of himself, as good a man as his father was." They all nod and several wipe tears from their eyes.

When Fullerton rises to make his summation, Hannah leaves the courtroom just as his ringing voice pronounces his greeting to the jury. I imagine she's near the breaking point and can't bear to hear what the prosecutor will say about her boy.

One hour later, when the jury returns with a verdict of "Not Guilty," Duff throws his arms around me, burying his face in my coat. Barely audible through his weeping, he asks, "How can I ever pay you for what you've done?"

"You don't owe me a thing, but I made a promise today, boy. Now it's your job to keep it."

He nods. "I will, Sir. I will."

I smile. "You better. I whipped your pa many years ago, and don't you think I can't do the same to you, even in my mature years."

With my arm draped over his shoulder, we head off to find Hannah and deliver the joyful news.

Chapter Twenty Nine

W hen I return home from the Armstrong trial, Billy Herndon waves a note at me and says, "Look at this. Your friends have been working."

I take the paper and read it. It's a letter from Norman Judd to the Republicans of Illinois.

> *In 1855 Mr. Lincoln threw his votes to Trumbull in order to defeat a Douglas man for the Senate, creating upon us a moral obligation which we have no wish to avoid.*
>
> *The Republican State Committee therefore resolves spontaneously and heartily to call a general state convention for the purpose of nominating Abraham Lincoln as the first and only choice of the Republicans of Illinois for the U.S. Senate, as the successor of Stephen A. Douglas.*

Never before have either Whigs or Republicans aimed to settle on a single nominee for the office of United States Senate. Judd's letter encourages his party to do just that.

A lump rises in my throat. I tell Billy, "Reckon I'd be crying if my reservoir of tears hadn't been drained back in Beardstown."

Before appearing at the state convention to accept the Republican Party's nomination, I prepare a speech and take it to the office for Billy to read.

When he finishes reading it, he shakes his head. "It's politically the wrong thing. You come within a hair of saying war is certain."

I throw up my hands. "I've chosen to anchor my argument on a universally known expression, something that will strike home in the minds of men and rouse them to the peril of the times. But never do I intend to advocate bloodshed."

He shrugs.

I glare at him and stuff my speech back under my hat. "It is indisputably true that the Nebraska Act has surely made the slave question harder to resolve, and I will deliver it as written."

He sags back into his chair.

At eight o'clock that evening, June 16, 1858, I stand before one-thousand delegates at the Illinois Republican Convention to accept the young party's first nomination for the United States Senate. My stomach is twisted in knots.

Mr. President and Gentlemen of the Convention,

If we could first know where we are, and whither we are tending, we could then better judge what to do, and how to do it.

We are now far into the fifth year since a policy was initiated with the avowed object and confident promise of putting an end to the argument over slavery.

Under that policy the agitation not only has not ceased, but has constantly increased.

In my opinion, it will not cease until a crisis shall have been reached and passed.

"A house divided against itself cannot stand."

I believe this government cannot endure permanently half slave and half free.

I do not expect the Union to be dissolved—I do not expect the house to fall—but I do expect it will cease to be divided.

It will become all one thing or all the other.

Either the opponents of slavery will arrest the further spread of it, and place it where the public mind shall rest in the belief that it is in the course of ultimate extinction; or its advocates will push it forward, till it shall become alike lawful in all the States, old as well as new—North as well as South.

The delegates rise and give me an unspirited ovation. I study their staid expressions, laced with worry. After I descend from the platform, Leonard Swett, my Maine-bred, Logan County lawyer-friend, greets me. He strokes his wiry beard and scowls. "Nothing could have been more unfortunate or inappropriate."

I let out a heavy sigh.

The next day, newspapers report sharper criticism from the national Republicans. Greeley responds, *You have repelled Douglas who might have been conciliated and attached to our side. Now go ahead and fight it through.* He's been courting Douglas to join the Republican ranks since President Buchanan set about cutting the Little Giant down to size.

Billy's warning echoes through my thoughts when an editor for *The National Era* writes, *Lincoln is a man of inflexible political integrity. He is too open and honest to succeed.*

An even less sympathetic opinion comes from the *Peoria Daily Telegraph—Honorable Abe Lincoln is undoubtedly the most unfortunate politician that has ever attempted to arise in Illinois. In everything he undertakes, politically, he seems doomed to failure.*

I press the heel of my hand against my forehead. "What does Providence have against me?"

Later that evening, I sit by the home fire, reflecting on William Cullen Bryant's *Thanatopsis* and settle on these lines:

What if thou shalt fall, unnoticed by the living,
and no friend take note of thy departure?
All that breathe will share thy destiny.
The gay will laugh when thou art gone,
the solemn brood of care plod on,
and each one as before
will chase his favourite phantom;
yet all these shall leave their mirth
and their employments,
and come and make their bed with thee.

Although my campaign is off to a rough start, I take comfort in counsel John Stuart gave me during my early days in the state legislature, "No defeat is ever as final as it seems." I vow to forge on. The cause is too worthy for failure.

Fortunately, Judge Douglas isn't faring much better. The national Democrats are abandoning him over his feud with Buchanan, and local partisans are teetering as well. In April, when the State Democratic Convention nominates Douglas for re-election, several dozen delegates walk out under orders of the Postmaster of Chicago, a recent Buchanan appointee. The renegades hold their own convention and nominate Buchanan's choice, Judge Breese.

To prepare for my campaign against Douglas, I pore over the district election results from the 1856 presidential canvass. Since the U.S. Senator is chosen by the state legislature—consisting of fifty-eight house seats and twenty-five senators—we must win the majority of those elections to defeat Douglas in January. The '56 results buoy my spirits. Even though Buchanan won the state's Presidential Electors, his opponents received thirty-thousand more votes. What's more, Republicans and Whigs combined to win a majority of the state house and senate districts. If we can repeat those numbers, we can secure the Senate seat.

I rally my friends, telling them our strategy must focus on the middle section of the state. Abolitionists hold a solid advantage in the north, so we're certain to win the seats in those counties. The southern counties are populated largely by southern-sympathizers who would never cast their ballot for an anti-slavery man like me. The middle counties are the stronghold of the old Whig party made up of folks who shy away from extreme positions. I caution my supporters that, if the Whigs buy Douglas' portrait of me as an abolitionist, my chances with them are dim. My worries appear justified when the Whig candidate for Governor, Buckner Morris, endorses Douglas.

Campaigning begins in earnest on July 9 when the U.S. Senate adjourns, and Douglas returns to Chicago to deliver a speech at the grand five-story Tremont House. I make tracks to the burgeoning young metropolis and stand at the edge of the crowd below the second story terrace as he begins to speak. On seeing me among his supporters, the Little Giant invites me to join him on the balcony. When I do so, he lauds me as "a kind, amiable, and intelligent gentleman, a good citizen and an honorable opponent." Out of politeness, I decline his invitation to address the assembly.

Soon after he launches into his speech, he turns and points to me, saying,

> I am free to say to you that, in my opinion, this government of ours is founded on the white basis. It was made by the white man, for the benefit of the white man, to be administered by white men, in such manner as they should determine.

It is clear to me, if not to the throng below, that he is taking direct aim at my criticism of the Supreme Court's Dred Scott decision, which said the Negro has no part in the Declaration of Independence. His supporters howl their approval.

The next evening I address a modest crowd from the same balcony. I conclude by rebutting Douglas' declaration of a white man's government.

> I should like to know, if taking this old Declaration of Independence, which declares that all men are equal upon principle and making exceptions to it, where will it stop? If one man says it does not mean

a Negro, why not another say it does not mean some other man? If that declaration is not the truth, let us get the Statute book, in which we find it and tear it out!

After lingering in Chicago for a few days, Douglas sets out on a tour of the central counties, canvassing votes for candidates who will support him when the legislature elects our Senator. I follow, unaccompanied and with no baggage. He travels in style on the Illinois Central Railroad directors' private car with a banner strung up on the side announcing, *S.A. DOUGLAS, THE CHAMPION OF POPULAR SOVEREIGNTY*; a baby brass howitzer manned by two gunners in red militia shirts is mounted on a tagalong flatbed to sound his arrival.

On his arrival in Bloomington, he's greeted by a throng of cheering admirers. No one makes any fuss over my presence, until Douglas notices me among the spectators as he begins to deliver his address. When he asks if I wish to make a speech to his supporters, I decline. I save my remarks for a more favorable audience the next evening after he departs.

I shadow Douglas as he moves on to Atlanta, Lincoln and Springfield, following the same pattern as in Chicago and Bloomington. When he sees me in the audience, he invites me to speak, and I decline, waiting until the next day to make my pitch under more agreeable conditions.

After a little more than a week of Douglas taking the crowd, and me gleaning his leftovers, I follow him back to Chicago. While there, I meet with Norman Judd who presses me to challenge Douglas to a series of face-to-face debates.

I fold my arms across my chest. "My recent experience shows that speaking at the same place the next day after Douglas is the best thing. I rebut him, but he has no chance of taking a second shot at me."

Judd stares up at me with his eagle eyes and taps the side of his aristocratic nose. "I can smell opportunity from a mile away, but I'll give you your way for now."

Judd's a stocky fellow with an authoritative bearing whom I've watched wear down the opposition while debating his cause in the State Senate. I know his concession isn't his last word.

Two days later as I prepare to return to Springfield, I read that Judd's friends at the *Chicago Tribune* have joined the chorus of those calling for debates. I go directly to his office to chastise him for enlisting the newspaper to pressure me. Before I can get in the first word, he grins as he hands me a copy of the *New York Tribune*. "Greeley has joined the debate bandwagon, too."

I tell him, "Douglas is the idol of his party. If we go face-to-face, his popularity and imperious style will carry every debate. The newspaper men will say 'Judge Douglas said so-and-so' and write it up as a triumph for him."

Judd steps up to me, his eyes only come up to the base of my throat, and plants himself like a boulder. "The committee's appetite demands something more than second-fiddle appearances in towns Douglas has just left with a Napoleonic air."

I shake my head and sit at his desk. "Get me some paper and a pen."

Still smiling, he hands me a sheet of his stationery.

"A blank page, please," I say in a deliberately icy tone. On the paper he supplies me, I write a brief note to Judge Douglas, challenging him to a series of debates. Judd delivers it on my behalf.

Before tendering his reply to my challenge, Douglas takes his tour down to Decatur. When I track him down, he's dining at the Oglesby House restaurant, and he invites me to join him. However, my hopes of settling the question of our debates are dashed by an onslaught of Democrats who parade by our table, offering him congratulations on his speech and well-wishes for the canvass. We complete our meal without a single word exchanged between us regarding the campaign.

The next day, Douglas heads up to Monticello to make a speech. As I'm lingering behind, having breakfast, I'm handed a copy of the *Chicago Times* which has published Douglas' response to my debate challenge. After digesting his litany of complaints and excuses, I write out a reply and make tracks north to catch up with him.

Our paths cross as Douglas is headed back south

from Monticello, having already concluded his speech. As I begin to address his complaints, he interrupts and tells me he'll be spending the night at the home of Frank Bryant. His host, a dyed-in-the-wool Democrat, lives in Bement, a flat, treeless patch of land I've just passed through. We agree to meet there after I've held my rally up in Monticello later in the evening, and I hand him the reply I'd written down in Decatur.

Late that evening, Douglas and I sit together in the parlor of Bryant's cottage, and he begins by complaining, "Lincoln, I don't understand why you didn't make this challenge earlier. You've been aware of my travels to the various county seats to meet with the Democratic committees for the purpose of scheduling my campaign stops. You followed me to each of those places and could have brought up the matter on several occasions."

I lean back in my chair. "I've been quite content to tag along and get the last word on you each time you spoke. It's the Republican Committee that is pressing for these debates."

He brushes his hair back behind his ears. "I imagine you would be quite content to continue as you have. You put me in the position of having to anticipate any new charges you might lay on me."

"As your agents can certainly report, Judge, my message doesn't change. You and the Slave Power have a conspiracy to spread slavery across the entire continent, and we must stop you."

"You have no evidence of any such agenda. If there's a conspiracy afoot, it is you and this straw man Buchannan intends to put forward, working to defeat me by dividing the Democratic Party."

I lean forward. "I've had no conversations with anyone from the President's administration who's conspiring against you."

Douglas swirls a mouthful of whiskey and gulps it down. "As soon as I agree to these debates, Buchanan's people will demand a share of the platform for their man."

"Then we'll both tell him he can't."

His eyes narrow. "And there's this matter of you dogging me around the state. It has to stop."

"Over the course of the nine debates, I'll not follow you."

"Seven debates. We already did the first two—Chicago and Bloomington."

"We have a deal."

Douglas stands and extends his hand. "Deal. I'll send you a list of the places and dates."

Three weeks later as my carriage bounces through Ottawa's dusty, unpaved streets to the venue of our first debate, my progress is impeded by a vast concourse of people jamming into the town square—more than could possibly get near enough to hear. I'm forced to disembark and push my way past a sea of supporters and Douglas partisans alike, leaving several brawls in my wake. My ears are assaulted by peddlers hawking merchandise and bands straining to make their music heard above the boisterous masses. There are no chairs for spectators to be seated and no trees to offer shade from the blistering sun.

When I arrive at the platform, where the wooden awning already collapsed under the weight of a gang of drunken ruffians who had insisted on climbing atop it, cheers erupt. I greet Judge Douglas and whisper, "I fear the crowd will be rougher on us than you or I could be to one another."

Douglas is the first to speak. He's allotted an hour for his main presentation. I will follow with ninety minutes and he will close with a half-hour rebuttal. He puffs out his chest and begins by reading a message from Lyle Dickey, the local torchbearer for Henry Clay's Whig principles. Dickey is both physically imposing and casts a large shadow over our state's politics. Dickey's message says:

> *The Republican Party in Illinois, unfortunately, has passed under the control of the revolutionary element of the Abolition party, and of those who have adopted or paid court to that element. The leaders, and to some extent the voters, of the Republican Party have been poisoned—debauched by the baneful sentiments and delusive distraction of that dangerous faction.*

The Democrats roar their approval. I hang my head. We need Whig support from the central counties to win this contest.

After the crowd quiets, Judge Douglas continues in an angry, bombastic style labeling me as a dangerous radical who dishonorably opposed the Mexican War ten years ago. He accuses me of conspiring to abolitionize the old Whig and Democratic Parties and claims my opposition to the Supreme Court's Dred Scott decision banning Blacks from citizenship would lead to massive immigration by Blacks into our state. He goes on to pose seven questions, most of which are designed to prove I favor Black equality and oppose the Constitution.

When my turn comes, I stand slump-shouldered, remove my spectacles to clean them and say to the assembly, "I now must wear these confounded things on account of my old age."

Laughter rises from the audience.

I gesture toward Douglas and say, "It is somewhat intimidating for me to stand here next to a great man, while I am yet a small man."

There is more laughter, this time mixed with hissing and booing. A small skirmish breaks out a ways back in the crowd.

"Judge Douglas makes a serious accusation, against which I am prepared to defend myself. He says I kept a saloon as a young man in the village of New Salem. That is not true; however I did work at a little still house at the head of the hollow."

Nearly everyone in the audience has a good laugh.

"Now as to the charge of the saloon, I think I can clarify the matter. I believe Judge Douglas is referring to a grocery I once owned where we sold whiskey by the dram. If that is so, I must say in my defense that I would have *kept* the grocery business if I could have. But due to circumstances, which I regret, I lost it."

Hoots and belly laughs break out all over the square. Even Douglas snickers.

For the remainder of my time I ignore Douglas' questions and accusations. Instead, I remind everyone of the lofty principles of the Declaration of Independence and the precious gift of liberty that was intended by our forefathers to be enjoyed by everyone.

On rebuttal, Douglas lambasts me for not answering his questions and challenges me to renounce the Black Republican platform. He claims my failure to make such a renunciation proves I favor repeal of the Fugitive Slave Act which requires free-states to return runaway slaves to their owners, the emancipation of slaves in the nation's capital, and that I wish to deprive citizens of their rights to carry slave property into the territories.

When the debate ends I'm roundly criticized even by my own friends. Fellow Circuit lawyer Henry Clay Whitney complains that I behaved like a dodger on the platform. "Next time," he says, "don't handle him so tenderly. You have got to treat him severely, and the sooner you commence, the better and the easier things will go."

I tell him and my other friends, "For the first time in this canvass, Douglas and I crossed swords here. The fire flew some, and I am glad to know I am still alive."

A week later, the skies have turned gray, the air damp and chilly. When Douglas arrives on the speakers' platform, he's dressed in plantation style with a new-looking ruffled shirt under a close-fitting blue coat, sporting a wide-brimmed soft hat. I finger the brim of my worn stove-pipe hat as I look down at my rough boots, exposed almost to their tops by my too-short, baggy pants. I tug at the cuffs of my thread-bare shirt sticking out too far from the sleeves of my coarse tattered coat. Mother's nagging about my uncouth appearance rings in my ears.

This time, I lead off with an hour address and finish with a half-hour rebuttal. Douglas' speech is sandwiched between my two.

I begin with short, crisp answers to each of Douglas' seven questions from the previous debate. Each question had been framed with the preamble, "Have you pledged?"

Each time I say, "I have not pledged," Douglas' frown deepens and his face grows sterner. At the conclusion of my denials, I go on to explain my position on each matter.

I say in regard to the first question, I believe the people of the southern states are entitled to a fugitive slave law under the Constitution and have never advocated its appeal, though it might be modified to be less objectionable without diminishing its effectiveness.

On the second, I say that I hope to never be in the sad position of having to pass on a law admitting a new slave state. Furthermore, I would be glad if there was never to be another slave state admitted, and if slavery were to be kept out of the territories before they are admitted to statehood, it is unlikely we would have any more.

My answer to the third question is included in my reply to the second.

On the fourth matter, I favor abolition of slavery in the District of Columbia under the following conditions: first, it shall be done gradually; second, it shall be done by a majority vote of the citizens of the District; and third, there shall be compensation to unwilling slave owners.

In regard to the fifth question, I say I have not sufficiently pondered the question of ending the slave trade between the states to take a position on it.

On the sixth matter, I have made my views on prohibiting slavery in territories sufficiently clear in the past. There is no need to comment on it further.

Finally, as to whether I am opposed to the acquisition of more territories unless slavery is first prohibited therein, I suppose I could add nothing to what is already in writing to make my position better understood.

At the conclusion of my responses, I ask Judge Douglas a question of my own. "Can the people of any United States Territory—in any lawful way against the wishes of any citizen of the United States—exclude slavery from its limits prior to the formation of a state constitution?"

"He won't answer," someone calls out.

I bite my lip to stifle a grin. If he answers "yes," he says the Supreme Court was wrong in its Dred Scott decision. Such an answer would confirm his opposition to the President who is from his own party, though it carries the risk of some moderate voters getting the impression that Popular Sovereignty can limit slavery's expansion. If his response is "no," he disavows his own principle of Popular Sovereignty and must agree that the Court will be right when it says that no state legislature, including our own, can exclude slavery.

During Douglas' turn, he answers yes to my question, and Judd glares at me from his seat in the front row. His countenance tells me he believes by giving Douglas the opportunity to affirm the view that slavery's extension can be halted, I have lost the debate and likely the election.

From the stand, Douglas teases me about only having four questions while he posed seven. He says, "But as soon as he can, he'll convene his council of Black Republicans, no doubt including Fred Douglass, to come up with more, which I will happily answer."

My jaw tightens, and several from the crowd yell, "White, white."

The Judge continues, "Douglass is a good man. The last time I came here to make a speech, while I was talking on the stand to you people of Freemont, I saw a carriage, and a magnificent one too, drive up and take a position on the outside of the crowd. A beautiful young lady sat on the front seat next to a man, and Fred Douglass, the Negro, sat on the back seat. Now it appears the owner of the carriage was in front, driving the Negro."

Cheers ring out from the crowd and someone shouts, "Right, what have you to say against it?"

Douglas retorts, "What of it! All I have to say is this, if you Black Republicans—"

They clamor again, "White, white."

"If you think that the Negro ought to be on a social equality with young wives and daughters, and ride in the carriage with the wife while the master of the carriage drives the team, you have a perfect right to do so and you ought to vote for Mr. Lincoln."

As Douglas continues to use the phrase "Black Republican" I drum my fingers on the edge of my seat, and the Republicans in the crowd become more agitated and demand, "White Republicans. White Republicans, sir!"

Douglas' veins bulge over his collar. "I wish to remind you that there was not a Democrat here vulgar enough to interrupt Mr. Lincoln when he was talking. I am clinching Lincoln, and you are scared to death for the result. I have seen your mobs before, trying to interrupt and prevent a fair hearing. I defy your wrath!"

When I stand tall for my rejoinder, vociferous cheers greet me. I say, "The first thing I want to say to you is a word regarding Judge Douglas' declaration about vulgarity and blackguardism expressed by some of you folks in the crowd. He says no such thing was done by any Democrat while I was speaking. Now, I only want to reply that while I was speaking, I used no vulgarity or blackguardism toward any Democrats in the manner Judge Douglas has repeatedly done toward my Republican friends."

The Republicans in the audience explode with great laughter and applause.

After the debate is finished, a young man introduces himself to me as Chester Dewey of the *New York Post* and offers his congratulations. "Well done, Lincoln. The New York Republicans who were in love with Douglas are rather more inclined to take a different view now. You made it clear the Little Giant continues to stand on the side of slavery's extension."

I give him a hardy handshake. "Thank you. We could use their encouragement."

The remaining debates are similar to the Freemont encounter. Douglas strives to convince his audiences that the Republicans and I advocate perfect equality of rights and privileges between the Negro and the white man. The charges are intended to scare conservative Whigs from voting for Republican candidates who might send me to the Senate. I bite my lip and deny his charges, knowing I risk alienating abolitionists in the northern counties.

Douglas also tries to convince the state's Whigs he's closer than I am to Whig doctrine. He claims the principles of Popular Sovereignty are the same as those endorsed by the Whig founder, Henry Clay. Lastly, he accuses me of trying to abolitionize Whigs and moderate Illinois Democrats.

I stand to my full height and make sweeping gestures as I contend Popular Sovereignty will expose free white Illinoisans to unnatural competition from slavery. I call Douglas' principle an invention of the devil, a pretense for the benefit of slavery. If successful, his doctrine would lead to an Africanized continent, if not an Africanized hemisphere. In much the same way that slavery pushed poor white Kentucky farmers into an unforgiving wilderness, slave holders will shove the descendents of those pioneers into the western most seas, and some of them into the Antarctic.

A week after our final debate, I arrive in Carthage where Douglas had been a few days earlier and hear of the Senator's appalling performance. I'm told that while he was speaking, Douglas demonstrated unmistakable signs of intoxication. He was unsteady on his feet, and his words were pronounced with such difficulty that no one could understand what he was saying. The chairman, after some hurried conference with others on the stand, pulled Douglas' coat, said something to him which brought the speech to an end. The chairman then explained to the audience that the speaker was suddenly indisposed and would not be able to finish his speech at that time.

I ascend the same platform on which Douglas made a fool of himself the prior week. It had been erected in front of two windows of the court house. Over it, a bowery of tree boughs had been constructed in order to shield the speakers from the rays of the sun. The boughs had recently been replaced, since the original ones had withered.

After speaking a few minutes to a rather dull audience, I step back a little from the front of the platform, squaring my shoulders in an attempt to straighten my slouched posture. As I do, my head bumps the boughs above me. I smile and turn my head to one side; then with a sudden movement, I thrust my head up and through the bowery. The crowd howls with laughter at what must appear to be some queer creature whose head is detached from its body. With everyone now relaxed, I continue my speech.

A week later, I'm in no mood for levity. My heart contracts over news of Douglas' last minute endorsement by John J. Crittenden, the silver-haired Whig Senator from Kentucky who is heir to Henry Clay's political legacy. And a few days later, when the grueling canvass and tedious night of vote counting end, the Senate contest is too close to predict. The margin of victory is in the hands of a small group of newly elected legislators whose loyalties are too tenuous to count on.

During the ensuing weeks of arm twisting, the chances of sending a Republican to the Senate begin to wane. I seek encouragement in my opponent's setbacks, recalling that President Buchanan's retribution against Douglas supporters certainly cost the Senator some votes. Patronage appointees who owe their offices to Douglas were replaced in two waves, one in July and the other in October. Twelve of the twenty-six highest paid postmasters, as well as the U.S. Marshalls and federal attorneys for the Northern and Southern Districts of Illinois, are sacked. Twelve local Treasury Department officials are also fired.

On a late December day, charcoal skies cover the horizon, bringing with them the scent of winter storms. The weather matches my sullen mood, and I dither at the law office for several hours, unable to apply myself to a single case. When Billy Herndon drops the *New York Tribune* on my desk, Greeley's latest admiration of Douglas gets my goat.

I slam the paper down and say, "I'll be over at Judge Treat's office for a game of chess."

After Treat and I trade checkmates for a couple hours, little Tad interrupts us. "Mama says you should come to supper."

I peer at him over my spectacles. "Tell her, I'll be right along."

He makes a face and runs home.

A half hour later, Tad is in Treat's office once more. A new game is in full swing. He stamps his feet and shouts to usurp my attention. "Mama said come right now."

Without looking up, I repeat my previous instruction. "Tell her I'll be right along."

Tad kicks the chessboard, scattering the pieces on the floor.

Judge Treat glares at Tad, then at me.

I stand, collect my coat, and take Tad by the hand. We sing as we walk home.

A few weeks later on a gloomy January morning, the

legislature convenes to make its Senatorial choice. Braced for disappointment, Mother refuses to attend the session. I enter the hall tight-jawed and downcast. After the votes are tallied and Douglas wins another sterling victory, I return home where Mother pays me no notice. I pour a cup of coffee and retreat to the parlor to sit by the fire in silence, holding a copy of *Richard III* in my lap, left open to the lines,

> *Bad is the world, and all will come to naught*
> *when such ill-dealing must be seen in thought.*

The next day, I'm called to a meeting in the Springfield office of Illinois Secretary of State Ozias Hatch—a tall, bearded bachelor who's as welcome in my home as family. Also present are: Jackson Grimshaw, who, like Billy Herndon, is impetuous in the face of injustice; Ebenezer Peck, a former Democrat who spent his childhood in Canada; and Norman B. Judd. They are more formal than I expect from my friends.

Judd gets right to their purpose. "Lincoln, we all would like to see you as the Illinois candidate for the Presidency. Can we use your name in connection with the nomination and election?"

I swallow hard. "Well boys, I doubt whether I could get the nomination even if I wished it."

"Lincoln," says Judd, "We all know you well, we believe in you, we love you as a friend, we admire your sterling qualities, and have faith in your fitness for the highest office in the land."

I rub my hands along my pants legs and clear my throat. "Reckon if we held the election in this room right now, I might win. In spite of that, I just proved I can't defeat Douglas here in Illinois. What makes you think a bunch of sophisticated easterners are going to get behind a common prairie lawyer no one's heard of?"

Secretary Hatch opens his valise and pulls out a fist full of documents. "They have heard of you. Your debates with Douglas have been published by newspapers all over the country. As for getting beaten by Douglas, did you examine the numbers? Republican candidates for the legislature outpolled Douglas' men by 190,468 to 166,374 for House seats, and 53,784 to 44,750 for Senate seats.

"If the districts were apportioned according to population, you would have won forty-one votes in the House and fourteen in the Senate, enough to capture the Senate seat. It was the reapportionment plan of '54, not Douglas, that beat you."

My pulse echoes in my ears. I stifle a grin. "I see you boys are serious about this. Can I think on my answer?"

They indulge me, and I hurry home with a spring in my step. The icy crust on the ground doesn't slow me.

When I give Mother the news, she reaches up and pulls my face close to hers so she can smother me with kisses. After her affections are exhausted, she pulls back and searches my eyes. Hers glisten through a residue of joyful tears.

It's a sight I rarely see. I kiss her forehead.

She draws her lips in a narrow line and says, "There's much work to do. We must give it every ounce of energy we have."

I nod. "It will not be an easy road."

She beams as she says, "I knew you would make me Mrs. President some day."

My heart skips. I imagine how disappointed she'll be if we fail, and it's Douglas who beats us.

Late the next day, I call on Judd to grant my permission to place my name in the field if the committee thinks it proper.

Three months later, I meet with members of the Illinois Republican State Central Committee, and we lay out a plan to win the nomination. I am to take steps to squash whatever efforts might be made by the Republican newspapers to coordinate any endorsements of my candidacy. In addition, I will also make as many speeches outside of Illinois as can be arranged with the purpose of advancing public discourse on the great issue of slavery. To avoid the kind of critical attention being applied to other Republican candidates, we agree to not make any further comments during the coming year about our efforts to secure the nomination. We hope these strategies will avoid a premature groundswell of support.

For the next several months, I bury myself in cases to shore up my personal finances and lessen my anxiety.

Chapter Thirty

Herndon and I are hired to defend a man who's on trial for murder. Our client, Harrison, got into a fight with a fellow named Crafton, drew a knife and stabbed him. Crafton died a few days later. We plead self-defense on Harrison's behalf.

Our case rests on the testimony of Rev. Peter Cartwright, the square-jawed, weather-faced Methodist preacher I defeated in the 1846 election for United States House of Representatives. My opinion of him has been that he's an attention seeking *Bible* thumper who finds it easier to see the speck in another man's eye than the log in his own. He measures truth by the ends it achieves.

During deposition, Rev. Cartwright tells a story which could exonerate Mr. Harrison. The victim, Crafton, supposedly confessed to the preacher that he attacked our client and he alone was responsible for the outcome of the fight.

As he takes the stand my left heel bounces irrepressibly under the table. There's no telling what he'll say in front of the jurymen. At the conclusion of his testimony, I let out a deep sigh. He amends his story as to only one detail. He says that Crafton, on his death bed, forgave Harrison, and the jury acquits Harrison. For months afterward, I contemplate the mystery of forgiveness, a miracle I have always denied.

Not many nights later while I'm reading the newspaper in the parlor at home, Mother berates me for forgetting to stoke the fire. When I protest she had not brought the matter to my attention previously, she says, "Mr. Lincoln, I have told you now three times to mend the fire, and you have pretended that you did not hear me. I'll make you hear me this time." She picks up a stick of firewood, and strikes me on the head, leaving a cut on my nose. I clean off the blood and slink up to bed. Long ago I learned the best remedy for her abuse is distance.

The next day, I'm sure the lawyers in court notice my wounded face, although no one asks how I acquired the ugly gash. I nibble on my lunch and once again mull forgiveness.

On another occasion, Mother is entertaining some aristocratic company from Kentucky and sends Bobby over to my office to have me to pick up some breakfast meat. Along the way home with my purchase, I run into the State Auditor Jesse Dubois, who is a good friend and neighbor. He walks home with me and we go into the kitchen through the backdoor. As I'm laying out the meat for the cook to examine, Mother storms up to us and berates me. "What kind of meat is this?" she shrills.

I glance at Dubois. "It's what the butcher had."

"It won't do," she says.

"Why not?"

"I will not serve to our dignified guests something that I would hardly feed to a dog."

"Why Mother, this is a very adequate piece of meat."

Her face turns red. "Adequate? Adequate, you say." She picks up a wooden spoon and begins accosting me about the head. She shouts, "You cannot make yourself president by settling for only adequate."

I cover my face with my hands and run out the backdoor. Dubois—a plump fellow who would rather watch horses race than stretch out his own legs—is close on my tail. Once we're a good distance away from the house, we begin walking, and silence fills the space between us. We don't speak even at my office while Dubois helps clean the blood from my face. As I'm rinsing out my blood-stained shirt, he breaks the quiet and invites me home for supper.

"No thank you," I say. "I'm not hungry, and there's a mountain of cases here to keep me occupied."

He looks, his eyes full of pity. "Why do you let her treat you so miserably?"

I hang my head. "If you knew how little harm it does me and how much good it does her, you wouldn't wonder that I am meek."

After he leaves, I open Shakespeare's *The Tempest* and am transfixed by the words:

> *...the rarer action is*
> *In virtue than in*
> *vengeance...*

In early September Norman Judd comes to my office with invitations from the Republican committees in Columbus and Cincinnati to speak in their cities. He thinks we should accept, since Douglas has launched a campaign across Ohio to drum up votes for local Democratic candidates.

I sit back and stare at the ceiling, "A speech in Cincinnati would be a very big thing. It's the seventh largest city in the country."

"Yes," he says. "Ten newspapers. Count—ten of them to publish your speeches. I wouldn't be surprised if dozens more reprinted it across the northern tier and up and down the eastern coast."

I look at him and grin. "Reckon we don't have a choice, then."

"It'll be like the first days of your campaign in '58. You'll roll into town on Douglas' heels a few days after he's given a big speech." Judd hands me a folded copy of *Harper's New Monthly Magazine* he's been holding behind his back. "Douglas wrote a long article in here. Read it for yourself, but it makes him look like a compromise candidate."

I flip through the pages of the magazine. "He must think he has the Southern vote locked down—who else would they go for? If he can splinter our infant Republican Party with this kind of moderate rhetoric—turn our free-soilers against the abolitionists, set former Whigs arguing with moderate Democrats who've bolted from his ranks, have German immigrants and nativists at each other's throats—he'd be standing in the wings waiting to pick off our disaffected members."

Judd nods. "After claiming Popular Sovereignty is exactly what the Founding Fathers intended, he goes on to accuse you and Senator Seward from New York of insisting that war is inevitable."

I lean forward and plant my hands on my desk. "I never said any such thing."

Judd glares down at me. "You know full well what he's referring to."

I meet his stare.

He parrots back lines of my nomination acceptance speech, the veins in his neck bulging. "In my opinion, it will not cease until a crisis shall have been reached, and passed ... A house divided against itself cannot stand ... I believe this government cannot endure, permanently half slave and half free ... the opponents of slavery will arrest the further spread of it ...."

I roll up the magazine and wag it at him. "By the time I stand before the folks in Ohio, I'll have answers for every lie he tells in here."

On September 16, I stop in Columbus on my way to Cincinnati and speak to a small audience on the east terrace of the State House. I loop my thumbs under my suspenders.

The Giant himself has been here recently.

Laughter erupts from the crowd. I let them settle, and once all is quiet I take a long, deep breath, gazing out into the horizon. I pull my shoulders back and erect myself.

*Judge Douglas ought to remember when he is
endeavoring to force this new policy of Popular
Sovereignty on the American people that there was
once in this country a man by the name of Thomas
Jefferson, supposedly a Democrat. He's one whose*

*ideas and principles are not prevalent among
Democrats today.*

I pause, giving my words time to sink in, before
stretching out my arms as if summoning my listeners to
gather close.

*Thomas Jefferson did not share Judge Douglas'
view of the insignificance of slavery. In
contemplation of this evil thing among us Jefferson
exclaimed, "I tremble for my country when I
remember that God is just!"*

*There was then a danger to this country, and there
is a danger now—a danger of the avenging justice
of God on that little question which is unimportant
to Judge Douglas.*

I step forward to the edge of the platform.

*Thomas Jefferson supposed there was a question of
God's eternal justice wrapped up in the enslaving of
any man or race of men. Those who enslave their
fellow man brave the arm of Jehovah. When a
nation dares the Almighty, every friend of that
nation has cause to dread His wrath.*

*Choose ye between Jefferson and Douglas as to
what is the true view of this evil among us.*

The next evening, a host of well-wishers gathers at
the depot as my train enters Cincinnati. After being feted
by a brass band and a cadre of local dignitaries, I'm
spirited off to my hotel. Later, a torchlight parade carries
me to the Fifth Street Market where pyrotechnic displays
and bonfires illuminate the night. The crowd is larger than
any that witnessed my debates with Senator Douglas a
year ago. Cannons announce my arrival.

As I ascend the platform I look south across the Ohio
River only a few hundred yards away. Reflections from the
fires dance in its currents. Beyond the river is my boyhood
Kentucky home, little brother Tommy's grave, and the hills,
creeks, and woods I roamed with Austin Gollaher. My heart
skips, and a flood of memories pinches my throat. There's

the farm Father couldn't make a go of. There's slave country. A mist covers my eyes.

I begin my speech by repeating the controversial lines I gave at the Senatorial nominating convention of '58 for which I've taken much abuse from my supporters and much condemnation from rivals. Those words didn't get me elected when I used them before; nonetheless, they remain true, and I defend their truth tonight. I stand tall and declare,

A house divided against itself cannot stand.

I believe this government cannot endure, permanently half slave and half free.

I do not expect the Union to be dissolved—I do not expect the house to fall—but I do expect it will cease to be divided.

It will become all one thing or all the other.

I gaze over the crowd and reach out as if embracing them.

I have not said that I do not expect any peace upon this question until slavery is exterminated. I had only said I expected peace when that institution was put where the public mind should rest in the belief that it was on a course of ultimate extinction.

I said I believed, from the organization of our government until a very recent period of time, the institution had been placed and continued upon a path toward extinction. I said that we had comparative peace upon that question through a portion of that period of time, only because the public mind rested in the belief of its ultimate extinction, and that when we return to that belief, I suppose we shall again have peace as we previously had.

I drop my hands to my side and walk forward toward my listeners as an unarmed man would do.

I have assured Judge Douglas directly, as I now assure you, that I neither then had, nor have, or

*ever had, any purpose in any way of interfering
with the institution of slavery where it exists.*

*I believe we have no power, under the Constitution
of the United States, or rather under the form of
government under which we live, to interfere with
the institution of slavery, or any other of the
institutions of our sister States, be they free or slave
States.*

I bow my head and my shoulders slump. My heart
pinches at the injustices suffered by the Negroes, and I'm
weighed down by the estrangement slavery has wrought in
our land.

*I say to my Kentucky friends—understand this—the
issue between you and me is that I think slavery is
wrong, and ought not to be outspread. You think it
is right and ought to be extended and perpetuated.*

Someone from the crowd shouts, "Oh, Lord!"

*I'm not speaking of the good people of Ohio. That is
my Kentuckian I am talking to now.*

I reach out my hands, as if beckoning my Kentucky
kin to draw near. I say they should be whole-heartedly for
Douglas because he molds public opinion to their ends
better than any of them could.

*There are a few things which he says that appear
to be against you, and a few that he forbears to say
which you would like him to say. But you ought to
remember that the saying of the one, or the
forbearing to say the other, would loosen his hold
upon the North, and by consequence, he would lose
his capacity to serve you.*

*I call your attention to the fact—for a well
established fact it is—that the Judge never says
your institution of slavery is wrong. There is not a
public man in the United States, I believe with the
exception of Senator Douglas, who has not at some*

time in his life declared his opinion whether the thing is right or wrong, but Senator Douglas never declares it is wrong.

I take a few steps backward and drop my hands to my side.

He leaves himself in your favor by not declaring the thing to be wrong. And, he keeps open the chances for luring the sentiment of the North into your support by never saying it is right. This you ought to set down to his credit, little though it be in comparison to the whole of which he does for you.

I remind them of Douglas' notion that *there is a line drawn by the Almighty across this continent where He has signed the soil; on one side of which the soil must always be cultivated by slaves.* Below that line slavery is right and has the sympathy and direct authority of the Almighty. I nearly choke on these words, unwilling to accept a God who would be such a cruel master, one who authored the abuse by one human against another.

I tamp down my emotions and try to employ logic to expose the trap Douglas' principle would catch us in.

Whenever you can get these Northern audiences to adopt the opinion that slavery is right south of the Ohio, they will readily take the perfectly logical extension of that argument, that whatever is right on that side of the Ohio cannot be wrong on this. If you have property on that side of the Ohio, under the seal and stamp of the Almighty, when it escapes over here, it is wrong to have constitutions and laws "to devil" you about getting it back.

So Douglas is molding the public opinion of the North to acknowledge that all laws and constitutions over here which recognize slavery as being wrong are themselves wrong, and ought to be repealed and abrogated.

I believe it is safe to assert that five years ago no living man had expressed the opinion that the Negro had no share in the Declaration of Independence. If that be true I wish you then to note the next fact: that within the space of five years Senator Douglas, in arguing for his principle of Popular Sovereignty, has got his entire party, so far as I know, to say that the Negro has no share in the Declaration of Independence. That is a vast change in the Northern public sentiment upon that question.

A voice rings out from the crowd. "Speak to Ohio men, and not to Kentuckians!"

I reply. "I beg permission to speak as I please."

If only he could see I am speaking to Ohio men. The Southern mind is already set on slavery, but the Northern view is yet susceptible to Douglas' cleverness. Judge Douglas is like the old snake oil vendor, who having gotten folks to drink his elixir, he is not satisfied until they've bought the whole snake, as well.

In Kentucky and in many of the slave States, you are trying to establish that slavery is right by reference to the Bible. Now again, Douglas is wiser than you. He knows that whenever you establish that slavery is right by the Bible, it will occur to some Northerners that slavery in the Bible was without reference to color; and he knows very well that you may entertain the idea of enslaving white people in Kentucky as much as you please, but you will never win any Northern support for it.

Douglas makes a wiser argument for you: he argues the rightness of slavery of the black man; the slavery of the man who has a skin of a different color from your own. He thereby brings to your support Northern voters who could not for a moment be brought by your own argument of the Bible.

I pause to survey the crowd. Faces of young and old, men and women stare back at me, reflecting the glow of torches and bonfires that illuminate the stage. A handful of glistening black foreheads speckle the sea of white. My throat tightens as I walk forward to the edge of the stage.

Judge Douglas makes a wiser argument for you: he makes the argument that the slavery of the black man—the slavery of the man who has a skin of a different color from your own—is right. He thereby brings to your support Northern voters who could not for a moment be brought by your own argument of the Bible. Will you give him credit for that? Will you not say that in this matter he is more wisely for you than you are for yourselves?

I inhale a deep breath as I make a sweeping gesture with my right hand,

Judge Douglas has also declared that in every contest between the Negro and the white man he is for the white man, but that in all questions between the Negro and the crocodile he is for the Negro. He did not make that declaration accidentally at Memphis. He made it a great many times in the canvass in Illinois last year.

The first inference seems to be that if you do not enslave the Negro, you are wronging the white man in some way. I say that there is room enough for us all to be free, and that it not only does not wrong the white man that the Negro should be free, but it positively wrongs the mass of the white men that the Negro should be enslaved. The mass of white men are really injured by the effects of slave labor in the vicinity of the fields of their own labor.

In the struggle between the Negro and the crocodile, he is for the Negro. Well, I don't know that there is any struggle between the Negro and the crocodile. I believe Judge Douglas' idea is a sort of proposition in proportion, which may be stated thus: "As the Negro is to the white man, so is the crocodile to the Negro; and as the Negro may rightfully treat the crocodile as a beast or reptile, so the white man may rightfully treat the Negro as a beast or a reptile."

*Now, my brother Kentuckians who believe in this,
you ought to thank Judge Douglas for having put
that in a much more acceptable way than any of
yourselves have done.*

I pause to wipe my spectacles.

*Again, Douglas' great principle, "Popular
Sovereignty," as he calls it, gives you by natural
consequence the revival of the slave trade whenever
you want it.*

*If carried to its logical conclusion, Judge Douglas'
principle gives the sacred right to the people to buy
slaves wherever they can buy them cheapest, even
in Africa.*

*THIS IN SPITE OF THE UNANIMOUS DECLARATION
OF CONGRESS THAT BUYING SLAVES IN AFRICA
IS A CRIME EQUAL TO PIRACY, PUNISHABLE BY
HANGING.*

Another voice from the crowd rings out. "Don't foreign nations interfere with the slave trade?"

I reply, "I understand it to be the idea of Democrats to whip foreign nations whenever they interfere with us."

The man responds, "I only asked for information. I am a Republican myself."

I chuckle. "You and I will be on the best terms in the world, but I do not wish to be diverted from the point I was trying to press."

*So now that I have shown you that Douglas is more
wisely for you than you are for yourselves, you
must take him or be defeated. But if you do take
him you may be beaten anyway.*

I rise to my full height and look about at their faces.

*We, the Republicans and others forming the
opposition of the country, intend to "stand by our
guns," to be patient and firm, and to beat you
whether you take him or not. We know that before*

*we beat you fairly we have to beat you and him
together. We know that you are "all of a feather,"
and that we have to beat you all together, and we
expect to do it. We don't intend to be very impatient
about it. We mean to be as deliberate and calm
about it as it is possible to be, but as firm and
resolved as it is possible for men to be. When we do
as we say "beat you," you perhaps want to know
what we will do with you.*

I hold out my hands.

*I will tell you, so far as I am authorized to speak for
the opposition. We mean to treat you, as near as we
possibly can, as Washington, Jefferson, and
Madison treated you. We mean to leave you alone,
and in no way interfere with your institution.*

*We mean to abide by all and every compromise of
the Constitution. We mean to remember that you
are as good as we—that there is no difference
between us other than the difference of
circumstances. We mean to recognize that you have
as good hearts as we claim to have, and to treat
you accordingly.*

I rub the back of my neck.

*I have told you what we mean to do. I want to
know, now, when that thing takes place, what do
you mean to do? I often hear that you mean to
divide the Union whenever a Republican or
anything like it is elected President of the United
States.*

Someone calls out, "That is so."
I answer back, "'That is so,' one of them says. I
wonder if he is a Kentuckian."
Another shouts, "He is a Douglas man."
I step forward and lean toward the audience.

Well, then, I want to know what you are going to do

*with your half of the country? Are you going to split
the Ohio down through, and push your half off a
piece? Or are you going to build up a wall some
way between your country and ours, by which that
movable property of yours can't come over here
anymore and be lost for good?*

*So you divide the Union because we would not do
what you think is right on the subject of your
runaway property. When we cease to be under
obligations to do anything for you at all, how much
better off do you think you will be?*

I plant my hands on my hips.

*Will you make war on us and kill us all? Why, I
think you are as gallant and as brave as any men
alive; that you can fight as bravely in a good cause,
man for man, as any other people living; that you
have shown yourselves capable of this upon
various occasions. But, man for man, you are not
better than we are, and there are not as many of
you as there are of us. You will never whip us. If we
were fewer in numbers than you, I think that you
could whip us; if we were equal, it would likely be a
drawn battle; but being inferior in numbers, you will
make nothing by attempting to master us.*

I grip the lip of the platform with the toes of my
shoes and lean as far forward as my balance will permit.

*We do not seek to master you. We must not
interfere with the institution of slavery in the States
where it exists, because the Constitution forbids it,
and the general welfare does not require us to do
so. We must not withhold an efficient Fugitive Slave
law, because the Constitution requires us, as I
understand it, not to withhold such a law. But we
must prevent the outspreading of the institution,
because neither the Constitution nor general
welfare requires us to extend it. We must prevent
the revival of the African slave trade, and the*

enacting by Congress of a Territorial slave code. We must prevent each of these things being done by either Congresses or courts. The people of these United States are the rightful masters of both Congresses and courts, not to overthrow the Constitution, but to overthrow the men who pervert the Constitution.

After closing my speech to thunderous applause, I'm whisked off to my hotel where Congressman Tom Corwin greets me. His family is the cornerstone of Ohio politics, and he's a backer of Ohio Governor Salmon Chase's presidential aspirations. The Congressman grabs my hand and says, "That was a great speech. You're just the man to head the Republican ticket, and I'm certain I can swing Congressman Schenck to your corner, as well."

My heart stops. The only words I can find are, "Thank you."

He clasps my arm. "Let's go someplace to talk."

After he and I discuss my nomination strategy for several hours, I can hardly wait to get home and share the details with Mother.

Two mornings later at half-past ten, I'm handed a copy of the *Cincinnati Gazette* as I board a train to Indianapolis where I'm to deliver an evening speech. The *Gazette* has reprinted my entire speech. While I'm in Indiana, I learn the *Illinois State Journal* has printed excerpts, and the *Chicago Press & Tribune* has published the entire *Cincinnati Gazette* version of the speech. The *Chicago Journal* runs a favorable review by a reporter who attended the event in Cincinnati.

I return home a few days later and walk home from the train depot; my feet glide as if they barely touch the ground. The moment I step through the door and give Mother the news, she chides me for being exuberant over the success of my Cincinnati speech. She purses her lips and warns me not to disappoint her as I did when I gave the Senate seat to Lyman Trumbull.

Within the week I travel to Wisconsin to address crowds in Beloit and Janesville. On my way to the train depot, Billy Herndon chases after me, waving a copy of

National Intelligencer—Washington's leading newspaper. They've reproduced my entire Cincinnati speech. On the train, I sit back in my seat, grinning. I don't recall ever before having so much energy as now courses through my veins.

Chapter Thirty One

After returning from Wisconsin, I join the Circuit in Clinton, Illinois for a session that lasts several days. During my time in Clinton, reports spill in of Republican election victories in Pennsylvania, Ohio, Indiana, and Minnesota. The townspeople toast me a raucous celebration as "Long Abraham the Giant Killer." I worry that the accolades are premature, but I smile, nonetheless.

The next evening I step off the train in Springfield, walk off the platform past the brick depot, and head down the gas lit street toward home, my breath visible in the late autumn chill. At home, I put down my old tattered carpet bag and peruse a stack of mail. Buried in the middle of the pile is a telegram.

> *Hon. A. Lincoln*
>
> *Will you speak in Mr. Beecher's church Brooklyn on or about the twenty ninth (29) November on any subject you please pay two hundred (200) dollars.*
>
> *James A. Briggs*

Beecher. Henry Ward Beecher. Brooklyn. New York. Harriet Beecher Stowe. *Uncle Tom's Cabin.* I walk to the parlor and collapse into a chair. I read the telegram several times before Mother bustles into the room, the boys bounding in her wake. She stops at the window and plants her hands on her hips. "What is that racket?"

I snap my head around to see what's gotten her into a huff. Bobby, Tad, and Willy are pressing their faces into the window pane, laughing and waving. A band is serenading us on the street outside our house.

I stand and join Mother and the boys.

Shouts and cheers mix with the music, growing louder until the band is nearly drowned out. Mother turns to me, a smile having replaced her drawn expression. "They're calling your name, Father."

I continue to stare out the window for a moment, then turn to her and say, "Reckon they are, Mother."

Together, Mother, the boys, and I step out onto the front porch. Cheers fill the night.

"Go," Mother says, still smiling. "Go be with them."

I kiss her cheek, pat each of the boys on the head, and lumber down the steps into the sea of well-wishers.

Later, in my reply to the telegram from New York, I request more time for preparation. I want to bring them a speech such as I've never before delivered—free of political stumping and unadorned by prairie humor. It should be a serious lecture fitting the highest intellect the east has to offer. The organizers agree, and say they'll anticipate my arrival in late February.

When I tell Billy Herndon about the lecture at Beecher's church, he warns that New Yorkers have little interest in a president who hails from the west.

I can't tell whether Billy's blushing comes from anger, jealousy, or too much whiskey.

He says, "I smell a rat. Rumors are that Greeley doesn't think Seward can beat Douglas. He's hoping you can siphon off enough of Seward's support to create an opening for Edward Bates at the convention. He thinks Bates is the one who can win next November."

I cock my head, "If that is his intent, I'll just have to be sure my speech convinces him I'm the best man to face Douglas."

"You'll need a new suit," he says.

I shrug. "I'm not sure I see Greeley's hand in this. He's not about to get mixed up with any place that's called 'The Grand Central Station of the Underground Railroad.'"

Billy screws up his face. "Maybe you shouldn't either."

"Why not? What better place to tell abolitionists to tame their radicalism than in their own den?"

He shakes his head. "Suppose the worst you can do is anger a bunch of delegates who won't vote for you anyway."

There are a number of other invitations besides the Beecher one; so many it's impossible to accept them all. The most curious one comes from Thurlow Weed, New York's political boss and manager of Seward's presidential campaign. His letter to Norman Judd, who's organizing my supporters, says, "Send Abram Lincoln to Albany immediately."

I tell Judd to say, "*Abraham* Lincoln isn't available."

Senator Simon Cameron of Pennsylvania is more direct. He asks me to run as his vice president. *We* decline.

One of the invitations I accept is to speak at Leavenworth in the Kansas Territory. I stand on the rostrum to address the crowd on December 3, the day after the abolitionist John Brown is hanged. Some folks expect me to take his defense, but my contempt for radicalism, regardless of the cause, has not changed since I addressed the Young Men's Lyceum in Springfield more than two decades ago.

Our brothers in the south say if the Black Republicans elect a President, they won't stand for it. They will break up the Union. That will be their act, not ours. To justify it, they must show just cause. Can they do that? When they attempt to make justification, they will find that our nation's policy toward them is exactly the policy of the men who made the Union. Nothing more or less.

If we shall constitutionally elect a President, it will be our duty to see that they submit. Old John Brown has just been executed for treason against the state of Virginia. We cannot object, even though he agreed with us in thinking slavery is wrong. That cannot excuse violence, bloodshed, and treason.

So, if our brothers in the south undertake to destroy the Union, it will be our duty to deal with them as old John Brown has been dealt with. We shall do our duty.

When I return home from the Kansas Territory, I ask Billy Herndon to handle my cases while I spend hours each day at the State Library. He shakes his head and asks, "How long will it take?"

I shrug. "A few days."

At the library, I pore through stacks of books and congressional journals, searching for evidence that our Founders intended slavery should not exist where it had not yet taken root when the nation began.

Three weeks later I stop in the office, and Billy greets me with a big grin. "Am I glad to see you back. I'm swamped here," he says. The trace of white that remains in his eyes sparkles; the edges are laced with red from overwork and too much whiskey.

"Sorry, I'm not finished yet. Besides, the challenge will do you good." I don't bother to remove my hat. "I stopped in to get your opinion on something."

Billy scowls.

"I read that General Washington said of slavery, 'There is not a man who wishes more sincerely than I do to see a plan adopted for the abolition of it.'"

He sits down hard behind his desk. "And?"

"And in the Virginia legislature, Patrick Henry said, 'Slavery is detested. We feel its fatal effects. We deplore it with all the pity of humanity. Let all these considerations press with full force upon the minds of Congress. They will search this Constitution and see they have the power of manumission. There is no ambiguous implication, no logical deduction. The paper speaks to the point; they have the power in clear and unequivocal terms.'"

Billy buries his purple-veined nose in a stack of papers.

"Well?" I say.

He glares up at me. "Well, what?"

"Where do you suppose I should place those quotations in my speech?"

Through clenched teeth he says, "Near the front."

A few weeks later when it's time to go on the Circuit, I stop in the office again.

Billy slams both hands down on his desk. "Is it too much to hope that you're here to help me carry this heavy case load?"

"I'm sure you're doing just fine." I take the notes for my speech from under my hat. "Did you know that Virginia, New York, Massachusetts, and Connecticut each ceded territories to the general government prior to the Constitution, and those cession agreements carried stipulations limiting, but not doing away with the general government's power to regulate slavery within the ceded territories?"

He shakes his head.

I continue. "Not only that, but when the Ordinance of 1787 was passed by the Congress of the Confederation, it prohibited the extension of slavery into the northwestern territories won from Great Britain during the revolution. Four members of that Congress later became signers of the Constitution."

Billy shuffles some papers on his desk. "I imagine your audience in New York will be grateful when you inform them of those facts."

I wrinkle my nose. "I'm sure they already know. I just want to demonstrate I'm equal to them."

He looks up at me. "Have you stopped to consider that some of our clients will be equally grateful if you could give them some attention?"

"Yes. I suppose. Though, no one has expressed any grievances, at least not to me."

"So, how much longer?"

"That reminds me, Billy. I've been meaning to ask— can you take the first couple of stops on the Circuit when it begins?"

He slams his fist on the desk. "How much longer is this going to go on?"

I glare at him. "As long as it takes. This is the biggest speech of my life, and I am determined it will be the best."

He puts his head down on his desk.

On the way over to the library, I scoop up little Holly, one of the neighborhood girls, and carry her on my shoulders. I tell her, "It seems that Mr. Herndon is getting a taste of how it feels to carry the heaviest part of the load ... and all for a very important cause."

"Am I heavy?" she asks.

I smile. "Not in the least ... say, would you like to hear me read a piece from my speech?"

She drums her fingers on the top of my hat. "What's a speech?"

I remove my hat and pull out my notes.

"Here's the ending part. I shall read it."

It is more than presumptuous to claim Congress deliberately framed and carried out two things at the same time which are absolutely inconsistent with each other. The bill enforcing the Ordinance of 1787 was passed at the same time, and by the same Congress which approved the first ten amendments to the Constitution. It cannot be argued that they intended to simultaneously confirm and deny the federal government's authority to regulate slavery in the territories.

Nonetheless, Senator Douglas relies on the Tenth Amendment to justify Popular Sovereignty, claiming the people have a sacred right to carry slaves wherever they choose. Moreover, the Supreme Court in the Dred Scott case planted themselves on the Fifth Amendment, declaring Congress has no power to make slaves free even when they are outside the jurisdiction of any of the slave states.

These notions were not even spoken of ten years ago. Now they are being thrust on us as if they are cornerstones of our nation. The truth is that twenty-one of the Constitution's thirty-nine signers

*confirmed by their votes as members of Congress
that the federal government has the authority to
regulate, even prohibit, the extension of slavery
beyond where it was in place when the country
was founded. The remaining signers never voted on
any bill related to slavery, though many of them
were firm in their belief in the wrongness of it.*

When I arrive at the steps to the library, I set little
Holly on the ground and say, "Well what did you think?"

She looks up at me and points to my shoulder. "I
think that's a long way up. Are you really a giraffe?"

I laugh and pat her on the head.

Chapter Thirty Two

On Saturday morning February 25, I disembark the ferry at the Courtland Street terminal in New York City and lug my trunk several blocks past bleak shanties. These piece-meal shelters make desolate prairie towns seem almost idyllic. When I immerse myself in a scurrying throng on Broadway, the city turns out to be busier, louder, and different from two years ago when Mother and I were here on vacation. Much of what used to be has been torn down and replaced with new, taller structures. A new crop of towering edifices have sprung up out of nothing. Befuddled, I stop a couple of times to ask blue clad constables for directions to the grand six-story hotel called Astor House.

On the ferry two men had boasted about the city's growth. It's now home to more than eight-hundred thousand people. My ciphering tells me that's two-and-a-half percent of the entire nation's population. I wanted to tell them that across the southern region of our land there are at least seven slaves for every inhabitant of their city. More are being bred each day to spread slavery's scourge across the continent.

The same men bantered about the importance of southern trade to the city's economy. They also praised the voters for electing a pro-slavery Democrat as mayor. One of the men, a banker, just returned home from a business trip to the South, claimed that northern banks have pumped more than two-hundred million dollars in loans into the southern economy. He should be made to understand that several generations of slaves have contributed a great deal more to both regions' wealth with their unrewarded labor.

After arriving at Astor House and laying down two dollars for my first night's lodging, I pick up a copy of the *New York Tribune* and read an announcement on page four about my speech. It says I'll speak at the Cooper Institute in New York City instead of Beecher's Plymouth Church across the river in Brooklyn. The Young Men's Republican Union has taken over sponsorship from the church lyceum committee. I fret the speech I have prepared to deliver in two days at Rev. Beecher's church might not be appropriate for a miscellaneous political audience. After depositing my trunk I set out to find someone who can shed light on the change in plans.

From Astor House, I walk south on Broadway, then east on Ann Street to the offices of the *New York Independent*. Figuring they won't be open to the public on a Saturday afternoon, I knock loudly. When a voice responds, "Come in," I open the door and walk inside.

Seated at a desk, with his head down, is a finely dressed gentleman—too well dressed to be a common newspaper editor. He must be the moneyed silk trader who owns the paper. If that's so, he's also a friend and benefactor of Rev. Beecher.

I ask, "Is this Mr. Henry C. Bowen?"

"Yes," he answers. He remains seated at a desk with his back to me, focused on his work.

"I am Abraham Lincoln."

Bowen spins around and stares up at me.

"Mr. Bowen, I am just in from Springfield, Illinois, and I'm very tired. If you don't mind, I will just lie here on your couch."

He nods, and I make myself as comfortable as conditions allow, hanging my legs over one end and propping my head at the other.

Bowen walks over and studies me. "What can I do for you?"

"Well, Bowen, I'm reminded of a story. You see, there was once two brothers, each marrying sisters on the same evening. During the ceremony, some of their friends sneak upstairs and exchange the beds which have been deliberately prepared for the two couples by the boys' mother. When the celebrations are finished, and the bulk of the guests have drifted back to their homes, attendants escort the brides to their respective beds, which they at once identify by their familiar furnishings. Upon hearing the attendants' word that the girls are ready to receive their husbands, the mother directs her sons upstairs according to her earlier arrangement, one to the bed on the right and the other to the left.

"As the family lounges downstairs, their ears peeled for the sounds of marital consummation, they are accosted by a frantic commotion. Racing upstairs, they find the two boys flailing in a pile on the floor as their brides sit wailing in their beds, covers drawn up to their chins. When the confusion is unraveled and the crying abates, the family stands in shame over the egregious error."

Bowen throws back his head and laughs.

"You see, Mr. Bowen, having discovered that my lecture scheduled for Monday night has been moved from Beecher's church to the Cooper Institute, I feel just like those two young men."

He collects himself and explains the switch was made to accommodate a larger crowd. "You must be disappointed you won't be speaking at Plymouth Church. So if you'll join me for Sunday service, I'll be glad to introduce you to Reverend Beecher."

"I very much appreciate the invitation," I say, getting up from the couch. "Mrs. Lincoln will be delighted; before I left Springfield, she insisted that I must go to his church."

"Then it's fixed," he says.

"Yes, but for now, I reckon I better get back to Astor House to rewrite my speech in the main. I don't think what I have prepared for the church folks will do for the audience that may now show up."

The following morning, I walk down to the Fulton Street pier and pay two cents for the ferry crossing to Brooklyn. Once on the other side, Plymouth Church is another two mile hike. On my arrival, I'm ushered to Mr. Bowen's pew.

The perfunctory standing, sitting and hymns are familiar, thanks to Mother's insistence that I join her in church on occasion. That familiarity does not give them meaning, however. By contrast, Rev. Beecher's preaching is a delight; it is passionate without abandoning logic. At the end of the service, I congratulate him. I also tell him I had hoped to meet his famous sister. He laughs and says he will speak with her about sending me a copy of her famous book, *Uncle Tom's Cabin.*

The next evening, fifteen hundred people, each having paid twenty-five cents for admission, jam into the Great Hall at the Cooper Institute. Precisely at eight o'clock, I follow the white-bearded, seventy-seven year old poet and newspaper editor William Cullen Bryant onto the stage.

When I take my seat on a tiny chair, I look into the crowd and see the *New York Tribune* editor, Horace Greeley, who supported Douglas in the recent Senate contest. Tonight he's one of the meeting's sponsors. The bespectacled king-maker, whose mane flows to his shoulders like a lion's, must regard me as a timid schoolboy, dressed in a rumpled, ill-fitting black suit, with my gangly legs wrapped around the rungs of my chair.

As Bryant rises to introduce me, I recall the closing lines from his *Thanatopsis* which I memorized over a decade ago during our stay at the Todd mansion in Lexington.

> *So live, that when thy summons comes*
> *To join the innumerable caravan*
> *Which moves to that mysterious realm,*
> *Where each shall take his chamber*
> *In the silent halls of death,*
> *Thou go not, like the quarry-slave at night,*
> *Scourged to his dungeon,*
> *But, sustained and soothed by an unfaltering trust,*
> *Approach thy grave like one*
> *Who wraps the drapery of his couch about him,*
> *And lies down to pleasant dreams.*

He introduces me with words nearly as eloquent. "It is a grateful office that I perform introducing to you an eminent citizen of the West, hitherto known to you only by reputation. He is a gallant soldier of the political campaign of 1858, and a great champion of the Republican cause in Illinois.

"These children of the West, my friends, form a living bulwark against the advance of slavery, and from them is recruited the vanguard of the armies of Liberty. I have only to pronounce the name, Abraham Lincoln ...."

Applause greets me as I walk slowly to the rostrum. I swallow, offer my greeting, and forthrightly state my purpose.

> *The facts which I shall deal with this evening are mainly old and familiar; nor is there anything new in the general use I shall make of them. If there shall be any novelty, it will be in the mode of presenting the facts and the inferences and observations following that presentation.*

Beads of moisture form along my lips, though my mouth is dry as I unfold my speech and proceed to do exactly as I promise. Holding true to the facts, I demonstrate that the intent of our Founders was to prohibit the extension of slavery and to see it die a slow and natural death. At the conclusion of my lecture I admonish the audience.

> *Let us be diverted by none of those contrivances ... such as groping for some common ground between right and wrong ... such as appeals calling on not the sinners, but on the righteous to repentance ... such as imploring men to unsay what Washington said and to undo what Washington did.*

> *Neither let us be slandered from our duty by false accusations, nor frightened from it by menaces of destruction to the government, nor of dungeons.*

> *Let us have faith that right makes might, and in*

*that faith let us to the end dare to do our duty as
we understand it.*

My heart bonds with the rhythm of the crowd's
ovation as the people rise in one great wave and cheer,
their hats and handkerchiefs waving high above their
heads. When their enthusiasm seems spent, voices cry out
for more speakers to be heard.

The first to step forward is Horace Greeley. He calls
me "a specimen of what free labor and free expression of
ideas could produce," and I bite down on my lip to stay a
flood of tears.

Following him, James Briggs speaks for the
organizers of the event. Although he is publically for
Governor Chase from Ohio, he announces that "one of
three gentlemen shall be our standard bearer in this year's
canvass for President of the United States—the eloquent
Senator William Seward from New York, the able Salmon
Chase, or the unknown knight who in 1858 on the prairies
of Illinois met the Bois Gilbert of the Democracy, Stephen
A. Douglas, and unhorsed him, Abraham Lincoln." The
rapid hammering of my pulse thunders in my ears. I never
imagined myself standing before such an audience in New
York, hearing my name uttered as an equal to such touted
men.

The next morning Horace Greeley's *New York Tribune*
trumpets, "The Speech of Abraham Lincoln at the Cooper
Institute last evening was one of the happiest and most
convincing arguments ever made in this City."

In the afternoon, William Cullen Bryant's *New York
Evening Post* declares, "The Framers of the Constitution in
Favor of Slavery Prohibition—The Republican Party
Vindicated—Great Speech of Hon. Abraham Lincoln."

Euphoria buoys me until the realities of fickle
politics slap me across the face. Less than forty-eight
hours after my lecture in New York, Senator Seward
delivers a major speech in Washington City. The following
afternoon on my arrival in Exeter, New Hampshire, for a
speech in the city where our son Bob is attending
preparatory school, I'm handed a copy of the *New York
Tribune*. Horace Greeley's praise of Seward's speech

deflates me. He calls it "more striking than any witnessed this winter." I search out a copy of Bryant's *New York Evening Post* to find him crowing Seward's speech was "distinguished for its certain noble impassiveness which shows the author is as superior to his opponents in moral nature as he is in intellect."

Over the next several days I make six more speeches in the states of Connecticut and Rhode Island. Mostly, I repeat the same two-hour lecture I gave at the Cooper Institute. Although many have read reprints of my New York speech, large crowds endure bitter weather to hear it first-hand and cheer me when I am done. They lift me from gloom to a plane shy of my Cooper Institute ecstasy.

In the town of New Haven, I offer a new homily to explain my view of keeping slavery out of the territories.

> *If we find a snake in our children's bed, we likely will not take up a stick and begin striking it. If we do so, we risk harming our little ones with our blows and getting them bit in the process.*
> *Furthermore, if we make them a new bed to sleep in, we do not gather up a batch of snakes and nest them in the bed before putting the children down.*

A large audience hears me proclaim, "I want every man to have a chance—and I believe the Black man is entitled to it—to improve his condition.

On my return trip to Springfield, I stop in New York City to collect my two-hundred dollar honorarium for the Cooper Institute speech. While there, I take the ferry to Brooklyn and attend another service at Rev. Beecher's church, arriving late and finding the pews are filled. After being directed upstairs to a gallery next to the organ loft, a kindly usher gives up his seat for me. Once the usual rituals are dispensed with, Rev. Beecher makes his points and illustrates them with unsurpassed clarity. When he concludes, I consider that humanity may have never before hosted such a productive mind.

After the service, I return to New York and pay a visit to the infamous Five Points slums. There, I tour the renowned House of Industry, a six-story charity mission which offers refuge to abandoned and abused children in exchange for honest toil. My host is Hiram Barney, a member of the committee which hosted my speech at the Cooper Institute. With iron-gray hair swept back from his broad forehead and a square, pugnacious jaw, he radiates strength and unwavering purpose.

Mr. Barney leads me to a little Sunday School class being held there, and the teacher invites me to say a few words to the children. After sharing stories of my own deprivation on the prairie as a child, I tell them of the hope they can look to by applying themselves in earnest. My eyes mist over as their faces light up. On receiving the teacher's appreciation I say, "These little ones give me courage."

Before leaving the city I'm accompanied on a stroll by James Briggs, the young Republican who sent me the invitation to speak at Rev. Beecher's church. As we come to the main post office, he stops and turns to the old building saying, "I wish you would take notice of what a dark and dismal place we have here. I think your chance of being the next president is equal to that of any man in the country. When you are president, will you recommend an appropriation of a million dollars for a suitable location for a post office in this city?"

My knees quiver as if under a heavy weight. I tell him, "When I was east, several gentlemen made about the same remark to me that you did today about the presidency; they thought my chances were about equal to the best. I am humbled you think of me in that light."

Chapter Thirty Three

On returning to Springfield, my patience is tested. Seward's supporters have noticed the broad circulation of my speech at Cooper Institute. They now impugn me for accepting the two-hundred dollar honorarium from its organizers. I'm vilified as "disgraceful" and "greedy."

As controversy over my fee continues to brew, charges are laid in the press that I am a "two shilling candidate who charges his own friends two shillin' apiece to hear him talk about politics." We had planned to make my candidacy public at a more appropriate time through newspaper endorsements. Now the word is out in an unflattering way. Since candidates for the land's highest office customarily refrain from giving speeches after their intentions are known, everything I wish to say from this point forward must be done through surrogates.

After making a clear and accurate account of the arrangements for my speech, I tell my friends, "I wish no explanation made to our enemies. What our opponents want is a squabble and a fuss, and they can have it if we explain, but they cannot have it if we don't. Give no denial and no explanations."

A few weeks later I'm bedding down at the Junction House in Decatur, Illinois, with John Moses and Nathan Knapp, two old friends and supporters from Scott County.

We're here for the State Republican Convention. Moses and Knapp, both lawyers, are delegates while I'm merely a spectator.

As I stand at the washing bowl splashing water on my face, Knapp says, "Well, Lincoln, tomorrow's going to be a mighty big day for you."

I dab my forehead with a towel. "Reckon it won't be too different from most days."

Moses takes the towel from me and steps in front of the bowl. "There's talk of you leaving here as Illinois' only choice for nomination as president."

I scratch my ear. "Everyone knows that Seward will be the nominee."

Knapp sits down on the bed. "When Seward speaks it's like a professor lecturing you on things he's only read about. On the other hand, the things you say sound like they're freshly mined—something you've actually lived. Don't be surprised if you come out of the Chicago convention on top."

"I'm not sure I consider myself fit for the presidency." I pick up my carpetbag and rummage through it, searching for nothing in particular.

Moses shakes his head. "You don't know your own power. Always worried about pushing yourself into positions you're not equal to. Just look at how far you've come, though. You've done it all with no great effort."

I smirk, "You have me confused with Douglas."

Knapp chuckles. "Douglas? The same Douglas you say doesn't even know himself? How did you put it? 'Like a skillful gambler, he plays for all the chances. He never lets the logic of principle displace the logic of success.'"

I lay my hand on his shoulder, smiling. "See there, you prove my point. Douglas is the man of success."

Moses hands Knapp the towel and says, "You wouldn't leave the job of beating him to a rabid abolitionist like Seward, would you?"

Knapp pauses at the washing bowl. "With the Democrats so badly split that they couldn't nominate a candidate in Charleston, it seems the risk isn't in losing to Douglas, it's in electing the wrong Republican."

I ask, "What's the right Republican?"

Knapp wipes his face. "One who articulates our founding principles as clearly as you, who understands the Democrats will drive us headlong into despotism. We must repel them, or they will subjugate us."

Moses lies on the bed. "We need a man who can match Douglas' oratory and who can expose his deceit. Douglas is like dealing with a man you can see and touch, but when you examine his tracks you think he isn't there."

Knapp adds, "As when he insists that Congress prohibited slavery in the territories, though they understood they ought not do so."

I grin. "You're using my own speeches against me."

Knapp continues, "Didn't you say last summer that the Democrats would delight a convocation of crowned princes plotting against their own citizens?"

"Yes. The Democrats of today hold the liberty of one man to be absolutely nothing when it comes in conflict with another's right of property. Republicans, on the other hand, are for both the man and his property; but when the two principles are at odds, the man before the dollar."

Knapp plops down on the bed next to Moses. "The Democrats seem to have switched sides. When they were the party of Jefferson, they believed as we do now."

"Damned Jackson corrupted them," says Moses.

I nudge Knapp to slide over and make room for me on the bed. "I remember once being much amused at seeing two intoxicated men engage in a fight. After a while, they removed their coats and continued their rather harmless contest. When the long affair was over, each man got into the other's coat. If the two leading political parties of today are identical to the ones from the days of Jefferson and Adams, they have performed about the same feat as the two drunken men. Unfortunately in this day, saving the principles of Jefferson from total overthrow is no game."

Moses turns on his side and faces away from Knapp and me. "If I were you, Lincoln, I would not go about it as you did the other night in Springfield."

"What do you mean?"

"You said in your speech that it strains logic for the Democrats to say on the one hand that the federal government cannot intervene to declare slavery illegal, yet they clamor for the government to outlaw polygamy."

"Why, that is the truth,"

Knapp sits up. "I applaud them for standing up against moral decay, and I hope a great many folks agree with me."

I roll to my side with my back to them. "Why are all the beds so short?"

The next morning Knapp and Moses go over to the Convention, while I eat breakfast with Richard Oglesby, one of the young Decatur men who has organized the meeting.

Oglesby takes a sip of coffee and repeats much of what the two Scott county delegates told me the previous night. He pleads with me to be in the convention hall after the noon recess. I assure him I will be there.

Just before two o'clock in the afternoon, I walk down South State Street to the make-shift convention hall, a wigwam made out of lumber and a borrowed circus tent. It measures one-hundred-and-twenty by fifty feet, taking up the width of the street and portions of the vacant lots on either side. I enter and crouch in the back, surveying the crowd of several thousand. The wigwam is so tightly packed I can barely see the array of prominent men seated on the hastily cobbled platform.

Without fanfare, a straw ballot is taken to indicate the delegates' preferences for who should be chairman of the convention. The poll indicates my old friend Joe Gillespie—who once joined me in jumping out the window to escape a quorum—will win the official voting. Judge Palmer, the temporary chairman, invites him to the stage as preparations are made to take the formal ballot. Joe's ascent to the platform is met with a standing ovation.

After waving to the delegates and spectators, Joe takes his seat, and everyone in the hall sits as well, except for Richard Oglesby.

Oglesby calls out, "Mr. Chairman."

I hold my breath. Our earlier conversation begins to take on meaning.

Judge Palmer replies, "What business do you have before the convention?"

"Mr. Chairman, I am informed that a distinguished citizen of Illinois, and one whom we ever delight at honoring, is present. I wish to move that he be invited to a seat on the platform. That man is Abraham Lincoln."

My heart races as some three-thousand folks, seven-hundred of whom are delegates, rise to their feet giving a thunderous ovation. The roar of applause shakes every board and joist of the wigwam.

When order is restored, the motion is seconded and approved. Those standing near me make a great effort to jam me through the crowd, which is once again standing and cheering. Tears of joy want to spill out of me, but I swallow hard, fighting to hold them back. A handful of friends circle around me, hoping to usher me forward. Well-wishers press in around me such that my friends can no longer move me ahead. At my side, Hill Lamon wraps his arms around my waist and jerks me off my feet. Others come to his aid, and together, they hoist me into the air. I am passed forward from one swell of hands to the next. I'm floating over the sea of delegates, like a flatboat riding the current of the great Mississippi.

On stage, I turn and wave to the audience, soaking in their cheers. While their hoopla continues, unabated, I take a seat in a small chair, the only one not occupied. I wrap my feet around the chair's legs and make an earnest effort to become inconspicuous.

A short time later, order is restored, and preparations are being made to take a ballot to nominate a candidate for governor. I slip off stage and walk over to Jim Peake's jewelry store to take a nap.

Soon after falling asleep, Hill shakes me and tells me I must return to the convention.

I rub my eyes. "What's up?"

"Come and see," he says. "Oglesby has it firm in his mind that the entire Illinois delegation will be voting for you at the Chicago Convention."

I get up and follow him back to the hall. Even a block away the noise from the place is deafening. My pulse quickens. I am now coming to comprehend the meaning of Hill's words, of what Oglesby intends. He is now attempting what Moses talked about last night.

As we step through the entrance, hats, books, and canes are flying in the air, and two men are making their way through the throng to the platform carrying a banner fastened between two poles. My heart begins to pound in my chest. When the two men reach the platform and turn to face the feverish crowd, I recognize one of them as John Hanks and make out the words on the sign.

ABRAHAM LINCOLN
THE RAIL CANDIDATE FOR PRESIDENT IN 1860
TWO RAILS FROM A LOT OF 3,000 MADE IN 1830
BY THOS. HANKS AND ABE LINCOLN …

I point to the sign and laugh. "His name is John, not Thomas, Hanks."

Again, I'm lifted by a sea of hands and passed toward the stage. This time, the crowd's delirium is so intense that part of the awning over the platform falls onto the heads of those standing beneath it. Undaunted, the delegates continue to propel me forward.

After much jostling, I make it onto the stage and wave at the crowd, unsure of what they expect.

In response to my gesture, they begin shouting with one voice, "Identify your work!"

I shake my head, grinning, and go to the chair where I'd been seated before.

The demands grow louder, "Identify your work!"

My grin fades as I sit down and tell the men nearest me, "I cannot say that I split these rails."

I wave again to the audience, but they refuse to give up their demand. Turning to John Hanks who's still holding up the sign, I say, "Where did you get these rails?"

Hanks grins. "At a farm you helped build down on the Sangamon."

I furrow my brow. "That was a long time ago. It's possible I split these rails, but I cannot identify them."

More shouts erupt from the crowd, "Identify your work! Identify your work!"

I suppress a smile as I ask Hanks in a loud voice, "What kind of timber are they?"

Hanks shouts, "Honey locust and black walnut."

I say in a voice loud enough to carry to the back of the wigwam, "That is lasting timber, and it may be that I split the rails."

The crowd howls its approval.

I get up and examine the rails, eying them closely. A hush falls over the assembly as I run my hands inside the notches. When I'm done I grin and proclaim, "Boys, I can say I have split a great many better looking ones."

The men on the platform laugh heartily, and I join them. Those in the audience yelp and holler and kick up their heels, dancing in front of us.

After a few minutes of celebration, Gillespie, who now holds the gavel as Chairman of the convention, comes over to me and says, "Might as well let them carry on with the fun. We'll re-convene in the morning and finish our business."

I nod, and he announces to the delegates, "We are adjourned until tomorrow."

I continue to sit on the stage and watch in disbelief at the commotion my name has caused. After a time, I leave the platform and pass through a back door that leads out to the street.

The next morning Richard Yates, who was nominated by the convention as the party's candidate for governor, announces that I am his preference for president. He promises to support me at the national convention in Chicago two weeks hence.

I nod my gratitude.

A resolution is read and approved by acclamation.

Resolved that Abraham Lincoln is the choice of the Republican Party in Illinois for the presidency, and that the delegates from this State are instructed to use all honorable means to procure his nomination by the Chicago Convention, and that their vote be cast as a unit for him.

Chairman Gillespie gavels the convention adjourned and walks over to offer his congratulations. We embrace, and I whisper to him, "My God, I now think this thing can be done."

He steps back, grinning. "We will give our lives if we must, to see to it."

Two weeks later, many of my friends are in Chicago at the national convention while I remain in Springfield. It is customary for men seeking their party's nomination for president to be absent from the conventions. So my stomach is in knots as I wait for dispatches of the results at the offices of the *Illinois State Journal*, formerly the *Sangamo Journal*. The *Journal* editor, Edward Lewis Baker, not the same as my friend Ned Baker who has removed to Oregon where he is now a member of the U.S. Senate, has made an arrangement with the telegraph office to have dispatches from Chicago delivered directly to him.

My friend Simeon Francis sold *The Sangamo Journal* to Baker whose purchase was financed by his father-in-law Ninian Edwards. Ninian is also Molly's brother-in-law. I gloat over how Ninian, a former Whig turned Democrat, must gnash his teeth knowing Baker uses his paper to promote my candidacy. Just like Simeon Francis used to do, Baker tests my ideas in editorials without me having to take the blame if they fall flat.

As I wait at the *Journal* for Baker to return from the telegraph office, I sit in a black bentwood hickory armchair supported by four twig legs. The seat made of branches is comfortable enough, but my body is too knotted with tension to take much pleasure in it. Before my arrival at the *Journal*, three dispatches were received from Chicago. The first announced the delegates had arrived in the wigwam. The second reported the names that were placed before the convention. I swallowed hard when I read the third dispatch giving the first round votes—Seward 173 ½, Lincoln 102, Cameron 50 ½, Chase 49, Bates 48. I told the boys before they left for Chicago that we could get the nomination if we gathered at least one-hundred votes on the first ballot.

My heart pounds in my ears when Baker arrives. He's poker-faced as he hands me the dispatch, his eyes fixed on mine. I breathe deeply and subdue every muscle in my face to hide even the slightest hint of expression.

I read it aloud. "Seward 184 ½. Lincoln 181."

A third ballot is needed since 233 is a majority.

I grin as the news spreads around the room. Hoots and cheers take on a life of their own. I say to Baker as he heads back to the telegraph office, "I can taste it."

Scarcely enough time passes for Baker to walk the short distance to the telegraph office and return before shouting and cheers fill the street outside. As we strain to decipher their words, several men push through the door. One yells, "Lincoln is nominated!" Another cries "Glory to God! Lincoln is nominated!" Behind them comes Baker waving a small scrap of paper in the air.

I bite my lip, straining to hold back tears. Those around the *Journal* office chant "Read the dispatch."

Baker hands it to me.

I will myself to. When I am composed, I say, "I felt sure this would come when I saw the second ballot."

The chant begins anew, "Read the dispatch!"

In a solemn voice, weighed down by the great responsibility being thrust on me, I read, "Lincoln 349—"

The remainder of the dispatch is drowned out by cheering.

I sit again in the bentwood hickory chair, dazed, accepting the congratulations of friends who file by to assure me of their support for the coming campaign. After a while, I stand and give a short speech which I conclude by saying, "There is a lady over yonder on Eighth Street who is deeply interested in this news. I will carry it to her."

The next day, a delegation from the convention calls at my home to receive my acceptance of the Party's nomination. I hand over a written statement to Newton Bateman, the Superintendent of Public Instruction. "Would you kindly tell me if I've used correct grammar?"

Newt studies my reply and says, "It is all correct, with one slight exception—almost too trivial to mention."

"Well, what is it?"

He points to what he calls a split infinitive. "It would be better to transpose the 'to' and 'not' in that sentence. You should say 'not to' rather than 'to not.'"

"So, I should turn those two fellows end for end, eh?" He nods.

I take out a pen, make the correction, and hand the paper back to Newt. "You have my humble acceptance."

Just then, little Tad works his way up to my side and whispers very loudly in my ear that Mother has prepared tea for our guests in the dining room. I look around the room and observe a number of the men straining to hide their discomfort over the boy's intrusion into our solemn business. I smile and assure them, "You see, gentlemen, if I am elected, it won't do to put that young man in the cabinet —he can't be entrusted with state secrets."

One month later Stephen Douglas becomes the Democratic Party nominee for president. His victory, however, comes at a great cost to his party. The southern delegates bolt and hold a convention of their own. They are angry over Douglas' refusal to declare that slavery is right, and they nominate Vice President John Breckinridge to head their ticket. The arithmetic of the Electoral College now favors a Republican victory.

My first act as the nominee is to hire young George Nicolay to be my secretary at a wage of seventy-five dollars per month. He recently worked for Secretary of State Hatch, who has made him available to me for the duration of the campaign. Nicolay's steely eyes caught my attention when I first encountered him at the *Pike County Free Press*. He was working there as a printer's apprentice when I rode the Circuit. Pale, lean, and nearly a foot shorter than me, he's all business and a hard fellow to put one past.

For an office, we cram two desks into a room in the Governor's suite on the second floor of the State House. We share a spacious reception area with tiny Newt Bateman, whom I call "the Big Schoolmaster."

Our quarters are so tight we can't shut the door for formal meetings. I stand in the reception room when more than a couple of folks stop in to ask for jobs or offer their encouragement. Sometimes, the line of well-wishers and office seekers extends all the way down the staircase to the front entrance, and my entire day is consumed greeting them. It grieves me to turn anyone away, but young Nicolay ferrets out those who would only waste my time. A descendant of good German stock, he has a knack for sniffing out opportunists. We get as many as eighty letters in a day, and Nicolay decides which ones to answer. He also writes appropriate replies. I review the ones he declines to answer, and occasionally, veto his decision.

I adhere to an established custom for presidential candidates to limit travel and speech making during the national canvass. Instead, I correspond with friends, political allies, and newspapermen advocating the Republican cause. On July 4, I write Dr. Anson Henry, my friend and former family doctor whose treatments for the "hypos" left me half-dead. He also introduced me to Dr. Drake, whose advice on my condition has been invaluable.

> *Our boy, in his tenth year, (the baby when you left) has just had a tedious spell of scarlet-fever and he is not yet beyond all danger. I have a headache and a sore throat, inducing me to suspect that I have an inferior type of the same thing. Our eldest boy, Bob, has been away from us nearly a year at school and will enter Harvard University this month. He promises very well, considering we never controlled him much.*

Mother and I are proud Bob has made such a great success of his education. He's nearly finished with his studies at Phillips Exeter Academy in New Hampshire, and will be attending Harvard College in the coming fall. I tell him if he is diligent in his studies, he shall learn more than I ever did as a lad, but he will never have so good a time.

When Bob's friend, George Latham, fails to win admission to Harvard, I write to him. My personal acquaintance with failure qualifies me on the subject.

> *I have scarcely felt greater pain in my life than on learning yesterday from Bob's letter that you had failed to enter Harvard University. And yet there is very little to deter you if you will allow no feeling of discouragement to seize and prey upon you. It is a certain truth that you can enter and graduate in Harvard University, and having made the attempt,*

*you must succeed in it. 'Must' is the word. I know
not how to aid you, other than to offer the
assurance of someone of mature age and much
severe experience that you cannot fail if you
resolutely determine that you will not.*

Very truly your friend,

A Lincoln

Judge Douglas, never one to stand on either tradition or principle, crisscrosses the country making political speeches and pressing his case directly before the people. He attacks abolitionism in the north and disunion in the south, hoping to sway moderate voters to throw in with him. He paints me as a "Black Republican" and the Southern Democrats as rabid demagogues.

A few weeks after my nomination, William Seward calls on me in Springfield, assuring me of his support. He's on his way to Minnesota and Wisconsin to bolster our standing there, and he'll stop in Indiana on his return to New York. We met once in 1848 while canvassing for the national Whig ticket, so I'm not surprised by his noble bearing and pretentious attire. Seward excels over me as a standard bearer for Republicanism in that regard. However, his short wiry frame, slumped shoulders, and shifting eyes are not attributes I recall from our previous encounter. Perhaps my recollection has been eclipsed by his enormous reputation.

When we get down to business, I lay out for him a recent discovery I made while analyzing the composition of Electors from the various states. "I am convinced," I say, "that we can win this thing if we take sixteen of the eighteen northern states plus California and Oregon."

Seward examines my tally sheet and smiles. Without looking at me he says, "Yes, New York's thirty-five electoral votes will be the key. With the Democrats feuding among themselves as usual, we can depend on Thurlow Weed and his apparatus to deliver those votes without much trouble."

I fold up the tally sheet and stuff it in my pocket. "Nevertheless, we mustn't give any slack."

He nods. "As I said, New York is in capable hands."

Chapter Thirty Four

One week before Election Day, I receive a message from Thurlow Weed in New York pleading for more funds to press the campaign there. Weed says, "Douglas' man Sanders claims they are gaining so rapidly the result is now impossible to foretell."

I groan. "How ... how did this happen?"

Nicolay looks up at me. "Apparently, the Democrats across New York have set aside their feuds and are rallying behind Douglas. He's tempered his Popular Sovereignty message and has been whipping up Unionist sentiment, starting to sound almost like you." He hands me a copy of *Harper's* magazine. "His North Carolina speech is all over the New York papers."

I read aloud a few lines of the *Harper's* account of the speech. "Douglas claims to be in favor of 'executing in good faith every clause and provision of the Constitution and protecting every right under it—and then hanging every man who takes up arms against it.'" I shake my head. "He has been cultivating Northern minds for years and steering them off track. Without directly saying it, he accuses Republicans of forcing the Southern people to take up arms against the government in order to protect their Constitutional rights."

I throw the magazine onto the desk. "We don't propose to take away any rights. We only want to stop the extension of slavery into the Territories. The only right to hold slaves that ever existed was the protection of it in the places slavery was found when the Union was formed. His Popular Sovereignty is just a contrivance to force something on us that was never intended."

Nicolay takes his seat behind the desk. "New York is vulnerable because its economy is knit together with that of the South."

I rake my fingers through my hair. "If Douglas wins New York, we lose. Without those thirty-five Electoral votes, the thing will get thrown to the House, and we don't control enough state delegations there to win. Neither does Douglas. It'll be between Breckinridge and Bell."

Nicolay picks up a pen and shakes his head. "Two pro-slavery men."

I look out into the hallway. "If that happens, there'll be no returning to our Founders' vision."

"How shall I reply?" he asks.

"Tell him the money's on its way."

While Nicolay is at the telegraph office sending the dispatch to Thurlow Weed, I poke my head into Newt Bateman's office and say, "You, Big Schoolmaster, just come here, won't you?"

When he joins me in my office, I push the desk aside far enough to close the door and show him a book containing a canvass of the City of Springfield. "This book shows how each citizen of the city plans to vote in the coming election. Let's take a look. I want to see in particular how the ministers have declared themselves."

Newt's eyes widen. "How did you come by this?"

"Friends."

As I turn the pages, I ask him to confirm for me the names of ministers or elders or members of various churches. I make careful notes on a sheet of how they intend to vote.

When I add up the tally and give it to Newt, his expression turns grim. "Why," he says, "twenty-three of the city's ministers are against you, and only three are with you."

"A vast majority of their members oppose me, too."

Newt shakes his head. "It doesn't make sense."

"Newt, I know I am not a Christian, but I have read the *Bible* carefully." I pull a *New Testament* from my pocket. "These men know full well that I am for freedom in the Territories, freedom everywhere, as free as the Constitution and the laws will permit. They also know my opponents are for slavery." I shake the *Testament* in Newt's face. "Yet with this book in their hands—in the light of which human bondage cannot exist for even a moment— they are going to vote against me. I do not understand it at all."

Newt replies, "I cannot explain it either, except to observe that some men are not ruled by reason, or by God, but by their own self indulgence."

I pace the room, tamping down my anger with each stride. After a while I stop and lay my hand on Newt's shoulder. "I know there is a God and that He hates injustice and slavery. I see the storm coming, and His hand is in it. If He has a place and work for me, and I think He does, I believe I am ready. I am nothing, but Truth is everything. I know I am right because I know Liberty is right. Christ teaches us so. I have told them that a house divided against itself cannot stand, and they will find it to be the truth."

Newt looks up at me. "A great many of us believe that God has placed you among us for the great purpose of bringing the slave system to its knees."

I pick up the canvass book and wave it at him. "Douglas don't care whether slavery is voted up or down, but God cares. So does humanity. So do I. With God's help we shall not fail. I may not see the end of slavery, but it will come, and I shall be vindicated."

I put the canvass book back on the shelf. "As for these men, they will find out that they have not read their *Bible* right. A revelation could not make it plainer to me that either slavery or the Government must be destroyed. It seems as if God has borne with the evil of slavery until every teacher of religion has come to defend it from the *Bible* and claim for it a divine sanction. Now, the cup of iniquity is full, and vials of wrath will be poured out."

I collapse into a chair and bury my head on the desk. Darkness and silence overwhelm me. When I peek up, Nicolay is gazing calmly at me from the open doorway. I look around for Newt, but he is no longer in the room.

Several days afterward a visitor from New England chides me for remaining silent on the day's great issues over the months since my nomination. He complains that many people are alarmed at the prospect I might be elected and the nation will be torn asunder. He urges me to reassure folks that I am not a danger to the Republic.

I throw up my hands. "This is the same old trick by which the South breaks down every Northern victory." I glare over at Nicolay. "If I were willing to barter away the moral principle involved in this contest and assure my own victory by making some new submission to the South, I would go to Washington without the favor of the men who were my friends before the election. I would be as powerless as a block of buckeye wood."

In measured tones I tell my visitor, "Those who will not read, or heed, what I have already publicly said, would not read or heed a repetition of it. What is it I could say which would quiet their alarm? Is it that no interference by the government with slaves or slavery within the states is intended? I have said this so often that a repetition of it is but mockery. All it would do is foster an appearance of weakness and cowardice."

When Election Day arrives, I rise at my usual time and join Mother, Willy, and Tad at the breakfast table to eat an egg and toast. The boys make their usual fuss.

Mother stirs her coffee and muses, "I don't think I shall know how to behave tomorrow if I wake and find that I am to be Mrs. President."

"I'm sure that you'll find yourself acting just as you always do." I chase the last morsel of toast with a gulp of coffee and get up from the table.

"What will you be doing today?" she asks.

I put on my coat and hat. "Just as I always do ... go to the office and greet visitors. Although, I think I shouldn't vote today. It's unseemly for a man to vote for himself."

"Don't forget your shawl," she says. "It's a mite chilly out."

I throw the shawl over my shoulders and head out the door. My breath forms a tiny cloud as I descend the steps and turn onto the walkway. Dead leaves turned brittle by an overnight frost crackle underfoot.

At my office in the State House, Nicolay is already at his desk. He peers up at me. I wave my hand at the myriad gifts piled everywhere. "Reckon if we win, this place will be stacked to the gills tomorrow. We might not even be able to get in."

He laughs—an uncommon thing for him to do.

We are visited during the day by a number of well-wishers. Billy Herndon is one of them. When he asks if I've voted, I look out the window at the crowd lined up outside the courthouse, waiting to cast their votes. Poll workers for each of the candidates are hawking their party's printed ballots, pitching their man's laurels and insulting opposing candidates.

I shake my head. "It's a long standing custom that a candidate ought not to vote for himself."

Billy winks. "At least vote for the other Republicans who are on the ballot."

I sit at my desk. "With all Republican names on a single ballot, everyone will think I've voted for myself."

"Before you drop your ballot in the box, simply cut off the top portion that has your name."

I sit back in my chair. "An excellent idea."

About three o'clock in the afternoon, I peer out the window and see the line is now short, so I head over to the courthouse to vote according to Billy's plan.

On my arrival, a crowd swarms me, cheering and shouting "Old Abe! Uncle Abe! Honest Abe!" Even the Democratic poll workers cheer me despite the shouts of "Giant Killer" coming from my supporters. I look around for Hill, someone big enough to hide behind, but am blocked by Republican agents exchanging blows over who will hand me their printed ballot. Several stout fellows struggle at lifting me off my feet to carry me up two flights of stairs to the courthouse polling room. I clutch onto my hat.

The commotion arouses several of my friends including, Billy, Nicolay, Hill, Secretary of State Hatch, and a young five-foot-six law student named Elmer Ellsworth. They shove folks aside to open a path for me to proceed. Amidst an ongoing din of cheers, my friends usher me upstairs to the "Republican" window in the jammed polling room.

After announcing my name to the election clerk, I hold my ballot over a glass bowl, and Billy hands me scissors. I snip off the top portion of the ballot and watch the bottom fall into the bowl. A roar goes up from the crowd. I greet their cheers with a broad grin.

That evening I hunker down in the cramped, second-story telegraph office to wait for results; supper is the last thing on my mind. The young handle-bar mustached operator, John Wilson, hands me the first news from Thurlow Weed in New York. "All is safe in this state." I'm unsure of his meaning. Maybe he means there have been no riots. Next Simon Cameron reports from Philadelphia that we have won the vote there.

Within minutes of Cameron's news, a dispatch from Alton, Illinois declares, "Republicans have checkmated Democrats' scheme of fraud." On hearing the latter news, I take a stroll down to Watson's Oyster Saloon for a bite to eat.

At Watson's, Republican wives have laid out a lavish table of confections. Mother, who helped the other wives, is seated back in one corner, holding a place for me. Every other chair in the dining room is occupied, though they empty as everyone rushes up to greet me and offer tentative congratulations. Mother's lips draw a tight line as various women beg permission to give me kisses on the cheek. Her eyes turn cold when I give in to their affections, saying, "Reckon that's a form of coercion not prohibited by the Constitution or Congress."

As telegrams arrive throughout the evening, they are read aloud. Each reader stands on a chair to deliver the incoming news. After midnight, the telegraph operator rushes into Watson's and hands me a dispatch. I gaze around the room at all the expectant faces, restraining a smile, though I imagine everyone can hear my heart pounding. Mother's face is more anxious than all the others.

Having no need for additional elevation, I stand in front of my seat and read aloud. "From Philadelphia. The city and state for Lincoln by a decisive majority." Before anyone can let out a cheer, I point my forefinger in the air and say, "I think that settles Pennsylvania. Let's hope the news from New York continues to be good."

Shouts and huzzahs ring out from around the room. Women and men burst into tears, then laughter. A crush of friends presses around me, offering heartfelt congratulations. Crying and laughing continue all around the room. Men fall into each other's arms dancing and singing. I choke back tears of joy as the wild scene grows into even greater bedlam.

A few minutes later, I slip past the sea of well-wishers and make my way back to the telegraph office to wait for more results. At the door I whisper to Norman Judd, "As good as the news is, I'm not fully certain that we have won. I'll feel better when New York gives us a final tally." My mouth is as parched as prairie grass in a summer drought.

Along the short walk back to the telegraph office, Springfield's sleepy residents can be seen peeking outside through just lit windows. They've been aroused by church bells pealing throughout the city. Word of the likely Republican victory spreads rapidly.

Minutes after I enter the telegraph office, a dispatch arrives from New York. "We tender you our congratulations upon this magnificent victory." I read it aloud and sink into a chair, absorbing the gravity of the moment. My spirit is lifted, but my shoulders are laden down under a yoke of enormous responsibility.

As the dispatch is passed around, the tiny room erupts once again in wild celebration which soon spills out into the streets, spreading over to the courthouse and across the entire town. A cannon is fired in the distance to declare the victory is official.

I sit silently for a few moments then stand, somber. Lyman Trumbull, who six years ago won the U.S. Senate seat I coveted, embraces me and shouts, "Uncle Abe, you're the next President."

My mouth curls into a smile. "Well, the agony is mostly over, and soon we'll all be able to go to bed." I amble downstairs and pause on the street under a gaslight. I fill my lungs with cool air before walking home.

If I had plans to retire for the night, my friends have other things on their minds. Despite the chilly night, they gather outside my window blowing whistles and horns, singing and dancing in the street until we invite them inside for refreshments.

All we have to offer them is water to drink, but they don't seem to mind. Mother, who would ordinarily be mortified over the poverty of our cupboards, is nonetheless cheerful, having realized her dream of being Mrs. President. When the last reveler leaves, I climb the narrow stairs to my bed and lie awake deciding whom I will invite to serve on my Cabinet.

Shortly after daybreak, I go to the law office and tell Billy Herndon of my planned appointments. He says, "They will eat you up."

I shake my head. "No. They will eat each other up."

Billy sits back in his chair. "Your Cabinet may be the least of your problems."

My head begins aching. "That's not hard to see."

"If disunion comes, we must keep foreign capitals out of the fray."

I grimace. "Unless they come to our aid."

Billy leans forward. "We'll need our own diplomats. The ones we'll inherit owe their offices to the party that has fought hard to uphold slavery. Their loyalty belongs to those who are eager to celebrate your failure."

"Reckon, then, we have some big work to do."

A few days after the election, Nicolay hands me Thurlow Weed's *Albany Evening Journal.* He warns me, "Weed's pushing for compromise with the southern states."

"What kind of compromise?"

"He's for everything from compensation for fugitive slaves to the repeal of personal liberty laws and extending the Missouri Compromise line to the western coast."

I toss the paper on the desk. "How can any Republican in this hour of victory, even if in the face of danger, think of abandoning what we have just won?"

Weed is not the only one suffering twinges of contrition. Wall Street is up wildly one day, then down the next. Newspapers on both sides of the ocean report anxiety over secession, asking what will become of cheap cotton.

Chapter Thirty Five

Speed's congratulatory letter raises a lump in my throat. My affection for him pinches my chest. He begins by saying,

As a friend I am rejoiced at your success—as a political opponent I am not disappointed.
But all men and all questions sink into utter insignificance when compared to the preservation of our glorious Union. Its continuance and its future will depend very much upon how you deal with the inflammable material by which you will be surrounded.

My knees buckle. The vision of my old Speed and his Kentucky taking up arms against the Union flashes through my mind. I sink into my office chair and close my eyes. Tears seep out and trace the creases in my cheeks.

Later in the morning, well-wishers begin to drop in to the office in a constant stream, sometimes like a river swollen with flood waters. Each visitor has his own morsel of advice. When I'm asked to give reassurances to the South and to the Border States, I fold my arms across my chest and reply, "The Republican newspapers are now, and for some time past have been, republishing copious extracts from my many public speeches. Any newspaper in the country could also publish them. I am not at liberty to shift my ground—that is out of the question. If I thought a repetition would do any good I would make it, but my judgment is, it would do harm. The secessionists, believing they had alarmed me, would clamor all the louder."

One fellow strikes me as having an uncommonly pleasant countenance. I study him closely for several minutes, unable to discern the source of his peculiar aura. Noticing that it's about supper time, I invite him home. Mother fusses about the unexpected guest, a stranger no less, but I follow her back to the kitchen and say, "Don't reckon he'll eat too much. Looks kinda thin, don't you think?"

She peers out toward the parlor. "Humph."

After supper, my guest and I swap stories and jaw about politics. As usual, the boys crawl into my lap and squirm about, pushing each other as if playing a game of king-of-the-hill. Our guest is kind enough to tolerate the boys' play and not press me for assurances or other declarations. On national matters, our conversation doesn't stray far from my positions that are widely broadcast. Mostly, we banter about local affairs until we retire for the night.

Petitioners who don't call on me at the office write letters. The subjects are the same as ones raised by those who come in person. Three letters on the topic of my appearance are refreshing in that I can act on them without much fear of jeopardizing my standing with the Electoral College.

First a woman complains of my ugliness. I say to Nicolay, "It is allowed to be ugly in this world, but not as ugly as I am."

A few days later, a letter from a group calling themselves "True Republicans" suggests that I cultivate whiskers and wear standing collars. They say I should do so for the benefit of the cause.

The third letter comes from an eleven year-old girl. She echoes the True Republicans' suggestion that I grow a beard. On my next visit to Billy Florville, my barber, I tell him, "Let's give them a chance to grow."

One day, a southern merchant is among the sea of callers. He argues more desperately than most that I should break my public silence. I tell him that if left alone to work in their own time, the southern unionists will succeed in bringing their states back into the fold.

He proposes I direct a surrogate to carry the message for me, just as many had done during the canvass. I heed his advice and write to Senator Lyman Trumbull, asking him to slip a message from me into one of his speeches as though he was saying it on his own account.

> *I have labored in, and for, the Republican organization with entire confidence that whenever we shall be in power, each and all of the States will be left in as complete control of their own affairs, and at as perfect liberty to choose and employ their own means of protecting property and preserving peace and order within their respective limits, as they have ever been under any administration.*

Word soon wafts up from Washington City that proposals for compromise are flying about Congress like crows swarming a newly seeded cornfield. The House of Representatives has formed a committee of thirty-three members, while the Senate now has a committee of thirteen. Both are aiming to make compromises that will avert disunion. I write to our men on the committees.

> *There is room to negotiate issues such as fugitive slaves, slavery in the District of Columbia, and the domestic slave trade. But, I will entertain no compromise regarding the extension of slavery.*
>
> *The instant we yield, they will regain the advantage we have now won. Every stitch of our labor will be lost, and sooner or later all must be done over. Douglas is sure to begin trying to bring in his Popular Sovereignty again. Have none of it.*
>
> *The tug has to come and better now than later. These aggressive actions by southerners to acquire territories in Cuba and Central America for the purpose of extending slavery prove their intentions.*

When Weed sends Seward to Springfield to lobby me on the question of extending the old Missouri Compromise line, he finds me reading anew the history of President Jackson's response to the 1832 Nullification Crisis. Back then, South Carolina passed an ordinance declaring federal tariffs unconstitutional and unenforceable within its "sovereign boundaries." President Jackson did not yield an inch. After gaining authority from Congress to use military forces against South Carolina, the state legislature repealed its Nullification Ordinance.

Following Jackson's tradition, a tough pill for this former Whig to swallow, I refuse to yield any ground. Seward leaves, shaking his head.

I turn to Nicolay. "I am not unmindful of the troubles we face. I wish with all sincerity that they did not exist. Nonetheless, I will not be bullied into altering my stance, not even by friends."

Neither do I welcome an upbraiding by our son, Bob. He writes Mother and me from Harvard University, scolding us over our recent trip to Chicago. He writes, "I see by the papers that you have been to Chicago. Aren't you beginning to get a little tired of this constant uproar?"

I tell Nicolay, "Reckon when I was a boy, I didn't think any higher of my father than Bob does of me. When you're an old man you'll see that many of life's duties are merely to be tolerated, while a few are truly joyful. I shook hands with thousands of well-wishers in Chicago. That was a drudgery at times, but the hope I saw on their faces makes up for thousands of days of aching in my bones." While in Chicago, I also met with Vice President-Elect Hamlin. Even though Hamlin and I heard each other's speeches during my term in Congress, this was my first meeting with the robust Yankee from Maine.

On December 20, Nicolay returns from his afternoon errands, grim faced. He hands me a dispatch from the telegraph office. My heart pinches as I read the news that the South Carolina legislature has passed a resolution to secede from the Union.

Nicolay asks, "What do you suppose President Buchanan is going to do?"

I shake my head. "Nothing. He claims secession is illegal, but professes he has no power to stop it."

"Speaking of incompetence ...." Nicolay hands me a letter someone sent to Secretary of State Hatch.

I put on my spectacles and read it.

Please consider me in among those you shall recommend to Old Abe for some job in his government. Poverty is no disgrace, but I find it damned inconvenient, and I should like something that would keep my nose and the grindstone apart for a while.

"I think the proper word is impotence," I burst into laughter.

Nicolay grins. "Laughter is good medicine in times like these."

A couple of evenings later, I'm at home in front of the fireplace having a casual conversation with Joe Gillespie. Sitting backwards astride an old straight-backed wooden chair, I lament the long wait until my inauguration, which seems even longer on account of Buchanan's bungling of the current crisis. I tell Joe, "I would willingly take out of my life a year for each of the months between now and my inauguration."

He cocks his head. "Why do you say that?"

"Because every hour adds to the difficulties I'm called upon to meet, and the present Administration does nothing to check the tendency toward dissolution."

Gillespie sits up in his chair. "You sound bitter."

I fold my arms over the back of the chair to form a resting place for my chin. "I have been called upon to meet this awful responsibility, yet I'm compelled to wait here until the Fourth of March next, doing nothing to avert the crisis or lessen its weight until it comes to rest on my shoulders. What's more, there are Republicans in Congress who advocate daily for compromise, as if they can make this whole secession business go away by surrendering to the enemy before we even begin to fight."

He leans forward, his eyes misty. "Is there anything I can do to help?"

I look up. "I have read the story of Gethsemane, where the Son of God prayed in vain that the cup of bitterness might pass from him. I am in the Garden of Gethsemane now, and my cup of bitterness is overflowing."

He reaches out and touches my arm.

I clasp his hand, fighting back tears. "Stay with me tonight. I fear I cannot endure such darkness alone."

Three days after Christmas, I'm all smiles over news I receive from Senator William Seward. After leading the compromise movement for months, he stands firm and votes against Senator Crittenden's proposal to appease the South with Constitutional amendments guaranteeing slavery in perpetuity. Seward also accepts my invitation to serve as Secretary of State.

The same week, Richard Yates, the new governor of our state and an old friend, pays a visit and asks Nicolay and me to find another office so he can reclaim the executive suite for the duties he's about to assume. I oblige him and offer my best wishes for his term.

On January 9, while Nicolay and I are transferring our headquarters to a comfortably furnished, newly painted and papered room in the Johnson Building around the corner, the national crisis deepens. The South Carolina state militia fires on an unarmed merchant vessel in Charleston Harbor because they believe it is secretly carrying federal troops and supplies to Fort Sumter. The same day, Mississippi's legislature approves secession. Florida and Alabama follow suit on successive days. The Buchanan administration continues to insist it is powerless to respond. I take a long walk to stave off a spell of darkness.

My Secretary of State Designate, Seward, wastes no time in taking back at least part of his recent gift to me. Nicolay hands me a newspaper from Washington City reporting Seward's recent speech in the Senate.

If it be a Christian duty to forgive the stranger
seventy times seven offenses, it is the highest
patriotism to endure without complaint the

passionate waywardness of political brethren so long as there is hope that they may come to a better mind. We who are empowered to act must do so now, without waiting for some particular person, to redress any real grievances of the offended states so the Union may be saved.

I look at Nicolay. "Write him a note congratulating him on his speech."

Nicolay furrows his brow. "Did I hear you right?"

I grimace. "Yes ... and after you have done so, send this letter to Congressman James T. Hale."

We have just carried an election on principles fairly stated to the people. Now we are told even before we take our offices, the government shall be broken up unless we surrender to those we have beaten. In this they are either attempting to play upon us, or they are in dead earnest. Either way, if we surrender, it is the end of us and of the government.

They will repeat the experiment upon us ad libitum. A year will not pass till we shall have to take Cuba as a condition upon which they will stay in the Union. They now have the Constitution under which they have lived over seventy years, and acts of Congress of their own framing with no prospect of their being changed; and they can never have a more shallow pretext for breaking up the government, or extorting compromise, than now.

There is but one compromise which would settle the slavery question, and that would be a prohibition against acquiring any more territory.

I take my coat and hat from their pegs on the wall. "Where you going?" asks Nicolay.

"I have some thinking to do." As I walk through the snow-covered streets, I ask myself the same question.

I find a secret place where I can write without interruptions for a couple hours at a time each of the several days. When my work is complete, I have a manifesto that will be my guiding star—something that will remain private until the right season.

> *Without the Constitution and the Union, we could not have attained the result, but even these, are not the primary cause of our great prosperity. There is something back of these, entwining itself more closely about the human heart. That something is the principle of "Liberty to all"—the principle that clears the path for all, gives hope to all, and, by consequence, enterprise and industry to all.*

> *The expression of that principle in our Declaration of Independence was most happy and fortunate. Without this, as well as with it, we could have declared our independence of Great Britain; but without it, we could not, I think, have secured our free government and consequent prosperity. No oppressed people will fight and endure as our fathers did, without the promise of something better than a mere change of masters.*

> *The assertion of that principle, at that time, was the word "fitly spoken" which has proved an "apple of gold" to us. The Union and the Constitution are "the settings of silver" framed around it at a later time. The frame was made, not to conceal or destroy the apple, but to adorn and preserve it. The setting was made for the apple—not the apple for the setting.*

> *So let us act, in a way that neither setting nor apple shall ever be blurred or bruised or broken.*

> *To so act, we must study and understand the points of danger.*

Chapter Thirty Six

D aily, the mail brings threats of impending peril. Nicolay reads to me an anonymous letter.

Caesar had Brutus. Charles I, his Cromwell. And, the President may profit by their example.

Friends also send warnings. I open a letter from Seward, still in Washington, who suggests,

Would it not be a coup d'état *were you to quietly, with only a carpet sack, get on the cars and drop down into this city someday next week or so?*

Seward makes the same appeal on several occasions. To determine whether I should follow his advice and sneak into Washington to avoid assassins, I send the Illinois State Adjutant General Thomas Mather there for a meeting with General Winfield Scott, commander of the federal army. Mather, as stalwart in friendship as he is in physique, earned my trust when he was president of the State Bank of Illinois.

He lifts a burden off my shoulders when he returns with a message from the elderly general who says he will "plant two cannons on either end of Pennsylvania Avenue, and if any of them insurrectionists show their faces or raise a finger, I'll blow them to hell."

With that matter settled I focus on bigger game, in particular, recruiting members of my Cabinet. My ability to concentrate improves when Mother travels to New York City to shop for new clothes and furnishings. I'm left at home to keep house and tend to the boys, who are half the handful she can be.

Of course, it's not as if my hands don't have enough to occupy them. On January 15, the news that Georgia has voted a secession ordinance is accompanied by a gloom that matches our prairie winter. Louisiana's secession on January 26 intensifies the darkness. This January has brought more trouble than that "Fatal 1st" of 1841, when Speed left for Farmington. I'm older and wiser now, and have no need for Dr. Henry's brutal treatments. Just the same, in my desk I keep a supply of little blue mercury pills like the ones he gave me to see me through my melancholy storms.

I meet the bitter news of spiraling disunion with a public announcement of our plans to depart for our nation's capital on February 11. I spend the remainder of my time here preparing my speech for the inauguration ceremony—except for one diversion.

On the morning of January 30, the day after Mother returns from her shopping excursion, I pack an old carpet-bag and put on a short coat and faded hat for a jaunt down to Coles County. I'm off to visit Mama, the only surviving love of my youth. Along the icy path to the rail station, I meet Henry Clay Whitney, a young lawyer who worked on my nomination committee. He's also headed for the train and will be pleasant company, at least for part of my journey.

Upon our arrival at the two-story brick depot, I realize I've neglected to buy a ticket, so Whitney offers to arrange for my passage while I check the luggage. I thank him and bend over to tie together the handles of my bag using some string.

A short time later when Whitney returns, he's accompanied by F.W. Bowen, the genial Great Western Railroad superintendent.

Bowen looks down at me as I'm now on my knees in the frozen snow, fumbling with my bag, my fingers numb from cold. He says, "Mr. Lincoln, I understand you're headed to Coles County this morning."

I look up and tell him that's so, upon which he offers me a free pass and invites me to his office. As Whitney and I follow him, I thank him for his generosity and ask how business is for the line. He tells me all is fine in the railroad business these days.

When I sit beside his desk in an old wooden chair, I lean back and sigh. "You are a heap better off running a good road than I am playing president. When I first knew Whitney, here, I was getting on well. I was clean out of politics and contented to stay so. I had a good business, and my children were coming up and becoming interesting to me. But now—here I am." With that, I turn sullen and don't speak another word until it's time for the train to depart.

Down line, we're joined by Cousin John Hanks and become engaged in storytelling and swapping jokes. As a result, we lose track of the train's progress and miss our stop. We ride on to the next depot and catch a return train.

At about six o'clock, after sunset, we arrive in Charleston where I'm staying the night at the home of Tom Marshall, a friend from the Circuit. Mama's home is a few miles out of town. Since my visit is unannounced, folks are surprised to see me walking down the street toward the Marshall's elegant brick home. When the word spreads, hundreds of well-wishers stop by to greet me.

The next morning, with bitter cold still hanging in the air, I meet Cousin Dennis Hanks and we borrow a two horse buggy for the ride to Mama's. He's the same chatterbox he was back when he moved into the half-face camp in Little Pigeon Creek. I tell him to bide his tongue when we reach the river crossing. The banks are hard frozen, and our wheels slip as the horses wade into the frigid water. Chunks of ice float by in the current.

I remember crossing an icy swollen river in an early spring decades ago. I was helping Father and Mama remove from Indiana to a new home in Decatur. Mama wanted to turn back when she saw how wild and deep the current was, but we pressed on. From Decatur they eventually came here to Coles County.

When Dennis and I pull the buggy up to the cabin that she now shares with her daughter's family, Mama barely waits for my feet to hit the ground before hugging me. It's not because she's delicate and stooped that she refuses to let go. Only after I stay my tears and say we should go inside does she release her embrace and clutch my arm like a drowning man latching onto a floating log.

After supper we all gather around the fireplace and catch up on family news. At some point, I give her a black cape I brought as a gift. While she unwraps it, I stand by her rocking chair, holding onto its frame. Tears flow down her cheeks as she folds the cape in her lap.

I smile down at her, my throat aching. She clutches my elbow and pulls me toward her 'til my face is next to hers. Next, she cradles the back of my head in her hand and kisses my cheek.

Tears trickle down my face. "I love you, Mama. No son could love a mother more."

The next day as we say a bitter-sweet good-bye, Mama wraps her arms around my waist, clinging tightly. "I fear I shall never see you again. Your enemies are certain to kill you."

"No, no, Mama. They will not do that. Trust in the Lord, and all will be well. We will see each other—again."

As I board the train for Springfield I'm told Texas has seceded. I ask myself, "Why are we given bonds of love, if in the end we are meant to part?"

While the mails and telegraph office feed us a steady course of bad news, the parcel deliveries that come our way are peppered with all manner of threatening "gifts." On one occasion, Mother unwraps a painting of my likeness wearing a hangman's rope for a necktie; my legs are shackled in chains, and my body covered with tar and feathers.

Not long afterward, I'm posing in the office for a sculpture of my bust when a package is delivered, wrapped in brown paper and tied loosely with string. I say to the elfish, impertinent sculptor Thomas Dow Jones, "What do you suppose is in it?"

"Don't open it," he says, edging away to collect his wide-brimmed hat and shawl. "There's always the chance it could explode."

"Where are you going?" I say, as I toy with the string.

"Nowhere," he says, returning to the parcel.

I scratch my head. "Should we soak it in water?"

"We should say our prayers if we do." Holding his hat and shawl behind his back, he bends forward, puts his face right up to the package and sniffs it. He appears to be more squirrel than human.

I laugh. "I remember once saying that prayers are nonsense. These days I've come to believe praying should be done whether or not one thinks they'll do any good."

He straightens up. "Go over there and wait."

I retreat to a corner of the room. "What are doing?"

"I'll hide it behind this clay model I've been working on. If it explodes when I open it, we might get a little messy, but we won't get hurt."

"Be careful," I warn, crouching next to a desk.

When Jones tugs the string undone, a pigtail whistle falls out of the wrapping.

He turns and stares at me.

I walk over to the workbench and pick up the harmless device, grinning. "It's a souvenir to remind me of something a newspaperman printed about me. 'No whistle can be made out of a pig's tail.'"

Afterward, I take the pigtail whistle home and try to make it work. When I give up, I hand the useless contraption to young Tad who immediately produces some musical tones. Within an hour he's playing fully recognizable songs.

When Bob returns from Harvard to join us for the journey to Washington he says, "Public life is nothing more than a gilded prison." Willy and Tad match each other's tantrums over leaving the family dog Fido behind with neighbors. I give them a photograph of the dog to take along. I wish the secessionists, and Bob for that matter, could be so easily soothed.

On February 9, while a Peace Conference is underway in Washington City, delegates from the six seceded states meet in Montgomery, Alabama and elect

Jefferson Davis President of the Confederate States of America. I say to Nicolay, "Nearly everyone I've loved has been torn away. Only my boys, Mama, and this precious Union remain. Now that I am about to take an oath to protect and defend it, it's being torn apart limb by limb."

He stares up at me. "It's not your doing."

His words are well intended, but of little comfort.

On the morning we leave Springfield for the nation's capital, I go to the law office for a long talk with Billy Herndon. First, we examine some papers and confer over certain legal matters he's working on. We also review the books and arrange for the completion of all unsettled and unfinished matters. I point out certain lines of procedure I wish for him to observe. Once these things are disposed of, I cross over to the opposite side of the room and throw myself down on the old office sofa. After many years of service, it has been moved against the wall for support. I stare at the ceiling in silence for a few moments before saying, "Billy, how long have we been together?"

"Over sixteen years," he says.

"We've never had a cross word in all that time."

Billy shakes his head. "No, indeed we have not."

"Others have tried to supplant you in our partnership over the years, but they were weak men who hoped to secure a law practice by hanging onto my coattails. In spite of your faults, which I've never criticized except privately, I have valued your trustworthiness and loyalty too much to be tempted by any of them."

"You've been like a father to me," he says.

"And you, like a son." I get up off the sofa and gather a bundle of books and papers to take with me. As I start to go, I turn to Billy once more. "That signboard down at the foot of the stairway—let it hang where it is, undisturbed. Give our clients to understand that the election of a president makes no change in the firm of Lincoln and Herndon. If I live, I'm coming back, and then we'll go right on as if nothing had ever happened."

He puffs out his chest. "I have always considered it an honor to have my name beside yours."

I linger for a moment, dabbing a tear, and take a last look at the old quarters.

When we arrive at the train depot to board the special cars that will carry us to Washington City, we're joined by Nicolay and Hill; the latter I've asked to accompany me as my bodyguard. I stand on the platform and say to a large crowd that's gathered to see us off,

My friends, no one, not in my situation, can appreciate my feeling of sadness at this parting. To this place and the kindness of these people I owe everything. Here I have lived a quarter of a century and have passed from a young to an old man. Here my children have been born and one is buried.

I now leave, not knowing when, or whether ever, I may return, with a task before me greater than that which rested upon Washington. Without the assistance of the Divine Being who ever attended him, I cannot succeed. With that assistance I cannot fail. Trusting in Him who can go with me and remain with you and be everywhere for good, let us confidently hope that all will yet be well.

To His care commending you, as I hope in your prayers you will commend me, I bid you an affectionate farewell.

I wave good-bye and take a seat on the train next to Nicolay. A lump rises in my throat. I pat his knee. "I will soon take an oath 'to preserve and protect the Constitution,' but already, the Union and its foundations are being rocked and its bonds ripped apart."

When I consider the great trouble that is before us, I am reminded of the Savior's lament as he stood upon a hill and gazed upon his beloved city, Jerusalem.

How often would I have gathered thy children together, even as a hen gathereth her chickens under her wings.

I gaze out the window, my eyes misting over as I watch my beloved countryside roll past. Memories, some joyful and others laced with pain, consume my thoughts.

Acknowledgements

I am most grateful for the invaluable contributions of many people who helped bring this story to life. Among them are two groups of dedicated authors—critique partners who hold my feet to the fire every week and challenge me to write my very best: Laurie Ezpeleta, Cheryl Feeney (Cheryl also did a yeoman's job as my editor), Brett Gadbois, Richard Heller, Michael Smith, Jan Walker and Barbara Winther. Van Rozay is my go-to-guy when it comes to storytelling and wordsmithing. Annmarie Huppert was an invaluable resource on the subject of complex post-traumatic stress, and Stacy Garza deserves special thanks for her work organizing the book launch. Ed Aro and his team at Gig Harbor Windermere Real Estate made an invaluable contribution to the launch effort as well.

Others who have supported me with their encouragement, financial support and critiques: Gary & Joan Albert, my sister-in-law Joan Andresen, my nephew Aaron Andresen, Kent Berg, my aunt and uncle Dotty & Bob Botts, Diptiman & Susan Chakravarti, my niece Kate Chang, my cousin Carol DeFelice and her son Matt DeFelice, Michael & Candace Donovan, Robin Foster, my mother Barbara Fowler, my brother and sister-in-law Glen & Heather Fowler, my niece Holly Fowler, Stacey Garza, my sister Donna Goetz, Don Havens, Brian & Michelle Greenley, Bob Hibbard, Robert & Nancy Hutchins, Steve Lynn and the gang at Morso Wine Bar, Matt McKellar, my college roommate Terry McMullen, Shinho Park, Tahirih PerryCook, my sister and brother-in-law Ruth & Larry Rice, my sister and brother-in-law Sandy & Laurens Thurman, my sister and brother-in-law Becky & John Shaw, my nephew Owen Shaw, Dan Smith, John Stoddard, and the baristas and gang at Starbucks Gig Harbor North.

For her inspiration and words of wisdom on the craft of writing, I give a special thanks to Kristen Lamb, founder of WANA International.

And special thanks to my family, without whose support I would have thrown in the towel dozens of times: my wife and proofreader Judi Fowler, my son and daughter-in-law Jason & Heather Fowler, my daughter and son-in-law Noelle & Adrian Brambila, my grandchildren Elijah, Lukas and Angelina Brambila, and my grand-dogs Mookey, Edgar, Wally, Keeley, Prim and Chonchis.

Additional Reading

Barton, W. E. (1920). *The Paternity of Abraham Lincoln: Was He the Son of Thomas Lincoln.* New York: George H. Doran Company.

Basler, R. ed. (1953). *The Collected Works of Abraham Lincoln.* New Brunswick, NJ: The Abraham Lincoln Association, Springfield, Ill; Rutgers University Press.

Bower, A. P. (2009). *The Last Stop: Lincoln and the "Mud Circuit".* Taylorville, IL: Oak Tree Press.

Burlingame, M. (2008). *Abraham Lincoln: A Life.* Baltimore: The Johns Hopkins University Press.

Burlingame, M. (1997). *The Inner World of Abraham Lincoln.* Urbana and Chicago: University of Illinois Press.

Campanella, R. (2010). *Lincoln in New Orleans: The 1828-1831 Flatboat Voyages and Their Place in History.* Lafayette, LA: University of Louisiana at Lafayette Press.

D. P. (1856). Official Proceedings of the Democratic Party National Convention. Cincinnati: Enquirer Company Steam Printing Establishment.

Douglas, S. A. (1860). The Dividing Line Between Federal and Local Authority: Popular Sovereignty in the Territories. *Harper's New Monthly Magazine* , pp. 519-536.

Epstein, D. M. (2008). *The Lincolns: Portrait of a Marriage.* New York: Ballantine Books.

Gore, J. R. (1921). *The Boyhood of Abraham Lincoln: From the Spoken Narratives of Austin Gollaher.* Indianapolis: The Bobbs-Merrill Company.

Greene, G. J. (1916). *Lincoln the Comforter.* Hancock, NJ: Herald Press.

Guelzo, A.C. (2002). Grand Rapids, MI: *Redeemer President.* Wm. B. Eerdmans Publishing Co.

Herndon, W., & Weik, J. W. (1889). *Herndon's Lincoln: The True Story of a Great Life.* Chicago, New York, San Francisco: Belford Clarke & Company.

Hogan, J. (2011). *Lincoln, Inc.: Selling the Sixteenth President in Contemporary America.* Lanham, MD: Rowan & Littlefield Publishing Group, Inc.

Holland, J. (1998). *Holland's Life of Abraham Lincoln.* Introduction by Allen C. Guelzo. Lincoln: University of Nebraska Press.

Holzer, H. (2004). *Lincoln at Cooper Union: The Speech That Made Abraham Lincoln President.* New York: Simon & Schuster Paperbacks.

Holzer, H. (2008). *Lincoln President-Elect: Abraham Lincoln and the Great Secession Winter 1860-1861.* New York: Simon & Schuster Paperbacks.

Holzer, H. (2004). *The Lincoln-Douglas Debates: The First Complete, Unexpurgated Text.* New York: Fordham University Press.

Journal of the Abraham Lincoln Association, Various Articles. (n.d.).

Kempf, E. J. (1965). *Abraham Lincoln's Philosophy of Common Sense: An Analytical Biography of a Great Mind.* New York: The New York Academy of Sciences.

Ketcham, H. (1901). *The Life of Abraham Lincoln.*

Lamon, W. H., & Teillard, E. D. (1895). *Recollections of Abraham Lincoln, 1847-1865.* Chicago: A.C. McClurg and Company.

Lapsley, E. A. *The Papers and Writings of Abraham Lincoln: Complete Constitutional Edition.* Project Gutenberg.

Myers, J. (n.d.). Abraham Lincoln and the Melissa Goings Case. *http://www.villageofmetamora.com/?hiscourt .*

Nicolay, J. G., & Hay, J. (1890). *Abraham Lincoln: A History.* New York: The Century Company.

Remsburg, J. E. (1893). *Abraham Lincoln: Was He a Christian?* New York: The Truth Seeker Company.

Sandburg, C. (1954). *Abraham Lincoln: The Prairie Years and The War Years.* San Diego, New York: Harcourt, Inc.

Sheahan, J. W. (1860). *The Life of Stephen A. Douglas.* New York: Harper & Brothers, Publishers.

Shenk, J. W. (2005). *Lincoln's Melancholy: How Depression Challenged a President and Fueled His Greatness.* New York: Houghton Mifflin Company.

Simon, P. (1971). *Lincoln's Preparation for Greatness: The Illinois Legislative Years.* Urbana and Chicago: University of Illinois Press.

Starr, J. J. (1922). *Lincoln's Last Day.* New York: Frederick A. Stokes Company.

Steiner, F. (1870). Religious Views of Our Presidents. *Index (Toledo, Ohio) .*

Tarbell, I. M. (1896). *The Early Life of Abraham Lincoln.* New York: S.S. McClure Limited.

The Abraham Lincoln Presidential Library and Museum; www.alplm.org/.

The Lehrman Institute, and The Lincoln Institute; www.abrahamlincoln.org;.

Walker, W. (1860). *The War in Nicaragua.* New York: S.H. Goetzel & Co.

Weems, M. L. (1833). *The Life of George Washington.* Philadelphia: Joseph Allen.

Wilson, D. L. (1998). *Honor's Voice: The Transformation of Abraham Lincoln.* New York: Aflred A. Knopf, Inc.

www.mrlincolnandfriends.org/.

About the Author

DL Fowler gets inside people's heads and writes about what he finds there.

The author of bestselling **Lincoln's Diary – a novel of suspense**, he spent his teenage years in Southern California in the shadow of Redlands' Lincoln Shrine. He now makes his home in picturesque Gig Harbor, Washington and travels frequently to America's heartland.

You can contact the author by visiting http://www.dlfowler.com or by scanning the QR Code below.

You can visit the author's blog at http://dlfowler.wordpress.com or scan the QR code below:

Your Opinion Matters

Other readers want to know about your experience reading Lincoln Raw—a biographical novel. A good way to give them your feedback is to post reviews on **www.amazon.com** and **www.goodreads.com**. Below are some questions to guide you in writing a meaningful review.

What part of *Lincoln Raw* did you most enjoy?

Do you believe biographical novels can be useful in studying history?

List three things you learned about Lincoln's life.

Were you surprised that Lincoln was not an abolitionist?

Were you surprised by Lincoln's religious views?

Would you recommend *Lincoln Raw* to other readers? Why?

Readers Guide

Following are some suggested points you might consider when discussing *Lincoln Raw—a biographical novel.*

What factors contributed to Lincoln's melancholy disposition?

What childhood incidents indicate Lincoln was naturally more sensitive to injustice and abuse than his peers?

What were Lincoln's views on religion, and how did they evolve over his life?

Compare and contrast Lincoln's views on slavery with those of abolitionists of his day.

How were the politics of Lincoln's day similar to or different from today's politics?

Before Lincoln left Springfield to be inaugurated president he wrote a manifesto. What difference did he see between the Declaration of Independence and the Constitution?

Discuss ways in which Lincoln's childhood and adolescent experiences influenced his relationships with women, and separately consider how early life experiences influenced his relationships with other men.

Consult resources on Post-Traumatic-Stress-Disorder such as *http://www.helpguide.org/mental/post_traumatic_stress_diso rder_symptoms_treatment.htm* and discuss whether Lincoln may have suffered from PTSD.

Discuss the advantages/disadvantages of using historical fiction in learning about history.

To arrange an in-person or video meeting with the author, go to http://dlfowler.com/contact-me .

Made in the USA
San Bernardino, CA
13 November 2014